A DEADLY MERMAID FETISH

PAMELA MONES

Woodhall Press
Norwalk, CT

A DEADLY MERMAID FETISH

PAMELA MONES

Woodhall Press
Norwalk, CT

Woodhall Press, 81 Old Saugatuck Road, Norwalk, CT 06855
WoodhallPress.com

Cover design: Jessica Dionne Wright
Layout artist: Wendy Bowes

Library of Congress Cataloging-in-Publication Data available

ISBN 978-1-954907-25-6 (paper: alk paper)
ISBN 978-1-954907-26-3 (electronic)

First Edition

Distributed by Independent Publishers Group
(800) 888-4741

Printed in the United States of America

To my mother, who showed me where the Sandman lives.

Chapter 1

The four a.m. call shattered the solitude of the darkened bedroom. No matter that it was Bob Marley's voice singing "Three Little Birds" from the nightstand. For a homicide detective, it meant only one thing: Evil had stolen peace from the night and sucked promise from the day. Somewhere, a life stripped of hope and denied its dreams.

Miranda clawed for her cell phone, catching it before it hit the floor.

"Hello," she groaned, gathering the soft covers around her as if they would shield her from the fresh horror about to strike.

"Miranda?"

"Of course it's me, Matt."

She rolled onto her back, pinched the bridge of her nose, and tried to clear the dryness from her throat. Her tongue felt thick.

"What's happened?"

"A dead mermaid washed ashore on Lido Beach."

"Too early for jokes, Matt. A mermaid? A dead mermaid?"

"No joke, Miranda. I'm here at Lido. A young girl, dressed like a mermaid. A harpoon in her chest."

Miranda bolted upright, reality bleeding through her daze. "A harpoon? That's a new one."

She heard Matt's deep inhale. Words unnecessary.

"Okay. I'll be there in twenty minutes."

She clicked off and pressed the phone against her lips to cage her scream.

Her sister's suicide still haunting her. Farrah—a lover of all things mermaid.

Did I return to work too soon? she wondered.

Her yearlong absence from the department—ordered by her boss—had erased none of the rage she had suppressed over the years following her sister's suicide. Her gradual unraveling was the reason her boss had called her into his office to deliver an ultimatum just over a year ago.

"You need a break, Detective Morales. It's counseling and a year away from here, or a transfer out of the department. You've lost your edge. You're . . . distracted. We'll call it a sabbatical. Sounds like something smart people like you take instead of vacations."

She knew calling it a sabbatical would make her sudden departure easier for Chief Petri to explain to department gossipers, rather than divulging it was for psychological reasons. An action intended to protect her stellar reputation—not only within the homicide department, but up and down the chain of command.

The chief was right. She had lost her edge. Although she couldn't explain how, she refused to accept that it was due to mental instability.

Now, the shock of a young girl, dressed like a mermaid, had landed on a nearby beach, tearing open old memories she'd long buried. And like Pandora's box, they'd be hard to put back. An ordinary Sunday imploding her carefully controlled world. A startling reminder that death comes without warning.

Showered and dressed, she drove across the iconic Ringling Bridge toward one of Florida's world-renowned beaches, and the new nightmare awaiting her. The sun barely tinted the dawn, the teal of Sarasota Bay not yet shimmering from the sun's reflection.

Despite her exceptional reputation as a homicide detective during her almost fifteen years on the force, Detective Miranda Morales was well aware that even a homicide detective is not immune to the emotional turmoil that comes when old wounds crack open, or monsters emerge from their hideous caves. But she was determined not to lose her edge. This time.

Miranda parked her Audi in one of the ample vacant spaces in the Lido Beach parking lot and grabbed her tote bag off the seat, locking the car behind her.

The path of crushed seashells crunched underfoot as she tromped down the path leading to the white expanse of powdery sand. The forensic team was already at work, combing the area for potential evidence the tide might have washed ashore. Caution tape cordoned off a wide area designated as the crime scene in black, unfriendly text—do not cross. The sun had barely begun its rise, the cloudless sky, a melancholy gray-blue.

Lido Beach stretched wide and white along the glistening aquamarine Gulf of Mexico. On this predawn Sunday, and with the snowbirds having flown back to their northern nests, traffic across the Ringling Bridge had been almost nil. As she'd driven to the scene, images of a lifeless body dressed like a mermaid with a harpoon in her chest had formed.

"A mermaid," Miranda muttered as she kicked up the sand. "A dead mermaid."

"Hey, Matt," she said as she approached him, his back to her.

He turned, his indigo eyes stained with disbelief and lack of sleep.

"Hey, Miranda," he said, shaking his head, trying to find a smile that wouldn't come.

"What do you know so far?" she asked, skipping the usual

polite small talk. Matt would see right through her feeble attempt to play down what lay in front of them.

"Not much," he began. "A jogger called Dispatch about an hour ago, saying that he thought it was a 'real' mermaid at first."

A sudden screech of seagulls flew overhead as if urging them to look up, away from the repugnant image at the shoreline. Their ear-piercing calls were in sharp contrast to the rhythmic rush of the tide lapping the shore.

The two detectives moved in tandem toward the twisted shape. The sweep of the tide kissed the victim's bony elbow. A metal pole jutting up from her frail chest pointed defiantly at the sky, as if mocking them.

Miranda's eyes fixed on the battered body lying unprotected from the elements. Seashells and algae were encrusted in the mermaid's tangled, raven hair. Gashes and bruises were prevalent on her torso and arms, her thin, pale lips separated in mid-scream. Coral-colored toenails poked through the torn, ragged tail. A necklace matching the color of her toenail polish had somehow managed to remain secure around her neck during her journey. The tattered tail with its blue sequins shimmered like tiny diamonds as the light of a new day shifted. Bare patches were evident where sequins had once been.

"How could a young girl dressed like a mermaid end up on our beach?" muttered Miranda, as if expecting a voice from the cosmos to answer her.

Out of the corner of her eye, she noticed distant movement across the sand. A short, rotund man was lumbering toward them, his straw-colored trousers flapping like sails as a sudden gust of wind blew across the sand. A red satchel hung from his shoulder, bumping against his thigh with each stride.

Miranda nudged Matt, jutting her chin toward the figure.

"The new coroner," said Matt.

"Hmm . . . Know him?"

"I met him recently at one of his lectures."

"Reputation?"

"The best, according to his students," confirmed Matt.

Miranda watched the coroner approach, wondering if he would be a pain in the ass to work with, or a kindred spirit. Maybe somewhere in between, she decided.

"Let's go greet him," she said, ducking under the caution tape.

The pudgy coroner was damp with sweat and out of breath when he finally reached them.

"Whew!" he said, dabbing the moisture off his forehead with a white handkerchief and wiping his hands before returning the crumpled cloth to his front pocket. "I'm Dr. Jonathan Rubens." He reached his chubby hand out to Matt.

"I'm Detective Matt Selva, and," turning to Miranda, "this is Chief Detective Miranda Morales. She's going to be leading this investigation."

Dr. Rubens wiped his hands on his trousers before reaching out to shake Miranda's hand, a broad smile on his puffy, reddened face.

"Pleased to meet you, Detective Morales."

"Likewise," she said, returning the smile.

"So, what have we got here?" he asked, scanning the activity at the shoreline.

"A jogger discovered the victim during his early-morning run on the beach. The forensic team was already here when I arrived about half an hour ago," said Matt.

"Anybody touch anything? Move the body?"

"No, sir. They know better."

"Of course." He took a deep breath. "So let's see what we're dealing with," he said, following Matt and Miranda under the yellow crime-scene barrier.

As he reached the victim, he stood like a captain surveying the carnage of battle. Staring at the metal pole jutting from her chest, he shook his head.

"I thought I'd seen just about everything," he mumbled. "I'll remove that ghastly thing in her chest when she's at the morgue." He glanced at them, as if they needed an explanation. "Eliminate risk of contamination and potential damage to surrounding organs where it's lodged," he added, blowing a heavy breath into the salty morning air.

The coroner squatted next to the victim, exploring her shape. A sculptor evaluating the results of his labors. Noting the rise and fall of its contours. The bend of the arms. Sway of the hips. His gaze finally reaching the tattered tail.

"I'll also be able to get a better look at the condition of her legs after I remove the tail."

Miranda and Matt nodded.

Dr. Rubens's coffee-colored eyes searched for obvious clues to the woman's demise. He squeezed them shut. Silently damning the cruel god that had allowed such a tragedy. Then he stood up to stretch, wobbling from the sudden change in position.

Matt grabbed his elbow. "You okay, Doc?"

"It's too damn hot!" the coroner declared, removing his handkerchief again from his pocket and wiping his furrowed brow before bunching the hanky into a ball and shoving it back where it belonged.

He looked at his wristwatch. "Not even eight a.m. What a helluva way to start a Sunday."

A technician scurried by carrying an Igloo cooler.

Matt grabbed her arm. "Got an extra cold one in there?"

The tech opened the Igloo and gave Matt a bottle of cold water. He uncapped it and handed it to Dr. Rubens. With just a few gulps, the coroner drained it and handed the empty back to Matt.

"Thanks. Just what I needed." He took a breath. "Hope you're going to recycle that," he said, nodding at the empty bottle before turning back to the victim, her unseeing hazel eyes staring blankly into the void.

Dr. Rubens again squatted beside the victim, visually cataloging her overall condition. Following her frozen gaze upward, he shaded his eyes with a chubby hand as he looked at the cloudless sky growing brighter. A trail of sweat coiled down the back of his linen shirt.

He rummaged through his red satchel, pulling out a pair of blue latex gloves that glided easily over his moist fingers. Next he removed a magnifying glass and penlight from the bag, slipping the magnifying glass into his back pocket. He slowly separated the mermaid's lips and shined the penlight around the inside of her mouth. After checking the tongue and mucosa lining, he focused the light on the back of her throat.

"Looks like a bulge or lump of some kind in the lining of her throat," he muttered as he leaned in for a closer look.

"Thoughts?" asked Miranda, stooping next to him to look over his shoulder.

"Can't exactly say." He rolled his shoulders, readjusted his penlight, and studied the victim's throat for a few minutes. "Could be a seashell or something like it that got lodged there during what must have been a tumultuous journey."

Another flock of squawking seagulls flew overhead, unmindful of the tragic scene below them, and again spooked Miranda.

"You okay?" asked Matt, reaching out his hand to steady her.

She nodded, clasping his hand then immediately letting go, brushing the sweat from her hand onto the leg of her lavender slacks.

"You'd think I'd be used to their squawks after living here all these years," she said, annoyed at her clumsiness.

"I could live here a lifetime, I think, and still be startled by their sudden outbursts," said Matt in her ear.

"We need to get her out of the heat and into the morgue," said Dr. Rubens. "I'll know more once I perform the autopsy." He shifted his eyes between the two detectives. "The body holds many secrets . . . and it will eventually reveal them all to me." He paused to consider his words. "At least I'll be able to determine the likely cause of her death, if not how she arrived on our shore."

Matt remembered a recent lecture he'd attended along with a class of cadets. He'd been impressed by how the speaker had emphasized the importance of noting what might seem mundane and irrelevant to the novice. The body holds the answers to the perplexing questions surrounding a mysterious death, the guest coroner had told them. The dead can't tell us what happened, so we have to be the eyes, ears, and voice of the victim. Each anomaly must be examined critically to determine if it's merely a normal variation to be dismissed, or something that can't easily be explained. Each organ, tissue, and bone must be examined until the body reveals its secrets, helping the examiner unravel the complex, unspoken message the body has left behind.

Matt gazed out across the expanse of the blue-green Gulf of Mexico and took a soothing breath. "Let's hope our mermaid's message is loud and clear, Dr. Rubens."

The coroner stood up abruptly and dusted off his trousers, waving to the two morgue assistants carrying a stretcher across the sand. As he studied the faces of the two detectives, he remembered past images of unnatural deaths. "I've seen a lot of dead bodies during my twenty-five years, detectives, but nothing quite like this," he said, shaking his head as if to expunge those distressing memories. "So young. So tragic."

The two white-coated assistants set the stretcher down and followed the coroner's instructions, transferring the corpse onto the flat, narrow surface and guiding her extremities and sequined tail into the black vinyl bag.

"Careful with the pole, men," cautioned the coroner, as the harpoon swayed slightly with the movement. "Martin, stand on the side to steady it and help push with your free hand. Jackson, you can push from the end of the stretcher. I know it'll be tricky maneuvering across the unstable sand. I'll help you load the stretcher into the back of the van and then follow you in my car to the morgue."

He turned to Miranda and Matt. "I'll be in touch, detectives."

Chapter 2

Miranda and Matt walked along Lido Beach, leaving the forensic team and crime photographer behind to complete their work.

"The coroner has his work cut out for him," said Matt.

"For sure. And there's little we can do until we have some nuggets for clues."

The sky now revealed strands of white clouds in the blue sky. It was growing hotter as dawn yielded to the sun.

Miranda closed her eyes for a few seconds, trying to summon happy thoughts that could outweigh the heaviness each new case carried with it. Nagging threads of self-doubt itched to take hold of her confidence.

The victim reminded her of her younger sister, exacerbating the guilt she had carried with her ever since she'd found Farrah's body on the bedroom floor, blood caked around her wrists. Suicide was never easy to understand. Especially when it was someone you loved.

How could I have not sensed her pain? What signs did I miss?

"Whew!" said Matt, breaking into her thoughts. "Another scorcher." He rubbed the back of his neck with a pale blue handkerchief.

"It's Florida, Matt. What d'you expect?" she said, elbowing him.

He laughed. His warm smile and engaging, indigo eyes always pulled her back to the present. She was glad he was her partner, even if she rarely told him so.

"Let's go in," he teased, cocking his head toward the water. His own attempt to shove aside—even if just for an instant—the shock of a young, lifeless body contorted on the beach.

Miranda shot him a dubious look.

"Really. Jump in the Gulf? Like we haven't a care in the world?"

Matt pursed his lips.

"Okay, then. How about coffee and a bagel?"

"Much better idea."

Lido Beach was beginning to activate, a smattering of people marking their territory on the wide stretch of talcum-powder sand. Soon swarms of sun-seekers would cluster. People lucky enough to be oblivious to the tragedy that had preceded them. After all, it was Sunday—the day reserved for family, fun, and sand castles.

The Lido Cafe had just raised its wooden shutters, announcing it was open for business.

"What'll it be?" said the perky, young woman behind the counter.

"A toasted everything bagel with cream cheese and a coffee. Black," said Miranda without hesitation.

"Same," echoed Matt.

"Okay," said the waitress. "I'll bring it to your table when it's ready."

Matt paid and dropped a couple of dollars in the tip jar next to the cash register. The waitress winked her appreciation.

They went and sat down at one of the stone tables. Seagulls and egrets flew overhead in search of their own nourishment.

"I forgot how much I loved this beach," mused Miranda, gazing out at the glistening expanse of turquoise. "I'm so glad to be back here."

Matt rested his forearm on the table and studied her profile. Her slender nose dotted with freckles. The full shape of her mouth. Her auburn-streaked hair gathered into a ponytail. Her flawless olive complexion.

"How was the sabbatical?" he asked, interested.

"Let's not talk about it right now," she said, glancing at him. Forcing a smile. She wondered what he would think when he found out she'd been forced into taking the sabbatical. They'd only been partners for a short time when it happened.

Melancholy seeped into her as the image of the dead mermaid returned. Farrah always believed mermaids were real. She couldn't help but smile at that memory.

"What kind of monster could do such a hideous act, Matt?"

Matt sighed, words failing him.

The waitress brought over their food. They ate in silence, Miranda pecking at her bagel, no longer hungry. Matt, famished, savored each bite. She raised her eyebrows as she watched him devour the entire bagel.

"I didn't even have a chance to grab an apple before racing to the crime scene," he said defensively.

Miranda smiled and shook her head.

"We should probably head back," she said, her bagel hardly touched.

Matt collected their trash and tossed it in the metal bin nearby. They walked along the beach past the crime scene. The yellow caution tape was long gone. The forensic techs were already on their way back to the lab to begin their analysis.

"Need a ride?" she asked when they reached the parking lot.

"Nope," smiled Matt, pointing to his bicycle chained to a palm tree.

"Really? A bike?"

"Yep."

She glanced at the bicycle's thin wheels and bright blue frame, then at Matt, and smiled.

"Bicycle a lot?" she asked before getting into her car.

"As much as I can."

She turned on the ignition and lowered the window. Her chocolate gaze was somber.

"Monsters are among us, Matt." She paused. "And they often look just like us."

Matt sighed. "They might look like us, Miranda . . . but they don't have our soul."

She bobbed her head and smiled, waving to him as she drove away.

What kind of monsters have visited you? wondered Matt as he watched her until she was out of view. He unchained his bike and rode to his condo a mile away.

Chapter 3

The gunmetal-gray drawers lining one wall of the Sarasota County Morgue resembled filing cabinets on steroids—but unlike filing cabinets, these drawers were refrigerated. Most of them were empty, but one or two contained once-breathing human beings now waiting for their families to hear the dreadful news.

A small office enclosed with clear, glass windows was opposite the refrigerated drawers. An amber desk light cast a funereal glow through the open door, spilling out into the den of the dead. Fluorescent lights hanging from the popcorn ceiling in the cavernous room did little to create a sense of welcome. Autopsy instruments were perfectly positioned on the metal tray beside the stainless-steel table where Dr. Rubens, dressed in green scrubs, prepared to unlock the mermaid's secrets.

"What happened to you, little one?" he muttered to himself, while his deep-set, brown eyes examined her small, pale breasts, juxtaposed against the grotesque pole jutting from her bony ribs. Her abdomen was bruised and bloated. The ragged-edged mermaid tail was still in place.

He snapped on a pair of blue latex gloves and reached for the shower nozzle dangling from a coiled rod above. He turned on the faucet and a spring-like rain flowed over the body, washing cracked and broken shards of seashells and tangled clumps of seaweed out of her black hair. Debris drifted down the gutter running along the side of the stainless-steel table, as if a summer storm had just ended. Her delicate toes, peeking out through the tattered fins, never twitched as the gentle spray massaged them. He paused at her hips, marveling at how the ragged waistband had managed to remain attached to the tail that kept her legs captive inside the tapered, narrow sheath.

"Okay, my friend. Let's get this bugger off."

He turned off the hose and returned the nozzle to its hook. His attempt to remove the tail proved more of a struggle than he'd bargained for. The hidden zipper along the side was corroded and wouldn't budge. He wondered if the material used to make the tail had shrunk from being in the water too long. Or, perhaps it was intended to be skin-tight.

Admitting defeat, he took the shears from the sterile tray and carefully guided the sharp blades along the seam. As he reached the frayed fins, he noticed that the coral color of her toenails contrasted nicely with the sapphire sequins adorning the tail. He imagined her bending at the waist, her small foot on a stool while she methodically applied the polish to each nail.

He carefully unwrapped the tail, surprised that her long, slender legs were as smooth and unscarred as the porcelain doll he'd gifted his young niece for her birthday a few years ago. He sighed deeply and closed his eyes, closeting the sadness overtaking him.

"When this case is solved, my little mermaid, I'll have this room painted in your honor. Sweet colors. Coral, like your toe polish. A blue ceiling to mimic the sky. Anything to brighten this dreary room," he whispered into her unhearing ear. Winking playfully, as if she could appreciate his whimsy.

He studied her pale, delicate features. His eyes lingered on the metal pole jutting out of her bony chest. "How did you become the target of this monstrosity? What horror brought you here?"

Letting out another sigh, he pulled his face protector down, activated the microphone, and began recording his findings. "A female, approximate age, thirteen to sixteen, washed ashore during the night or early-morning hours on Lido Beach. Jutting out from the ribs, amid the scars and multiple contusions on her chest, is a metal pole. Most likely the weapon that caused, or led, to her death. The bloating and discoloration of the abdomen, along with the savage marks covering her face, arms, and torso, suggest a traumatic and savage journey. The exact length of time she was in the water—unknown. No obvious injuries on her lower extremities, most likely protected by the mermaid tail. Dark circles resembling ligature marks encircle both ankles. Half-moon scars under her breasts suggest she has, or had, breast implants." He paused. "A bit young, though, for implants. Make a note of that, Jonathan," he recorded as a reminder for when he wrote his formal report.

His eyes were again drawn to the metal pole pointing to the ceiling. "Now to remove this ghastly thing." He gripped the base of the weapon where it entered her chest, steadying it as he coaxed it from between the jaws of her rib cage. The chest was unwilling to let go. "Heavy bastard," he mumbled, finally extracting the weapon.

A dull clunk echoed as something dropped onto the table. He set the weapon down beside her and picked up the object with his forceps. He held it up to the light, eyeing it from all angles. Inspecting it like an entomologist studying a rare insect. Then, he placed the object into a metal bowl, describing what he'd found.

"An irregular-shaped object, approximately 0.635 centimeters in diameter, apparently wedged between the tongs of the harpoon in her chest cavity, is encased in membrane and fibrous tissue. The object feels firm. Like a stone. Or marble." He glanced again at the object in the bowl. "The specimen will be sent to the lab for analysis."

Next, Dr. Rubens examined her mouth. The beam of his headlamp focused on the back of her throat where he remembered detecting an unusual lump during his preliminary examination at the crime scene.

Angling the metal arm of the magnifying glass over her mouth, he maneuvered the forceps toward the lump, patiently teasing it away from the membrane lining the throat.

"Got it," he muttered, standing up straight, tilting his neck from side to side to loosen the tightness pinching the nerves. He held the forceps up to the light, again shifting the angle for a better view.

"A pea-sized object—similar in firmness and irregularity to the object from the prongs of the harpoon—was removed from the lining of the victim's throat." He shrugged, then set it carefully down into a second metal bowl and continued to dictate. "It will be sent along with the other specimen to the lab for analysis."

He methodically continued to explore the surface of the victim's body, positioning the victim on her side. He noticed what first appeared to be a bruise on her left shoulder. Then, looking more closely, he saw that it appeared to be an image. He retrieved his magnifying glass and began recording.

"A frog tattoo with bulging red eyes is inked on the victim's left shoulder. Spidery black veins etched on its back. The tattoo measures 30.61 mm—the diameter of a half-dollar." He scanned the body for more tattoos. "Seems like the frog is a loner."

He returned her to her back and picked up the scalpel. With a steady hand and precise grip, he sliced open the victim's chest with a coroner's familiar Y-incision.

"Okay, little one, let's see what secrets you're hiding."

Chapter 4

Miranda, relieved to be back in the calm embrace of her home, stepped into a cool shower, washing away the sweat and sand clinging to her like barnacles on a boat. Visions of the disheveled, battered mermaid with the savage-looking harpoon in her chest refused to loosen and swirl down the drain along with the remnants of Lido Beach.

Bob Marley's "Three Little Birds" spilled from her iPhone into the room just as she stepped out of the shower.

"Ugh," she groaned.

"Morales," she said, holding her phone with one hand while towel-drying her thick, auburn hair with her free hand.

"It's Dr. Rubens, Detective."

She stopped drying her hair and sat on the edge of her bed. "Any news, Doctor?"

"I have a couple of things I'd like to show you. Can you come over to the morgue?"

She glanced at the clock.

"I'll be there within the hour."

She opened the lower cabinet for her blow-dryer and then decided she'd put the top down on her Audi and let the wind finish drying her hair. Her chocolate eyes roamed over the clothes on the rods in her closet. Casual and colorful sundresses on one side. Sleeveless blouses and light-colored capris and slacks on the other side.

She chose a tangerine tank top and crisp, white slacks. Not too shabby, she thought as she glanced in the mirror.

She rushed downstairs, grabbed her keys, and put down the canvas top of her Audi.

Let's hope the coroner has some good news.

The stench of the morgue gagged her as she pushed open the metal door.

I'll never get used to the smell of death, no matter how much disinfectant and air freshener they use.

She walked toward the table where Dr. Rubens was in the midst of the autopsy. The naked corpse was bathed in the appalling glare of the unforgiving overhead fluorescent lights. The tattered tail was gone, and the victim's blank hazel eyes stared up at the harsh light that magnified the brutal gashes and scars on her torso, face, and arms, confirming that she'd experienced a tumultuous journey.

"Hello, Detective Morales," he said softly, sensing her presence without looking up. "Thanks for coming."

"I wish I could say I was glad to be here, Doctor." She paused and looked around the room. "Can't somebody requisition a little paint to cheer up this dreary place?"

She heard his muffled laugh drift out from behind his transparent face shield.

"Funny you should say that, Detective. I had a similar thought myself earlier."

Miranda positioned herself on the opposite side of the autopsy table. As she scanned the victim's battered body, her sister's image appeared. Tears threatened to expose her grief. She quickly locked the memory back in its box, but not before tears wet the rims of her dark eyes.

She wiped them away, but not before Dr. Rubens noticed.

He said nothing, lifting his protective mask and resting it on top of his balding head. His eyes expressed what words could not. He had his own nightmares to shield, stemming from decades of dealing with the dead. Knowing that each case could be the one that would make him call it quits.

Witnessing the evil people are capable of doing becomes a heavy burden. Emotions could prevent him from doing his job well. Routine thinking is required to create a shroud of detachment, he had told himself. Yet emotions continued to swirl wildly inside him.

"Follow me," he said, setting down the forceps and motioning with his arm as he walked toward the counter along the far wall. The blue-sequined mermaid tail—splayed open—lay flat on display.

Miranda's eyes roamed the tail, admiring its sleek design and hand-sewn sequins that covered the entire surface. Even the unflattering fluorescent lights could not diminish the twinkle of the tail's glimmering sapphire discs.

"The craftsmanship of the costume is exquisite," she muttered.

"Might be, Detective, but I'll tell you one thing: Removing that masterpiece was no small feat. Slippery bugger. I finally had to cut it off." He pointed to the clothing tag stitched inside the tattered waistband. "This is what I wanted to show you."

She leaned in.

"Mermaid's Delight. Tampa," she read aloud. "That could be useful."

"But that isn't the most interesting thing I found," he said excitedly, making his way back to the autopsy table. Miranda following in his wake. He picked up the forceps and clamped it onto the irregular-shaped object in one of the metal bowls and held it up to the light.

Miranda squinted. Sharpening her focus.

"Any idea what it is?"

He shrugged and handed her the forceps and magnifying glass.

"Beats me. See what you think," he said, rubbing his chin with his gloved hand. "I thought a stone, perhaps? It's firm. Dropped from the tongs of the weapon when I extracted it."

After peering at the object for a minute, Miranda handed the forceps and magnifier back to him, saying, "I expect Forensics will come up with something more definitive," she said. "Care to take another stab at it, Doc?" She lowered her head, embarrassed by her careless phrasing. "Sorry, Dr. Rubens. No pun intended."

The coroner raised an eyebrow. "Well, what I can say is that whatever the object is, it's encased with chest tissue, obscuring its true texture and shape. The pitted surface you can see slightly below the thin coating might be bone fragments from her ribs. But the paramount question for me is, was the object inside her before the weapon struck her, or, was it part of the weapon itself? A decoration of some sort?"

Miranda nodded.

Next, the coroner clamped his forceps on the object in the second metal bowl.

"Here's another little mystery," he said, handing the forceps back to Miranda. "You may recall that I noticed a strange lump in the victim's throat on Lido Beach this morning? This is it."

Miranda held the specimen up to the light, turning it at different angles.

"Any opinions on this one?" she asked, handing the forceps back to him.

"Nada," he said, shaking his head as he returned the object to the bowl.

"The two objects look to be the same size and shape," she said. "Could they be made of the same material?"

He shrugged. "Hard to tell, really. They could be anything." He glanced at her. "She could have even swallowed something during her watery ride."

"Well, if it would help to get some answers faster, I can drop the specimens off at the lab on my way home," offered Miranda, checking her watch. "Detective Selva and I will check out Mermaid's Delight." She took a deep breath and smiled. "Finally. Something tangible to get us moving toward some answers." Her eyes flushed with anticipation as she looked directly into the coroner's intense gaze.

"Good luck with that, Detective. And thanks for offering to drop off the specimens at the lab. Hold on a minute—I'll get the form from my office."

While Miranda waited, she went over to the autopsy table and stared at the ghostly young girl. A chill swept through her just as Dr. Rubens returned. He paused, giving her time to feel whatever she was feeling. But Miranda, immediately sensing his presence, turned toward him, pressing her lips together. He squeezed out a sympathetic smile and nodded.

"I've signed the chain-of-command form, Detective," he said, handing it to her. "Depending on the results of the analysis, we might get a better idea of our victim's travels. If we're lucky."

"I hope so, Dr. Rubens. Hopefully it will identify what the objects are, but, unfortunately, not how they got inside her."

"True. But something's better than nothing. Right?"

She smiled. "Yes. Of course. Anything else before I leave?"

"Ah," he said eagerly. "I almost forgot." He rolled the victim onto her right side, gently, as if she could feel the weight of his hands. "Look here," he said, pointing his index finger at the mermaid's left shoulder.

"A tattoo?"

"Yes. It looks to me like a toad, or a frog."

"Hmm." She leaned in closer. "The black veins threading through its body are so faint." She stared at the image for a few seconds, struck by the details etched in such a small area. "And those bulging red eyes are so . . . weird." She glanced up at the coroner looking over her shoulder. "Any idea what it could mean?" she asked as she straightened up.

Dr. Rubens stepped back and shrugged.

"Tattoos are as common as fleas these days, Detective, so it's not surprising she would have one. The important thing is to discover, why a frog?" He looked straight into Miranda's chocolate eyes. "People often choose their tattoos based on very personal reasons. Things that are important to them, for one reason or another." His eyes returned to the tattoo for a few lengthy moments, as if expecting the frog to explain itself. Then he looked again at Miranda. "If you can discover the meaning behind the tattoo—if indeed there is one—perhaps it will lead you to some answers."

"Is it conceivable the image is just decorative? Maybe a frog is just a frog?"

"Maybe. But I'd put my money on it meaning something to her, even if it doesn't answer the question of why she arrived on our beach with a harpoon in her chest."

A fresh thought made him smile.

"I've never known a beautiful, young maiden—or mermaid—to be enamored with a frog. Unless, of course, it turns into a prince."

Miranda laughed out loud. It felt good. Her shoulders relaxed. But only until the coroner suddenly boomed, "The Virginia Museum of Fine Arts!"

"What?" said Miranda, puzzled by the outburst.

"A special exhibit at the museum in Richmond. My sister lives there and I visited her a year or so ago. My niece is fascinated with tattoos, so I took her with me to view a temporary exhibit on the Japanese Art of Tattoos. The intricate patterns inked on people's bodies astounded me! Human canvases. Extraordinary designs with such complex, unimaginable radiance. Images so detailed they looked like the people were actually wearing clothes." He glanced at her, flushed, and cleared his throat. "I dare say, no body part had been overlooked by the tattoo artist on the plaster models. Remarkable artisans."

Miranda smiled, imagining how the male and female anatomy might be disguised, hidden beneath the artist's skillful use of colored inks masterfully drawn.

"So, no fig leaves, I take it," she teased.

The coroner grinned.

"Were there any tattoos of frogs?" she continued, trying to follow the coroner's train of thought.

"Not specifically. However, the museum had printed a catalog to accompany the exhibition." He tapped his curled lips. "I think I bought one for my niece. I'll ask her to check it for images and information pertaining to frogs and toads that might have been referenced in the exhibition."

"Hmm," nodded Miranda, thinking. "Certainly a good place to start. Thanks, Doc."

Miranda's gaze lingered on the frog image a bit longer, imprinting the inky image of the tattoo in her memory before Dr. Rubens placed the victim on her back again. Dr. Rubens watched her expression grow more sullen.

Suddenly aware of his gaze, she straightened her stance.

"Just thinking how tragic it is, the death of someone so young."

He pressed his lips together and nodded.

"I'd better be off," she said.

Dr. Rubens collected the two small glass jars and transferred the specimens, sticking a label on each one.

"I'll be in touch as soon as the lab reports are back," he said, handing her the jars.

"Thanks, Doc."

She stepped outside the metal doors of the morgue and into the summer heat. Bob Marley's "Three Little Birds" flowed from her cell phone, the melody instantly lifting her spirits.

"Hey, Matt," she said after checking the caller ID. "We're taking a road trip to Tampa. Come by my house in an hour. I'll drive."

"But—"

Miranda disconnected before he was finished.

Chapter 5

The forensic lab was busier than a beehive in summer, reinforcing the grim reality that bad things happen every day. Even in paradise. Regardless of the season. As she rounded the corner of the long hallway leading to the office of the director of the forensic lab, Miranda rammed into the handsome photographer she'd eyed, fleetingly, at the crime scene.

"Oh, sorry," she blurted out, feeling a warm blush spread on her cheeks.

He smiled.

"No problem. I should have been watching where I was going."

"Oh, no . . . no—completely my fault."

He paused.

"You're one of the detectives I saw on Lido Beach this morning, right?"

"Uh, yeah. Detective Morales. Miranda."

He reached out his hand to her.

"Pleased to meet you. Quite a gruesome scene."

She nodded, suddenly feeling awkward.

He studied her features like he was framing her for a photograph. Very photogenic, the voice inside him whispered.

"I was wondering if maybe we could meet for a drink sometime?"

His flirtation surprised her.

"A . . . a drink?" she stuttered. "Umm, well, I've got to drop off these specimens for analysis, then go to Tampa . . . then . . ."

"It's just a drink, Detective," he said, "not a marriage proposal." He took a card out of his pocket. "Text or call me if you're interested."

Miranda took his card and slipped it into the back pocket of her slacks.

"Sure. Okay. Yeah, I'll do that."

She had no intention of getting mixed up in that kind of complication. Her last, and only serious, romantic encounter had careened her toward a deep depression. The rawness of its abrupt ending still haunted her. Part of the mental baggage that she carted with her, and what had helped contribute to her forced sabbatical.

The photographer winked at her before walking away.

She watched his confident stride until he was out of view. Then, she knocked on the lab director's office door.

"Hey, Miranda," smiled Dr. Warren Levy, as he opened the glass door. He reached out his hand. "So good to see you after so long. Please, sit down. I take it your sabbatical is over?"

She inhaled deeply. Does everybody know about that? She forced a smile.

"Uh, yeah. I think everybody should take one," she said without meaning it.

"Ah. I'm afraid the powers that be wouldn't let me come back if I did that."

They both laughed.

"I doubt that. You'd be too hard to replace."

"That's very kind, Detective. So, what brings you to our gemology lab?"

"I'd hardly call your lab 'humble.' You have some of the brightest minds and the most cutting-edge technology. And your staff does a brilliant job with the evidence that comes through here. Much of your lab's success is due to your leadership."

She handed him the two small jars containing the specimens.

"These mysteries need your undivided attention. And pronto, if you please."

"Pronto, is it?" he teased, smiling and lifting his well-groomed dark eyebrows. He studied the objects, holding each jar up to the light. "Any ideas?"

"Not really. The coroner thought one, or both, could possibly be some kind of stone. They're both covered with gook, so it's hard to tell."

"Gook?" he repeated, amused. "Very scientific." His bright blue eyes sparkled as the light struck them at just the right angle.

Miranda lowered her eyes to conceal her embarrassment.

"Where'd they come from?"

"One was extracted from the back of our victim's throat. The other was apparently lodged between the tongs of the harpoon Dr. Rubens removed from her chest during the autopsy."

"Harpoon?" he said, settling back in his chair, eyes wide. "Not a weapon you see every day."

Miranda nodded, relaxing a bit as Dr. Levy continued to visually inspect the specimens.

"What do you know so far?"

"Our vic's a . . . a mermaid."

His eyebrows shot up again.

"A harpoon—and a mermaid?"

"I know, I know. It sounds . . . fantastical. She's not a real mermaid, of course. The victim washed up on Lido Beach late last night or early this morning wearing a mermaid costume."

"Ah. And . . ." He paused. "There's got to be more."

"Not really. Other than she was in pretty bad shape. Wherever she started her journey, it wasn't a pleasant ride."

He took a deep breath, his eyes studying hers. "Nasty business we're in."

"How long will it take to analyze the two specimens?" she asked pointedly.

"We'll get right on it. A mermaid must be a priority. Pronto, right?"

Miranda rolled her eyes.

"Please call me as soon as you know something, Dr. Levy."

"Always do, Detective Morales."

Chapter 6

Miranda opened her front door to see Matt's hand raised mid-knock, a growl rumbling in his throat.

"Where the hell have you been, Miranda?" he snapped. "I figured you'd call me after we left the crime scene and got ourselves cleaned up. Get together to discuss the case. It's been well over an hour since then!"

"Before you throw a hissy fit, Matt, step inside and I'll fill you in."

Matt stomped into the foyer, arms folded across his chest.

Miranda was unfazed by his tantrum.

"Dr. Rubens called me just as I got out of the shower. He asked me to come to the morgue."

"Without me?" hissed Matt.

"I figured you could catch up on your rest since you were at the crime scene so early." She glanced at him, gauging whether or not he was buying her excuse. He wasn't. Apologies didn't come easily to her. But Matt was different. He deserved one.

Matt blew out a heavy breath, corralling his urge to spew angry words at her.

"I didn't mean to hurt your feelings, Matt. It wasn't personal. Just expedient. I'm . . . I'm sorry. I had to go straight away." She paused. "I guess I wasn't thinking."

"Jesus, Miranda! I thought we were partners! Do you take me for some kind of rookie wimp?" Insecurity was clearly at the heart of his disgruntlement. His underlying fear that he wouldn't live up to Miranda's expectations—even though he had no clue what her expectations of him were. It had never come up before.

"We are partners, Matt. I'm truly sorry. I respect you as an equal." She gave him time for her words to seep in. "And I especially admire your dedication. Not only to the job, but to me."

He bent his head down, digesting her apology. He was acutely aware of the cocoon she'd spun around herself since they'd first become partners. Keeping the world at bay. Work her only outlet. Issues she never hinted at but he could sense. He looked up at her with his puppy-dog, indigo eyes.

"Well, just don't shut me out." He paused, briefly averting his gaze before locking eyes with her. "So, what did you discover at the morgue?"

"I'll fill you in on our drive to Tampa. On the way, I want you to find out what you can about a shop called Mermaid's Delight. I'll need the address." A smidgeon of guilt nudged at her as she soaked in his dejected expression, knowing he had a right to be miffed.

Matt looked at her.

"Mermaid's Delight, because?" Resentment still lingering.

"Because Dr. Rubens found a clothing tag in the mermaid tail when he removed it, from Mermaid's Delight. Where we're headed." She looked over at him, suddenly filled with a sense of her betrayal. "I really am sorry, Matt."

Matt pulled out his iPhone without assuaging her guilt and Googled the shop's name.

Once they were settled in the car, Matt plugged the address into Waze.

"Make sure the shop's open on Sundays. Please," she added, glancing at him.

His eyes were glued to the phone as the landscape zoomed by.

She knew he was pissed. He'll get over it, she decided. But it didn't stop her from regretting her decision to go to the morgue alone.

They rode in cool silence for several miles.

"Are you ready to listen, or are you going to stay grumpy?" she finally asked.

Matt expelled fumes of latent hostility, refusing to look at her.

"I'm ready," he grumbled.

"Okay, then," she said, rolling the tension from her shoulders. Clearing her throat, she mentally organized what she had learned at the morgue into a logical, straightforward framework. "Dr. Rubens extracted two objects from our victim. One came from the lining of her throat. The other dropped out when he removed the harpoon from her chest."

Matt shot her a look. She had his full attention.

"I remember him saying he thought he saw something in her throat at the crime scene. Did he have any idea what the objects could be?"

"Not really. He thought the one in her throat could be some kind of stone, or ocean debris."

"What about the other one, caught in the harpoon?"

"That one's more of a mystery. Even though it looked similar in size and shape to the one in her throat, he wondered if it could have been part of the harpoon itself."

"Meaning?"

"Like maybe it was a decorative feature on the harpoon that broke off when it struck her rib cage."

Matt nodded, picturing the thrust as the harpoon penetrated the chest.

"Or maybe it's part of the mermaid costume itself?"

Miranda turned to him with a broad smile.

"That's a brilliant idea, Matt. Neither Dr. Rubens nor I considered that possibility."

"Don't try buttering me up."

She laughed.

"I'm not trying to butter you up. It's conceivable that the top of the costume covering her breasts contained adornments, just as the mermaid tail was adorned with hand-sewn, sapphire sequins. We don't know for sure because the top was missing when she washed ashore. Once we know what the objects are, perhaps we can make more sense of it."

They each developed plausible scenarios involving the mysterious specimens for a time. Then Miranda continued with her whereabouts after leaving the crime scene.

"I dropped the two objects off at the forensics lab on my way home. Dr. Levy assured me he'd make the lab analysis a top priority."

Matt nodded. His frustration was softening. He resumed his research on Mermaid's Delight, reading aloud bits and pieces of relevant sections he'd Googled while Miranda drove.

"Costume shop in Tampa. Sells mermaid apparel and accessories. Owned by Trixie Monroe, a graduate of the prestigious Parsons School of Design. Got her start in the costume business when she met a producer of cult movies who commissioned her to make costumes for his fantasy and science-fiction films."

He glanced over and saw Miranda nodding.

"The professional connection with the film industry catapulted Monroe to fame and fortune in a short period of time as other film and theater people sought out her talents." He stopped reading for a few seconds. "Looks like a lot of movie people are fascinated with mermaids."

Miranda's focus was split between the traffic and him.

"Just get on with it, Matt."

"Trixie Monroe has dressed mermaids throughout the United States, Europe, and Central America for over a decade. Her exquisite designs command thousands of dollars for a single costume."

His eyes scanned the remainder of the article.

"Now this is interesting. Monroe was a former Miss Panama. Moved to Tampa in 2009 where she opened her shop."

He tapped on the photo of the designer embedded in the article and turned it toward Miranda.

"Not sure how current this is, but this is her."

Miranda's eyes drifted from the road to Matt's phone.

"Hmm . . . she could have been a beauty queen . . . when she was younger."

Matt stared at the image for a few seconds before clicking out of the article.

"Did Dr. Rubens find anything else during the autopsy?" he asked.

"Yes. A rather intriguing detail," she said, with all the drama of a good storyteller.

Matt shifted in his seat, twisting to face her.

"A frog tattoo, about the size of a half-dollar." Matt's eyes remained fixed on her as she described the details. "With bulging red eyes that seemed far too large for its small head. It was inked on the victim's left shoulder. Weird-looking creature," she said, squirming, as if she suddenly felt the slime of a wet frog crawling down her back. "At least Dr. Rubens and I agreed it resembled a frog. Or a toad."

"Sounds a bit creepy, or at the very least, odd. Did Dr. Rubens have any thoughts?"

"He only remarked, 'Tattoos are as common as fleas,' " she said, mimicking Dr. Rubens's voice.

Matt laughed, amused that the coroner's voice had made such an impression on her. Miranda continued to surprise him with the things that intrigued her.

"He also noted that, in his experience, people often choose tattoos based on their personal beliefs. Political dogma, religiosity—that kind of thing. He said that if we could uncover the meaning behind the frog tattoo, we might learn more about what was personally significant to our mermaid."

Matt wasn't sure he bought the theory, but he let it percolate for a time.

"Well, come to think of it, that actually makes sense when you think about it," he said. "My roommate freshman year at college had a tattoo that covered most of his back. It shocked me, to be honest, when he took off his shirt one day."

"Really? What was it?" she asked, captivated.

"It looked like a sea monster from some horror movie. Anyway, that was my instant reaction. Contorted in the shape of a whale, yet with sharp claws and the scales of a dragon. Ferocious-looking, for sure. When I ask him about it, he said it represented the 'tumult and discord of water.' I couldn't look at him the same way after that."

"Did he explain what it meant? Why he chose such a creature to literally carry on his back for the rest of his life?"

"I don't remember exactly, but it had something to do with Leviathan. Apparently a water creature that killed his female mate and served her to the so-called righteous—at a banquet."

Recalling his roommate's story sent a shiver down his spine.

"He said it had something to do with procreation."

He looked at Miranda.

"Honestly, it didn't make much sense to me. He said he was a devout Jew, and Leviathan was mentioned in the religious teachings of his faith. Something about the restoration of Israel."

His eyebrows pinched together and he shook his head.

"It was long time ago. I could have the whole story mixed up, so don't hold me to it."

"Hmm . . . still sounds like a strange choice for a tattoo," said Miranda.

"He did say that, at least for him, it symbolized a deep religious belief that was linked to the destruction of the world." He looked at her and paused. "Years later I heard that he'd become a Navy Seal."

Matt shrugged, wondering if Miranda had any tattoos. He'd never been a fan of them, especially when he imagined how they'd look once the person got old. Skin wrinkled and flabby. It's one thing when the skin is smooth and taut. Quite another when . . .

Suddenly he saw a sign for the Tampa exit. He turned up the audio for Waze just in time for Miranda to hear the instructions: "Keep right at the exit in seven hundred feet, then stay right toward Tampa."

Miranda followed the commands, ending with "You have reached your destination."

Miranda pulled into the parking lot in front of Mermaid's Delight and parked.

"Ready to explore the magical world of mermaids?" she said, opening her door.

Chapter 7

They paused outside the mermaid shop, peering at the window display where rubber mannequins with creamy white "skin" were draped with what Miranda assumed was the latest in exotic mermaid attire and accessories.

"I know I was annoyed that you didn't ask me to go to the morgue with you."

Miranda looked at him, puzzled.

"I thought we covered that already?"

"We did, and I'm fine with it. But I'm thinking it might be better if I stayed behind on this one."

"Because?"

"Because Trixie Monroe might be more willing to talk mermaids if I'm not around. You know, just another customer interested in mermaid stuff, rather than two detectives showing up, investigating a murder."

Miranda smiled.

"Sounds a little sexist, Matt. Maybe Trixie likes mermen, too," she teased. "But you do make a good point. What do you have in mind for yourself?"

He cocked his head toward the shop next door, Mel's Book Emporium.

"Research. I'll browse the shelves looking for books on mermaid folklore and tattoos, while you dive into the pleasures of Mermaid's Delight and Trixie Monroe's fantasy world."

She groaned at his pun.

"I don't want to give you the impression you're not an equal in this investigation," she said.

"Think of it as divide and conquer," he replied, winking. "Text me if you need me to rescue you."

The bell jingled over the front door as Miranda entered Mermaid's Delight.

The attractive woman behind the sales counter assisting a customer looked just like the photo on Matt's iPhone. Elegant and regal, befitting a former Miss Panama. Tall and slender, with an ivory complexion and bright red, full lips, her sleek black hair caressed her narrow shoulders. A runway model half her age couldn't exude more allure.

Trixie Monroe looked over and nodded at Miranda.

"I'll be right with you," she said, smiling. "Have a look around."

Miranda drifted from rack to rack, listening as the shop owner dismissed the customer's desire to opt for the mermaid tail she had chosen herself, rather than the one the designer had recommended. Trixie Monroe radiated arrogance—or perhaps it was merely the self-confidence that Miranda herself had never mastered.

The variety of costumes and accessories was impressive. Mermaid tails with gaudy embellishments, colorful beads and finely stitched embroidery. Silk scarves, hand-painted with sensuous mermaids, dripped from satin-covered hangers. Earrings shaped like sea creatures dangled from carousels sitting on glass countertops. Faux gemstone necklaces were artfully displayed on black velvet pads glittering under the LED lights, lighting designed to exaggerate and enhance their sparkle. Everything was carefully displayed to tempt mermaid enthusiasts to forget the budget they'd promised themselves they'd stick to before crossing the threshold into fantasyland.

A silver charm bracelet in one of the cases grabbed Miranda's eye. A tiny mirror, a mermaid comb, a seahorse, a grinning dolphin, a graceful stingray, and a starfish attached to a delicate, silver chain. The price tag was turned facedown, forcing the customer to ask, “How much?”

Instantly her estranged mother’s stern voice poked into her thoughts.

If you have to ask the price of something, Miranda, you can’t afford it.

Then, thoughts of her sister broke through.

If only Farrah could see these marvelous mermaid costumes.

“Dreaming?” said a sultry voice behind her.

Startled, Miranda jumped.

“Sorry. I didn’t mean to scare you.

“I was just lost in a memory,” said Miranda, catching her breath.

“Mermaids are enchanting. Bewitching creatures, luring sailors to their death like moths to a flame.” The designer’s cool, green eyes surveyed Miranda. A headmistress inspecting a student accused of a forbidden act.

Miranda felt chilled to her core, and instinctively crossed her arms over her chest.

“I’m Trixie Monroe,” the woman said, reaching out her hand with its perfectly manicured nails painted blood-red.

Miranda reluctantly shook her hand without sharing her own name.

Now that she saw her up close, Miranda noticed an almost alabaster glow to her complexion. The woman’s eyes were cold and calculating as she tried to hide a condescending aura behind her plastic smile.

“What an extraordinary shop you have, Ms. Monroe.”

“Yes, I think so. Are you looking for something in particular?”

“Actually, I was interested in this blue-sequined mermaid tail,” Miranda said, standing in front of a rack holding a tail similar to the one the victim had been wearing.

"You have exquisite taste."

Trixie Monroe removed the costume from the rack and held it up for Miranda's inspection.

"It's absolutely stunning," said Miranda, biding her time before asking the questions that would really get to the heart of why she had come to Mermaid's Delight. "Do you make all of these yourself?"

"I design some of them—actually, just the custom orders," she said smugly. "All the regular merchandise is made . . . elsewhere. The United States, China, Taiwan."

"So, this particular blue one—did you design it?"

Trixie cleared her throat and notched her chin higher.

"Yes. A custom order I handled myself." Her eyes grew wary. She was beginning to sense this was not an ordinary customer. She was guarded, but undaunted by the questioning.

"Ah. So did the person who custom-ordered this one decide not to take it after all? That's why it's on the rack with the others?"

The designer shifted her weight to the other foot, growing irritated now.

"Are you interested in purchasing the mermaid tail, Ms. . . ."

"Morales," said Miranda, handing her a business card.

Monroe looked at it, then glared at Miranda, returning the blue tail to the rack.

"You're a detective?" she said, her tone uneasy. Her shoulders had stiffened.

"That's right. Detective Miranda Morales. I was hoping you might be able to help me."

"I can't imagine how I could possibly help you."

"I'm investigating a murder."

The woman bristled. Her outward calm extinguished, her posture was now defensive and defiant.

"What would I know about a murder?"

A force to be reckoned with, thought Miranda. Tread carefully.

"The victim is a young girl. She was wearing a mermaid tail with a label from your shop."

"Tragic, I'm sure, Detective." She paused. "My merchandise is sold all over the world. I have no idea where it goes after it leaves my shop."

Miranda took out her iPhone.

"I'd like to show you some pictures."

It wasn't a request. Without hesitation, she turned the savage photo toward Monroe.

A bloated, bruised face filled the screen. Black, tangled hair encrusted with algae and beach debris.

The woman recoiled and shoved the phone away.

"How could you expect anybody to be able to identify something like that?" she protested.

Miranda wasn't surprised by the designer's reaction to the gruesome image, but still found her lack of empathy appalling. Her initial dislike for Trixie Monroe was growing.

"She's a human being, Ms. Monroe. Not an object."

She didn't flinch.

"I'm sorry, Detective," she said, lifting her chin. "I'd like to help you, but I have no idea who that . . . person might be."

Undeterred, Miranda swiped to the photos Dr. Rubens had sent her. The shop's label stitched to the waistband. Another photo showing coral-colored toenails poking through the ragged, torn fin. Patches where blue sequins had once been.

"Disgusting!" seethed the designer.

"I understand, Ms. Monroe. Do you recognize the tail as one that had been custom-ordered, like the one you just showed me?"

She ignored Miranda's question.

"Such a shame. So defaced and damaged."

Miranda wondered if her remarks were meant for the victim or the tattered tail.

Then Trixie Monroe turned her cold gaze on Miranda.

"What did you ask me?"

"If you had custom-designed the tail in the photo. It looks just like the one you took off the rack."

"There's no way I could tell from that hideous picture. It could have been sold through some other shop altogether."

"But your tag is sewn on the costume the victim was wearing."

The designer huffed and shrugged her shoulders.

"Dozens of designers copy those of us at the top of the food chain in the fashion world," she said, clasping her hands in front of her. "If the tail in the picture is mine, it could have been one of several I shipped to a post office box in Miami several months ago."

"Is the one here in your shop part of that same order?"

"Maybe."

"Was it returned for some reason?"

Trixie Monroe squirmed.

"That's hard to say. My assistant handles all deliveries and returns."

"Well, if your custom orders are all original, how do you explain that the one hanging on the rack—the one like the one on the dead mermaid—could have been sent to Miami?"

"I didn't say the one on the rack was a custom order. You're putting words in my mouth."

Miranda sensed the shop owner was blocking her.

"Would you check your records, please, Ms. Monroe? See if a tail like the one on the victim was part of the custom order sent to Miami?"

"That's private information, Detective. You need a search warrant to see my records."

"Technically, yes. But if I come back with a search warrant, I could confiscate all of your records. If you cooperate now, however, I'll soon be out of your hair."

The threat was a gamble since Trixie might not be aware of how hard it could be to get a search warrant.

Trixie Monroe blew out a breath, defeated, her eyes shooting darts into Miranda's steady gaze.

"If I recall, one of the tails wasn't ready to ship with the others. It was sent later. The one hanging on the rack is not the same quality as the one I made especially at the request of a customer." She paused. "I never ask what the special occasion might be for such orders, or who wears them once they leave my shop."

The designer turned and reluctantly opened the top drawer of the filing cabinet behind the sales counter. Thumbing through the files, she slid out the invoice she was seeking, keeping it out of reach of Miranda.

"Six custom-ordered tails were sent to Mermaid Fantasea, P.O. Box 211, Miami. The order specified style, ornamentation, and precise measurements for each tail." Trixie Monroe glanced up at Miranda. "All six costumes were about the same size," she said, returning to the invoice. "One order specified the blue sequins had to be hand-sewn, with a contrasting turquoise waistband of braided silk with Swarovski crystals and other embellishments."

Trixie looked up again into Miranda's challenging gaze. "The one in your photograph seems to be missing the turquoise braid. If it is, indeed, the same one in this order." A contemplative look veiled her face. "A shame," she muttered. "Swarovski crystals are quite expensive."

Miranda reached for the invoice and folder in Trixie's hands, but the designer instinctively pulled them back.

"Confidential. You will have to get a warrant if you want to see this information. I've told you everything that's here," she said, pressing the folder close to her chest.

Miranda knew the shop owner was testing her.

"Anybody sign for it?"

She took a deep breath, calculating how best to answer. Although resigned to the interrogation, she was unwilling to give more details.

"We insure our shipments, but we don't always require signatures. All custom orders are paid for up front. Before we ship them. Seems to work best for . . . everyone." Trixie paused. "For this order, I was specifically told to leave my label off the tails."

"I would think the label would be a status symbol for you," said Miranda. "And good advertising for your shop. Are you saying that the costume on the victim couldn't have been part of that shipment because it did have your label on it?"

"No. Just that sometimes I ignore those kinds of requests," Trixie said, defiantly. "I'm proud of my merchandise. My label is my brand. All six tails did have my label sewn into the waistbands. Removing my label would be like unstitching the swoosh logo from a Nike sneaker."

Would someone really want to add their own label to Trixie's tails? Miranda thought. Certainly easier than copying the design and making them from scratch.

"So you disregarded the request to eliminate your clothing tag on all the tails?" Miranda asked.

"I'm afraid that's all I can tell you, Detective . . . Morales," she said, her eyes drifting to Miranda's business card on the counter. "If there's nothing else . . ."

"Thanks for your time, Ms. Monroe," said Miranda flatly, aware that she had reached the end point of the interview. "You have my card. If you remember anything that might help, please call me. Anytime."

"Of course, Detective," she said, doubting she'd ever have reason to call the brash detective.

Just as Miranda was walking away from the counter, a young woman entered the shop through the privacy curtain at the back. Miranda guessed the young woman was an employee, about nineteen years old. Pretty, in a girl-next-door kind of way, except for the flashy green glitter flakes dusting her hair.

"Hello, Ms. Monroe. Sorry I'm late," said the woman, catching her breath. "Car trouble." She smiled when she saw Miranda, and in a low whisper asked, "Is she a new customer?"

Trixie grimaced, realizing Miranda had stopped short of her exit.

"This is Detective Morales, Brenda. She was . . . interested in my designs," she said, skirting the issue of the dead mermaid. "She was just leaving."

"Detective?" said Brenda, alarmed, wringing her small hands together. "Is something wrong?"

"Nothing that concerns you."

Miranda kept her eyes on Brenda, deciding whether or not to question her about the victim.

"Well, actually, Ms. . . ."

"Sinclair," said Brenda.

Ignoring the shop owner's dismissal, Miranda returned to the counter.

"I'm investigating a murder, Ms. Sinclair."

"Murder?" Brenda's mouth gaped open.

"It doesn't concern us, Brenda," Trixie Monroe scoffed. "I left a list of things for you to do in the office. You need to get started on it right away."

Miranda shot the designer a scathing look.

"I beg to differ with you, Ms. Monroe. This does concern you, in that your label was on the victim's tail. I'd like to show your assistant the photo of the girl."

Trixie put her hands on her hips, her frustration clearly evident. "I forbid you to show that ghastly picture to Brenda. I'm telling you, there's no way she knows who that . . . person is!"

"I'd appreciate it if you would take a look at the photo, Ms. Sinclair. I admit it's unpleasant, and I apologize," said Miranda. "I wouldn't ask unless I thought you might have seen her." Miranda clicked the photo on her iPhone and approached Brenda. "This girl washed up on Lido Beach early this morning. She was wearing a mermaid tail with a tag from this shop."

"I told you to go to the back room, Brenda. You can start

with the inventory."

"Ms. Monroe, if you continue to interfere with my investigation, it will not bode well for you." Miranda paused to let the threat sink in. "I need Ms. Sinclair to look at this photo."

"Hmmph," grunted the designer, stepping back.

Miranda handed the phone to Brenda.

"Oh my God!" Brenda gasped, slapping her hand over her mouth. "I think I'm going to be sick!" She raced off to the bathroom, her hand over her mouth.

"I hope you're satisfied, Detective Morales. Now Brenda will be useless for the rest of the day."

"It's not a matter of whether I'm satisfied or not, Ms. Monroe." She stared into the shop owner's angry eyes. "It's a matter of identifying a young girl wearing a mermaid costume with your tag in it, and finding out how she ended up dead on one of our beaches."

"I'm sure I can't help you with that. Neither can Brenda. So, if there's nothing else . . ."

Miranda glared at her. Bitch with a capital B.

"I'll be back," said Miranda. You can bet your fancy ass on that.

As Miranda turned away from the sales counter, Brenda came out of the bathroom, ashen-faced and trembling.

Miranda slid a business card across the counter.

"Please call me if you think of anything, Ms. Sinclair. Anything at all."

Brenda picked up the card and glanced at it, forcing her lips into a fragmented smile.

"Good day to you both," Miranda said bluntly. The bell over the door jingled as she stepped outside into the fresh air without looking back.

She expelled a puff of pent-up irritation and texted Matt: "Finished here. Meet me outside."

Just then she heard a shrill whistle. Turning around she saw Matt holding a large book under his arm.

"Good timing," he said.

Miranda growled.

"That doesn't sound good."

"What a diva!" she growled, then glanced at the book under Matt's arm. "What'd you find?"

He held up the book with the cover facing her.

"Iconography and Symbolism in Ancient Cultures," she read aloud.

"Research," he said with a smile.

She wasn't sure if she should be amused or amazed.

"Well, you can continue your research on the ride home. But let's have lunch first. I'll fill you in over a sandwich."

Matt looked at his watch. "Two-thirty. No wonder I'm starving."

They got into the car and drove to a nearby restaurant.

"What's your pleasure, partner?" she asked, glancing at Matt.

"A double cheeseburger with fries and a Coke."

Miranda placed Matt's order, then hers. As she waited at the window, her Bluetooth flashed Unknown Caller.

"Morales here." Static and intermittent gasps vibrated through the Bose speakers. "Hello? Who is this?"

"Detec . . . Mor . . . les?" said a crackly voice. "This is Bren . . . Sin . . . from Mer . . . Delights. Can you hear me?"

"Yes, but you're breaking up, Brenda."

"I must be . . . bad . . . zone." A long pause, with the static increasing, then subsiding. "Mermaid camp . . ."

"Brenda? Are you still there?" Miranda said, reaching for the bag of food being handed to her through the window.

"Yes. Sorry. I stepped out of the shop to call you. I wanted to tell you that Ms. Monroe has been doing business for some time now with a mermaid camp a few miles away from here. The camp director might be worth talking to. Maybe she'd recognize the . . . the girl in the picture." Her voice was laden with sorrow.

"Why do you think that?" asked Miranda, watching Matt as he peeked into the bag. Mouthwatering aromas filled the car.

"A lot of young girls attend her mermaid camp every year. It's been around for some time. Maybe the . . . mermaid in the picture attended one of the camp sessions."

"What's the director's name?"

"Dallas, I think." Brenda paused. "No, that's not it." Another pause. "Georgia. Her name's Georgia. I'm sure of it. I don't remember her last name. If anybody knows mermaids, it'll be her."

"What's the name of the camp?"

"Sirens of the Deep. It's a few miles south of Mermaid's Delight, just off the highway. It should be well signposted. I think it's open till maybe five o'clock tonight. Sunday's a popular day for visitors."

"Sirens of the Deep," repeated Miranda. "Thank you, Brenda."

"Oh, one more thing, Detective. I overheard Ms. Monroe on the phone right after you left. Something about a mermaid fantasy? Not sure what it means. She never mentioned it to me, but I heard her say something about a meeting planned sometime this week. At least that's what it sounded like to me. Exactly when I couldn't say."

"Do you know where?"

"No. I assume the Tampa harbor." She paused. "Actually, come to think of it, I did hear her say something about a yacht. So the meeting might be on one of the boats docked at the harbor."

"Thanks, again, Brenda. If you hear anything else, please call me."

"I will. I've got to get back to the shop."

Miranda looked at Matt. "Google 'Sirens of the Deep,' will you?"

"More mermaids?" he groaned.

"You love it." She grinned.

"Yeah. Like a sharp stick in the eye," he muttered under his breath.

Chapter 8

From her office window, Georgia Holmes watched as two strangers walked up the path toward the administration building. She checked her hair and makeup in the mirror near the front door. First impressions mattered, and she was forming her own.

Nice-looking couple. Reminds me of a movie star. Tom Cruise? A young Hugh Grant, maybe? Yes. Same thick hair. Handsome features. He'd make a divine Neptune. I can picture the woman with him, dressed in a mermaid costume. Slender waist. Shapely hips. Perfect breasts. A model for a billboard ad for my camp. If only I could afford the luxury of advertising.

A wave of depression swept through her, suddenly aware of her own shortcomings. Wishing she were taller-thinner-younger. That her cropped, salt-and-pepper hair looked less matronly. She had thought about coloring it many times but had never made the leap. She was loyal to her stylist, who had no imagination. The fact that, as camp director, she was surrounded by young, beautiful campers made her even more self-conscious. Now, at sixty, she wondered if it was too late to even bother. *I am what I am.*

She turned to the clock on the wall. The voluptuous mermaid painted on the clock face stretched out her arms to signal the current time: 4:45 p.m.

"Damn," she muttered. "I can't be late for my massage."

"Everything okay, Ms. Georgia?" asked Destina Walker, her petite, forty-something secretary. She was typing away at her desk in the reception room, watching the director's fixed gaze out the window.

Georgia was too immersed in the couple's approach to hear Destina's question.

Destina shrugged and resumed her typing.

As Matt and Miranda neared the building, Miranda poked her chin at the mosaic archway. Mermaids and sea creatures painted on the sign announced SIRENS OF THE DEEP—WHERE MERFOLK ARE BORN.

"Guess we're in the right place."

"Oh, good," he answered sarcastically.

As they walked up the three steps to the front door, Georgia Holmes swung it open, folding her arms under her large breasts, a tentative smile on her lips.

"Good afternoon. May I help you?"

"Good afternoon. I'm Chief Detective Miranda Morales, and this is my partner, Detective Matt Selva."

Georgia's shoulders tightened. Detectives? Her stony glare softened as she scanned Matt's features. Yes. Definitely. Hugh Grant.

"I'm Georgia Holmes, director and co-owner of the camp," she said, reaching out her hand to them. "What brings you here?"

"We're investigating a murder," said Miranda without preamble.

"A murder?" Georgia pressed her hand to her heart. "Oh, my. How tragic. But what do I have to do with a murder investigation?"

Miranda pulled her iPhone out of the back pocket of her slacks.

"I have a couple of photos I'd like to show you, Ms. Holmes."

She opened the phone to the same photo she had shown to Trixie Monroe and Brenda Sinclair at Mermaid's Delight.

"Do you recognize her?" she asked, passing the phone to Georgia.

Georgia put on her eyeglasses, attached to a lanyard embroidered with mermaids. She pulled the phone closer, gasped, then turned away, shoving the phone back toward Miranda. She removed her glasses and pinched the wide bridge of her nose, her face drained of color. Suddenly she felt wobbly.

Matt grasped her arm. "Take some deep breaths, Ms. Holmes. Slowly now," he encouraged softly. "We'll get you inside so you can sit down."

Miranda pushed the door open wide enough for the two to enter together. She followed.

"Miss Georgia! Are you okay?" exclaimed her secretary, jumping up from her desk.

"Yes, Destina . . . I'm fine. Please bring a pitcher of cold water and some glasses to my office."

"Of course," Destina said, wary.

Georgia sat down in the high-back chair behind her uncluttered oak desk and motioned for the two detectives to sit in the armchairs facing her.

Matt glided his hand over the smooth shape of dolphins on both arms of his chair.

"Hand-carved," said Georgia, smiling proudly, momentarily turning her thoughts away from the horrible photo she'd just seen.

Matt smiled and nodded, his fingers gently riding over the deep grooves and crevices, marveling at the meticulous detail and fine craftsmanship.

Pictures of camp life were scattered around the spacious room. Georgia posing with a line of young girls dressed as mermaids. Girls of varying sizes preparing to dive into a huge swimming pool wearing their colorful tails. Other photos showed campers sitting on blankets under trees, reading magazines. Small groups were gathered at picnic tables, engaging in assorted activities. A shadow box filled with sand dollars, starfish, and sharks' teeth hung on the wall next to a large window that overlooked gardens bursting with native flowers. A mural of tropical fish and playful dolphins swimming among coral reefs covered one long wall, leading the eye to a cluster of mermaids around a large, flat rock. One mermaid poised seductively on top of a rock that sat in the middle of a vast ocean.

Destina entered the office carrying a tray with a pitcher of water and some glasses.

Miranda cleared her throat, clasped her hands together in her lap, and leaned slightly forward.

"I want to apologize for not having prepared you for that photo, Ms. Holmes. I understand the picture is quite disturbing." She glanced at Matt, then back at Georgia. "Sometimes we forget that most people aren't used to the savage things we see as part of our job."

Georgia's shoulders drooped as she grew calmer. She put her forearms on her desk and folded her hands in front of her. She took a deep breath to ready herself.

"It was terribly shocking," she said, holding back tears. "So, how do you think I can help you?"

"A young girl washed up on Lido Beach during the night, or sometime early this morning," Miranda said.

Georgia's eyes widened. "The girl in the photo?"

"A label from a costume shop was stitched inside the waistband of the victim's mermaid tail," continued Miranda.

"What has that got to do with me?"

"The label was from Mermaid's Delight in Tampa. Do you know the shop?"

The edge of Georgia's mouth twitched.

"So, Trixie Monroe sent you!" she exclaimed, angrily. "It's just like her to get me involved in something sordid!" She paused, her sea-green eyes darting from Miranda to Matt. "What made her think I'd know the girl?"

Miranda's eyebrows flicked up. So Georgia Holmes has issues with Trixie Monroe.

"Actually, it wasn't Ms. Monroe who suggested we come here," she said, avoiding the mention of the shop clerk's name. "But it does seem reasonable, don't you think, that a girl wearing a mermaid costume might have attended your camp, especially considering the camp's proximity to Mermaid's Delight?"

Georgia took a deep breath and let it out slowly. She poured a drink of water from the pitcher to wet her mouth.

"I suppose that's a reasonable assumption," she confessed. "Let me see the pictures on your phone again," she said, reluctantly putting her glasses back on. Leaning forward, she reached for the phone Miranda had slid across the desk.

"We know it may be difficult for you to recognize the girl, especially in her condition, but it would be extremely helpful, Ms. Holmes, if you could tell us anything," Matt said.

Georgia looked at the photos, then closed her eyes and bowed her head.

"Take your time, Ms. Holmes. We know this isn't easy."

Georgia raised her head, tears in her eyes, and slid the phone back toward Miranda.

"I'm sorry, detectives, but I'm afraid I can't help you. I've never seen the girl in the pictures." She stood up abruptly and walked around her desk. "Now, if there's nothing else? I have another appointment."

She opened the door to the reception room. "Ms. Walker will show you out. I'm sorry I couldn't help you."

Miranda picked up her phone from the desk and put it in her pocket. As she turned to leave, she noticed Matt engrossed in a picture on the corner of the director's desk. The director was arm in arm with a handsome man with an olive complexion, wearing a Panama hat and a straw-colored summer suit. His oversized sunglasses, along with the hat, made it difficult to discern his features. He stared, unsmiling, at the camera. Mermaid Fantasea was painted on the side of the yacht behind them.

Georgia twisted around and saw them looking at the photo. "Are you coming, detectives?" she snipped.

Miranda elbowed Matt, and as she brushed past Georgia, she whispered, "You two make a handsome couple."

"Whatever do you mean?" she said, a blush spreading across her plump cheeks.

"The photo on your desk. You look very happy."

Georgia's demeanor hardened.

"Good day, detectives. Good luck with your investigation."
As Miranda and Matt headed back to the parking lot, Miranda said, "She knows a lot more than she's saying."

Feeling the director's laser-beam focus on them, Miranda abruptly turned around.

Georgia was standing in the office doorway, arms folded, just as they were when she had first greeted them.

Miranda walked casually back toward her and smiled.

"Would it be okay if my partner and I took a look around your camp before we leave? My younger sister and I loved mermaids when we were little. She would have been ecstatic to have had the chance to be a mermaid at your lovely facility."

Georgia, hesitant, rolled her shoulders and huffed, but she seemed proud that Miranda appreciated the camp.

"Go on—but the camp closes to visitors in half an hour. Make sure you're out by closing time."

Miranda nodded. "Thank you. We will."

Georgia's attentive green eyes followed the two detectives as they headed down the flagstone path toward the mosaic arch, welcoming them to merfolkland. Their unexpected visit had unsettled her more than she realized. And the picture of the dead mermaid had alarmed her. Its grotesqueness set her nerves on edge. She tried, but failed, to shake away the gruesome images of the dead girl's vacant, unseeing eyes. The bruises and gashes that marred her thin, bare arms. Her long, coal-black hair encrusted with debris. The tattered mermaid tail.

Shivers twisted down her spine. She was grateful that her massage would loosen her twisted muscles and ease her turmoil until she no longer pictured the brutality humans could inflict on one another.

Chapter 9

Beyond the ornate arch, pastel-painted cottages dotted the perimeter of the expansive campground. Bougainvillea with spectacular fuchsia blooms complemented the elegant silver palms lining a stretch of the path. An Olympic-size pool encompassed a large part of the center of the campground, clearly the focal point of the bucolic setting. Orchids and other exotic plants in Tuscan-style pots sat at strategic locations around the pool.

A mosaic path of square tiles with motifs of sea turtles, whales, dolphins, sharks, and seahorses led to a few picnic tables with brightly colored umbrellas unfurled for protection from the sun's harsh rays. A life-size mermaid sculpture with outstretched arms stood in the center of a nearby pond, ducks paddling without a care around the water fountain.

Behind a high wall a few feet away, laughter spilled into the late afternoon air.

Miranda nudged Matt.

"Let's go see what mermaid campers look like."

Matt sighed as they reached a forked path about twenty feet from the arched entrance.

"I'll go left, you go right," she said.

Three young girls in their early teens were sitting at a picnic table, giggling as they strung colorful beads onto long, white cords. Whispering. Shuffling through the collection of beads on the table. Choosing the perfect one to add to their necklaces. Miranda put her index finger to her lips.

He nodded.

They watched silently, cataloging the girls' features and mannerisms. Long chestnut curls dripped over one girl's snow-white shoulders, cascading down her chest and barely covering her well-developed breasts that spilled over the top of her bikini. The girl next to her had red, poker-straight hair parted down the middle. Her breasts were less developed. The third girl, her back to Matt and Miranda, had corn-silk tendrils that twirled like satin ribbons down her slender back, delicate wisps clinging to her untanned arms. Every so often they'd laugh out loud, squealing with delight as they found the next bead to add to their collection.

Suddenly a gust of wind blew across the table. The girls shrieked as they tried to keep the beads from rolling off the table. The strong wind had exposed a dark mark on the corn-silk-haired girl's left shoulder.

Miranda moved like a cat toward the picnic table, nudging Matt and jutting her chin toward the girl with her back to them.

"Looks like one of the campers has a mark of some kind on her left shoulder," she whispered.

"The blonde?"

Miranda nodded.

Eager to confirm her suspicion, she walked over to the table. Matt stood beside her.

"Hello," said Miranda, smiling warmly.

The girl with the corn-silk hair flinched and twisted to face them.

"Sorry. I didn't mean to frighten you," said Miranda.

The girl turned back around to resume threading her beads.

"Hi," replied the girl with the chestnut curls from across the table. "Are you the new camp counselors?"

"No, we're just looking around. Mind if we watch for a few minutes?"

"Whatever," said the chestnut-haired girl.

"Yeah, whatever," said the red-haired girl.

The blonde kept her eyes averted, intent on beading her necklace.

Miranda sat down on the edge of the bench next to the blonde girl, looking across the table at the two girls stringing beads. Matt remained standing beside her.

"What are you making?" asked Miranda, browsing the assorted trinkets spread out on the table.

"Necklaces," said the red-haired girl. "It's a tradition that the campers make their own jewelry to wear during the fashion show. The rest are sold in the gift shop."

Miranda glanced at the chestnut-haired girl seated next to her.

"You're all campers here?"

"Yes," said the girl with the chestnut hair. "We have to finish these necklaces by the end of the week."

"What's the hurry?"

"The celebration marking the end of our camp session is this weekend. We have a talent show and everything."

"Ah. May I?" asked Miranda, pointing to one of the finished necklaces on the table.

"Sure," said the red-haired girl, stringing beads while smiling flirtatiously at Matt.

"It's quite lovely," Miranda said, admiring the necklace before returning it to the table. Turning toward the girl with the corn-silk hair, she asked, "Which one did you make?"

The girl sorted through the collection of beads, ignoring Miranda.

"She doesn't talk much," said the chestnut-haired girl as she threaded her own beads. She missed the blonde girl's snarl at her from across the table.

"Her name's Lila. She made that one," said the red-haired girl, pointing to a necklace containing colored sea glass, painted shells, and shiny seahorses lying on the table.

"That's stunning. Do they sell pretty well in the gift shop?"

"Sometimes," said the chestnut-haired girl. "A visitor bought one of Gina's last week," she said, cocking her head toward the camper next to her.

Gina smiled unabashedly.

"And Tammy made a pearl necklace as a gift for a special friend," Gina said, returning the chestnut-haired girl's compliment.

"Lucky friend," smiled Miranda.

"Did you know pearls can be black?" asked Tammy, spontaneously.

"Uh, yes. Is the friend you made the pearl necklace for still here at camp?"

"No. She got sick or something and left camp abruptly. I didn't even have time to put the clasp on it." She paused and looked up at Miranda.

"When did she leave?"

Tammy and Gina eyed each other.

"Soon after she got here," said Tammy.

"Sounds like you were good friends."

"Kind of," said Tammy. "But not really. She did mention that she liked pearls, though. I found some black ones at the bottom of one of the trinket baskets and made a necklace for her just before she left."

A pudgy, solitary figure wearing a Panama hat and sunglasses, standing in the shadows of the bougainvillea shrubs in the distance, caught Lila's eye. She accidentally bumped shoulders with Miranda seated next to her as she wiggled nervously on the bench.

Miranda looked up and spotted the stranger, but he turned away.

Lila's breathing grew more rapid and her hands trembled. She dropped some beads, which rolled across the table and fell into the grass beneath the bench.

Matt and Miranda bent down to collect the fallen beads. Miranda whispered to Matt, "Look closely at Lila's left shoulder when you stand up. Looks like a tattoo of a lizard to me."

"You look like you just saw a ghost, Lila!" said Gina.

Matt stood up and casually leaned in to eye Lila's shoulder as he set the beads back on the table. He nodded to Miranda as she took her seat beside Lila.

Gina had come over to check on Lila and was rubbing her back. Miranda noticed that Gina also had a tattoo on her left shoulder, but a strong breeze blew a wisp of red hair across her shoulder, concealing the tattoo before Miranda could make out what it was.

Lila sat there, frozen. Silent as death. Gripping the necklace in her delicate hands, with goose bumps dotting her pale arms. Then, mechanically, she began threading beads onto the white cord once again, her breathing back to normal.

Gina returned to her seat opposite Lila, still vigilant.

"I think we're all a bit nervous about the upcoming talent competition."

Miranda scanned the distant landscape where Lila had been looking but the stranger had disappeared. She picked up the conversation again with the campers.

"By the way, my name's Miranda," she said, studying the threesome. "And this is Matt."

Matt smiled, slightly embarrassed, uncomfortably aware of Gina's flirtation.

"Are you two married?" asked Tammy bluntly.

Miranda laughed.

"Uh, no. We're just partners."

"Partners? Like you're-in-love-but-not-married kind of partners?"

Matt cleared his throat and shifted his stance.

Miranda smiled. "Actually, we work together. That kind of partners."

"Ah. That's good news," said Gina, winking at Matt while coyly pulling a strand of hair over her breast.

Matt looked away, trying to ignore her overtures.

Miranda, aware of the girl's advances, smiled to herself.

"So, you mentioned there's a talent show? What's that all about?"

"It's awesome," said Gina. "There's an underwater ballet, and a beauty pageant. The talent competition is the finale." She pursed her lips and tapped them with her index finger. "The ballet is really difficult," she said. "Wearing a mermaid tail while swimming and holding your breath underwater—it's exhausting."

"Holding your breath for such a long time is the toughest part," said Tammy. She tilted her head. "Very few campers can do it."

"But there's always one mermaid who does it better than anybody else," said Gina, sounding envious.

"Are you one of them?" asked Miranda.

"No," laughed Gina. "But Miss Georgia told us about one of her mermaids who'd learned to hold her breath for much longer than any other camper who'd ever attended her camp." Miranda raised an eyebrow.

"That's remarkable. What's her name?" asked Miranda.

Gina shrugged.

"I don't know. Miss Georgia never mentioned her by name. Or why she had to leave when the camp session had barely begun." Gina paused, scrunching her mouth. "Too bad, too. She missed the chance to compete for the Queen Mermaid Ambassador title."

"And wear the bejeweled crown during the trip around the world . . . on a yacht," gushed Tammy.

"A yacht. Really?" Miranda said, remembering the picture on Georgia's desk.

"Yes. The Queen Mermaid Ambassador, along with a chaperone, travels around the world for a year, promoting the importance of cleaning up the oceans and protecting sea creatures."

"Wow! An important job." Miranda glanced across the field. She nudged Matt, and nodded toward the flowering bougainvillea. The stranger had reappeared.

"Do you think that's the guy in the photo on Georgia's desk?" he whispered.

"Hard to tell with the sunglasses. Same Panama hat, though. He certainly seems interested in the girls."

"Hmm . . . I wonder if Georgia knows him?"

The campers had already resumed their former chattiness, Gina's provocative behavior toward Matt yielding to the task of necklace-making.

Matt checked his watch and elbowed Miranda.

"We should probably be heading back, Detective," he said, louder than he intended. "It's getting late."

"Wait! You two are detectives?" said Gina abruptly. Her eyebrows arched. "What are you doing here?"

"We're just following up on a couple of anonymous calls reporting some recent burglaries in the area and thought we'd see if anybody here at the camp had noticed any problems," said Miranda, in an effort to not raise any red flags.

She quickly turned the conversation in a different direction. "Gina, I noticed you have a tattoo on your shoulder."

Gina was suddenly self-conscious. As if having a tattoo was a bad thing.

"My parents gave me permission."

"Well, I have a tattoo," Miranda lied again.

"What kind?" asked Tammy.

Lila, for the first time, focused on Miranda's chocolate eyes. "A . . . songbird. To tell the truth, we're actually here to find out if a girl with a frog tattoo on her shoulder ever attended this camp."

Fear filled Lila's striking blue eyes as she stared at Miranda. Her breathing became more rapid, almost panting.

"What did the girl with the frog tattoo look like?" asked Tammy.

Miranda started to pull the phone out of her pocket, wondering if she should show them the gruesome photos.

She glanced at Matt, and he sucked in his lips and shook his head almost imperceptibly. She put the phone away.

"Maybe we can come back with some pictures to show you."

"You should come to our upcoming camp celebration," said Tammy.

"You'll be blown away by the underwater ballet," added Gina.

Lila's shoulders stiffened, her eyes still on Miranda.

"We'll see," said Miranda. "Thanks for talking with us."

As she and Matt reached the archway, she turned and waved at the campers.

"By the way, Detective," Gina called out, "it's a serpent." She twisted slightly, pointing to her left shoulder.

"A serpent! Thanks." She gave Gina a thumbs-up.

"What was that all about?" asked Matt.

"I noticed she had a tattoo, but her hair was blocking it." She stopped abruptly and glanced at Matt. "Now I'm wondering if Tammy also has a tattoo. I need to go back."

"What are you talking about?"

"The tattoos, Matt. Don't you think it's strange that Lila, Gina, and our Lido Beach mermaid all have tattoos? On their left shoulder. I need to know if Tammy has one."

"Hold on a minute, Miranda. Don't you think you're overreacting—grasping at straws? Remember, Dr. Rubens told you that tattoos are as common as flies."

"Fleas," Miranda corrected him.

"Okay. Fleas, then," he puffed, exasperated. "It's been a long day, Miranda. Why don't we regroup tomorrow and see where we are? Whether or not she has a tattoo won't change anything for the moment."

Miranda was willing to hold off showing the campers the photos of the dead mermaid, but she was not willing to put off learning if Tammy also had a tattoo.

"I'll be right back."

Gina and Tammy looked surprised at her hasty return.

"Excuse me, girls, but I wondered if you also have a tattoo, Tammy." She scanned the curious eyes fixed on her.

"What do you care?" grumbled Tammy.

"I'm . . . researching tattoos. For a class I'm taking." Miranda hated lying, but it was necessary. "I happened to notice that Lila has a tattoo. A lizard—or a salamander, I think?"

Lila recoiled, immediately pulling a lock of her corn-silk hair over her left shoulder to cover her tattoo.

"Oh," said Tammy. She obligingly turned to expose her shoulder to Miranda.

"Ah, a turtle."

"I call it a tortoise. Sounds more glamorous."

"Well, it's pretty cool. Thanks for showing me."

Tammy shrugged, fidgeting with the beads on the picnic table.

Miranda rushed back to Matt.

"Well? Satisfied?"

"Yep! A turtle. Or tortoise, as Tammy prefers. And, it's on her left shoulder, as well. So, not only did our vic have a tattoo of a frog on her left shoulder, but all three campers also have reptile tattoos." She stopped to face Matt. "Why reptiles and not a mermaid, or a starfish, or some other sea creature?"

"You've stumped me there," he said.

"The tattoos have got to mean something, Matt. We just need to figure out what." She frowned. "Did you notice how Lila bristled when I mentioned her tattoo?"

Matt shrugged. "Lila seems a bit . . . high-strung."

"Yeah. She's certainly not the typical camper that comes to my mind."

"Well, we'll try to sort all of this out tomorrow."

They got into her car and headed back to Sarasota.

Miranda was frustrated with Trixie Monroe and Georgia Holmes and their refusal to cooperate. She still felt the trip was worthwhile, especially knowing that all the girls had tattoos.

"I have a feeling this mermaid thing is bigger than it appears, Matt."

She looked over at him, flipping to the front page of his book from Mel's Book Emporium and starting to riffle through the pages.

"I have a feeling you're right," he said, and began reading.

Chapter 10

Miranda kept her eyes on the congestion as they headed south on I-75.

"Must be an accident up ahead," she muttered, wondering why Waze hadn't alerted her.

As they crawled forward for the next few minutes, her mind was stuck on the three campers at Sirens of the Deep. Mermaid dreamers. The terror she'd seen in Lila's eyes had unsettled her. And there was something about the camp itself that bothered her.

Maybe it was just the camp director. Her demeanor was distant. Devious. A mix of motherliness and cunning. She couldn't quite put a finger on exactly what gave her that impression, but her own instincts rarely failed her. Georgia Holmes's mermaid camp was more than an idyllic, whimsical landscape where children could live out their mermaid fantasies.

She glanced at Matt who was humming to himself, engrossed in his reading.

I've never heard him hum before, she thought. It struck her how very little she actually knew about her partner of the past few years. Despite watching each other's back, they shared very little about their private worlds.

"Finding anything useful?" she asked, casting a quizzical eye at him.

"Fascinating stuff," he said, without looking up. "This chapter's all about cults."

"Really?"

"Yeah," he said, looking over at her. "I'm thinking maybe a cult could be involved in the mermaid's death. The tattoos might be a clue. Despite being as common as fleas, I agree that it seems oddly uncommon for our victim and all three campers to have tattoos of reptiles on their left shoulders."

"Well, a frog is actually an amphibian. Not a reptile."

"That is true. But frogs live on both land and in water."

"Does your book say anything about what such tattoos could symbolize?"

"The symbolism surrounding frogs is intriguing," he said, flipping the page.

"What about lizards and salamanders—the tattoo on Lila's shoulder? And the serpent, and—"

"One tattoo at a time, my pretty," said Matt, mimicking the Wicked Witch in *The Wizard of Oz.*

Matt read aloud from the section on frogs while Miranda drove.

"Frogs represent fertility."

"Fertility? Hmm . . ."

"Apparently because they lay a huge amount of eggs."

Miranda looked dubious.

"Frogs also symbolize resurrection," he continued.

"C'mon, Matt," she said, shaking her head. "Sounds like hogwash."

"No, really, Miranda. It says that a frog goes through three stages of development. Like being born again. A resurrection."

"So, what about reptile symbolism?"

"I haven't gotten that far."

"Maybe we're trying too hard," she said, blowing out a breath.

"Consider this, Miranda. Maybe our victim was on board a ship. Distraught. Depressed. Maybe she decided to commit suicide by jumping overboard?"

"Maybe," she said, without conviction.

Her younger sister's suicide from years ago was bleeding into her thoughts.

She pressed the CD button on the dashboard. Music, the great healer. Bob Marley, her favorite mood lifter.

She sang along to "Three little birds" and shoved the memory back into its tomb.

Matt closed the book, slumped down in his seat, and listened to Miranda and Marley sing. The perfect antidote to stress. He closed his eyes and gave in to sleep, the early start to the day finally catching up with him.

The next thing he heard was Miranda saying "We're home."

He opened his eyes and sat up, a bit foggy. What had seemed like a few minutes had turned into almost an hour. He realized they'd arrived at Miranda's house. He rubbed his face, picked up his book that had slid to the floor, and opened the door.

"Thanks for the ride, partner."

"No problem," she said. "My house tomorrow. Nine a.m. sharp. Call me if you discover anything brilliant in that book of yours."

Even before Matt had slipped the key into the door of his eleventh-floor condo, he could hear Muscle panting on the other side. He was relieved that his neighbor, Katy Sukowski, had agreed to take him to the dog park when he had texted her from the crime scene that morning.

A petite, pretty woman in her late twenties, Katy had moved into Matt's condo building shortly after he had moved in last year. An easy friendship followed. They had exchanged keys, both agreeing it would be a good idea in the event of an emergency. So far, this was the first time he'd had to ask her for such a big favor, and she immediately came to the rescue.

Muscle squealed when Matt opened the door, his whole body wiggling like a bowl of Jell-O. He nuzzled Matt wherever he found an open target, saliva dripping from the leash clutched between his teeth.

"Okay, buddy," Matt said, tugging the wet leash out of the dog's mouth. "Let me wash up and change. Then we'll go for a run." Despite his own exhaustion, Muscle had needs, too.

He'd never had a dog growing up, but now that he had one, he couldn't imagine his life without a pet. The only problem was his unpredictable work schedule. Having Katy as a backup was a blessing.

Dressed in shorts and T-shirt, he gulped down a cold Corona he'd grabbed from the fridge and stuck a bottle of cold water in the side of his backpack. He slipped on his aviator sunglasses. Dusk had already deepened to darkness, but putting on sunglasses had become a habit. He stuck his phone in his backpack, clicked the leash to Muscle's collar, and off they went.

Matt loved living on Lido Key. The wide, white beach and aquamarine Gulf of Mexico that he could see from his condo softened the tension he could never completely leave at work. He marveled at how quickly the water could change its hue between dawn and dusk. He'd grown up in a small town in Michigan. Adopted. Father a cop. Mother a social worker.

His dad had hoped his son would become a cop. Matt had other ideas. Nothing firm. No plan. "Still percolating," he'd tell his dad when the subject of law enforcement came up.

But Midwestern winters were getting more brutal, so he decided he'd begin looking for opportunities in warmer climates as soon as he graduated high school. As fate would have it, he ended up attending a law enforcement recruitment seminar during his last year of school that had set him on the path his father had hoped he would travel.

He landed a job in Atlanta right after graduation, where the chief had assigned him to desk work. He smiled, recalling his boss's reason for keeping him off the streets. "Get your bearings before you head out to discover the world ain't as innocent as you think it is, kid," his boss had told him.

But when his boss discovered his new recruit's sharp, analytical mind, he encouraged him to apply for a promotion. Matt quickly made his way up the law enforcement ladder to detective, passing the exams first in his class. But after a few years in Atlanta, he decided he wanted a bigger challenge, in a less-congested, less-frenetic city.

He continued to migrate south. Took a job in Jacksonville, Florida, before setting his sights on Sarasota. He wasn't sure the small city would offer him enough of whatever he thought he was looking for. But soon all the pieces began to fit together.

"Come on, Muscle. Let's put some pep in our step," urged Matt, running behind the fit, black Lab. "It's been a dreadful day, and it's not over yet. My partner gave me an assignment and I don't want to disappoint her in the morning," he said, talking into the breeze Muscle left behind.

Reptiles danced in his head as the run eventually changed to a casual walk back to the condo. Muscle, exercised and fed, followed Matt into his small office and dropped down on his doggy bed next to Matt's chair. Matt rubbed Muscle's silky, black head, whispering in his ear, "Frogs and lizards and reptiles, oh my."

Muscle's ears twitched. He groaned, too tired to care, ready to dream whatever it is dogs dream about.

Matt sighed, opened his computer, and typed mermaids and reptiles into the search engine. He clicked link after link, scanning articles until his eyes burned.

Finally he closed the lid on his laptop.

"That's all, folks," he muttered, shuffling off to his bedroom with barely enough energy to take off his sweaty clothes. He knew a shower was in order, but instead he flopped down on his unmade bed. He hoped tonight would be free of nightmares.

Muscle climbed up on the bed to his usual spot beside him. Loyal friends forever.

Chapter 11

Monday morning came too soon. Miranda wished she could have slept longer, but it was no use. Staying in bed would provide little relief from her nagging thoughts.

She rolled to the edge of the mattress and sat up for a few minutes, easing herself into the new day. Then, she got up and opened the curtains to a bright, powder-blue sky. Instantly she felt more energized, and headed for the bathroom.

The image in the mirror soured her mood. Her chocolate eyes were cloudy. Her flawless olive skin was dry despite the moisturizing night cream she applied each night. She leaned in for a closer study and detected a few new creases lining her forehead. Her crow's feet spread at the edges of her eyes.

"Age is creeping up on you, Miranda," she said to the mirror.

She sighed, deciding she had more important things to do than perform a critical self-assessment after such a demanding day yesterday.

She stepped into the glass-enclosed shower. The blue LED showerhead gently sprayed hot water over her curves and down her shapely, athletic legs. Stored-up tension escaping from her muscles, but the horrific images of the dead mermaid remained stuck in her head.

Toweled dry and naked, she gargled with some mouthwash before spitting it into the sink. She brushed her teeth and combed her long, auburn-streaked hair, gathering it into a ponytail.

"A little touch of mascara should help," she said to her mirror image.

The plum-colored capris and pink sleeveless blouse she pulled from her closet instantly transformed her from sluggish and self-critical to cheerful and refreshed.

The weather app on her iPhone predicted another scorcher of a day.

What did you expect—freezing with a chance of snow? You live in Florida, for God's sake.

She brewed a fresh pot of coffee and took a cup to her home office, where she clicked the computer awake. Trixie Monroe and Georgia Holmes needed further examination. While she and Matt had learned little from yesterday's interviews with the two women, visiting Sirens of the Deep had offered some insight into the workings of the mermaid camp. And Trixie's shop clerk, Brenda Sinclair, had provided some useful background information concerning her boss's mermaid business.

Miranda preferred working at home, away from the continuous buzz and interruptions at police headquarters downtown. She was grateful her boss, Chief Dominic Petri, had given her some leeway after she'd returned to the homicide squad three months ago.

Few people in the department knew that her yearlong sabbatical had been forced. At least, as far as she knew.

"Your usual analytical brilliance is dimming," the chief had told her when he summoned her to his office back on that dreadful day. "Get your head back in shape, or be gone."

She knew she'd become unfocused, short-tempered. Aloof, even. Reclusive at times. While she never fraternized with colleagues as a general rule, the chief said he worried that she was "digging a dark hole" for herself.

She knew a sabbatical would not calm the turmoil of her personal life. Past regrets. Estranged parents. Her sister's suicide. Work was her therapy. Sharing her life story with a rent-a-friend was not her style.

But the sabbatical was a direct order, not a suggestion. And so was the order for counseling.

Recalcitrant, she begrudgingly agreed to keep the appointment with the department's psychologist. Dr. Jenna Belfort prescribed the yearlong hiatus from the homicide department. The time away would be "constructive," was how she'd presented the directive to Miranda.

Nonetheless, Miranda took it as banishment. The intermittent therapeutic relationship between her and the psychologist proved rocky. In the end, Dr. Belfort reluctantly signed off on her case, even though she was unconvinced that her patient had committed herself to tackling her personal demons.

When Miranda had finally returned to work, Chief Petri let her read a copy of Dr. Belfort's condensed report:

Detective Miranda Morales is an intelligent, introspective, deep thinker who is completely aware of her own deficiencies. Like most people, she has demons which she is fully capable of controlling. Yet her sensitivity, coupled with her recalcitrance, make her battle to control them unpredictable at best. That she chooses to deal with these issues on her own terms makes forming a therapeutic relationship with her futile.

Thus, I firmly believe that the best therapy for her is to return to the homicide division where she can use her insight, analytical skills, and intellect as allies. They will help her to navigate the darkness she faces on the job and, in the process, shed light on her own darkness. Only by facing her foes—real and imagined—will she regain her confidence and focus.

I believe she will gradually discover the source of her own nightmares and, in turn, unlock the strength inside her to finally confront—and eventually tame—them, if not

eradicate them altogether. That is, if she makes the commitment.

Miranda looked at the him and nodded.

"Thank you, Chief Petri, for the opportunity to return to the homicide department. I know I have a lot of work to do, professionally and personally. I won't let you down."

Now was her chance to prove it to him by solving the Lido Beach mermaid case. A case that threatened the very lifestyle of those who chose to live in the city she loved. Low crime. Culture. Sunshine. Beaches. A city of wealthy philanthropists and talented artists and performers. Sarasota had enough to keep the police force on its toes, but far from the level of crime found in other regions of the country.

It was no wonder that the Lido Beach mermaid's arrival on one of the area's most popular beaches had rattled the community. Nothing this dramatic had ever happened in the sedate, artsy community. It could certainly threaten the city's robust tourism industry should fears spread. At least, that was the worry coming up the chain from the mayor's office to the tourism office. One scathing editorial about the quality of the investigation and the ability of law enforcement to crack the case could have "serious consequences for the city's economic engine," the mayor had told his staff.

Just as Miranda sat down at her computer, the doorbell chimed.

"Perfect timing," she said as she swung open the front door with a welcoming smile. "Hope you got a decent night's sleep. Coffee's in the kitchen. Help yourself and join me in my office."

Matt carried a steaming cup of coffee and his computer bag down the hallway to her office and settled himself at the makeshift desk Miranda had created for him. The floral-patterned upholstered sofa under the window invited conversation. He wondered if Miranda ever had friends or family over for visits.

"Nice couch," he said, removing the speckled composition notebook from his canvas bag.

"What?" asked a distracted Miranda.

"Your couch. Looks like a nice place for an afternoon nap."

"Hmm," she said absently.

He opened the notebook to a page covered with sketches of reptiles, with scribbles in the margins and arrows pointing in haphazard directions.

Miranda spotted the copious notes and drawings in his notebook.

"Looks like you've been doing your homework." She paused. "Or were you just doodling?"

"Maybe some doodles," he said, smiling, "but mostly a jumble of thoughts I put on paper while they were fresh in my mind this morning."

"Did you get the e-mail I forwarded to you last night from Dr. Rubens? I was too exhausted to give it my full attention. Figured we could discuss it this morning."

"No, I didn't see it." He immediately clicked to his e-mail and found the attachment. He opened and scanned it as Miranda talked.

"Basically he cites the cause of death as drowning," said Miranda.

He looked at her, eyebrows pinched. "That's it?"

"It's just a preliminary report, Matt. He's still awaiting toxicology and a few other things before he submits his final report."

"Well, of course she drowned." His voice was tinged with sarcasm. "But I would've thought it was the harpoon that killed her."

"I know, I know," she said. "But before we get too critical, let's start at the beginning." She looked at Matt. "It's easy to skip over important details when you're in a hurry. Let's read it together."

They read the report in silence.

A few minutes later, Miranda said, "So, he concluded drowning caused her death, but emphasized that the weapon pierced her lung and thus contributed to her drowning." She glanced at Matt. "I guess that means that even if she had perfected the ability to hold her breath underwater for unusually long periods—like the rare camper at Sirens of the Deep—she still wouldn't have been able to save herself. If she had a punctured lung and couldn't breathe, strong arms and legs wouldn't have been enough to save her."

Matt leaned back in his chair, puffing out a breath he'd unconsciously locked inside his own lungs.

"Added to the not-so-small challenge of a pierced lung, she was also encumbered by the mermaid tail," he said.

She looked at him pensively. "I've been giving some serious thought to your latest theory."

"What's that—the one about cults?"

"Not that one. Yet. The one where you posited that she might have jumped overboard. I don't buy the suicide idea." She paused. "But what if something, or someone, frightened her. Threatened her. And jumping in the water was her only means of escape."

"Or maybe someone pushed her?"

Miranda chewed on her bottom lip, considering that possibility. Then she came up with a new one.

"Or, maybe she was kidnapped. Taken on board some kind of ship and held captive. And she somehow escaped." She glanced at Matt. "I'm staying with the jumping-ship theory."

"Of course we don't know whose boat, or what kind. We don't know why they kidnapped her, or where, exactly, they might've been taking her. And most importantly," said Matt, "we don't know why she was wearing a mermaid costume."

"And if she jumped by choice—not because she was suicidal—she must have believed she could swim safely to shore."

Matt nodded. "But where did the harpoon come from?"

"That's the million-dollar question, Matt."

They both pondered various scenarios. Jumped. Accident. Pushed. Kidnapped. Hunted.

"Regardless of the reason," said Matt, "she must have had professional training at some point. A swim coach? Maybe she was trying out for the Olympics? A female Michael Phelps?"

"Hmm . . . intriguing idea. She must have had some coaching. Not only for swimming, but techniques for holding her breath underwater for long periods." Miranda paused. "Unless she was training for some kind of clandestine mission? But why the mermaid costume, then?"

"Maybe . . . a spy?" He stared at Miranda, blowing out a breath. "But that's . . . preposterous."

"I wasn't thinking that kind of mission. Maybe part of some kind of cult initiation?"

"Well, before we delve headfirst into the cult theory, let's imagine it was a just a simple party on somebody's boat," suggested Matt. "Alcohol flowing like Niagara Falls. Then something suddenly changed. Someone snapped."

He recalled parties he'd attended in college where events had spun out of control like a tornado twisting across the Kansas plains.

"We both know the tragic results of over-imbibing," he continued. "Playful teasing turns to lust. Loss of control. Emotions flaring like rockets on the Fourth of July. It happens all too often."

"And, if she were confident she could safely swim some distance wearing a mermaid tail, she must have had practice wearing one," said Miranda.

"Unless she wasn't expecting to have to swim to save her life. Or didn't have time to remove it before she jumped."

"But the harpoon is still troubling. It certainly doesn't fit with an innocent frat party."

"Good point," conceded Matt. "There's only one place that comes to mind where someone could get that kind of training."

"Sirens of the Deep," they said simultaneously, the sparks in their eyes igniting like steel striking flint.

"Georgia Holmes would surely remember if such an exceptional swimmer had been one of her campers," said Matt. "Do you think she's stonewalling us?"

Miranda's phone pinged, alerting her that a new e-mail had arrived.

She turned to her computer and opened it on the larger screen.

"Looks like Dr. Rubens just sent more pictures of our mermaid. All cleaned up."

Matt pulled his chair closer for a better look.

"Despite the traumatic journey, she looks a lot better than when we saw her on Lido Beach. But still pretty raw."

"I think we need to return to Sirens of the Deep and show these to Georgia and the campers," said Miranda.

She checked the time. Almost ten thirty.

"I'm curious how Georgia Holmes will react to these new images. And this time we're not leaving without showing them to the campers."

Chapter 12

Young girls darted from one cottage to the next, giggling as they collected fellow campers for their morning swim practice. It was a more frenzied atmosphere than when Miranda and Matt had shown up yesterday.

They decided to skip Georgia's office and go directly to the picnic area, where they sat down on one of the benches, watching the flurry unfold around them. They waited for the swim session to end so they could show the three campers the cleaned-up photos of the victim.

"Isn't that where the three campers sat making necklaces yesterday?" asked Matt, angling his head toward one of the tables.

Miranda nodded, recalling how terrified Lila was after noticing the stranger in the distant shrubs, watching them. Kicking herself for not having checked him out.

"May I help you?" called a voice from behind them.

Matt and Miranda turned to see Georgia Holmes walking toward them.

"Ah. It's you, detectives," she said, her tone one of surprise mixed with annoyance. "What brings you back to my camp so soon?"

"Good morning, Ms. Holmes. Nice to see you," said Miranda, standing up and stretching her hand out in a greeting, Matt mirroring her.

She shook their hands. Her grip was loose and unfriendly, and she eyed them suspiciously.

"Did you forget something?"

Miranda took her iPhone out of her purse and tapped the screen. New photos of the victim appeared. The victim's legs were free of the tattered mermaid tail, but the gashes and bruises on her face and arms were still shocking. The Y-suture line evident on her chest was a gruesome reminder that the young girl had undergone an autopsy. Puncture wounds left by the harpoon in her chest appeared less raw. The victim's long raven hair, now washed free of debris, fell along her colorless arms. The scalp flap to expose the brain had been returned to its natural curve of the hairline, her unseeing hazel eyes now closed.

"We hoped you'd take another look at these less-disturbing photos of the victim, Ms. Holmes," Miranda said, extending her phone to Georgia.

"Why don't we sit down first," said Georgia.

As they sat down on the wooden bench, the director hesitated, then took Miranda's phone, closing her eyes for a few seconds before swiping through the images. Sorrow filled her eyes when she looked over at Miranda and returned her phone.

"Do you recognize her?"

Georgia's tear-rimmed eyes shifted between the two detectives.

"It's . . . difficult to say," she said softly. "People can often look different out of context." She cleared her throat, as if something had suddenly gotten stuck there. "So many young girls come through my camp. If they have troubles before they arrive, I expect they bring those troubles with them."

Miranda glanced at Matt.

"Take your time, Ms. Holmes. It's really important that we find out who this young girl is," he said, encouragingly.

Georgia dabbed at the corners of her eyes with a tissue she held tight.

"She could have been one of our campers," she sniffled. "Her features resemble one of the girls who attended the camp some time ago. I can't recall exactly when." She paused. Tears were starting to run down her face. "So many girls come through my camp, it's hard to keep them straight." She wiped away another tear as it slid down her cheek. "They have such a passion for mermaids." She giggled nervously. "Believing mermaids are real. Hoping they can become one themselves." She took a deep breath. "If it's the same girl I'm thinking of, she was friendly and outgoing. Enthusiastic, even. All the campers liked her. The young ones and the older ones." Georgia's mind drifted somewhere beyond the photo, to a private memory. "She made friends easily, and was always eager to help however she could."

"So you do remember her, Ms. Holmes?" asked Miranda.

"It might not be the same girl," she said, perturbed. "But if she's the one I'm thinking of, she was definitely a strong swimmer. Learned her lessons well. Took no time getting used to wearing a mermaid tail in the pool." She had a gleam in her eye. "But our instructors still managed to teach her some of the more difficult maneuvers that most of the other girls couldn't master. Quite remarkable how she carried herself for someone her age. How easily she adapted to the water."

"Did the instructors teach her how to hold her breath for long periods underwater?" asked Matt.

"Yes. All the campers learn how to do that. But her control was incredible. She could stay underwater without surfacing for a breath for the longest time. One of the instructors dived in one day to make sure she was okay." She paused and sighed. "Everything seemed to come so easily to her." Her tears had dried and she looked at Miranda. "But as I said, that was some time ago."

"What else can you tell us about her?" asked Matt, coaxing Georgia to dig deeper. "Family? Friends? Anything she might have said that, in hindsight, might provide clues as to what might have happened to her?"

Georgia unclasped her hands as she began to relax.

"I don't know much about the campers' families. Occasionally I get to meet some of them, but usually the girls are eager to have their family members leave once registration is complete. They're happy to be on their own until their families return for the end-of-camp performance and then take them, and their memories, back home."

Miranda surveyed the grounds as Georgia spoke. Her eyes were drawn to Lila who stood taller than the other girls at the side of the pool. Her corn-silk hair was twisted into a knot that grazed her thin neck. Lila turned around and stared across the lawn, then quickly turned away when Miranda met her gaze.

"By the way, Ms. Holmes, I noticed a stranger in the distance while Detective Selva and I were talking with the girls. Do have any kind of security at the camp?"

"I guess we should, but well…it costs money you know. The camp has been struggling a bit the past couple of years. But you're right."

"What can you tell me about the tall, thin girl with the platinum hair?" asked Miranda, nodding toward the pool.

Georgia followed her gaze.

"Lila. Stunning, isn't she?" She paused, giving herself more time to think. "A bit aloof, though, I'd say. She stays on the fringes, except when the other two campers standing next to her are around. The instructors call them 'the inseparables.' While the other two girls are quite talkative, Lila rarely speaks." Georgia paused again. "As a matter of fact, I can't say I've ever heard her talk at all. But then the girls interact far more with the counselors and instructors than with me. So maybe she talks to them."

"Actually, we met those three yesterday. I was hoping we could show them the cleaned-up photos of the victim," said Miranda.

Georgia shook her head. "Absolutely not! There's no way they'd recognize her, even now that she's been 'cleaned up,' as you say." She glared at Miranda, her look unyielding. "They're too young to witness such an appalling sight! Especially of someone so close to their own age. I assure you, detectives, none of the campers would know her."

Mother Goose protecting her flock, thought Miranda.

"How can you be so sure?" she pressed. "You said the girl in the picture attended your camp. Isn't it conceivable one of the girls might recognize her?"

Georgia sucked in her cheeks and squeezed her eyes into narrow slits, her shoulders fixed. "I said she might have attended my camp, not that I was certain. And besides, if she had been one of my campers, she would have come at a different time from these girls. None of the campers here this session would have met her."

Georgia Holmes was growing more defensive by the minute. She was clearly hiding something, but Miranda decided it was unwise to pressure her any further about the matter. Matt's mantra circled in her head. You can catch more flies with honey than you can with vinegar. She nudged him. Help me here, Matt.

Matt cleared his throat. "We talked briefly with Lila and her two friends yesterday, Ms. Holmes. They were making necklaces at one of the picnic tables. We chose not to show them the pictures then, especially after seeing your reaction."

"Ah, yes. The necklaces," she beamed, nodding. "That's what all the hullabaloo is about," angling her head toward the group of campers dangling colorful mermaid tails at their sides. "They're about to do a dress rehearsal for the ballet performance coming up this weekend. Our end-of-camp celebration."

"For the underwater ballet?" asked Miranda, eager to hear Georgia's version of the event.

Georgia raised an eyebrow. "You know about that?"

"Yes. One of the girls mentioned it."

"It's quite a spectacular evening," said Georgia proudly. "The finale of the event is the talent competition. It's a way to give the campers a sense of closure." She drifted off for a few seconds. "The winner is crowned based on the tally of scores for three combined events—the underwater ballet, the beauty pageant, and the talent show." She took a deep breath and smiled broadly. "The crowning of the Queen Mermaid Ambassador is what everyone gets excited about." She paused again. "Why don't you come and see for yourselves. It's this Saturday. Light refreshments and music start at five. The show begins with the underwater ballet at six. The beauty pageant and talent show come afterwards, followed by the crowning of the queen to close the celebration. The whole program lasts about two hours."

"Sounds . . . delightful," said Miranda.

"I don't think you'll be disappointed," said Georgia, a sparkle in her green eyes that fixed on Matt. Definitely a young Hugh Grant. "People from all around the world come to see our magnificent mermaids perform the ballet."

Miranda glanced at Matt, then back at the director. "We'll plan to see you on Saturday, then."

As they walked back to the car, Miranda grumbled, "Next time I won't ask her permission to show the photos to the campers. Let's go get some lunch and come up with Plan B."

Chapter 13

The cerulean sky over Tampa Bay was magnificent in its clarity. Not a single cloud dared to detract from its brilliance. A hostess led Matt and Miranda to an outdoor table with amazing views of the harbor and gave them a menu. The waterfront was animated with tourists gawking at the floating yachtominiums docked along the plethora of slips. Other people sat on benches admiring the egrets and herons soaring overhead. Pelicans were nosediving for fish, and seagulls screeched, begging for crumbs.

They reviewed the offerings on the menu, then Miranda gazed out at the harbor, casting her thoughts away from yesterday's nightmare, enjoying the clear water and bustle of people exploring this tropical paradise. As her eyes roamed the dock, a luxurious yacht navigating toward one of the slips caught her attention.

She nudged Matt, angling her head toward the harbor.

She reached into her purse. "Damn," she muttered. "I left my binoculars in the car. Order me a turkey club, a side salad, and a lemonade. I'll be right back."

When the waitress arrived at the table, Matt ordered for Miranda, then gave his own order for a quarter-pounder with cheese, fries, and an iced tea.

By the time Miranda returned, he was sipping his iced tea. He hadn't taken his eyes off the impressive yacht, watching the captain maneuver the vessel into place.

A young girl with a long, black ponytail and string bikini was leaning on the railing, awestruck by the activity along the waterfront promenade. He smiled, amused at how the girl waved and called out to people strolling about, admiring the yachts.

Miranda, flushed and perspiring, wisps of auburn-streaked hair sticking to her moist cheeks, dabbed her face with the napkin once she sat down. She took a gulp of lemonade from her frosty glass and sighed, leaning back in her chair and then twisting slightly for a better view of the harbor. She discreetly lifted the binoculars to gaze out at the activity like any tourist taking in the local scene. She lowered them when the waitress arrived with their meals, lifting them again as soon as the waitress left.

As she refocused the lenses and peered at the yacht, she saw a bulky figure wearing a captain's uniform step onto the upper deck. He was looking through his own binoculars to survey his surroundings. She caught him searching in her direction and abruptly turned away, blowing out a breath, sitting rigid in her chair.

"Damn," she said, tempted to lift the binoculars again.

"What's wrong?" asked Matt through a bite of burger.

"I think someone's watching us."

"What? How could they be? Nobody knows we're here," he said, wiping ketchup from his chin.

"The yacht tying up at the harbor. Looks like the captain's scouting the scene and he caught me looking at him."

"He probably thinks you're just another gawking tourist."

Miranda's sixth sense was aroused. She wanted desperately to pick up her binoculars but feared drawing attention to herself. In the end, her need to know won out, and she picked up the binoculars again.

When the captain's eyes fixed on her, she quickly set the binoculars on the table and leaned against Matt, brushing her hand affectionately along his arm. Pretending to be more interested in the handsome man beside her than with what might be happening on the yacht. At least, that's what she hoped the captain would think.

"Don't look over at the harbor," she whispered to Matt. "I wonder if that could be the yacht Brenda mentioned would be coming to Tampa? She told me she thought she overheard Trixie mentioning a meeting . . . and the Mermaid Fantasea."

Matt leaned back for a look, but Miranda pulled him closer. Kissing him on the lips. "I think he saw me looking at him," she said, talking through the kiss. "Let's wait and see what he does."

Matt squinted at her and tried to pull away, wondering if she'd suddenly lost her mind. But she wrapped her arm around his neck.

"I want him to think we're just a couple of lovers on a day out in the sun."

"Don't you think you're being a little . . . paranoid, Miranda?" he asked, through Miranda's lips pressing on his.

She pulled back and feigned a laugh. Then pecked him on his cheek, as if teasing him, before pulling away. Laughing at the joke he didn't make as she took a bite of her sandwich.

Matt played along as they continued their light banter, unaware that the captain had just entered the cafe dining room.

Dressed in a crisp white uniform, the captain scoured the outdoor patio until the hostess greeted him. He nodded toward an outside table. As he passed by their table, he glanced at Miranda, saluting her with two fingers touching the brim of his cap.

"Buenos días," he said, smiling.

Miranda nodded and smiled back.

"He knows. He knows I was looking at him through my binoculars," she whispered as the man sat down at the nearby table.

"So what?" he said softly.

Shortly after the captain had sat down and ordered a drink, a husky, dark-skinned man came into the cafe and rushed directly over to the captain's table without sitting down. They talked for a few minutes, then the man abruptly left.

The captain drained his beverage, opened his wallet, and slid some bills under his plate, then got up, glaring at Miranda on his way out.

"Something's up. I can sense it."

"Like what?" asked Matt, pushing the remaining bits of his burger into his mouth.

"I'm not sure. Just an uneasy feeling."

Matt emptied the glass of iced tea and sat, a contented man, stomach full and thirst quenched. He knew Miranda's gut feelings were uncanny. She would share her thoughts when she was ready.

Then a thought of his own, unrelated to the captain's mysterious exit, popped into his head.

"How many custom-made mermaid tails do you think Trixie Monroe has made for the mermaid company in Miami?" he asked.

She paused, her fork full of salad greens in midair.

"An intriguing question, Matt. I have no idea. But I imagine that custom orders would be expensive. So how many could she realistically get?"

"Maybe we can find out who some of those special customers are?"

"Hmm . . ."

She recalled recent events. The lone stranger in the shrubs at Sirens of the Deep. The camp director's reticence to let the campers see the photos of the victim. The yacht now in the harbor. The captain showing up at the cafe. The bulky stranger conversing with the captain. The captain abruptly leaving without eating his meal.

"Let's take a walk, Matt," she said, motioning for the waitress to bring the check. "I want to check out the name on the yacht out there."

They headed toward the promenade crowded with bicyclists, mothers pushing strollers, and older couples walking hand in hand. Everyone admiring the views, letting their worries go out with the tide. At least for the next few hours.

They wandered aimlessly, giving her time to connect some of the dots.

The Tampa–St. Petersburg area had a lot to offer, and she realized how rarely she took advantage of it. The traffic could be a nightmare. Why create headaches when everything I want is in Sarasota? Pristine beaches. Art. Opera. Restaurants. Theater. She loved city life, but on a much smaller scale than Tampa.

Her thoughts drifted to a long-ago trip she had taken to New York City, to visit Ground Zero. Between feeling the remorse of that chilling day—the helter-skelter of confused people seeking shelter, the huge plumes of smoke blocking the sun—she had no urge to return to a jungle of skyscrapers that kept out the natural light of day.

By contrast, Sarasota had a serenity that mixed with the gaiety of life offered by beaches and boats. Graceful palm trees, dazzling aquamarine water, and plenty of sunshine.

"I can't imagine how people can afford yachts the size of some of these," said Matt, breaking into her thoughts.

Being a successful, world-renowned surgeon like my father is one way, thought Miranda. But she kept it to herself.

"A lot of wealthy people live under the radar here in our fine city, Matt. People aren't always what they seem."

"I suppose you're right. I certainly don't know any of them. If only . . ."

"You might be better off not knowing them. Ever think about that?"

As they neared the luxurious yacht, all seemed unusually somber for such a bright, sunny day.

Miranda nudged Matt's arm, cocking her head toward the name painted on its side.

"Mermaid Fantasea," he muttered.

"Look closer," she said.

"Mermaid Fantasea—with a Roman numeral two."

Miranda nodded.

"Yep. Where there's a second one, there must be a first."

"Maybe's there's even more," noted Matt.

She rolled the idea around in her head. "I don't recall Brenda mentioning anything about multiple yachts, do you?"

He shrugged. "I didn't notice whether the one in the picture on Georgia's desk had a number on it."

"We need to learn more about the Mermaid Fantasea Corporation," Miranda said, "and whether they own a fleet of yachts bearing the same name. Brenda mentioned that Trixie would be attending a meeting here sometime this week, and she heard the name 'Mermaid Fantasea.' But she had no idea what any of it meant."

"Maybe that's why the captain left the cafe so abruptly? Because Trixie's here?"

"I'm just tugging at straws again, I guess, Matt. Trying to piece together the puzzle."

Her sixth sense was kicking in.

"I'm not sure we can learn anything more here that will help our investigation. We should get back to Sarasota, try again to show the campers the photos of our victim."

"Since you accepted the director's invitation to the camp's celebration this Saturday, we could do it then," said Matt.

"I was hoping to do it sooner rather than later. But you're right, Matt."

They had just reached the parking lot when a two-seater white Mercedes—top down—zoomed into the lot, parking a few cars away from Miranda's Audi.

"Someone's in a hurry," said Matt as Miranda unlocked the car.

Miranda paused, watching as a tall, elegant woman wearing a red, wide-brimmed sunhat, floral sundress, and large sunglasses emerged from the car and scurried past them.

"That's Trixie Monroe," said Miranda.

"Are you sure? How could you tell with the hat and sunglasses?"

"You don't forget a woman like Trixie Monroe."

"What do you want to do?"

"Let's wait a few minutes. See if she boards the yacht."

She checked her watch as she settled into the driver's seat. It was almost two o'clock.

"If nothing happens in the next few minutes, we'll head back home."

Matt put on his seat belt as he glanced out at the yachts in the harbor. They watched as Trixie made her way toward the pier.

"Have you ever been on a yacht, Miranda?"

"My father owned one when we were children."

She had no idea if he still had it. Nor did she care. She had severed her relationship with her parents right after graduating from high school, several months after her sister's suicide. She had chosen to attend college as far away from them as possible.

"Despite my sister and I having mermaid fantasies, we preferred being on land. I suspect my father didn't really want us on his prized possession anyway."

Matt raised his eyebrows at Miranda's unexpected personal reveal. He knew little about Miranda's family life, or any of the secrets she might have tucked away in her private world.

"My sister, Farrah. She died . . . too young," said Miranda. "Maybe I'll tell you about her sometime." Maybe, she thought without looking at him.

She reached into her tote bag behind Matt's seat and got out her binoculars, focusing on the Mermaid Fantasea II.

"Shit," she said, shoving the binoculars to Matt. "Take a look."

"At what?"

"The yacht!" she said, jutting her chin toward the harbor.

Matt adjusted the binoculars and watched Trixie flailing her arms as she faced a short, bulky man dressed in a colorful, tropical shirt and pale slacks, his features hidden under the brim of a baseball cap and sunglasses.

"Looks like they're having a heated argument," said Matt, returning the binoculars.

"Damn! I wish I could get a better look at him!"

When she looked through the binoculars again, the man had grabbed Trixie's arm with one hand and was rapidly poking her shoulder with the index finger of the other.

"He's definitely peeved about something."

They watched as Trixie angrily twisted away from the man and stormed down the ramp, toward the parking lot.

Miranda slid down in her seat as the designer stomped past them.

Matt, not having met her at her shop, studied her as she fumbled in her bag for her keys.

"She's not quite as young as she looked in the picture," mumbled Matt.

Trixie unlocked the car and tossed her bag and red sunhat on the passenger seat. Her tires squealed as she raced out of the lot, scattering crushed stones and dust into the dry air and startling pedestrians midway through the crosswalk. One of walkers raised his middle finger and yelled curses at the mad-woman who had almost run them over.

"Time to go, Matt," Miranda said, turning on the ignition. "We need to know if there are other Mermaid Fantaseas out there—and if the yacht in the harbor is the one Brenda mentioned, we need to find out what Trixie's up to."

They followed Trixie at a safe distance for several miles. Miranda pulled back when Trixie finally turned into the driveway of one of the many magnificent homes at the end of the cul-de-sac in an upscale community not far from the harbor, the spacious grounds of each McMansion stunningly landscaped. Many had direct views of Tampa Bay, and most were enclosed behind protective, ornate iron gates.

Miranda parked close enough for them to discreetly watch the designer.

Trixie threw open her car door and slammed it behind her. She marched up the flagstone path leading to the front door of the Tuscan-style mansion. The door opened to greet her as she stepped onto the portico.

"Either this is her home, or somebody's expecting her," said Matt. He scanned the nearby homes in the posh neighborhood. "Guess there's a lot of money in the mermaid trade if she can live in a place like this."

"Must be," said Miranda without conviction, wondering about the shop owner's apparently lucrative business and lavish lifestyle. "Conveniently located near the marina, too."

"And the mermaid camp," he added.

They watched the house for some time, but everything remained still.

"Looks like Trixie's staying put for a while. We should head back home."

"Good. I have plenty more research to do."

"Like what?"

"I'm growing more and more intrigued by tattoos, reptiles, and cults."

"Ah. Myth busters. Symbols. Your new book."

"Something like that," he smiled.

"Okay. Let's go back to my house and regroup. Maybe your book will provide some answers."

Just as Miranda pulled away from the curb, a tall man with an olive complexion, smartly dressed and with a confident stride, approached the house.

She jabbed Matt. "Did you see where that man came from?"

He looked up, confused. "I have no idea. I wouldn't have noticed him if you hadn't poked me."

Miranda frowned as they drove away. Something about the man looked familiar to her.

Chapter 14

Back at Miranda's place, she went right to her office computer while Matt took his place at the makeshift desk beside her.

She opened the screen to the last image she'd viewed before going to bed the night before: a photo of a miniature frog. Dr. Rubens had piqued her interest with his tale of the tattoo exhibit he'd seen at the Virginia Museum of Fine Arts in Richmond.

She decided to delve deeper into symbolism and tattoos, starting with the frog inked on the dead mermaid's shoulder.

Matt likewise drilled further into his own research.

After an hour had passed, Miranda looked over at Matt.

"Let's compare what we know so far," she said.

"Okay. I'll start," he said. "We have a dead mermaid. A harpoon. Mermaid wannabes. All with tattoos on their left shoulder."

"A frog. A lizard. A serpent. And a turtle. Sorry, tortoise," she corrected herself. "So, the question is, what do the tattoos have to do with mermaids?"

"Let's just set mermaids aside for a minute."

"Okay," said Miranda, her brow furrowed.

Matt scrolled through the assorted images he'd saved to his desktop, landing on an enlarged photo of a frog.

"That's looks way different from the frogs I've been researching," said Miranda. "This one is more . . . peculiar."

"That's because it's a red frog. It's one of the poisonous frogs that live on an island in the remote regions of the Republic of Panama. It's the only frog I could find with bulging red eyes like the one you described on the Lido mermaid's shoulder."

He read aloud from the text describing details of the red frog. "Certain Indian tribes native to Panama extract the poison from the red frog to use on the tips of darts and arrows when fighting their enemies." He glanced at her. "I wonder if our vic could have been poisoned?"

"Interesting thought. I'll ask Dr. Rubens if there's any evidence of poison when he gets the toxicology report back. Anything else noteworthy?"

"Let's see," he said, scanning more of the text. "As we already know, a frog symbolizes fertility and resurrection. But this article states that early Christians considered the frog both good and evil, as well as a symbol of the sins of envy and greed."

"Hmm . . . do you have your book with you?"

"Never leave home without it."

Matt opened the book to the table of contents and turned to a page he'd marked with a Post-it note. Miranda leaned over his shoulder, scrutinizing the picture of a green frog, opposite a picture of a red frog.

"Does it say anything about frogs having a connection to mermaids?"

"So far, nothing about frogs and mermaids, but it says Asians believe putting a jade frog under the tongue of the deceased will ensure their safe travel from Earth to the spirit world." His eyes drifted to another paragraph. "The frog carries with it the positive attributes of the moon." He paused. "I never would have associated frogs with the moon."

Miranda pressed her back against her chair and folded her arms across her chest. "I think we're getting too deep in the forest, Matt."

Ignoring her, he flipped to another page he had marked.

"Hold on," he said, excitedly. "According to the Chinese

practice of feng shui, putting a frog in an east-facing window will foster childbirth and a happy family." He glanced at her. "Feng shui is—"

"I know what feng shui is, Matt," she said, cutting him off. "So, no reference to mermaids, but once again, to fertility. What about toads versus frogs?" she asked.

"Why toads?"

"Just wondering if frogs and toads symbolize different things. Maybe the tattoo on our mermaid is a toad, not a frog."

Matt flipped through more pages until he found a photo of a plump toad with big black eyes, a mottled bright yellow and dark brown, with tiny dots resembling freckles on its shoulders.

"The toad is believed to spit poison if it senses danger . . . it prefers dark, damp places. Some cultures believe the toad could transform itself into a witch."

He looked over at Miranda, remembering having read somewhere about gypsy witches who were thought to have originated in India during the Middle Ages. He wondered if he should bring it up, or if it would just add to the already murky waters.

"I've seen that look of yours before, Matt. What are you thinking?"

"Maybe if a toad can transform into a witch, witchcraft is the link between frogs and mermaids. Or even reptiles and mermaids?"

Miranda's eyebrows arched.

"You can't possibly be serious, Matt. Witches and mermaids?" She laughed out loud.

He felt the heat of embarrassment flush through him.

"Sorry, Matt. It just sounds so . . . preposterous."

He leaned back and ran his fingers through his thick, black hair. He clasped his hands behind his head and blew out a heavy breath.

"I think you're right, Miranda. We're probably spending too much time in the woods. Maybe the tattoos are just tattoos."

She straightened up and faced her computer.

"The tattoos have got to mean something, Matt! I can feel it. We've just got to keep digging. Assemble the bits and pieces of the puzzle into some sort of meaningful collage." She scrubbed her head with her long fingers.

"Well, do we know anything about the Lido Beach mermaid's ethnic background?" Matt asked. He wasn't willing to discard the notion of witchcraft quite yet. He stared at Miranda. "I keep circling back to cults—including gypsy witches. Maybe we're limiting our focus to mermaid cults, when the synergy surrounding our victim's murder is much more sinister and diverse."

She looked doubtful.

Undaunted, he continued. "Romani witches, for example, use charms and amulets to absorb their energy, which increases their powers. Though they're thought to have originated in India, they also have roots in Central and Eastern Europe. If our victim came from one of the countries known to still harbor cults that practice witchcraft, perhaps she was kidnapped from her country." He paused. "Like mermaids, gypsy witches have an affinity to water."

Miranda tilted her head from side to side to stretch the tight muscles in her neck.

"We don't know much about our mermaid's background," she said, "but your idea of cults, generally speaking, is an intriguing one." She puffed out a breath. "But let's not get too far afield. We still can't rule out that she might have jumped ship for some reason. It's the weapon—that horrific harpoon—that still stumps me."

Suddenly, Bob Marley's ringtone interrupted their discussion.

"Morales," she answered, curtly.

"It's Warren Levy, Detective. You sound a little . . . terse."

"Sorry, Dr. Levy. What's up?"

"I've just e-mailed you my reports and photos on the specimens you dropped off at the lab yesterday. Please confirm you got them."

He clicked off before she could respond.

She was too immersed in her thought process to check for his reports just then. Instead, she started tapping the keyboard with renewed vigor.

A few minutes later, she pounded her desk, shouting, "Trident!"

"Jesus, Miranda! You scared the bejeetlejuice out of me!"

"The harpoon, Matt!" she said forcefully, leaning back and anchoring her red-framed glasses to the top of her head.

"What about it?"

"We keep referring to the weapon as a harpoon. But what if it's a trident?"

"What does it matter whether the weapon's a trident or a harpoon?" asked a bleary-eyed Matt. "Our mermaid is still dead."

"I've just been reading about it, and it looks like they have very different purposes. The harpoon is used in recreational sport. The trident, with its three prongs, is specifically designed as a weapon." She paused and looked at him, eyes wide.

Matt shook his head. He was exhausted. "Come on, Miranda. It's getting late."

"Just listen for a minute, Matt. A trident is often used for underwater combat!"

He leaned forward, now all ears.

"Maybe they were role-playing some fantasy game and tempers flared as the competition grew more heated—acting out a computer game like . . . *Call of Duty*."

Matt's jaw dropped. "How do you know about *Call of Duty*? Are you some kind of closet gamer?"

"No, but I bought some shares in *Activision Blizzard* recently," she said playfully.

"Wow! Who knew?" Awe and sarcasm entwined as another layer of her personal life was unveiled. "I don't think *Call of Duty* has anything to do with mermaids."

"True," she noted, "but it does involve combat." She embraced his renewed enthusiasm. "Suppose, Matt, that the game-master leading the role-play changed the rules. Maybe wanted to add more thrills. More . . . danger. Danger in the form of a weapon, like a trident."

"I dunno, Miranda," he shrugged. "Seems like a weird thing for grown-ups to be doing."

"C'mon, Matt. Video games are not just for kids. We both know the outlandish behaviors people of all ages sometimes engage in, just for the thrill of it. Then, when something freak-ish happens, we are rudely awakened to the depths of some people's idiosyncrasies. We shake our heads thinking, 'Whoa, I've never seen that before." Until the next unimaginable, horrific deed reminds us that evil is out there." She paused to observe Matt's reaction. "We've seen it happen too many times."

Matt was too tired to challenge her, and she was too ramped up to quit.

"Think about it, Matt. Adults love role-playing games. Civil War reenactments. People dressing up, impersonating their favorite superheroes. Imagining they possess extraordinary powers to save humanity and the universe."

"Like Comic-Con?" he said, perking up. He was himself a Marvel fan.

"Maybe. Or Magic the Gathering. I researched the game when I was studying profiling at an FBI training session a few years ago."

"So Magic the Gathering involves role-playing, too?" He was familiar with the popular card game but had never played it.

"I'm not sure. Maybe in a different kind of way. But it doesn't matter. I'm just proposing that role-playing could somehow be involved."

"So you're suggesting what—that underwater warriors are attacking mermaids as part of some fantastical, mythical role-play?"

Miranda inhaled a deep breath, then expelled it like a deflating balloon.

"I dunno, Matt. I'm just trying to figure all this out! So far we've gotten nowhere. We need to catch a break."

Matt stood up and stretched. His joints were stiff from sitting so long.

"I'm beat, Miranda. Let's call it a day. Pick up all the loose ends tomorrow."

She sighed. Matt looked wrung out, his indigo eyes fading to gray, whereas she was getting a second wind. She felt she was on to something significant without knowing exactly what. Giving up now threatened to have it all be for naught.

Suddenly she bolted upright, remembering Dr. Levy's earlier phone call.

"Shit!"

"What?"

"Hold on just a bit longer, Matt. That call earlier was from Dr. Levy. He sent over the analysis of the two stones found in the victim."

She clicked on her e-mail and immediately sent Warren Levy an apology for her delayed response. Then she opened the first attachment.

"Let's have a look."

Matt's curiosity was piqued, his energy renewed.

A small photo of a dark, round object accompanied a report labeled Mermaid Specimen 1—Throat. She began reading aloud: "The object from the victim's throat appears to be a black pearl. Possibly a Truly black pearl, which is extremely rare. Unlike Tahitian pearls from the South Pacific, which are called 'black' pearls, they are not Truly black pearls, according to the lab analysis."

"I don't understand," Matt said. "Sounds like semantics to me. Black. Truly black. What's that supposed to mean?"

"Wait till I'm done," she said gruffly. "Sorry, Matt. I'm feeling edgy—and tired, too." She continued to scroll through the report as she read. "The stone found in the Lido Beach mermaid's throat appears to be the rarest kind of black pearl—a Hanadama, often called the Spherical Flower. It's considered to be the best pearl harvested from the Akoya oyster. Information from the Pearl Science Laboratory of Japan indicates that one of the Hanadama pearls in its specimen vault was stolen several months ago." She read the note written in bold type: "The Japanese laboratory will be sending an expert to determine if this specimen could be the stolen pearl."

She stared at Matt with unbelieving eyes.

Matt, stunned, sat rigid in his chair.

"This case gets weirder and weirder," he said. "Enlarge the photo, please, Miranda."

She zoomed in on it. The pearl's pewter luster was striking. Matt moved his chair closer.

"Wow!" she said, mesmerized. "It looks nothing like the gooey glob Dr. Rubens showed me at the morgue!"

"What about the second specimen? The one that dropped from the harpoon."

She opened the attachment labeled Mermaid Specimen 2—Chest, and again read aloud.

"Analysis of the second specimen shows turquoise, among the oldest gemstones in the world. While normally a rich blue, the turquoise in the stone removed from the victim's chest contains an intricate pattern of black veins resembling a spider's web. The veins running through it are created by particles known as a 'matrix' and indicative that this particular stone is of the highest-quality turquoise."

She paused, scanning through the report, choosing relevant bits to read aloud.

"Turquoise deposits of this quality have been found in Brazil, China, Israel, Mexico, and Tanzania. After thorough analysis, this particular specimen is definitely from outside the United States. It is quite different from the turquoise often associated with Native Americans and the Southwest. While veining is considered a less desirable characteristic of such turquoise to some gemologists, the spider-like pattern in this stone could be deemed more rare—and thus, more valuable to a collector."

She double-clicked on the image, revealing a brilliant turquoise oval stone in full screen, robin's-egg blue, with thin black bands spreading through it.

"It does look just like a spiderweb!"

"It's sensational!" said Matt.

"And according to the tape measure beside it, it's slightly larger than a jelly bean."

She reformatted the screen to view the black pearl and turquoise specimens side by side.

"They're magnificent!"

"Magnificent, yes," said Miranda. "But if it turns out the pearl is a Truly black pearl and belongs to the Japanese, our case might become an international one."

Too tired to care, he packed up his computer and slung the canvas bag over his shoulder.

"That's it for me, Miranda. Sorry—I'm beat. See you in the morning," Matt said, shuffling toward the front door.

Miranda followed. "Give Muscle a treat as my apology for keeping you here so long. And be safe going home." She kissed him on the cheek. "I really appreciate you sticking with me."

As the door closed behind him, he touched the warm spot on his cheek.

"What was that about?" he mumbled as he walked to his car.

Chapter 15

The Republic of Panama

Armando Perez had been working as an engineer for the Panama Canal Authority for almost twenty-nine years, having apprenticed at his father's side when he was just nine years old. He loved his job almost as much as his father had, but unlike Juan Perez, whose first love was his work, Armando's priority was his family.

He had never planned on becoming a father. He had watched his parents toil and barely scrape by, working multiple jobs to feed, clothe, and educate him and his two sisters. The burden of children is too great, he would remind himself.

"We would be great parents, Armando," his wife Estancia had insisted. "Our children would be strong and smart—like you."

"No, Estancia," he would say. "My job as chief engineer is demanding enough. Being responsible for a child would be too stressful!"

Armando wasn't selfish by nature, but he was unwilling to sacrifice his career for fatherhood. Conscientious, kind, intelligent, and hardworking, he had risen to chief engineer not long after being offered the job at the Canal right after graduating from university.

"You are much brighter than all of my other engineers put together," his boss would tell him with a slap on the back. "You will soon be my boss."

Armando was determined not to let his own dreams die the way his father's had.

Then, one ordinary day turned extraordinary when he noticed a beautiful woman in the visitors' pavilion, watching the ships pass through the Panama Canal. He was already late for a meeting, but the sight of her stopped him in his tracks. Their eyes froze the instant they met and the cosmos opened. Armando knew his life and everything in it would never be the same.

He walked over to her.

"Pardon, Señorita," he said softly. "Soy Armando Perez."

The young woman with caramel-colored skin and amber eyes smiled at him.

"Soy Estancia Marino."

They were married within the year. Estancia eventually convinced Armando they should have a child.

"We'll start with one and see how it goes," she pleaded when he told her it was too soon.

Now, thirteen years later, he couldn't imagine life without his beloved daughter.

Illyana was turning into a beautiful young woman, and that frightened him more than he realized.

Eduardo Diego, a close family friend, fanned the flame of his worries.

"With her light complexion and golden hair, she will catch the eye of many young boys eager to become men," said Eduardo, whispering in his ear as he sat next to him at the kitchen table, remnants of Illyana's birthday celebration evident. "An angel surely must have kissed her at birth."

Armando's laugh belied his anguish and the dark thoughts swirling in his head.

He looked across the table at his lovely daughter, engrossed in a magazine. He wondered just how he could protect her from the world's seedier elements. Doubts that he could keep her safe from both imagined and unimagined dangers beyond his control mushroomed inside him.

"I want to be like her," said Illyana, her voice breaking into his private distress, holding up a picture of a mermaid in the magazine. "She's so mysterious and beautiful, Daddy. Don't you think?"

Armando dragged himself out of his worries and glanced at the half-human, half-fish creature posing seductively on the page, staring directly at him. Silky, golden hair barely covered her voluptuous, bare breasts. Her large, emerald eyes were ominous and seductive. The moonlight reflected off her pewter-colored tail like tiny fairies flitting about in the darkening sky. A large-masted ship in the distance carried sailors about to be bewitched by this mermaid on a rock in the middle of the ocean. He recalled his father's stories about mermaids.

The danger comes at night, Armando, when the creatures glide up from the depths of the ocean. Their melodies and soft voices lure lonely sailors who long for a loving embrace. As the sailors reach out to them, the creatures drag them underwater, unaware that humans can't breathe without air, as they can. You must be careful, Armando. Mermaids are dangerous vamps.

"Daddy? Don't you think she's pretty?" asked Illyana.

Armando tried to smile to disguise his angst, but failed.

"You do know mermaids are just a myth, don't you, sweetheart?" he said, his soft brown eyes searching hers, the fear that only a father of a daughter could feel tearing at his heart.

"They are real, Daddy!" Illyana huffed, slapping the magazine down on the table. She gripped her upper arms with her small hands, pouting like a toddler whose toy had just been taken away.

Estancia tried to cut the tension in the room by redirecting the conversation.

"Anybody want more birthday cake? There's a few slices left."

Armando cast a disapproving look toward his wife. *Stay out of this, Estancia.*

Illyana, clutching the magazine, glared at her father, mother, and Eduardo, sitting around the table.

"No matter what you think, Daddy, they are real. You don't see them because you don't know how to look for them."

"Ah," said Eduardo, putting in his two cents. "So you've seen them, then, Illyana?"

Illyana scowled at him, took a deep breath, and pulled back her shoulders.

"Not yet, but I know they're there." She stared at Eduardo, unsure of whose side he was on. "They surface at dusk, singing their lyrical songs. Their melodies are carried on the wings of birds returning to their nests for the night." She paused. "You believe me, don't you, Uncle Eduardo?" she said, calling him by the honorary title her father had bestowed on his friend the day she was born.

"Well, I believe that you believe they're real, Illyana," Eduardo said. "Have you ever heard their songs?"

Illyana grew more vexed, chewing on a strand of hair she had pulled from behind her ear, then anchoring the damp strand behind her ear again.

"No! I haven't seen them. Not yet. Nor have I heard their songs. But that doesn't mean they aren't out there!" Her face turned red with rage. "But we will! We are patient."

"We?" gasped Estancia, her concerns mounting. The three adults' realized Illyana must have had an accomplice in this fairy tale.

"Shit," muttered Illyana under her breath. Stupid!

"Illyana?" said Armando, edgy. "Who else has been watching for mermaids with you? And where?"

She knew instantly it was too late to take back her words. The rapid-fire questions suddenly coming at her aroused panic. She knew Maria would be pissed.

She took a deep breath, wondering how much she should tell them.

"My friend Maria and I sometimes go to the marina after school. You know her from when she came home with me after school one day. It's calming to walk along the water after being stuck inside all day, studying." She glanced at the faces staring at her around the table. "People swear they have seen mermaids surface near the docks at dusk."

Armando looked at Estancia as if to ask Did you know about this?

"It's not really on your way home, Illyana," said Estancia, looking across the table at Eduardo and Armando.

"Unless, of course, you've discovered a shortcut?" said Eduardo.

"Who said they've seen mermaids? Who, Illyana?" demanded Armando, pounding the table, growing more agitated as dreadful scenarios started to invade his thoughts.

Illyana knew she shouldn't say anything more, but decided she'd tell them enough to stop them from worrying. Or worse, forbid her from hanging out with Maria.

"Maria said she knows a man who keeps his boat at the marina near the Bolivar Bistro. He takes tourists out to watch for mermaids. He told her he'd take us to see them whenever we wanted." Illyana watched her family's distress deepen. "Everybody knows him. He said tourists have seen them whenever he takes them out to this secret place where only he knows they surface."

Estancia pulled her chair closer to her daughter, putting her arm around her shoulders.

"But you've never gone there, Illyana, right? Or talked to the man yourself, have you?" asked her mother, fighting to keep her tone steady so her daughter wouldn't feel like a mouse caught in a trap.

Illyana shrugged off her mother's arm and averted her eyes.

Armando tried to swallow his emotions, the myriad of unthinkable outcomes threatening his reason. But this was his daughter. His only child. His efforts to be reasonable eluded him. Finally, unable to stop himself, he stormed over to his daughter, grabbed her by the arm, and screamed at her.

"You must never—never—go there again, Illyana! And Maria must not go there either. Do you understand me? I'm warning you."

She jerked away, turning her face to the side, refusing to look her father in the eye.

Her mother returned her protective arm to her child's shoulders, smoothing Illyana's hair as she caressed her, whispering, "Promise us, Illyana. Please promise, us. We all love you and only want to keep you safe."

Illyana finally looked into her father's eyes, one thought flooding her mind. She'd just broken a sacred oath, revealing the secret she and Maria had promised never to divulge to anyone. Illyana had completely blown apart this trust, and she knew her friend would never forgive her.

Feeling exposed and ashamed, she extracted herself from her mother's embrace and twisted out of the chair. She stomped toward the stairs, stopping at the bottom and turning to face her loved ones, all staring at her from the kitchen. Then, without another word, she started to head upstairs.

Armando, in a fit, rushed after his daughter. Eduardo raced after him, grabbing his wrist just as Armando reached for Illyana. Estancia covered her mouth, muffling her sobs as she watched from the kitchen.

"Let it go for now, Armando," Eduardo said softly, tugging at his friend's arm.

Armando snarled, shoved Eduardo away, and lowered his head. Defeated, he returned to his seat at the table, Eduardo in his wake.

"Go to bed, Illyana," Eduardo whispered. "It'll be okay. Your dad's just worried about you, as we all are. That's what people do when they love someone—protect them." He paused, speaking to Illyana's back at the top of the stairs. "We only want to keep you safe."

Illyana swallowed the tight knot in her throat and looked over the railing, listening to her mother crying in the kitchen.

"I'm sorry, Mamma," she called out softly. "I promise I will never make you cry, ever again."

She slammed her bedroom door, threw herself on her bed, and sobbed, "I'm not a baby anymore," punching the pillows. "They'll never understand! Never!" She pounded the pillows until they absorbed her pent-up anger.

Eduardo had returned to the table, his head low, his own fears no less than his friend's. They sat in silence, letting a false sense of calm filter into the room.

Having regained some composure, Estancia looked across the table at Armando and Eduardo.

"We should talk to Maria's mother."

"No!" growled Armando. "That's none of our business. We don't know her that well, or even know if Illyana's telling us the truth." He looked into his wife's puffy, damp eyes. "You know how dramatic girls can be at this age."

Eduardo sat quietly, watching and thinking.

"Illyana is growing up," he said. "We all knew this day would come—it just seems like it came too soon." Eduardo looked at Armando and Estancia with worried eyes. "The time has come to be vigilant, mis amigos. This is a dangerous age for young girls. The world is no longer the way it was when we were growing up."

Estancia's sobs deepened, her eyes swimming in tears. Armando went over to her and she nestled her head in his chest as he hugged her.

"I hope we're not too late, Eduardo," said Armando, desolate and defenseless.

Chapter 16

On the walk to Maria's house the next morning, Illyana thought about how stupidly she had behaved at her birthday party. She was angry at herself for telling her family about the mermaids, but it was too late; the damage was done. She prayed Maria would forgive her.

Maria Diaz bounced down the stairs to greet Illyana at the front gate, but immediately sensed something was wrong.

"You okay?"

Illyana lowered her head.

"What's the matter?" asked Maria, putting her hands on her friend's shoulders, forcing Illyana to look her in the eye.

Illyana lifted her tear-filled eyes slowly and took a deep breath. "I'm so sorry, Maria. So sorry."

"Sorry about what?"

"They know," she said.

"Know what?"

Illyana stared into Maria's confused gaze.

"You didn't!" Maria huffed. "You couldn't have, Ana! Urrrg-ggh!" Her face blistered with outrage. "We made a pact, Illyana. How could you?"

"I didn't mean to. It just . . . it just came out."

"You've ruined everything, Ana! Do you know that? Every-thing!" screeched Maria.

The two friends walked in silence the rest of the way to

school. Maria seething, Illyana kicking herself, knowing she needed to fix it, but with no idea how.

After several long minutes, she stopped in front of her friend and looked directly into her eyes.

"I have a plan."

Maria's angry eyes burned into Illyana's.

"A plan? Really? You have a plan?" But her curiosity soon outweighed her anger. "What kind of plan, exactly?"

"We'll tell our parents that we're staying overnight at each other's house one night," said Illyana excitedly. "I'll bring my sleeping bag with me. Then, we'll sneak to the marina, taking our sleeping bags with us. We'll hide in the shrubs near the restaurant, spend the night watching for mermaids. Nobody'll ever know. We'll go home in the morning before anyone realizes we were gone."

"Are you crazy?" barked Maria. "Don't you think they'll be keeping an even closer eye on you now that you told them about the mermaids?"

Illyana thought about that for a moment.

"Well, your mother doesn't know about it. And my parents trust me. I told them the truth last night, so they'd never think I'd lie about spending the night at your house."

"They used to trust you. That's all changed now!"

"I've never lied to my parents before, so they have no reason to think I'd make a habit of it now."

"I can't believe how naive you are, Ana. Now that they know I'm involved, your parents will be less likely to let you spend the night at my house."

Illyana was emphatic that her plan would work.

When Maria continued to resist, Illyana told her friend that even though she wanted her support, if necessary, she'd go to the marina alone.

Maria finally caved in, although she still had doubts—in addition to the fact that she was still furious at Illyana.

She decided she'd come up with a plan of her own.

Chapter 17

Panama had an abundance of nightlife amid its Manhattan-like skyline, but many people preferred to escape the noise and congestion of the city and relax at the charming Bolivar Bistro and Yacht Club, located a few miles outside of Panama City.

This was true even though the place didn't quite live up to its name. Although there were yachts scattered all around the harbor, there was no yacht club. The bistro was a casual, no-frills bar and open-air restaurant overlooking the harbor. It was a favorite watering hole among the locals, as well as those who sought a night off from their lavish lifestyle to enjoy a more laid-back yet appealing ambience. The wealthy anchored their yachts here partly because of its reputation for good food and an extraordinary wine selection.

The dozen or so tables—sans tablecloths—had flatware and thick paper napkins beside each place setting. A single orchid in a clear vase elegantly graced the center of each table. The spacious dining area under the charming thatched roof accommodated diners who showed up hungry and ready to quench their thirst. Conch shells and starfish decorated various columns of the large, open space. Ceiling fans in constant motion took advantage of the cool breeze that filtered up from the harbor.

While locals frequented the bistro most days, the club's success depended on the wealthy who would drop in after sailing from some tropical island they owned on their way to somewhere else. Clientele who sought the kind of anonymity they couldn't find in the fancy clubs in Panama City. Clandestine meetings and affairs of the heart that might too easily be discovered, or the risk of being caught in the company of high-class "companions" wearing provocative cocktail dresses that exposed cleavage and long, tanned legs. Saturday and Sunday nights were the busiest, when people celebrated the end of a work week and tourists found their way to the bistro after visiting the nearby Museo de la Biodiversidad.

None of the people who frequented the bistro knew precisely how Jonah MacTavish had come to own the place, and nobody cared. They enjoyed the tall, rugged-looking Scot's stories and appreciated his sense of humor and impressive vocabulary, even if they didn't always understand everything he said. And the fresh seafood and Peruvian dishes were always prepared to perfection.

Jonah MacTavish knew many of the club owners in Panama City where the nightlife bloomed once darkness descended, the lights from high-rise condos twinkling like tiny stars filling the cityscape. Some shared stories of their eyebrow-raising escapades, the deals made and missed, the dubious methods they used to "get things done." They confessed their sins after drinking more than they should have, joking with him like he was one of the in-crowd.

Jonah's easy, nonjudgmental, quiet manner made him popular with all sorts of people he'd met over the years. One of his close friends who owned a high-end club in the city recently told him about corrupt politicians crossing the threshold of his private club.

Jonah listened with polite interest, having already witnessed many despicable acts as a former merchant marine. When he'd had enough of the sordid side of life, he had decided to plant his roots in Panama, establishing the Bolivar Bistro and Yacht Club. Through hard work and a little luck, he had transformed the downtrodden hangout that had attracted fishermen content to eat mediocre meals and drink cold beer into one of Panama's top-rated bistros. He concocted exotic drinks from recipes he'd garnered from barmen he'd met during his travels, and the bistro's extensive wine list attracted oenophiles from around the world. He also offered live music whenever a local band was available, including a steel drummer who rivaled any in the Caribbean.

On this night, a few diners were fully enjoying the spectacular view of the Caribbean, engaged in laughter and conversation, while the busty barmaid served top-shelf spirits and imported wines to a small group of Americans sitting at the wraparound bar, the focal point of the dining room.

Jonah's newest patron had just walked into the bistro. He had introduced himself as Mano Sorkin, and gotten right to the point, asking Jonah if he'd be interested in having a silent partner in the restaurant.

"Looks like you run a class act here, amigo," he said. "And a great location for me, as I often travel through this area."

Jonah guessed the handsome, well-dressed man was in his late forties. Mano had said he was a "Brazilian businessman," but that he rarely spent time in his home country, saying, "Most of my business is between Central America and the States."

Jonah was savvy enough not to delve too deeply into what kind of business the Brazilian gentleman was in. He didn't care what the man's history was, or why he might be traveling to Panama. And no, he wasn't interested in having a silent partner.

Mano Sorkin chose a table and immediately ordered a bottle of Jonah's finest red wine.

There was another newcomer to the bistro tonight. Jonah had pegged him as a high-roller when the overweight man had first set foot in his restaurant. He wore an expensive-looking pair of loafers—no socks—and celebrity-style sunglasses, despite the Panama hat that would have provided enough of a protective shield from the sun's glare. The swagger in the stranger's walk exuded affluence, confidence, and arrogance.

Jonah could smell success nautical miles away, and was seasoned enough to conclude that massive wealth often stemmed from nefarious sources.

A husky man with a bronze glow walked close behind the heavyset man, glancing around the room as if he expected to see a familiar face. Or perhaps a threatening one. His eyes lingered on Sorkin sitting alone at one of the tables, but he made no gesture of recognition. His charcoal-colored slacks with a subtle sheen looked tailor-made. The light gray, short-sleeved, collared shirt that curved around his bulging biceps enhanced his skin tone. His black beady eyes could bore a hole through a person faster than a power drill through a four-by-four.

Jonah figured he must be the bodyguard.

"Welcome to the Bolivar Bistro and Yacht Club, gentlemen. I'm Jonah MacTavish, but my dad called me Skeeter. You can call me anything you want."

The two men laughed and followed him to a prime table with views of the harbor.

"May I get you something to drink while you look over our menu?"

"Bring us a bottle of your best French wine, por favor?" said the high-roller, with a Spanish accent.

"White or red?" asked Jonah, motioning for the waiter to bring over the wine list. "Fine wines are not easy to get in Panama, but we are fortunate to have assembled a superb selection."

The waiter handed the wine list to Jonah, who passed it on to the man in the Panama hat.

"Surprise me," he said, smiling up at Jonah without even a glance at the wine list. "Bring a red and a white."

Mano Sorkin, who had arrived half an hour earlier, was already enjoying his Chateau Leoville Las Cases 2010—a bold Bordeaux tinted with dark fruits and hints of mineral that blended with the fruit for a full-bodied experience. The price tag: $350.

Jonah returned with two wine bottles, holding them so the heavy man could examine the labels.

"Ah," said the newcomer, removing his sunglasses and slipping on his half-glasses to see the labels more clearly. "A perfect pairing," he said, nodding and smiling his approval.

Jonah bowed, pleased with compliment.

"I'll put the white burgundy on ice, although it's the ideal temperature right now if you'd like me to open it while you wait for your meal."

"Perfect!" exclaimed Castro.

As Jonah uncorked the wine, he looked out at a magnificent yacht in the marina that he hadn't noticed before, wondering if it might belong to one of his new patrons.

"That's quite a piece of art out there," Jonah said, jutting his chin toward the harbor, before pouring a taste of the Batard-Montrachet for the men to sample. "I don't recall ever seeing it here before."

The newcomer smiled, swirled the wine, tasted it, then nodded.

"Perfecto."

Jonah poured each man a glass and then returned the bottle to the ice bucket.

"It belongs to me," said the overweight man proudly. "Mermaid Fantasea. Bought it from a Saudi business associate a few years ago at a very good price."

Jonah smiled, suspecting the man's tale wasn't quite the whole truth.

"Well, it's a stunner, that's for sure. We get some good-looking boats here, but nothing quite like that."

"Thank you," the man said, smiling. He reached out his thick hand. "My name's Castro Montoya, and this is my . . . assistant," he said, clearing his throat, "Python."

Python grunted but did not extend his hand.

Jonah nodded at the bulk of a man.

"I'd be happy to take you on board someday," offered Castro Montoya, without meaning it. "We are traveling to Florida. So maybe on our return—if we come by this way."

"I'd be honored," Jonah said, with a bow. "Now I'll leave you to your server."

As Jonah turned toward the bar, he saw Sorkin discreetly lift his wineglass to Montoya, who returned the gesture.

Friends? Acquaintances? Silent partners? he wondered.

While mixing drinks at the bar, Jonah gazed out at the setting sun. He spotted a young woman in a bikini strutting on the top deck of the yacht Montoya said belonged to him. Her long legs seemed to stretch forever, and her full breasts overflowed the top of the bikini. Her silky black hair was pulled back in a long ponytail that swirled midway down her sculpted back.

He estimated her age to be sixteen, maybe seventeen. It was difficult to gauge from such a distance. She was leaning over the brass rail, laughing wildly and waving her arms at the jet-skiers zooming around the harbor.

Montoya unexpectedly jumped up from his table, clearly agitated. He punched Python's thick arm and cocked his head toward the marina, scowling.

"Mirakakoo!" hissed Castro Montoya, trying to control his contempt. "Get her away from that railing and lock her in her room. Now!"

Python bolted up from the table, rattling the glasses as he knocked it off balance. He raced toward the pier like a weasel chasing a rabbit.

Despite his massive build, the bodyguard was fast and agile. He raced up the yacht's ramp, yelling words Jonah couldn't make out. Once on board, he yanked the young girl by her bare arm. She tried to pull free, but he grabbed her behind the neck and forced her arm behind her back, pushing her through a small opening that Jonah figured led to the lower cabin. Then they were gone.

Jonah threw the dish towel down on the bar and rushed over to Montoya. A disgruntled customer wasn't good for business.

"Is everything okay, Mr. Montoya? The wine to your liking? I see your friend left in a hurry."

Montoya forced a smile to soften his angry eyes and set his shoulders. The last thing he needed was to make a scene. Still standing, he removed his wallet from his back pocket and placed an ample stack of bills on the table.

"That should cover the wine, amigo," he said, knocking over his chair as he stormed out of the bistro, heading toward the pier.

Mano Sorkin started to get up, but instantly sat back down. "Damn you, Castro!" he muttered to himself. "You're a fucking fool."

Jonah watched as Castro Montoya gestured wildly, one arm stabbing the air and the other pressing his cell phone to his ear. On board, he immediately stomped across the deck and down the stairs, the bikini with the long legs and silk ponytail now an illusion.

While Jonah continued mixing drinks, he kept his eyes on Montoya's yacht. A dim light shone through the small window curtain on the starboard side.

About half an hour later, Montoya returned to the upper deck, Python close behind. The two men stood at the brass railing, arms flailing, as they intensely scanned the area near the harbor, as if desperately searching for whatever they had lost.

Python suddenly pointed to a clump of bougainvillea bushes along the shoreline. Montoya looked through a pair of binoculars to the spot Python was indicating. Not finding anything, he lowered them and pounded the railing with his fist.

Jonah rushed over to the doorway for a better view. The jetskis had finally silenced as dusk faded to darkness. Then, as if riding on the wings of a breeze, a faint echo of voices and laughter filtered from the bougainvillea. Cries of shorebirds and the low murmur of tourists walking along the promenade mixed with the muffled laughs spilling from the bushes.

Montoya poked Python's thick bicep and shoved him toward the ladder. Python maneuvered adeptly down the narrow steps, and the minute his feet hit the dock, he tore across the path toward the laughing shrubs, a furious Montoya watching intently.

"Take care of the bar for a couple of minutes, Rebekah," Jonah called across the room to the buxom bartender. She was talking to a couple of regulars who showed up after work every day for a beer before trudging home to whatever chaos—or emptiness—awaited them.

Jonah took a few steps down the path toward the harbor, listening for more sounds coming from the shrubs. He stopped abruptly when he heard two male voices in a heated argument breaking through the bushes.

"Leave me the fuck alone, you moron!" one voice yelled.

A deeper, louder voice bellowed back, "Castro's gonna kill you when you get back on the Mermaid, you little fuck!"

Jonah looked over at the Mermaid Fantasea, noting it had a Roman numeral two on it. Pale moonlight was beginning to stream its silver glow across the harbor, intensifying Montoya's angry grimace as he watched the bougainvillea bushes, waiting for whatever was hiding there to appear.

Suddenly Python emerged from the shrubs dragging a lanky young man behind him. The boy's khaki shorts sat well below his waist. The front of his T-shirt sported an image that Jonah couldn't quite make out. He wore white, low-cut sneakers—no socks—on his feet.

When they reached the yacht, Python shoved the young man up the ladder and pushed him over the railing, sending him flying.

Castro Montoya smacked him on the back of the head when the boy finally got back on his feet. Then Python grabbed the youth by the arm and launched him down the stairs to the lower deck, Montoya trailing behind.

Jonah watched for another few minutes. The night had suddenly turned quiet.

After a few more minutes, he figured the show was over, telling himself it was probably a family squabble as he walked back inside and poured himself a whiskey—a double. He took it outside to one of the tables, letting his mind settle. Most of the patrons inside were finishing up their dinners and relaxing with coffee, a few still clinging to the bar.

Mano Sorkin stopped at Jonah's table on his way out.

"Problemo, Señor Jonah?"

Jonah looked up. "Nah. Just a couple of friends having some fun, I guess." Even though he was far from convinced the cause of the ruckus was that simple. "How was your meal, and the wine? I apologize for being distracted. I hope your server met your needs."

Sorkin gave Jonah a thumbs-up.

"Impeccable," he said smiling. "Everything was perfect! I will be back soon. Maybe then you will be ready to take me on as your silent partner."

The two men laughed and Jonah stood up to shake his hand. Jonah was struck by the velvet quality of the Brazilian's voice, and the firm but friendly grip of his handshake.

Sorkin took a business card out of his shirt pocket and handed it to him.

Mano Sorkin, Chief Executive Officer. Sorkin Import-Export, Calle Emanuel, Republic of Panama.

Several phone numbers were listed.

"Thanks, Mr. Sorkin," Jonah said, looking into his deep brown eyes. "You're welcome here anytime."

"Thank you again for a great meal and memorable wine. Enjoy this beautiful night," Sorkin said. He smiled, and paused to admire the tropical vista. The gentle evening breeze tickled the palm fronds that stretched along the waterfront. The round, silver moon was coming into its full glory as the sky grew darker.

Jonah watched him stroll toward the pier and stop in front of Montoya's yacht to light a cigarette. He paused there for a couple of minutes and gazed up at the Mermaid Fantasea. Then, he turned and walked toward the group of yachts lining the marina.

Jonah wondered which yacht belonged to Sorkin as he drained his whiskey and went back to the bar and what the Roman numeral two on Montoya's yacht referenced.

Chapter 18

"What the fuck were you thinking, Xander!" blasted Castro Montoya, pushing his nephew down onto the club chair below deck. Pacing wildly in front of him, Castro continued to mumble curses and vicious threats.

Python watched the interrogation from the cream-colored, leather couch across the room, his scornful black eyes pinned to the scrawny kid he had never liked.

Xander shrugged his lean shoulders. His head was bent low, and he was squeezing his thin hands together between his scuffed knees. A child caught with his hand in the cookie jar.

"I just thought—"

Castro slapped him across the face mid-sentence.

Xander palmed the burn on his cheek and whimpered. "I didn't do nothin', Uncle."

"Nothing? You're damn right you were doing nothing, you little shit! You were supposed to be keeping an eye on Mirakakoo! She was strutting around the deck like a smutty tart, calling attention to herself—to us—at the same time. Waving to everyone, cackling like a horny hen."

Castro was furious, wiping a hand through wisps of his black hair.

"I . . . I . . ."

He slapped Xander across the face again.

"Tell me just what you were doing in those bushes?"

Xander sheepishly raised his fawn-like eyes.

"Nothing. I was only gone for a few minutes. I thought Mirakakoo would be okay."

"What was the 'nothing' that was so important you couldn't wait until we got back?" growled Castro. "If you weren't my nephew, I'd tie a cement block to your ankles and dump you overboard."

Python laughed maniacally.

Castro grabbed Xander by the chin and squeezed it hard, glaring at him like an animal about to attack its prey.

"Tell me what you were doing out there, or I swear I'll slice off the tip of one of your fingers—maybe all of them!"

"Okay, okay, Uncle," sputtered Xander. "I . . . I saw this pretty girl go into the bushes while I was cleaning the deck," he stammered, clenching his hands so hard they turned white. He raised his arm to shield his face from another blow. "I was . . . I was just curious about what she was up to, that's all."

Castro's features twisted into a ferocious mask and he growled, nose to nose with Xander.

"Didn't I tell you not to draw attention to yourself—or to the yacht? The owner of the bistro up the hill is already overly curious."

Xander, abashed, lowered his eyes, clasping and unclasping his hands nervously.

"What else happened out there?"

"Nothing. The girl said she was watching for mermaids."

Castro swatted him across the side of his head.

"Mermaids? Mermaids? You little bastard."

"Honest—she said she was watching for mermaids," Xander repeated softly. "Her name is Maria."

Castro grabbed his scrawny nephew by the front of his shirt, pulling him up out of the chair. "What the fuck do I care what her name is?"

Xander felt his uncle's spittle splash his burning cheek.

"Does she know your name? That I would care about!"

"No, Uncle Castro," he lied.

Castro shoved him back down in the chair and stomped over to the bar and poured himself a glass of Scotch, spilling some of it over the rim onto the polished bar top. He picked up a cocktail napkin and wrapped it around his glass without bothering to wipe up the spill and sat down on the leather sofa next to Python.

Calmed by the alcohol, Castro got up and poured himself another drink and sat down on the bar stool. He stared at his nephew and shook his head. His eyes were unforgiving.

"Do you have any idea how much trouble you've caused? If you mentioned anything to that girl about what we're doing here, I swear, I'll—"

Xander jiggled his right leg. His hands were fisted on his knees and he was staring at the floor as if his voice had dropped to his feet.

"I'm talking to you, Xander! Answer me!"

Xander lifted his head slowly. He took a deep breath, then said, "I told her nothing, Uncle! Nothing!" Tears were rolling down his cheeks.

Suddenly, he bolted out of the chair and raced down the narrow hallway and slammed his bedroom door.

Castro gulped down his drink and poured another.

"He has no idea how messy things could get, Python. I'm already worried that the port authorities have been cracking down on shipments coming into their cities. All they need is some crazy reason to search the yacht and discover our . . . merchandise."

Castro looked around the club room.

"Where the hell is Mirakakoo?" His voice was angry, then alarmed. "What did you do with her, you moron?"

"I was out in the bushes getting Xander. She's probably lost in la-la land after snorting cocaine all morning," said Python, his voice deep and defensive.

Castro gestured for his bodyguard to follow him to the upper deck. The stars had already cluttered the night sky and the breeze was kicking up.

Mirakakoo was nowhere to be seen.

"Go check the bushes," ordered Castro, cocking his head toward the clump of fuchsia bougainvillea. "See if that girl Maria is still there. If she is, bring her to me. If she resists, give her a shot of this." He handed Python a syringe. "And don't call attention to yourself in the process! I don't want any more ruckus. I'll check around for Mirakakoo. She must be in her bedroom."

Python lumbered down the ladder to the dock and headed for the bougainvillea.

Meanwhile, Castro threw open Mirakakoo's bedroom door so hard the knob left a deep gash in the wall. She was lying facedown, motionless, her long black ponytail trailing down her bare back. Her slender arm dangled over the edge of the bed, her unmoving fingers grazing the carpet.

"Fuck!" he yelled, sitting on the bed next to her, shaking her frantically. "Mira! Mira! Wake up!" He grabbed her ponytail and lifted her head, then flipped her over like a pancake. Thick saliva coated her pale lips. Her face was pallid. Ghostly.

"Xander!" screamed Castro, rushing to Xander's room, pounding wildly on the door, turning the knob. Locked. He pounded harder. "Xander, get the hell out here!"

Terrified, Xander opened his door slowly, covering his face with a crooked arm, waiting for Castro's strike. But when he looked over his arm, he saw the horrified look on his uncle's face, and lowered his arm.

"What's wrong, Uncle?"

"I think Mirakakoo's dead!" Castro said, gripping his nephew's bony neck and shoving him down the corridor toward the girl's bedroom.

"Fuck!" gasped Xander when he saw Mirakakoo lifeless on the bed. "What did you do? What happened?"

In a flash he was beside her. "Holy shit—this isn't good." He put two fingers on her neck. "She's not dead—yet—but her pulse is very weak." He put his cheek to her mouth. A faint breath dusted his skin. "She's still breathing, but barely. She needs help. Fast!"

He shook Mirakakoo's floppy body, calling her name.

"Get me the syringe from the drawer in the nightstand. Quickly!"

Castro grabbed the syringe with a trembling hand. Xander clutched it and flicked the barrel to get rid of any bubbles, then thrust the needle into her bicep and emptied the contents of the syringe, watching anxiously for signs of life. A flutter of eyelashes. A gasp. A twitch of a finger.

"Nothing!" declared Castro, wheezing. "You've got to do something, Xander! You've got to save her."

"I'm taking her to the upper deck for some air. Call an ambulance."

"No! No ambulance and no upper deck! People could see us up there. We can't risk the authorities getting involved in this. We can't!"

Castro paced like a wild man, swiping his flushed face with a shaking hand. His breathing was labored.

"You never should have left her alone!" he said, swiftly turning to Xander. "I should have known you'd fuck up. You always do."

Xander's concern for Mirakakoo took priority over his fear of his uncle's fists. Still holding her draped in his arms, with one foot on the steps to the upper deck, he glared over his shoulder at Castro.

"What about Python, Uncle? He's the one who gives her this poison! Why do you keep him around? He's good for nothing!" Exasperated and angry, Xander ignored his uncle's order and carried Mirakakoo up toward the fresh air.

Castro stormed over to the bar and poured another drink, swallowing it in one gulp. His stomach burned. He was terrified and confused.

Xander gently lay Mirakakoo on the lounge chair on the upper deck and covered her with a beach towel, warm and dry from the day's heat. He pulled up a chair and sat next to her, stroking her bare arm. Her skin felt clammy against his warm hand.

"Mira . . . Mira . . . wake up. Come on. Wake up, please. Open your eyes, Mira. Please! Please open your eyes," he begged repeatedly, drying his eyes with his T-shirt, smudged with dirt and grass.

He lowered his head, as if in prayer, then looked at her chest rising and falling weakly. Her breathing was gradually growing stronger. He caressed her face. Held her hand. And whispered, "You're going to be okay, Mira. You'll be okay. Just breathe. Breathe. I'm here."

Mirakakoo's eyes opened to slits, then instantly closed again.

"Come on, Mira. You can do it. Breathe. Breathe," he urged, slapping her cheeks.

After a few feeble flutters, her dark eyes stayed open.

"Wha . . . what happened?" Her voice was dry as dust.

"I'll get you some water."

"No, wait," she said, grabbing his arm. "Tell me where we are."

"Panama. Remember?"

Mirakakoo closed her eyes again. "Panama?"

He handed her a glass of water.

"Drink. We're on our way to Florida, Mira. Now you must rest," he soothed her, silently making a promise to himself. *I swear I'll kill Python if he ever gives you that fucking shit again!*

Chapter 19

Jonah MacTavish was closing up the Bolivar Bistro, still perplexed by the strange behavior of his newest patrons, including the bodyguard he'd nicknamed the Incredible Hulk. Especially disturbing was watching the Hulk's abuse of that young boy he had dragged out of the bushes near the harbor.

His mind wandered as he wiped down the bar.

"Age must be catching up with me," he muttered, feeling his energy and sharp mind slipping away. He was glad he'd recently hired a graduate student from the University of Panama to help out part-time.

"Hey, amigo," said a voice calling to him from the open entry.

Jonah tossed the towel and smiled wide. "I was just thinking about you. You're not due here till tomorrow night. What's the occasion?"

Kai Rendell gave Jonah a man-hug.

"I thought I'd stop by, see if you needed an extra hand tonight, but looks like your closing up," he said, sizing up the empty room. "Slow night?"

"It was a lot busier earlier. How about a drink?"

Kai smiled and nodded.

Jonah grabbed a couple of cold beers and led Kai to one of the tables overlooking the marina.

"Beautiful night," sighed Kai. "I love the energy of the city, but there's no better place to chill than here after a week of exams," sighed Kai.

They clinked bottles, quietly admiring the tranquil scene spread before them. Lights blinked on distant boats scattered around the harbor, confirming that life was good—for some. The breeze rustling through the palm trees along the waterfront soothed away their weariness.

"You said it was a busy day. Tourists?"

"More like an interesting day. Tourists, yes, but a few newcomers with cultivated palates and thick wallets."

Kai smiled up at the stars poking through the night canopy. "That's some yacht out there," said Kai, tilting the neck of his Corona toward the harbor.

"The Mermaid Fantasea. I noticed it had a Roman numeral two on it. Owned by one of the newcomers I just mentioned. With an appreciation of fine wine and the money to pay for it. Showed up with his bodyguard." He glanced at Kai. "That's what I meant by interesting."

"How does a person earn enough to buy something like that?" asked Kai, thinking about his own pitiful finances. An education, even in Panama, is expensive. Seeing that it had one of the finest programs in archaeology and ancient civilizations, it had been his first choice as a place to pursue his doctoral degree. His professor was a well-respected academic from the United States who remained active in the field—another plus.

Jonah had his own theories.

"If it's not from a family inheritance, usually it's Wall Street types—hedge fund gurus," Jonah said. "Financiers scamming those with big ideas but few resources. Convincing us that they, and only they, hold the secret to amassing riches." He glanced at Kai. "I imagine huge financial rewards are not earned in the noble halls of academia." He smiled, nudging his friend.

"Well, there is big money in technology, you know," countered Kai, jokingly.

"Ah, the Mark Zuckerbergs, Tim Cooks, and the likes of Jeff Bezos and Bill Gates."

"And don't forget Elon."

The two friends laughed as they enjoyed the view and each other's company.

Somber thoughts of Castro Montoya and Python entered Jonah's mind. Their abrupt departure gnawed at him. And the mysterious girl with the mile-long legs roaming the yacht was another stumper.

He sighed, gulped down his beer, and walked to the edge of the steps. The cool breeze drifted up and brushed his sweaty cheeks.

Suddenly, Python emerged from a clump of bougainvillea, the same spot from which he'd dragged the young boy to the Mermaid Fantasea. The Hulk's thick arm was now wrapped around the shoulder of a young girl with dark, wavy curls. Her short-shorts showed off her toned and shapely legs. Python drew her closer as she stumbled beside him.

Kai walked up next to him. "Anything unusual going on down there?"

"Nah. Looks like some young girl testing her alcohol tolerance," Jonah said.

But the twist in his stomach told him it was more than that. Especially the way Castro, sipping his drink at the railing, watched their approach like a red-tailed hawk awaiting the return of his mate to the nest.

As the two reached the yacht, the girl stumbled and fell backwards. Python caught her and shoved her up the ladder. When she lost her footing, he grabbed her around the waist and toppled her over the brass railing. Python hefted himself onto the deck and picked her up, and Castro led them down to the lower cabin.

"How about another beer before I close up?" said Jonah, pulling Kai's attention away from the yacht. He was trying to slough off the unease inside him, even though his gut was signaling that something was terribly wrong.

He slapped Kai on the back as they headed inside.

"How are your studies coming along?" he asked Kai.

"Good. My professor was invited to speak at an antique collectors' club in Florida on Wednesday, which means I'll have some extra time to catch up on my thesis and help you out around here while he's away."

"Ah. Where in Florida?"

"Sarasota."

The sound of the Mermaid Fantasea's engine suddenly rumbling to life forced his attention away from Kai. He twirled around to see the massive yacht backing out of the slip, heading toward open waters.

"Shit!" he muttered.

"What's wrong, Jonah?" asked Kai, puzzled by his friend's unexpected outburst.

"Nothing. It's none of my business," Jonah said, irritated at himself for his cowardice.

Jonah poured them both a whiskey, hoping to quash his overwhelming feeling of impotence. The same feeling he'd had when his father forced him to pick up a rifle on his sixteenth birthday, knowing how much his son hated guns.

Chapter 20

Gabriella Navarre had just finished her business with her clients in Bocas del Toro, Panama, and was eager for the next phase of the operation. The day had proved fruitful, but not without some haggling over the terms of her contract. She had worked with the Colombia cartels before, but the leader of this cartel was particularly belligerent.

In the end, she had gotten what she wanted and took the afternoon flight back to Panama City, planning to stay a day or two at Shelter Bay Marina before flying to Florida. It was her preferred spot to relax during her travels between Central America and the United States, and close to Tocumen International Airport and her direct flight to Miami. It was also close to the Panama Canal, where she could keep track of the two vessels for which she had arranged passage through the Canal, on their way to Florida.

The Festival of Dagon was the main reason for her trip to Florida. She had become aware of obstacles that were threatening to impede plans for the celebration, plans she had thoroughly devised to finally bring together the various factions within the Mermaid Fantasea empire. If the expansion was to succeed, everything had to go off without a hitch. She had no intention of letting things implode at this stage of the operation. Even if they did, she knew the world was a big place; there were plenty of greedy entrepreneurs with deep pockets waiting in line to do business with her. Plus, she was too young to retire, even if she certainly could afford to do so. For now, she had storms to calm and raging fires to extinguish. And all the pots seemed to be boiling in Florida.

The dominoes were being set up, ready to fall in spectacular order. All she had to do was make sure each one was in its proper place, each player prepared for his or her respective parts. The worldwide expansion of the Mermaid Fantasea Corporation would be her greatest achievement thus far.

The small countries of the Central America region had long been a refuge for expats and wealthy tycoons trafficking in goods nobody wants to talk about—money, illicit drugs, stolen art, rare, priceless objects . . . humans. Colombia, Nicaragua, Costa Rica, and, more recently, Panama, among others, had for decades been associated with nefarious schemes and ruthless exploits enabled by corrupt officials with their hands out, willing to turn a blind eye for the right price without any regard for law or respect for human dignity.

The harsh spotlight had shined especially bright on Panama a few years ago with the release of the infamous Panama Papers, exposing the darkest side of organized crime and the Panamanian law firm that managed a massive network of high-profile global clients to achieve protection for their assets, sometimes accumulated by questionable means.

Even before the release of these documents, Panama was quickly, yet quietly, becoming a haven for expats who had given up on the promises made by their countries' governments that a better life was just around the corner. Panama, like Costa Rica, had an abundance of resources, although it had not yet been discovered to the extent Costa Rica had.

Panama's chief revenue resource was the Panama Canal, now under its own control after the agreement with the United States had expired. But Panama was also a major banking center and economic powerhouse. Its relatively stable government and modern skyscrapers—along with its exclusive clubs—attracted celebrities and international investors who had money to spend and secrets to hide. Shelter Bay Marina provided the perfect retreat and an ideal spot for doing business with its close proximity to the Panama Canal. And the amenities Shelter Bay provided suited Gabriella perfectly.

"Buenos días, Señora Navarre," said Fredriko Costa, Shelter Bay's young manager. "Como esta?"

"Muy bien, Fredriko. Eusted?"

"Bien, Señora. Will you be staying long in Panama this time?" he said, switching to English. He liked to practice the language whenever he had the chance, and was happy that she encouraged him to do so.

"Si. Yes, Fredriko. Do you have the latest schedule for my shipments coming through the Canal?"

"I'll check for you, Señora," he said, turning toward his office where transport records and ship schedules were kept. Fredriko was a handsome man in his mid-thirties. His skin tone was lighter than many of the other workers employed at Shelter Bay. Gabriella always enjoyed chatting with him, finding him to be bright, articulate, and a reliable source of valuable information. He had no idea what the stunning señora's business was, and he never asked, despite his deep curiosity surrounding why such a gorgeous woman would so often travel without an escort.

He did recall that on a few occasions, pretty, shapely young girls would accompany her, and he wondered if they might be her children. But since they were never the same girls, he figured they must belong to someone else. Maybe she was a caretaker of some sort? But no, she was too elegant for a job that required so much hard work and was not always pleasant.

After checking the shipment manifest, he returned to Gabriella. She was sitting under a large yellow umbrella, wearing a broad-brimmed sunhat and sipping a cocktail.

"Good news, Señora Navarre. The ship is on schedule to go through the Canal later today, arriving on the other side by late tonight."

"Good." The extra hundred dollars she slipped Fredriko now and then always ensured that her shipments received priority treatment.

"You are traveling alone again?"

Her mouth involuntarily twitched. "Yes, Fredriko," she replied matter-of-factly.

He bowed, sensing she was perturbed by his question.

"If I can do anything to help make your stay more comfortable, please let me know. I am always at your service."

"Gracias, Fredriko," she said, sliding another hundred-dollar bill into his pocket.

Half an hour later, he returned to give her an update.

"Your vessel is third in line now, Señora Navarre," he said, handing her an official-looking envelope. "The captain sent this a few hours ago. I trust it's not urgent."

"Thank you, Fredriko."

She opened the envelope, read the message, then quickly gathered her purse and briefcase. "Fredriko, please order me a taxi to take me to the airport as soon as the vessel clears the Canal."

ᏫᏘ

Gabriella paid the taxi driver when she arrived at the Paradise Cove Resort on Rocky Point Island, located just four minutes from the Tampa International Airport. The bellman collected Gabriella's luggage and carried it into the hotel lobby.

Standing at the hotel's registration guest waiting to check in, she wondered how her partners had managed to create such a mess. The operation had been planned with attention to the most minor detail.

As the female MacGyver—the nickname given to her by Mano Sorkin—she was at the top of her game for this mission. "No room for fuck-ups!" she remembered him saying.

The bellman unlocked the door to her room and set the larger suitcase on the luggage rack at the foot of the bed. After tipping him, she kicked off her red-soled, Louboutin stilettos and opened the mini-bar, removing two single-serve bottles of vodka and a tonic water. She was grateful that someone had filled the ice cube tray in the fridge. She hated traipsing to ice machines hidden in hotel corridors.

She washed her hands and took the beverages and ice-filled glass out to the balcony. She sighed as she spread her cramped toes on the tiled floor, warmed by the day's sun.

Travel always made Gabriella tense, but looking across the aquamarine gloss of Tampa Bay soon calmed her tangled nerves. The double-vodka tonic gradually drowned out her troubles and untied the knots in her neck and shoulders.

She leaned back and rested her feet on the rattan ottoman that matched the cushioned chair. She took a deep breath and smiled as her blue-green eyes drifted past the in-ground pool and white sand beach below, marveling that a poor, orphan girl from Colombia could rise to such prominence. And in such a short time.

Her cell phone broke into her trance.

"Hola."

"Meet me on the Mermaid Fantasea in an hour. I'll fill you in when you get here."

Chapter 21

Morning broke to the delightful sound of songbirds chirping outside her bedroom window. Miranda felt her spark of energy rekindle. Not quite ready to seize the day, she stretched her arms overhead and groaned. She'd had a decent night's sleep, which she attributed to having escaped to the solace of her herb garden for most of yesterday. Both she and Matt had decided they'd work separately after the past couple of days of intense theorizing.

Today promised to be fruitful. Miranda willed it to be so, and so it would happen. A murder needed to be solved before her boss lost faith in her.

The visit to Trixie Monroe's mermaid shop and Georgia Holmes's mermaid camp a couple of days ago continued to circle in her head, along with the three campers with their shoulder tattoos. A lot of unanswered questions needed answers.

Lila, the girl with corn-silk hair and a lizard tattoo, especially concerned her. The terror in her China-blue eyes when she'd seen the man wearing a Panama hat and sunglasses, watching them from the bougainvillea at Sirens of the Deep, had deeply troubled her.

Miranda was growing more and more convinced that both the mermaid designer and the camp director knew far more than they were admitting. She wondered if they were in cahoots somehow.

After their session on Monday evening, when they'd kicked around role-playing games, gypsy witches, and cults and reviewed results from the lab, she and Matt had agreed they'd work at home on Tuesday before meeting up again on Wednesday to continue their investigation.

Feeling the optimism of a new day, Miranda got out of bed and took a refreshing shower. She towel-dried her hair, put on a pair of white shorts and a sleeveless lavender blouse, and bounced barefoot down the stairs to the kitchen.

While the Keurig gurgled coffee into the pot, she headed to her office and tapped the keyboard. The photos of the turquoise stone and black pearl filled the screen. She took a deep breath, captivated by their magnificence.

She suddenly remembered she'd forgotten to collect her mail over the past couple of days. She unlocked the front door and reached into the metal box painted with songbirds.

"Junk, junk, and more junk," she mumbled, flipping through the useless fliers. As she sorted through the pile, she noticed a white envelope that appeared to be an invitation of some sort. She glanced at the return label and groaned. Her parents' address on Longboat Key. An area known to house the super rich and well-connected.

She had been estranged from her parents for much of her adult life, and shunned their lifestyle as part of the social elite in Sarasota. She couldn't remember the last time she'd seen them, despite living close by. She blamed them, as well as herself, for her younger sister's suicide. Coupled with that tragic event, they had refused to accept her choice of a career in law enforcement, rather than in medicine or law. That was the last affront she'd been willing to suffer. She wanted no part of their haughty, high-class attitude and superficial friends.

Her heart raced as she tapped the envelope nervously against her thumb. Her stomach tightened. "Fuck!" she blurted out. She took a deep breath and closed her eyes.

Just read it, Miranda.

Finally, she tugged the small card out of the thick, white envelope.

Dr. & Mrs. Fernando Morales cordially invite you to a cocktail reception
June 24, 7:00 p.m., at the Ritz-Carlton Ballroom in downtown Sarasota,
honoring Professor Graham Aramis Waterman, PhD.
Please RSVP for the cocktail reception
on the enclosed card.

~

A lecture, "Untold Stories and the Search for Antiquities of the Pre-Columbian Period in Panama," free and open to the public, will be held June 25 at 1:00 p.m. at the Van Wezel Performing Arts Hall in Sarasota.

Miranda gasped, checking the date on her watch. The party was tonight!

"No, no, no, no, no!" she growled. Her heart was pounding so hard she thought it would crack her ribs. She sat down in the nearby wooden swing and squeezed her eyes shut, commanding her heart to return to normal.

"Breathe. Breathe," she chanted, until her voice grew dry and scratchy.

Graham Aramis Waterman. Once, the love of her life. The man who had crushed all her hopes. Demolished her dreams. He was coming to town—her town—her selfish, thoughtless parents taunting her. Damn them!

She couldn't stop the painful past from breaking into the present. The memory of how she and Graham Waterman had met during their first year at the University of Washington in Seattle. Her major, forensic psychology. His, archaeology. Their love affair had lasted throughout college, and she'd had every reason to believe they would marry soon after graduation.

She had believed he would propose at a romantic dinner

he'd arranged for the evening of their graduation. Instead, he'd laid out his plans to attend a university in Panama City to pursue a doctorate in pre-Columbian artifacts.

"It's the break I was hoping for, Miranda," he'd said, as excited as if he'd just won the lottery. "The Universidad de Panamá has accepted me based on my undergraduate and graduate research."

She remembered thinking he was talking about Panama City in Florida's panhandle, but soon realized it was in Central America.

The final blow came at the very end of his announcement. "I think it's best if I go alone."

The only thing she remembered after that was waking up at the University of Washington Medical Center. A young nurse wearing pink cotton scrubs with small dogs printed on them was checking her vital signs. She remembered asking the nurse where she was.

Now, more than a decade later, she was faced with something she had fought to keep buried—struck by the paralyzing reality that her battle against a slumbering demon wasn't over. Anguish and despair came rushing back as she confronted the bitter truth that Graham Aramis Waterman had left a deep hole inside her that had never closed.

Fuck you, Erika and Fernando. And double-fuck you, Graham! I'll be damned if I let any of you back into my life again.

She shoved the invitation and envelope into her back pocket and stood up abruptly. The wooden swing banged hard against the railing. She went to the powder room, where the mirror reflected a pathetic face with red puffy eyes, mocking her. She splashed cold water on her face and ran a brush through her hair.

And the day had started with such promise.

She took the invitation and envelope out of her pocket and dropped them on the coffee table in living room on her way back to the office.

It was time to get back to work, but for the next couple of hours she had to force herself to concentrate. Painfully aware that she was stuck in mental quicksand. She thought about calling Matt to cancel their meeting, but decided his presence would help distract her from her torment. Struggling to focus, she finally gave up.

She got up and dragged herself to the kitchen and opened the fridge. The bottle of wine she'd opened last night was almost full. She poured herself a glass, then carried the bottle and glass out to the patio. It was nearing lunchtime, but her stomach was too tied up in knots to think about eating. Wine was her Prozac. Her silent friend.

She sat down on the chaise lounge and drained her first pour. Then poured another. She set the bottle on the patio floor, leaned back, and listened to the lull of the songbirds as a soft buzz slowly spread through her body.

Instead of unclogged brain cells and fresh insights, old wounds reopened.

Finding her younger sister lying on the bedroom floor with her throat slashed . . .

The heartbreak of a shattered romance . . .

She emptied the last of the bottle into her glass and gulped it down.

Miranda's front door was ajar when Matt arrived. Slowly he pushed it open, as if expecting something to jump out at him.

"Miranda?" he called out, closing the door behind him.

He cautiously made his way down the hallway and through the living room, eyeing the white envelope and small card on the coffee table. He continued toward her vacant office, calling her name, then out to the kitchen where he set his computer bag down on the table.

"Miranda?"

Through the French doors leading to the back patio, he saw her lying on the lounge chair, a wine bottle on the floor beside her.

He went outside and picked up the empty bottle. He felt her forehead and wrist. Warm. Pulse slow. Her eyelids fluttered but didn't open.

"Miranda. It's me. Are you okay?"

A low groan escaped her lips.

He set down the bottle and lifted her up off the chaise. He carried her to the living room sofa and gently set her down, covering her with a soft blanket.

He returned to the kitchen and sat down at the table, removing his computer and book from his canvas bag. He reviewed the forensic report on the two stones extracted from the mermaid, and read the coroner's report again.

Myths involving reptiles. Fertility rituals. Belief in the afterlife. Other dead ends, all too convoluted to lead them to a motive for murder.

He considered the one thing they hadn't explored more deeply—the weapon. Miranda was convinced it was a trident rather than a harpoon, that distinction somehow important to her. He shrugged, deciding he'd let her deal with that question mark.

The Japanese pearl expert who'd flown in from Japan had concluded that the black pearl found in the victim's throat was not the rare Hanadama pearl stolen from their lab vault a few months ago, though it was still valuable. The big question continuing to plague their investigation: How did two rare stones end up inside the victim?

He heard Miranda stirring in the living room, and went to check on her.

"Ugh," she said, leaning on her elbow and pressing the palm of her hand on her forehead.

"How are you feeling?" Matt said.

She tried to sit up but immediately dropped back on the sofa.

"Can I get you anything?"

"A handful of aspirin from the medicine cupboard in the powder room."

Matt returned with a glass of water and two aspirin.

"Thanks."

She sat up, swallowed them. She noticed the RSVP card on the coffee table.

"Shit!"

"Looks like you've been invited to something?"

She scowled at him.

"I'll get back to work in the kitchen. Lie back down until you're feeling better."

He returned to his computer and continued reviewing the forensic report. Then he moved on to reptile tattoos and mermaids.

A short time later, he heard Miranda go into the powder room.

He shook his head, worried about her mental state. He'd never seen her in such a desolate condition. He thought about the invitation on the coffee table. He wanted to know why it had upset her so much, but decided she'd tell him in her own time. Or not.

Miranda shuffled out to the kitchen and sat down in the chair next to him. She stared at him until he finally looked at her.

"I'm sorry, Matt. I have no excuse." She bowed her head and twiddled her fingers, then looked up at him with puffy, bloodshot eyes. "Long story."

"The important ones always are," he said, distressed at seeing her so vulnerable.

She cleared her throat. "I owe you some answers."

"You don't owe me anything, Miranda."

"Yes I do. We're partners. But I'd like to think we're also friends."

He leaned back and closed the lid of his computer.

"The invitation on the table—it's from my parents. I haven't seen them. For a long time." She glanced at him. "Even though they live just a few miles away."

Matt only nodded, wondering if that was part of why she kept her personal life so closed off—from shame, or self-preservation.

"An old flame of mine is coming to town to give a lecture tomorrow."

"Ah. What's the topic?"

"Pre-Columbian artifacts. He's an archaeologist, a professor at a university in Panama."

"Close by then. Panama City, Florida, I presume?"

"Panama City, Panama."

"Whoa. Central America. That sounds cool. Are you still in touch?"

Miranda flushed. "I used to follow him on Facebook, but opted out after I'd satisfied my curiosity."

"Ah," said Matt.

"A lifetime ago he took me out to dinner to celebrate our college graduation." She took a deep breath and lowered her eyes, her hands clasped tight.

"Uh-huh," said Matt, nodding, giving her as much time as she needed.

"I was expecting a marriage proposal." She stared into his eyes. "But instead, he dumped me."

"Ouch! That must have been . . ." He stopped himself. He had no idea what it must have been like.

She looked at him, sadness filling her chocolate eyes.

"That was the last time I saw him, or heard from him. Now, out of the blue, this invitation arrives."

"Anything I can do to help?"

"No. It's my nightmare to face. Alone." She smiled weakly at him. "But it's kind of you to offer."

They sat quietly for a time, each wrestling with what to do next.

Then she looked deep into his searching gaze.

"Okay," she said, slapping her hands on her knees and taking a deep, cleansing breath. Fortified and in control. At least, that's what she was struggling to project. "The pity party's over." She stood up, felt dizzy, and quickly sat back down.

Matt reached for her but she pulled away.

"I'm okay," she said, and headed for her office.

But he knew she wasn't okay. And he didn't know how to help her. He smiled, remembering the unexpected kiss she'd given him after their long day.

He carried his computer and book to his workplace in her office, prepared to review their case.

"So, this is what we know, or think we know," Matt began, summarizing from his notes. "Our vic wasn't poisoned. Cause of death was drowning—hastened by the weapon piercing her lung. A trident," he emphasized, glancing at her. "She's age fourteen to sixteen and was two months pregnant. According to her DNA, she's a mix of Eastern European and Scandinavian. She has half-moon scars under her breasts, but apparently not from implants. The ligature marks around both ankles are a mystery." He looked at her, making sure he still had her attention. "Two stones—turquoise and black pearl—were found during the autopsy, the pearl in her throat, and the turquoise in her chest. Origin and significance unknown. A frog tattoo is inked on her left shoulder."

Miranda nodded.

"That pretty much sums it up," said Miranda. "But there's still a lot we don't know. Who she is. Where her journey started. Why a frog tattoo. Why she was wearing a mermaid tail. And how she managed to wash ashore on Lido Beach with a harpoon—or a trident—in her chest."

"Okay. What's next?"

"We need to start pressing Trixie Monroe about her business with the Mermaid Fantasea company in Miami, and find out more about her relationship with Georgia Holmes. And we need to find out from Georgia Holmes who the man in the photo on her desk is. And what, if anything, he has to do with the Mermaid Fantasea yacht behind them in the picture."

"What's the plan, then?"

"We show the pictures of the victim to the three campers, despite Georgia's objection. This time I won't ask for her permission."

Matt checked his watch.

"It's late to be heading back to the mermaid camp. Let's go first thing tomorrow." He wanted to add that, with her hangover, she was in no shape to see anyone. But he didn't.

"Hmm," she muttered, wondering if she should tell him about the cocktail party at the Ritz that evening. That she was considering attending it, despite the gnawing voice in her head warning her not to. She wondered if she should invite him as her guest, then decided it was too risky—although she couldn't articulate exactly why.

"I guess you're right," she agreed. "I still think your cult theory is the most promising."

"I'll keep researching it. You get some rest before we meet up tomorrow."

"Good. Go home to Muscle. And don't worry about me. I'll be just . . . peachy."

Chapter 22

The handsome valet winked at Miranda as she handed him the keys to her Audi. While the Ritz-Carlton was close enough to her home that she could've walked, the kitten heels she had chosen to wear weren't meant for walking. Not to mention the humidity, even after sundown, and realizing she was already late.

Men and women dressed in their elegant cocktail attire were milling about the spacious ballroom. Clusters of guests laughed and sipped cocktails as they shared light banter and laughter. A podium on the stage marked the spot where the guest of honor would be introduced.

Miranda blew out a heavy breath and inhaled, mustering as much courage as she could. Stunning in her black, above-the-knee, strapless dress, her dark auburn hair demurely gathered in a classic French twist, she lifted a glass of champagne off one of the passing trays. She saw her parents moving about the room, chatting with guests. She swallowed her drink in two gulps, then quickly picked up another.

The tall, lean, sandy-haired man standing next to Fernando and Erika Morales looked unchanged from how she remembered him, except for a deep tan. He was more sophisticated-looking now in a tuxedo.

Her glass trembled in her hand, and her knees were weak. She suddenly wished she hadn't come, or that Matt had come with her. She visually explored the spacious ballroom but saw no other familiar faces. Not that she expected to.

Graham caught her gaze and their eyes locked. Erika Morales turned to see what he was looking at and saw Miranda standing just inside the ballroom entrance. She nudged Fernando, who was actively engaged in conversation with a beautiful young woman.

"Excuse me," said Graham, setting his empty champagne flute on a nearby table, parting the crowds as he made his way toward her.

Miranda swallowed hard. Here it comes. She braced her shoulders, feeling light-headed.

She downed her last drop of champagne and swooped up yet another, willing herself to be steadfast as he approached.

"Hello, Miranda. It's been a long time. You look gorgeous!"

He leaned in to kiss her but she instinctively pulled back.

He lowered his slate-blue eyes briefly, awkward and embarrassed, then raised them.

"Graham," she said casually, taking a sip of her drink, as much to steady her nerves as to cool her throat. "What an intriguing turn of events."

She hoped he didn't notice the glass trembling in her hand. She drained it and exchanged the empty for yet another and immediately took a sip.

Slow down, Miranda. This is not the place or time to lose control.

She breathed more slowly, lifting her perfectly sculpted jaw and struggling to make her smile appear authentic.

Graham noticed tiny lines creasing the edges of her eyes, and smiled to himself. Neither of them was getting any younger, and yet she still looked radiant.

"Uh, yes, intriguing is a good way to describe it, I suppose. Your parents' letter asking me to present my research to a local collectors' group came as a complete surprise."

"No kidding?" she said, sarcastically. "I assumed you'd stayed in touch with them after our final dinner together."

He stared at her.

She didn't flinch.

He cleared his throat.

"Uh, well, we've exchanged a few letters over the years. When your father asked if I'd like to present my work to the Antiquarian Collectors Group here in Sarasota, how could I refuse? Especially when he told me that his close friend has an extraordinary and rare collection of pre-Columbian artifacts."

"Of course. How could you?"

Her champagne buzz was beginning to make the ballroom spin.

"Are you okay?" he asked, taking her elbow.

She instantly withdrew her elbow from his hand.

"I'm . . . fine."

"You might want to take her home," whispered a waiter as he brushed past Graham carrying a tray of bubbly.

Graham flashed him a knowing smile.

"Excuse me," said Miranda curtly. "I've got to use the ladies' room," wishing she had something to hold on to on the way to the restroom. Thankfully the room was so crowded that nobody paid her any attention as she bumped against them.

When she returned, her parents and Graham were standing at one of the high tables, talking and smiling. Her father motioned for her to come and join them. She hesitated, then took her time to cross the short distance.

Fernando leaned in to kiss her and she immediately recoiled.

"Glad you could come, darling," said Fernando. Handsome, polished. Perfectly coiffed. Alluring in his tuxedo.

Miranda wiped away his hot breath. Darling? Fuck you! She could see that her father had not lost any of his charm.

Her mother was decorated with glittery jewelry like a movie star on Oscar night. Subtle signs of cosmetic surgery revealed that she was attempting to slow the aging process.

"We never got your RSVP," said Erika, snidely.

"That's because I just got the invitation, Mother. An afterthought, no doubt," she said. "Surprised I came?"

"You could have called, at least," Erika challenged.

Graham shifted his position, sensing the simmering friction between mother and daughter, and entered the conversation.

"Uh, your parents were just telling me you're a homicide detective, Miranda. How's that gig going?"

"The gig, as you call it, can be demanding at times. But it definitely has its rewards."

"I'm glad to hear you're happy." He turned to her parents. "You must be very proud!"

Erika slipped her gloved arm around Graham's bent elbow while peering at her daughter. "I wouldn't know anything about that kind of work."

"Thank you, Mother. I see you haven't lost your talent for condescension."

Erika shot her an evil eye, then turned back to Graham.

"Have you settled in at the Ritz?" she purred.

Graham shifted his weight. The room suddenly felt like a sauna.

"Yes. It's beautiful. I never could have afforded such a lavish suite on my professor's salary. So thank you."

"Fernando and I are so delighted you agreed to come," said Erika, moving close enough to Graham that he could smell her champagne-tainted breath. "The least we could do is make sure you're comfortable while you're in our great city."

Bands of sweat were collecting under Graham's collar. He swooped up two glasses of water as the tray passed by, handing one to Miranda. Fernando, wearing his political smile, held the base of his crystal champagne flute with the precision of the skilled surgeon he was.

"Your research has been invaluable to our understanding of the practices of ancient civilizations, Graham. I once entertained the idea of studying ancient healing customs as an extension of my medical training," Fernando said, with a chuckle. "But I soon realized I could serve humanity better by using modern practices. Leave the digging up of ancient rituals and herbal remedies to scholars like you."

A cordial laugh spread around the table.

Miranda just rolled her eyes.

"From what I've read about your work, Dr. Morales, volunteering your skills in other countries through Doctors for Equal Care, you're making a remarkable contribution to humanity," complimented Graham.

"There you are," boomed a voice approaching them.

Everyone's eyes shifted to the roar behind them.

"Am I interrupting some salacious gossip?"

The short, slightly overweight man approaching them was dressed in an Armani tuxedo, thin strands of dyed black hair combed over his bald head. His high forehead exposed deep furrows formed from years in the sun. The gleam in his round, brown eyes softened the harshness of his loud voice.

"Peter!" Fernando exclaimed, embracing his friend. "I was hoping you could come tonight and meet our distinguished professor."

"I could hardly miss meeting the world-famous Dr. Waterman," said Peter Millstine, reaching his hand out to Graham. "I'm delighted to finally meet you."

"An honor to meet you, Mr. Millstine. I'm eager to hear about your fascinating antique collection, perhaps even have a chance to see it before I return to Panama."

Peter smiled without committing himself.

Fernando turned to his daughter.

"You might remember Peter, Miranda. You were quite young when he was getting started with his antiquities business." He gently slapped Peter on the back. "Now he has an art gallery on Longboat Key and has founded the Antiquarian Collectors Group."

Peter stood back to admire Miranda in her body-sculpting dress. He lifted her hand and brushed it with a kiss. She tried to jerk it away but he had a firm grasp on it, staring into her unfriendly, chocolate eyes.

"I don't recall any of your friends, Father," she said. "You'll have to excuse me, Mr. Millstine. I've been away from the family for quite some time."

"No matter," said Peter, smiling. "Look at you now. All grown up into a stunning, young lady." Without taking his eyes off Miranda, he added, "Fernando and Erika, you must be so proud!" Fernando cleared his throat and shifted his stance.

"Yes . . . well, anyway," he said, turning to Graham, "Peter here has assembled an impressive collection of mermaid folk art—memorabilia, so to speak—and has developed quite a fetish for mermaids in the process."

"A mermaid fetish?" said Miranda, suddenly fully recovered from her overdose of bubbly. Her eyes were wide. "A bit . . . unusual, isn't it?"

"Well, I don't know about that," said Peter.

"I thought a fetish had something to do with aberrant sexual practices?" she asked brazenly.

She still had enough champagne in her system to be free of inhibitions and polite etiquette. She rarely attended social events like this, one of the reasons being her aversion to small talk.

The group squirmed at Miranda's rudeness.

Graham immediately seized the opportunity to rescue the collector from Miranda's brash remark.

"Well, actually, Miranda," he said with a casual smile, "psychiatrists are responsible for linking the term 'fetish' to sexual behaviors. We in the antiquities field consider a fetish in quite a different light."

"Really? How so?" she said.

"Well," continued Graham, "fetishism isn't my area of expertise, but I do know that most people—at least those outside the mental health field—consider a fetish more of an obsessive fascination with an object, without any particular connection to sexual . . . preferences."

"That's interesting," said Miranda, pausing while Graham held her stare. "Those of us outside the mental health field and inside law enforcement tend to link fetishes with sexual arousal. But I know from my psychology courses at college that the subject is open to interpretation."

Graham wondered why Miranda was pursuing such an awkward, if not offensive, subject at a time like this. He studied her, as if he were back in his classroom with a belligerent student, considering what tone was best to use in such a circumstance. He took a deep breath and resumed his professorial demeanor.

"In the context of ancient cultures, where tribal beliefs and practices were dedicated to worshipping fertility and rebirth, one might conclude that sexual arousal was part of such rituals. But in truth, these tribes used objects—or fetishes—to protect them, believing these objects were endowed with magical powers." He paused and scanned the group before continuing. "The leaders of these cultures were more concerned with survival and perpetuating their species than how future societies might construe their practices as deviant, or sexually aberrant."

Graham remembered times when Miranda would clutch onto an idea like a dog with a bone. Nonetheless, he was intrigued by the depth of her interest in the topic.

"Well," said Peter, with a throaty laugh, "I certainly hope none of you think I have an unhealthy bent toward . . . deviant sexual practices," he said clumsily.

"Of course not, Peter," said Erika, brushing his arm.

But Miranda's thoughts had already drifted to the Lido Beach mermaid and the frog tattoo symbolizing fertility and rebirth.

"Do you know if any ancient rituals involved reptiles and mermaids?" she asked bluntly, her gaze locked on Graham.

"Excuse me, Miranda," said her father, irritated. "I think we should give Graham a break from your interrogation, so he can enjoy the evening."

Miranda shot a venomous look at Fernando.

Graham cleared his throat.

A rumble of disapproval was clearly audible from Erika at Miranda's crass behavior.

"It's quite all right, Dr. Morales. It will get me primed for my lecture tomorrow," he said, smiling at Miranda. "I'm happy to continue, if the rest of you don't mind."

"Well, it's up to you," said Fernando, with nods from the others.

"Okay, then. As far as reptiles are concerned, tribes viewed them as objects of devotion and spiritual reverence, as they did other animals, such as mountain lions, owls, horses, and yes, mermaids," he said. "If you come to my lecture tomorrow, you'll learn a lot more about the power of beliefs and ancient customs that might seem perverse to us today, but played an essential role in many ancient cultures. You could list almost any object and find some person, tribe, or cult, somewhere in the world, who devoutly worship objects they believe are imbued with magical powers that promise them protection from whatever it is they fear."

"Well, Dr. Waterman," said Peter, shifting the conversation, "I have a confession to make." With a sly grin, he leaned into the group and said, in conspiratorial voice, "I recently acquired a rare talisman thought to belong to a South American water deity. I was hoping you'd take a look at it while you're in town. Authenticate it for me."

Graham's eyes lit up like sparklers on the Fourth of July.

"I'd be delighted, Mr. Millstine! And if possible, I'd love to see your entire collection of mermaid folk art," he said, reminding the collector of his earlier hint.

"Of course, of course. It would be an honor," said Peter, smiling like a boy eager to show off his newest toy.

The group nodded and smiled, except for Miranda, who was absorbing the vibe filtering among the small, elite group, sensing their concern that she might engage in another series of disrespectful cross-examinations. She decided to back off and let the show go on as her parents had planned.

"Why don't you tell us about your latest research, Graham?" suggested Fernando.

"Seems almost ironic," smiled Graham, lowering his head briefly before looking squarely at Peter Millstine. "I've been exploring the ancient Inuit Indians and tribes of Central and South America, specifically researching their objects of worship and the powers they attributed to them. I'll cover much of it in my lecture tomorrow. Please, I'd love to hear more about your talisman."

"Well, I believe it's something you know quite a bit about. To be honest, Dr. Waterman, your article, published last year in the *Antiquarian Collectors' Journal*—that's why I asked Fernando to arrange our meeting," said Peter. "Please, could you tell us how you collected your research for that article?"

"Well," said Graham, "my research was primarily from secondhand sources and information I'd gathered from published articles referencing the item—a very rare mermaid belt, currently housed in a private collection."

Miranda's eyes shot open to full alert at the mention of a mermaid artifact.

"Most research suggests the belt belonged to Masimi Aqua," Graham continued, "who, according to legend, was a mermaid spirit." He glanced at Peter. "A water spirit supposedly from South America."

Peter smiled proudly, a glitter in his eyes. "Before you continue, Professor, I must confess that I am that anonymous collector. The belt is the new talisman in my collection."

Graham gasped.

"Is it true the belt is adorned with a string of rare black pearls and gemstones?" Graham asked excitedly.

Peter nodded and smiled, his earlier disgruntlement forgotten.

"Yes, it is. And as you wrote in your article, legend has it that the belt would turn to seaweed if it were ever stolen, rather than given as a gift. As you also noted, mermaids are well known for their penchant for offering gifts—gold trinkets, miniature pottery figurines, even healing rituals." He paused. "They're especially known for giving the gift of prophecy."

"That's quite a story," said Miranda. "A mermaid spirit with a belt of gemstones."

Graham waited for Miranda to challenge him. When she didn't, Peter filled the void.

"Depending on whose legend you believe, Masimi Aqua left the magnificent mermaid belt onshore as a gift for her beloved," he explained. "Nobody knows who her beloved was, but experts seem to agree that the talisman is dated to the early fifteenth century. Perhaps earlier." He lowered his eyes, twisting the gold-and-diamond ring on his pinky finger. "For the record, the belt was given to me as a gift. So if the legend is true, I am happy to say it will not turn to seaweed while it remains in my collection." He glanced at Miranda. "Of course, if someone steals it . . ."

Laughter flowed around the group, while Miranda's mind returned to images of the dead mermaid lying contorted on Lido Beach.

"To your point, Dr. Waterman, the belt does contain a band of exquisite pearls," said Peter. "Black pearls, to be precise, as well as rubies, sapphires, and emeralds."

Miranda's eyes widened. The waistband on the Lido mermaid costume, if in fact it had had one, was missing. Only the "Mermaid's Delight" tag remained intact. Miranda wondered if the tail did indeed have such a waistband, could it have been adorned with the black pearl found in the victim's throat?

"How long have you owned the talisman, Mr. Millstine?" she asked.

Peter glared at her for what seemed an eternity.

"Long enough," he said simply, suddenly growing uneasy. He produced a smile nevertheless. "I'd like to learn more about you, Miranda, and why you're so fascinated with mermaids. I understand you're a lawyer?"

"Actually, Mr. Millstine, I'm a detective. Chief detective, of the homicide division," she said confidently.

Peter's demeanor immediately changed. "Ah, I apologize," he said, flushed. "I thought you were a lawyer. I guess I . . . misunderstood." He glanced at Fernando and Erika with eyebrows raised.

Erika and Fernando looked furious.

"It was actually my parents' desire for me to become a doctor. But I preferred a career in law enforcement." She set her jaw and glared at her parents. "I guess that's about as close to a lawyer as I'll ever get," she said sarcastically.

Erika's face twisted in anger and disgust.

"Ah, well," Peter stammered, "I . . . I'm truly . . . impressed. I know plenty of doctors and lawyers, but you're my first homicide detective." His smile failed to disguise his disdain.

Graham cleared his throat and edged closer to Miranda.

"I hope you'll be attending my lecture tomorrow, Miranda?"

Before she could answer, Erika cut in, checking her diamond-studded Rolex.

"Sorry to interrupt, but it's time to introduce Graham, Fernando," she said, nudging her husband with her elbow.

"Yes, of course," said Fernando.

He took Graham's arm and guided him to the stage, where he introduced him.

Graham approached the podium and greeted the crowd, thanking his sponsors for the invitation. He said a few words about his lecture the following day, then politely excused himself.

He walked over to join Miranda, who was standing alone at a high table far away from Peter and her parents.

"Can I see you later?" Graham whispered softly in her ear.

Before she could answer, her father came up behind them.

"I see you two are getting . . . reacquainted."

"I was just leaving," she said briskly, abruptly turning away just as her father's cell phone rang.

"Excuse me for a moment," he said, heading toward an exit door.

Graham immediately grabbed her arm. "I'm only in town for a couple of days, Miranda. Would you please join me for dinner before I go back?"

"I don't think that's a good idea, Graham," she said, retracting her arm, feeling like a vise was pinching her heart. "Good luck tomorrow. Safe travels back to Panama." She moved swiftly away.

He watched her leave, sighing deeply, his heart weighed down by years of unfinished business and lingering regrets.

Miranda stopped in the hallway to retrieve her valet ticket from her purse. The buzz in her head had strangely returned. She felt dizzy, so she sat down on a padded bench in the lobby, unaware that her father was a few steps away, his back toward her.

She turned when she heard his familiar voice, agitated, harsh and demanding.

"Bring her to my office immediately," he ordered, pacing the hallway. "And make damn sure nobody sees you. I don't want any fuck-ups, do you understand? I'll be there within the hour."

Miranda quickly stepped back inside the ballroom before her father could see her. She took a deep breath and counted to three before opening the exit door again, as if she were just leaving. When she stepped into the hallway for the second time, she feigned surprise at seeing him.

"Leaving so soon?" he said, his angry scowl replaced by a false smile. "Just when it seemed like you and Graham were getting along so well."

"I have a lot of work ahead of me tomorrow."

"Exciting new case?" he said, reaching for her arm.

She glared at him.

"Sadly, there's always a new case." She stared at him for a few seconds more. "I'm surprised you're asking; you've never taken an interest in me before."

He gripped her bare arm. "That's not true, Miranda."

Her chocolate eyes turned black. She twisted away from him. "Enjoy the rest of your evening."

He grabbed her again.

"Take your hand off me!" she ordered.

Fernando released his hold and took a deep breath. "I remember how you always liked mysteries and puzzles," he said, almost in a whisper.

"I doubt you remember anything about me, Father." She fought the urge to allow him to confess his past wrongdoings—to make up for his neglect.

He sucked in his cheeks, seeing the fiery spirit she'd had since she was a child. He took a another deep breath.

"Can't we just sit for a minute? Please?"

The guilt of a child stirred within her.

"I only have a second. I'm tired and I have a lot of work to do."

Miranda brought her valet ticket to the valet station, handing it to the same handsome man who had helped her when she arrived. Then she and Fernando sat down on the padded bench.

He tried to take her hand but she folded her arms across her chest.

"What do you want?"

"I read in the paper this morning about a young woman wearing a mermaid costume who washed ashore on Lido Beach last Sunday. I wondered if you were involved in the case?"

She hesitated. She hadn't read the paper, so she wasn't sure if it mentioned her as lead detective.

"Yes. I'm leading the investigation."

Fernando raised his eyebrows and nodded slowly.

"Ah. Perhaps Graham's lecture tomorrow will be of interest to you. After all, between him and Peter, mermaids seem to be the topic of the day."

Miranda peered at him for a few seconds, wondering again what had prompted this interest in her work. She hoped it wasn't his desire for her and Graham to reunite romantically, after all this time.

She had never been able to get a firm read on her father as a child. Fear had gripped her whenever he entered a room. She never knew whether he'd erupt in anger, mercilessly criticizing her for something she didn't understand, or if he'd ask her to leave the room so he could talk to her sister, making his preference for Farrah clear while ignoring her.

But she was older now and felt only contempt and distrust for the man standing before her. Her sister's suicide years ago had carved a deep chasm between her and her parents, and it had only deepened over the years.

"I doubt anything Graham has to say would help with my investigation," she scoffed. "Now, I've really got to go." She stood up. The dizziness was gone, although she felt an odd chill. She squared her bare shoulders, wishing she had brought a wrap with her, and headed down the hallway toward the exit.

Fernando rushed after her and blocked her way. Behind her father, she saw Graham looking at them from the ballroom door he was holding slightly ajar.

She turned back to her father, looking at him with eyes that had turned cold and hard.

"I've got nothing more to say."

He gripped her by the shoulders as if she were a child again. She winced at the tightness of his hold.

"Why won't you tell me?"

"Tell you what, exactly?"

"About the mermaid case."

"I'm not at liberty to talk about an active investigation," she replied curtly. Her anger churned the acid in her stomach. To stave off the nausea, she reluctantly sat down on the closest settee and took a deep breath. "Why the sudden interest in my work?" she asked.

He shrugged.

"I guess you could help by arranging an appointment for me to see your friend's collection of mermaid—how did you describe it? Memorabilia?"

Fernando's eyes narrowed.

"Peter has a few things on display in his gallery, but most of the valuable objects are locked up at his home on Longboat Key," said her father. "Not too far from our house. I'll see what I can do." He paused. "Maybe you could stop by to see me and your mother on the way."

She abruptly stood up and smiled as the handsome young valet arrived with her car keys.

She turned to her father. "Enjoy the lecture tomorrow."

As soon as she was out of his sight, Fernando pulled out his cell phone.

"What the fuck do you know about a dead mermaid washing up on Lido Beach?"

Chapter 23

The surgical suite in the Morales Medical Building in Bradenton, about ten miles north of Sarasota, had the latest state-of-the-art equipment to run a successful plastic surgery practice. According to statistics, Florida, New York, and California were among the top places in the country for cosmetic surgery. Those who wanted to cling to the fountain of youth seemed to cluster together, Florida, in particular, being a magnet for people desperate to hang on to their looks. Taut faces incapable of expression, oversized, shapely breasts intended to defy gravity, and countless other examples attesting to people's vanity.

As a child Miranda knew that her father was among the most sought-after plastic surgeons in the world, and was listed as one of the best plastic surgeons on Florida's Gulf Coast. Recognized as a top professional early in his career, the demand for his skills with a scalpel enabled him to open his first outpatient surgicenter in Bradenton a quarter-century ago, with others to follow in Tampa, Palm Beach, Boca Raton, and Miami.

While Dr. Morales traveled extensively around the world donating his time and talent, his reputation also enabled him to attract the best and brightest doctors to his practice, pretty much guaranteeing that his wealthy clientele would remain loyal to him. Only the best of the best were given a place in his operating room.

The long hours he worked with other volunteers at Doctors for Equal Care had exposed him to the savage conditions all too prevalent in third-world countries. Babies born with malformed faces, deformities resulting from warring sects setting fires to villages, leaving people maimed, if they survived at all. Birth defects from incompetent practitioners and poor dietary standards. Unsanitary conditions everywhere.

He was young when he committed himself to these humanitarian efforts, embracing the idealism so prevalent among youth. But over time, he'd seen the futility of trying to combat the injustice so rampant in these desolate countries, with leaders seeking to fill their pockets with riches on the backs of their people's suffering. He was always relieved to return home.

Now, having amassed a fortune of his own, all of that seemed like a lifetime ago. The lavish lifestyle he now enjoyed eclipsed that time in his life, his selfless goal at the beginning now replaced with the lucrative business of sculpting aging faces and shaping less-than-perfect bodies. Noses too big. Breasts too small. Lips too thin. Sagging skin. A multitude of reasons that enabled his lust for the high life to grow ever stronger.

This is why the frantic call that came during the cocktail party had enraged him. Emergencies were typically relegated to the newbies in his practice; everyone knew that.

But this call was a different matter altogether. Something he had to deal with personally.

"Peter will drive you home tonight—I have an emergency," he told Erika when he returned to the ballroom.

"What kind of emergency?"

"Just one of the new doctors worried about a patient he had in surgery this morning."

"Damn it, Fernando!" she huffed. "What about Graham?"

"Graham can take care of himself. He's staying here at the Ritz. He'd probably appreciate some quiet time."

"Fine!" she hissed. Peter Millstine wasn't one of her favorite people, but since he had to drive past their home on the way to his, it seemed expedient. "Don't be late!"

☙

By the time Fernando arrived at his office, a near-dead young girl lay under a crisp, white sheet on the table in the operating suite. Her pulse was thready, her skin clammy and gray.

"You idiot, Castro," Fernando fumed. "This is not my area of expertise. I'm a plastic surgeon, not a magician!"

"I'm sorry, Fernando! I didn't know what to do. I was scared! I tried to call Peter but it went to his voicemail. I had to call you. Thank God you answered your phone!"

"Tell me what happened. Who fucked up this time?"

Castro Montoya lowered his gaze, shaking his head.

"Fuck!" bellowed Fernando, performing a quick assessment of the young girl with the black ponytail and thin arms.

"She was shivering. I thought she was going into shock!" explained Castro. "We were heading to Florida from Panama. She seemed to be doing fine. Then suddenly she turned pale and feverish. Like I told you. She complained of stomach pain. Python thought she was having a seizure. My nephew said she had overdosed. Fortunately he was able to give her an injection to counteract it. She seemed to be doing okay for a while after that, but she suddenly took a turn for the worse once we'd docked at the harbor in Tampa." He wiped his sweaty face with his thick hand. "I . . . I couldn't risk taking her to a hospital, so I brought her to you."

Fernando held up the X-ray of the girl's abdomen he'd ordered on his way to his office.

"What does it show?" asked Castro, looking at the unrecognizable grayscale image.

"A foreign body. Something with a sharp point at one end. Let's hope it didn't puncture the bowel." He gripped Castro's arm. "Goddammit, Castro. This fucking mess shouldn't be on me!"

The anesthesiologist he'd notified of the emergency had already begun preparing for surgery by the time Fernando arrived. An intravenous drip was in place, and he'd just injected a drug into the IV to raise her blood pressure. An oxygen mask covered her mouth. Slowly she began responding to the treatment.

"Vital signs are stable so far," said Dr. Kashmin Abdullah, closely monitoring the patient.

Fernando nodded. "Good. Start the anesthesia."

Fernando trusted Dr. Abdullah, who'd been with him for over a decade. He paid him exceptionally well to ensure his confidentiality. Despite health-care regulations protecting patients' privacy, he knew all too well that not everybody in the health profession abided by them. Money was always the most powerful motivation for loyalty. It was especially important at inopportune times like this that secrecy trumped HIPAA regulations.

"This is much more serious than the usual mistakes, Castro!" Fernando blasted the man standing at the back of the operating room. "This has got to stop!" He had warned his partners when they formed their business alliance several years ago that he would not participate in certain aspects of their enterprise. Now it seemed things had gotten out of control.

Castro kept his head down, avoiding Fernando's hostile eyes.

"Go, Castro! Wait in the recovery room. You'd better say every prayer you know."

Castro Montoya shuffled out of the OR suite, his eyes rimmed with tears, unable to look at Mirakakoo lying helpless on the surgical table before he left.

"It's not my fault," he mumbled on his way out.

After more than an hour, Fernando finally removed the strange object that had been lodged deep under the skin of Mirakakoo's abdomen. He carried the slimy clump over to the sink, rinsing off the blood and membrane encasing it. Through the microscope next to the sink, a tiny shape covered in glorious, multicolored enamel emerged. There was a needle-like prominence at one end, a fan-like shape at the other. The iridescent lapis, gold, emerald, and ruby feathers shimmered. Tiny black beads for eyes. The stick-like legs ended in delicate bird's feet. The object was breathtaking in its elegance.

He tossed his bloody gloves in the trash bin, untied his surgical mask, and stormed into the recovery room.

Castro, startled, stopped massaging Mirakakoo's thin arm.

"We need to talk, Castro—now!" he said, yanking a terrified and puzzled Castro out of the chair and shoving him down the hall to the now-empty operating room. The double doors flapped shut behind them.

He thrust Castro hard against the wall with such force that one of the pictures fell to the floor, shattering the glass.

"Now, what the fuck's going on?" His bark echoed through the cavernous room.

Castro lowered his dark eyes to the floor that seemed to move beneath him. Fernando, within an inch of Castro's flushed, sweaty face, said, "I asked you a question, Castro—"

Castro instinctively drew back, lifting his eyes.

"It's not my fault, Fernando! I swear. I don't always know what they're up to. I just take orders. I am just a pawn in this chess game."

"Hmmph," grunted Fernando, his eyes wild. "You tell Mano that this is the last time I come to his rescue! Do you hear me, Castro? We're damn lucky she didn't need a blood transfusion. Or worse."

Furious, Fernando paced the room like a trapped animal, then swirled around, enraged.

"And find out how the fuck a goddamn hummingbird got inside this girl!"

Chapter 24

"What's wrong, Miranda?" asked Matt, noticing her faraway look as she sat spellbound in front of her computer.

"What?" she said, as if she'd forgotten Matt was in the room.

"You look like you were in Neverland. Anything you want to talk about?"

Miranda leaned back in her chair and swiveled around, her arms on her thighs.

"You're creeping me out, Miranda. What's bugging you?"

She sighed, pressing her fist against her mouth.

"I went to the cocktail party last night."

"Cocktail party?"

He took a deep breath and leaned back. "Ah. The invitation. I'm not surprised you went," he said. "Eager to get face-to-face with your former Romeo after so long apart?"

"That's mean, Matt. It's not like you."

"I just don't get you, Miranda," he said, running his hand through his thick, black hair. "You close yourself off to everyone around you, yet you easily open yourself up to the pain and misery of your apparently troubled past without hesitation." His tone was one of irritation mixed with defeat.

"I was curious. I thought I might learn something that could help with our case."

"You discussed our case with him?" He blew out a breath, clearly annoyed.

"His expertise is pre-Columbian history and tribal rituals," she continued, ignoring his irritation. "I thought he might be able to help us make a connection between reptiles and mermaids." She glared at him, but her chocolate eyes softened. "Or share his knowledge on ancient cults, perhaps giving us some insight into how they operate."

Matt shook his head. "A professor. A published PhD, studying mermaids?" He closed his eyes, exasperated. "Reptiles, I could understand, but mermaids? Now that's a first."

Miranda knew it sounded preposterous, but she also knew they needed all the help they could get if they ever hoped to solve this case. She fixed her eyes on him.

"There's also my father's strange behavior."

"What are you talking about?"

"He got a phone call during the party. I overheard him in the hallway as I was leaving. He was agitated."

"Why?"

"That's just it. He wouldn't say. But, more importantly, he introduced me to a friend of his. A wealthy collector. A collector with a mermaid fetish."

Matt hunched forward.

"A mermaid what?"

"A fetish. An obsession of sorts."

"Now that sounds weird."

"It's . . . complicated. But it might tie in with our research." She glanced at him. "Graham apparently published an article in some antiquities magazine about a rare talisman—a mermaid belt—attributed to a mermaid princess. He had no idea the anonymous collector who owned the talisman was the very same friend of my father's—Peter Millstine."

Matt was listening intently now.

"And," said Miranda, her excitement growing, "there's a legend tied to the belt."

"Legend?"

"Long story short, Masimi Aqua, a mermaid, gave her belt to the man who saved her. Apparently the talisman owned by

Millstine is a belt adorned with pearls and gemstones." She paused, eyeing Matt, who was sitting on the edge of his seat. "Graham's giving a lecture today at the Van Wezel. He'll be speaking about ancient rituals and tribal beliefs. Maybe even mermaids."

"Hmm . . . sounds a little far afield. . . and I don't recall seeing a belt on our mermaid's tail," he said.

"Maybe there was one originally, but it got torn away during her journey," said Miranda. "I thought that if there was a belt, perhaps the pearl Dr. Rubens found in her throat could have come from it?"

Matt looked intrigued.

"The lecture's in an hour. We're going," she declared.

Matt dropped Miranda at the entrance to the Van Wezel Performing Arts Hall. "I'll park the car and meet you inside."

"Okay," she said. "I'll be up in the balcony."

She was surprised to see such a large crowd in the auditorium. "I didn't know pre-Columbian history was such a popular topic," she mumbled as she headed for the upper level.

There was a podium in the center of the stage, next to a large screen. Low voices hummed in the lower gallery as anticipation grew.

The door at the back of the balcony creaked open and Matt walked over to the seat beside her just as a well-groomed, distinguished man walked to the podium.

"My father," whispered Miranda.

"Nice-looking guy. At least from here."

Miranda elbowed him.

"Welcome, everyone," said Fernando Morales, smiling out at the crowd. "I'm delighted to introduce our special guest this afternoon. His extensive study in the field of pre-Columbian culture and tribal customs has added enormously to our understanding of that historic civilization. This afternoon you will be the first to hear about his experiences as part of an expedition that uncovered a collection of rare artifacts, and how legend and fact are intertwined in these ancient civilizations. So, without further delay, I'd like to introduce Professor Graham Aramis Waterman."

Applause thundered through the auditorium as the two men shook hands. Fernando left the stage and took his seat in the front row. As the applause subsided, Graham adjusted the microphone, then smiled at the crowd.

"Ladies and gentlemen, I'd first like to thank Dr. and Mrs. Morales for their gracious invitation to speak to you today. I'd also like to thank all of you for sacrificing precious time to be indoors with me when you could be out on one of the award-winning beaches Sarasota is known for."

Soft laughter and light applause wafted through the auditorium.

Miranda shifted in her seat and took a deep breath.

"Now, if someone would dim the lights, I'll begin our journey into the world of the San Blas Kuna Indians of Panama and their remarkable history."

Graham clicked the first slide, showing an Indian tribe. The leader wore a crown of colorful feathers and held a long spear in his left hand, a bow and arrow in his right. His entourage wore elaborate long necklaces adorned with small trinkets. The men wore simple loincloths, and the women, their breasts exposed except for their necklaces, wore fabric wraps that fell just below their knees. Beaded bracelets were wrapped around their narrow ankles. A naked, cupid-like child carried arrows in a small quiver that peeked over his left shoulder. He carried a tiny bow in his right hand. The tribe was lined up in single file behind their chief.

"Throughout history, ancient people have believed that power and leadership result from supernatural forces called mana," Graham said, looking out at the attentive faces. "This so-called power went well beyond endowing leaders with the physical prowess and brute strength expected of the regular chiefs and tribal leaders.

"Both status and mana were believed to be inherited at birth, rather than automatically passed down through the generations. The threat to power, leadership, and status from others within the tribe, as well as those outside the tribe, intent on usurping that power, rested with the ability of leaders to constantly prove they were the chosen ones. That they had been endowed with unique traits that separated them from the common people."

He turned to glance at the image on the screen.

"The leader in this photo is the one we assume was endowed with the status and mana to lead this tribe—the chosen one."

Graham clicked to the next slide, which depicted a collection of small gold charms.

"Tribal members often wore gold ornaments like these to reflect not only their social status and power, but just as importantly, their belonging to distinct tribal groups. In ancient societies, gold was not viewed the same way it's viewed today among Western cultures, but rather symbolized the combined secular and sacred powers within the elite members of the tribes. Survival of the pre-Columbian Kuna society was dependent on keeping the commoners convinced that their chiefs had been imbued with unique qualities. Sustaining that belief was paramount to maintaining order within the tribe and enforcing the moral integrity of the people."

The next screen showed two images side by side: a small, square, metal box with a mermaid on the lid and a gold-colored bracelet.

"This seemingly innocuous object on the left, found at the bottom of the Pacific Ocean two years ago, is a silver box filled with miniature figurines. This slide shows a close-up of the lid," he said, pointing with his laser pen on the lid's surface. "Here you can see the detail of the snake wrapped around the mermaid's shoulders." Then he moved the red laser dot to the bracelet. "This stunning gold cuff is etched with a frog and lizard facing each other, with a turquoise cabochon separating them."

Miranda leaned forward, clearly captivated.

"See that?" she whispered to Matt. "Snake. Frog. Lizard. Turquoise. Coincidence?"

He nodded.

The next slide revealed a gold, miniature filigree frog with pierced limbs. The tiny gold wire that shaped the ears continued in a diamond pattern down its spine. Beside the frog was another miniature, this one a silver lizard with a single row of protruding spikes from its thin neck to the tip of its long tail.

"Reptiles are common symbols in ancient rituals," explained Graham. "These rare artifacts are thought to have been originally buried at a sacred burial site of the Kuna Indian tribe in Chiriqui, in northern Panama. We're still trying to figure out exactly how the box landed at the bottom of the Pacific Ocean."

Matt nudged Miranda. "The professor might just be useful after all," he whispered.

Miranda leaned back in her seat.

Audible whispers swept through the audience as Graham highlighted more images.

"The ancient Kuna Indians believed that reptiles symbolized the powers of earth, sky, and water, and were responsible for transforming ancient peoples from uncivilized and immoral to a highly ordered and spiritual community that developed knowledge and wisdom."

As Graham continued to explore the myths and legends surrounding the ancient tribes, he reached his final slide—a seductive mermaid sitting on a large rock jutting up from a calm sea. The pale light of a full moon reflected off her emerald-colored tail, and her scales glittered like tiny stars. Her gaze was fixed on a large-masted ship in the distance as a tiny sprite hovered over her head, reminding Miranda of Tinkerbell.

Matt nudged her again.

"Reptiles and a mermaid. The whole enchilada."

"Shush," said Miranda.

Graham's eyes lingered on the final image for a few silent moments, then scanned the audience sitting in the dimness. "Few myths have been as mystifying and powerful as mermaids." He paused. "Fact or fiction? Myths and legends arise from many sources, and for many reasons. They arouse deep emotions. They've been both praised and demonized throughout centuries.

"Some people believe in mermaids as strongly as others believe extraterrestrials live among us. Or that the Loch Ness Monster still thrives in Scotland. That magical creatures live above and below us in places we have yet to discover." He paused again. "We might be surprised by the secret societies that exist among people we know, living right next door. They have private passions and embrace doctrines that have been passed down through the centuries. They participate in sacred rituals that honor their long-held convictions, outside the confines of traditional religion."

Again Graham paused and looked at the image of the mermaid on the screen.

"Rituals can represent the grateful praise for the gods who bring rain for a healthy crop. Or they can reflect hatred, ignorance, and hostility tied to a past they don't quite understand. Like life itself, everything has many sides, and many purposes. Some practices that might seem demonic or barbaric to one sect are embraced by another, while others embrace beliefs in powerful protectors and faithful guardians, ensuring their safety and the future of their race. The quest to explore how and why ancient cultures adopted certain doctrines and engaged in rituals we consider peculiar today is what I have dedicated my life to."

Graham's fingers were gripping the edges of the podium, and his voice grew more intense. "Is there magic in the universe? Astronomers continue to discover new reasons to believe in the magic and mystery of the cosmos, a world where each culture can interpret such mysteries in their own way.

We must learn to accept—and not judge—any society based on their customs and practices." He took a breath. "Thank you all for coming. I'd be happy to stay to answer a few questions. Lights, please."

Matt had been mesmerized by Graham's presentation. He wondered how Miranda might be feeling after seeing him as a professor rather than a once-upon-a-time Prince Charming.

Miranda stood up slipping her purse over her shoulder.

"Don't you want to stay for the questions?" asked Matt, surprised.

"No," she said, giving a brief, backward glance at the stage before exiting the balcony.

ᘓ

Matt parked in front of Miranda's house a few blocks away from the Van Wezel. He glanced at Miranda, acutely aware that she had traveled to invisible places he could not go. Exactly what was simmering inside her beautiful head he couldn't say, or even imagine.

"Are you okay?" he asked quietly, turning off the ignition.

She didn't respond.

"I can understand why you thought Dr. Waterman might be of some help with our investigation," he said, stealing a glance.

"What?" she said, as if coming out of a fog.

"Dr. Waterman. Graham. I thought he made some fascinating points, including the idea of cults."

Miranda blinked, her eyes now fixed on his.

"What do you mean?" she asked. She looked tired, or overwhelmed. Seeing the former love of your life after so long would have rattled anyone.

"His talk about rituals," Matt said, forging ahead. "And the power of beliefs. I mean, isn't a cult just a tribe that embraces staunch beliefs in, well, many different things?"

"Hmm," she muttered. The silence felt heavy and awkward.

"What do you say we get together tomorrow?" Matt

finally suggested. "Give us both time to digest what the professor just presented—maybe focus on some new trails of inquiry and discovery." He turned to her. "Are you even listening to me, Miranda?"

She turned and smiled at him.

"You're an amazing partner, Matt. I appreciate all of your . . . support."

He nodded, flattered and embarrassed, but no less confused.

She patted his hand. "Thanks for coming to the lecture with me. It was really good of you."

As she got out of his car, all he felt was a sense of unease.

Chapter 25

The full moon cast a wide swath of silver across Sarasota Bay as Graham Waterman stared out of his hotel window. The majestic skyline of tall condominiums stretched along the coastline. He'd been restless and awake since 3:30 a.m., his mind filled with thoughts of his former love.

She had looked so beautiful at the cocktail reception. Her sensual black, strapless sheath had revealed her tanned, shapely shoulders and outlined her full breasts, stirring something inside him. More than a sexual arousal. Yes, he felt the urge of desire, but it was more. The free-falling auburn hair he remembered had been bundled up in a sexy twist. The sway of her slender neck combined with everything else about her had ignited a yearning inside him that he hadn't felt in years. An elegant and intelligent woman beyond his reach. He wondered if he'd made the biggest mistake of his life.

At the end of his lecture he had watched her leave the auditorium with a man. It had bothered him, and he was surprised by that. He wished she would have stayed behind, at least tell him what she'd thought of his presentation. Their conversation at the reception had centered on everything but what he'd truly wanted to talk about. The past. The now. The future.

He'd been moping around his hotel room, resorting to his computer to distract him from thoughts of her, but it had proved to be futile. He'd given up on going back to bed. His mind was in too much turmoil, and being alone in a hotel room only amplified his torment.

He stared at himself in the mirror. Tiny lines he'd noticed

before suddenly appeared deeper than he remembered, and he was greeted by new aches each morning. But his gray-blue eyes and trim body still attracted attention, even though none of the women he allowed into his world appealed to him for very long.

He blamed his demanding schedule for why he had never settled down. Now he was becoming painfully aware that he'd never gotten Miranda out of his system. His attempts to ignore his feelings for her were hollow.

The sun had started to peek over the horizon. A spray of gold was breaking through thin clouds by the time he'd showered and dressed. He decided to Google Miranda before heading out to seize a new day.

What he found astounded him. One entry in particular:

Miranda Morales was only the second woman to graduate first in her class at the FBI International Terrorism Unit. Her skills at deciphering complex codes and accurate profiling are considered well above average. Her capacity to combine her keen intuitive talents with solid scientific inquiry will surely lead her to a successful future in law enforcement.

He decided it was time to explore the city Miranda loved so much. He hadn't wanted to eat breakfast at the hotel, so the woman behind the desk in the lobby suggested the Yellow Mango across the street.

Traffic along the north-south connector between Sarasota and Bradenton was barely awake. A few runners, walkers, and bicyclists were heading toward the Ringling Bridge to get in their exercise before the heat of the day became too unbearable. Florida, like Panama, has a climate that brings thunderstorms and high humidity.

He remembered reading that, historically, the bridge linking the historic downtown to Longboat Key had been a subject of heated opposition when it was first proposed. Now it had become an iconic structure. The highway to heaven, he'd thought upon arriving a couple of days ago.

"The Pacific Ocean is nothing compared to the aquamarine waters of the Gulf of Mexico and Sarasota Bay," he remembered Miranda telling him whenever she talked of her hometown. She'd been homesick from the day she first arrived in Seattle. The rift between her and her parents had driven her to the opposite coast, and from what he had observed at the cocktail party, kept her apart from them even now. "Seattle's too dreary," she used to say.

He sat down at a table in the small garden of the Yellow Mango and ordered coffee and a croissant. He picked up the local newspaper from an empty chair and browsed the front page. Nothing much drew his interest; the usual problems confronting cities and small towns around the country. Panama had its own share of troubles. Gangs. Drugs. Murder. Corruption at all levels of government, often intertwined. He wondered if paradise truly existed anywhere in the world.

A headline below the fold caught his eye: "Dead Mermaid Washes Ashore on Lido Beach." Curious, he read the full story:

Lead homicide detective Miranda Morales has offered no comment about the mysterious appearance of a dead girl dressed like a mermaid who washed up on Lido Beach last Sunday. Chief of the Sarasota Police Department Dominic Petri and Bruce Borneo, the state district attorney, have shunned attempts by reporters to obtain more information. The only details provided were that a jogger had discovered the body in the predawn hours on Sunday. The body was taken to the Sarasota Medical Examiner's Office for an autopsy. Calls to the coroner's office have not been returned. Four days into the case, no arrests have been made.

Graham leaned back in his chair, sipping his coffee and popping the last bite of the croissant into his mouth. Something about this struck him as familiar. He'd read about Panamanian police being involved in an ongoing investigation into the rise of abductions of young girls in Panama and neighboring Colombia. Their disappearance was linked to a cartel that had resurfaced in Central and South America over a year ago. One of the apparent victims had been found in a dumpster near the Panama Canal. Later reports revealed she had been wearing what authorities described as remnants of a mermaid tail, based on the frayed fabric resembling fins.

Law enforcement in Panama had also discovered evidence that an import-export company was involved in the theft of priceless artifacts from the National Museum of the Republic of Panama several years ago. Authorities had concluded that the kidnappings and the museum robbery were unrelated, without offering reasons for that conclusion. As far as Graham could remember, the investigation was ongoing.

Could these cases be connected to Miranda's, or am I looking for an excuse to contact her?

He finished his coffee and studied the walking map of Sarasota he'd picked up at the hotel's front desk. He had no idea where Miranda lived. Besides, she'd been brushing him off, and he didn't want to cause her any more pain.

The waitress returned with his credit card and receipt, which he stuck it in his pocket. As he did, he felt a piece of paper he didn't remember being there. He unfolded it and saw that it was a note from Fernando, with Miranda's home address and phone number.

Just FYI was hand-scribbled on the paper, and signed simply, F.M.

He expelled a heavy breath, and muttered, "If not now, when?"

Graham got to Miranda's place just before nine a.m., a single-story house in a cozy neighborhood of pastel-painted cottages. The yellow wooden swing on the front porch and the blue mailbox hand-painted with colorful birds and butterflies amused him.

Miranda had always been an early riser, so he hoped showing up at this time of the morning, unannounced, would be okay. Second thoughts began to swarm inside him. Standing immobilized on the sidewalk, staring up at the house, his heart raced as he obsessively checked the number above the front door against the number on the paper.

You're stalling, Graham.

His deep breath did little to calm his jitters. He considered turning around and going back to the hotel. Then the phrase returned—If not now, when?

He started up the steps, a thousand thoughts racing through his head. Maybe she's at work? Maybe she's living with someone? Maybe it's the guy who was with her at my lecture? Anxiety overtook him. He did an about-face and was going back down the steps when the front door opened.

"What are you doing here?" Miranda asked, arms folded across her chest. "How did you find out where I lived?"

She was wearing a sea-blue tank top and pale yellow slacks, her feet bare. Her auburn hair was uncombed, and her face was as fresh as the morning light.

"I . . . I was out for a walk," he stammered. "Your father must've stuck this in my pocket," he said, holding up the crumpled piece of paper.

Damn you, Fernando!

"Ah, your ally. How thoughtful of him."

Sarcasm her usual defense mechanism.

"I'm sorry. I shouldn't have come," he said, just above a whisper, and turned back down the steps.

Miranda felt her heart tear open. Despite undergoing therapy, she was totally unprepared for coming face-to-face with the person with whom she had entrusted her life and shared her deepest, darkest secrets. Glaring at the casually dressed, gorgeous man with the slate-blue eyes looking up at her, she felt her legs wobble. She had once believed forgiveness trumped betrayal, but forgiveness never came easily to her.

Maybe it's time I try harder.

"Do you want to come in?" she said to his back, hoping he'd just keep walking, while at the same time hoping he wouldn't.

He stopped and turned around, looking at her with a mix of regret and gratitude.

"Are you sure?"

She nodded, holding the door open.

He hesitated. If not now, when?

She led him to the kitchen.

"Coffee?"

"Thanks, but I just had my third cup at the Yellow Mango."

"Ah."

She looked warily at him, poured herself a cup, and motioned for him to sit down.

"So, what do you want?" she asked bluntly.

He cleared his throat.

"Well, I just read about the case you're working on in this morning's paper. The mermaid who washed up on the beach."

He paused, giving her the chance to shut him down. She didn't.

"The article said you're the lead investigator . . . I wondered if that's why you took such an interest in Peter Millstine's talisman and mermaid fet—uh, fascination, at the cocktail party?"

"In part," she said, trying to remain detached.

He paused, staring at her. So many memories zooming inside him.

"My timing was never very good," he said, lifting his eyes like a wounded deer. "I—"

"Don't go there, Graham. What did you really come here for?"

He took another deep breath.

"I thought maybe I could somehow help with your investigation."

She remembered her father's comment as she left the event at the Ritz.

"Did my father put you up to this?"

"Uh, what? No. I just thought, if you had questions, I might be able to help. I know a bit about mermaids," he teased. "Maybe I could answer some of your questions."

She glared at him.

"Or maybe Peter Millstine could," she shot back.

He looked straight at her. "Peter? Why him?"

She shrugged. "Because he's a collector and has a talisman supposedly belonging to a legendary mermaid." She paused. "And...he struck me as a bit . . . weird. Creepy." She studied his eyes. "What was your impression of him?"

"Well, he did seem a bit defensive, especially when the conversation drifted toward fetishes. Understandably so, though." He waited for her biting retort, but her glance was more pensive than judgmental. "It certainly was awkward, to say the least."

"My gut tells me it was more than him feeling awkward."

"Your intuition was always reliable, Miranda."

"Not when it came to us."

She knew it was a low blow.

"Sorry." A shameful heat spread through her. Her cell phone rang. Without checking caller ID, she answered curtly, "What!"

"I have news," said Matt, then quickly changed his tone. "Why so grumpy?"

"Sorry, Matt," she said, looking at Graham.

"You do remember we're supposed to go to Tampa this morning? Revisit the mermaid camp. Right?" said Matt.

She hadn't remembered.

"Of course I do. Come to the house in a half-hour," she said, and clicked off.

"My partner," she said to Graham. "We have some leads to follow. He'll be here soon."

Recalling her father's conversation she'd overheard in the hallway, she said plainly, "What's your opinion of my father?"

Graham shrugged. Pursed his lips. "I don't know him very well. Seems friendly. Certainly smart. Why do you ask?"

"I heard him on his cell phone as I was leaving the party. I could only make out a few words." She paused, wondering how much she should reveal. "Angry words. Sounded like he was arranging a clandestine meeting."

"I saw you talking to him. What did he say exactly?"

"Something like 'Make sure nobody sees you.' He was particularly . . . unglued."

"Do you think he might be having an affair?"

"No. I got the feeling it was more sinister than that."

"You don't think sex can be sinister?"

He knew instantly that he'd stepped way out of bounds.

He averted his eyes and cleared his throat before looking into her penetrating stare.

"Well, he did leave the room rather abruptly after getting the call," Graham said.

"Did he say anything when he returned to the ballroom, after I'd left?"

"No. He just asked Peter if he would drop your mother off at the house on his way home." He tapped his mouth, thinking. "He did tell her that the call was from one of his new doctors, related to a surgery he'd done that morning. Something like that."

She shook her head. "He was lying. If that were the case, why would he be so secretive?"

She paused, looking across the table at him.

"Do you remember anything else he said?"

"Umm, something about a transfer of goods. I only caught bits and pieces."

"My father's a plastic surgeon, not a merchant," she said. "What kind of goods could he be talking about?"

"New surgical equipment for his office, maybe?"

"But again, why would that require a call at that hour?"

Graham shrugged. He could tell by the look on her face that she'd keep digging until she found an answer.

"I want to show you something," she said, standing up, wondering if she was stepping into a minefield. But she had to take the chance. "Come into my office for a minute."

She showed him the two stones pictured side by side on

her computer screen. “What do you think of these?”

“They’re remarkable!” Graham moved closer, his eyes roaming over the objects.

A loud knock on the front door startled both of them. She checked her watch.

“It’s my partner. See what you think while I answer the door.”

She welcomed Matt with a guilty smile. He was holding two cups of Starbucks coffee and a small white bag.

“I brought us breakfast.”

“Oh,” she said, opening the door wider. “Come in. There’s somebody I’d like you to meet.”

Graham stood up when Matt entered her office.

Matt froze.

Miranda pressed her lips together, then looked at Graham.

“Graham, I’d like you to meet my partner, Detective Matt Selva. Matt, meet Professor Graham Waterman.”

Chapter 26

The drive to Tampa was silent for several miles, the tension sizzling.

Miranda was relieved Matt had offered to drive, as she had a lot on her mind.

First, there was the whole Graham thing—she was relieved Matt hadn't brought up the matter of seeing him at her house. Next, they had formulated a new plan for questioning Georgia Holmes and Trixie Monroe. And then there was her father's strange behavior at the cocktail party, which was still bothering her.

Personal matters needed to be shoved to the background to make room for more pressing issues. It was imperative that they show the photos of the dead mermaid to the three campers at Sirens of the Deep. Also, she wanted to ask Georgia about the man in the photo on her desk, and if the yacht pictured with him had a Roman numeral after the name Mermaid Fantasea. Then, they'd go to Mermaid's Delight to pressure Trixie Monroe regarding her mermaid business affiliates. She had refused to cooperate when asked about the mermaid tail found on the victim, denying it was one of her designs, despite her shop's label stitched on the waistband.

Matt tapped the steering wheel, his mind a jumble of troubling thoughts and new theories. Cults were his main focus, But Graham Waterman was the source of his new discontent.

Finally Matt broke the silence.

"Why does it worry you so much that your father was having a clandestine meeting?" he asked. This was certainly a safer topic than her former lover.

She squeezed her hands in her lap.

"It's just a feeling," she said. "He wouldn't see patients that late at night. Doctors always have a recording telling callers to dial 911 if they're having an emergency after-hours." She glanced at Matt's profile. "And doesn't it seem odd that my parents would have kept in touch with someone from my past?"

Matt shot her a look but said nothing.

"Why wouldn't Graham let me know that he was coming to town? If I hadn't gotten that invitation, I never would have known he was here." She huffed. "Can you imagine how I would have felt if I'd read about his lecture in the newspaper after it was all over?"

"Okay, Miranda," said Matt, exasperated. "I don't have answers to your questions. All I know is, we have to focus on this investigation and sift through what we know, as convoluted and abstract as it may be."

She looked at him, thinking how selfish and insensitive she'd been, droning on about her former lover instead of concentrating on their case.

Then, like clouds parting after a storm, a lightness spilled through her. She suddenly realized that she cared more about Matt than Graham.

"You're right, Matt. We . . . I . . . need to focus. I'm sorry."

He took a deep breath, then blew it out. "So, tell me what else you learned."

She pulled herself together.

"Well, for one thing, that collector Peter Millstine gives me the creeps." She shivered. "His obsession with mermaids. His agitation when the conversation turned to fetishes." She stared out the front windshield. "And doesn't it seem strange that suddenly the cosmos has gathered together reptiles, a mermaid talisman, a black pearl and a turquoise stone—two rare gemstones—all at the same time that a dead mermaid, two months pregnant, washes ashore with a trident in her chest?"

Matt rubbed his chin. "Coincidence?"

Miranda rolled her eyes.

"Okay. No coincidence, then," conceded Matt. "But as far as your old—the professor is concerned, it does seem a little strange that your parents would stay in touch with him. Especially after treating you so callously, and the devastating effect the breakup had on you." He paused and side-glanced at her before returning his eyes to the road. "But, there's nothing unusual about your parents having a wealthy collector friend who happens to have an interest in mermaids. Even if he does creep you out."

He let his words settle her before continuing, wondering how to phrase the next bit without sounding insensitive.

"I can understand why Graham might not have wanted to contact you."

Her eyes became slits. "What do you mean by that?"

"I don't know. Maybe he's feeling more pain than you think over the breakup," he said.

Miranda scowled, unwilling to dowse the burn growing inside her.

"Maybe. Maybe not. But, putting Graham aside, my gut tells me something peculiar's going on." She remained silent for a beat. "And, as far as Graham feeling any pain and sorrow over me, I seriously doubt that."

"I think the lady doth protest too much," he mumbled to himself.

Miranda growled, but Matt continued his attempt to make sense of what she was describing. "As far as your dad's alleged secret meeting, just think about it, Miranda. He's deeply involved with humanitarian work. Maybe the meeting had something to do with that?"

"My dad's too inherently selfish to inconvenience himself unless there's something in it for him. He'd never allow himself to be dragged away from a social event, or the chance to rub shoulders with the cultural elite in Sarasota. Whatever it was, his behavior disturbs me."

Miranda's phone rang, interrupting their discussion.

"Morales." A long pause on the other end. "Hello?" she said again before she heard the whisper break through. It was the shop clerk at Mermaid's Delight. She put the call on speaker.

"Detective, it's Brenda Sinclair again. Sorry to bother you, but I overheard Trixie talking on the phone last night before I closed the shop. She sounded really upset. Frightened, even. She's supposed to meet somebody in Tampa. Somewhere near the harbor. I don't know exactly what time, but I think it's around two o'clock."

"Do you know who she's meeting?"

"No, but I heard her mention the Mermaid Fantasea again. I've got to go," she said, nervously. The line went dead.

She turned to Matt, checking her watch.

"We won't have much time to spend at the mermaid camp, but I really want to show these pictures to the three campers."

Matt squirmed in his seat. "I should tell you that I got a call late last night from Georgia Holmes. Totally out of the blue."

"What? Why didn't you tell me?"

"I'm telling you now. I figured we were planning to go there anyway. And besides, you've been all tied up with . . . with your own stuff," he said, gruffly.

Miranda glowered at him. "That's not the point."

"Maybe the shock of seeing . . . the professor at your house this morning distracted me, and I forgot about it."

"That doesn't explain why you didn't call me right after she called you!"

"I'm sorry, Miranda." He was growing tired of her recent mood swings. "You haven't been straight with me lately. First, you go to the morgue without me. Then, you go to a cocktail party to reunite with your old lover without mentioning it. And to top it all off, he was at your house this morning!"

She glanced back and forth at him a few times. Time passed in tense silence.

"I'm sorry, Matt. I'm sorry about all of it. I have no excuse.." She waited, hoping for what, she wasn't sure. "This past year, when I was away—it was not at my request, but an order."

Matt looked at her. "An order?"

"Chief Petri felt I needed a . . . break." She took a deep breath and let it out slowly. "It's been a tough few years for me. I guess I never really recovered from my sister's suicide." She squeezed her eyes shut. "And now, the shock of Graham arriving here . . ."

Matt reached out and took her hand. And she let him.

"I'm so sorry about all of that, Miranda. I can't imagine what you've been through. I know it's difficult for you to talk about things. But right now, we have to keep it together if we're ever going to solve this complicated case."

She looked at him, her vulnerability palpable. She smiled, knowing he was seeing her fully. The emperor without clothes. She squeezed his hand before letting go.

"So, back to Georgia Holmes's phone call," she said.

"Yes," he said, pausing to collect his thoughts. "She insisted I not tell you that she'd called me."

"That's it? What was she calling you for in the first place?"

"She didn't say exactly. Wanted to discuss the matter in person. Whatever the reason, she sounded jittery."

"Well, since we're being honest with each other, you should know that I showed Graham the pictures of the black pearl and the turquoise stone when he stopped by the house."

"I know. I saw him looking at the pictures on your computer."

"Well, for the record, I didn't mention any details about the stones, or our investigation. But, interestingly, he said they looked familiar."

Matt's eyebrows shot up. "In what way?"

"He thought they looked similar to ones that had been stolen from a museum heist in Panama a few years ago. Said it made international news, but I don't recall hearing about it. The black pearl resembled two pearls that were eyes on a miniature gold frog."

"Like the one in Graham's slide presentation?"

"Yes. He also said the turquoise resembled the stone that formed the shell of a rare tortoise miniature. Again, like the one in his slide. Both the frog and tortoise date from around the twelfth century and have never been found."

Matt nodded as he digested the details.

"One more thing. He said that one of his students in Panama had e-mailed him that Interpol recently discovered stolen artifacts they suspect were part of the Panama museum heist."

"Where?"

"They got an anonymous tip pointing them to a warehouse outside of Panama City, Panama. The items had been crated and were ready for shipment to the United States. He figured Graham would be interested, since he knew Graham had been researching the miniatures before the heist." She paused, then said, "When they raided the warehouse and itemized the contents, the frog and the tortoise miniatures were not among the recovered treasures. So, the multimillion-dollar question is, are the black pearl and turquoise found in our dead mermaid part of that museum heist?"

A thought flashed through Miranda's head.

"Call Georgia and tell her you're on your way to meet with her right now. Ask her to meet you at the cafe where we had lunch the other day. She doesn't have to know you told me about the meeting. I'll stay out of sight."

"But what about showing the campers the photos of our vic?"

"It's more important to find out what's bothering Georgia, and to not miss Trixie, who's due to show up near the Tampa harbor around two o'clock—if what Brenda says is true." She looked at Matt. "The camp's not far from the cafe, so hopefully Georgia will agree to meet you there before Trixie arrives. We'll just have to show the photos to the campers later. One more day isn't going to change anything."

"Whatever you say," he said, handing her his phone since he was driving. "Find her number in my contacts and call it. I'll use my Bluetooth."

The camp director answered within three rings.

"Sirens of the Deep, Georgia Holmes speaking."

"Ms. Holmes. It's Detective Selva. I had some business at the Tampa marina, but I'm available now. Can you meet me at the cafe where we met the other day?" He looked at Miranda. "Yes, I'm alone. No, I didn't mention our meeting to my partner." He listened for a couple of minutes before hanging up.

"She'll be here in half an hour."

"Great! We have time for a quick drink first."

Chapter 27

"Thanks for coming, Detective Selva." The light filtering through the cafe window heightened the green in Georgia Holmes's frightened eyes. "I'm terribly worried about the future of my camp."

"I'm afraid I'm not following you, Ms. Holmes. It looked to me like everything was in order when Detective Morales and I were there a few days ago. The campers appeared engaged in camp activities—swimming, crafts."

"It's not that." She fiddled with her napkin, briefly averting her eyes. "The dynamics of running a camp like mine are . . . complex."

Matt placed his forearms on the table and clasped his hands.

"Ms. Holmes, tell me as best you can what's bothering you." Georgia blew out a deep breath.

"Something strange has been going on with Trixie Monroe the past several weeks, Detective Selva. I've sensed it for a while now, but just can't figure it out. I'm especially concerned for my campers."

"Your campers? Has something happened to them?"

She gulped a mouthful of iced tea while keeping her eyes glued to his.

"Nothing like that, I'm happy to say." She rolled her thin, pale lips and shifted position, her breasts now pressing against the edge of the table. "I think Trixie is mixed up in something illegal. Something . . . dangerous."

"How so?"

"Oh, I don't know," she said, squirming. "I've known her for a long time. But ever since she began doing business with the Mermaid Fantasea company a few years ago, she's been . . . different. On edge all the time. Impatient. She almost bit my head off when I asked her about the custom orders I was supposed to deliver for her this week."

Her hand trembled as she sipped her iced tea.

"What can you tell me about the man in the photo on your desk. The two of you are posed in front of a yacht?"

He paused.

Georgia's eyebrows shot up.

"Yes. The Mermaid Fantasea."

"Is there a number after the name?"

"Yes, a Roman numeral one. Is that important?"

"Just curious."

"The man is Mano Sorkin. Trixie introduced him to me several years ago. She said he was very excited to hear all about my camp and might be interested in becoming a major sponsor." She glanced up from her twiddling fingers. "The camp's been losing money since my husband died suddenly, nine years ago. Mr. Sorkin, he took an interest in the camp and became a benefactor. He's served off and on as one of our judges for the past few years. He's been very generous, but there's something about him I don't quite trust."

"You looked quite taken with him in the photo," said Matt, with a smile.

Georgia blushed.

"When I first met him, I thought he was so handsome and polite. A true gentleman. A rarity these days." She looked directly at Matt. "That is, with one or two exceptions."

Matt smiled and lowered his eyes. He was never comfortable with compliments.

"He's supposed to be coming to the talent show Saturday night as one of the judges. But I'm feeling very uneasy about the whole thing." She looked directly at Matt. "I'm really scared, Detective."

"Well, Ms. Holmes, my partner and I plan to come to the event, so we'll be there should anything happen. But what makes you so scared?"

She shrugged. "Woman's intuition, I guess." She laughed. "I'll be less frightened knowing you and Detective Morales will be there. Thank you, Detective Selva. I'm probably just overreacting." She looked at her watch. "Now, if you'll excuse me, I have to get back to camp. I have a great staff, but I prefer to do spot checks to ensure everything is ready before the big celebration."

Matt stood up and shook the camp director's warm, trembling hand.

"One more thing, Ms. Holmes, before you go."

She paused, looking wary.

"How well do you know the families of your campers?"

Georgia frowned, confused.

"Well, not very well; only what I've read on their applications. Why do you ask?"

Matt smiled warmly. "Just trying to get a feel for how close you and your staff get with the campers."

"Ah. Well, while they're at my camp, they become like children to us."

Matt nodded.

"I'll look forward to seeing you . . . and, of course, Detective Morales, at the celebration this Saturday." She lingered, staring at Matt as they stood next to the booth. "By the way, I've thought about it, and I do believe the girl in your photo was one of my campers last year. Hard to tell from that photo, but I checked my files, and the picture in her folder looks very similar to the one you showed me. If it is the same girl, Trixie Monroe sponsored her." She paused. "The camp can be a bit pricey for some, so some of the campers need sponsors."

"Ah," he smiled. "Thanks for sharing that with me."

She touched his arm affectionately. "See you Saturday, then."

Matt sat back down in the booth. He motioned for the waitress to come to the table.

"I'm going to join that young woman out on the deck," he said, nodding toward Miranda. "Would you bring my check over there, please?"

"Of course."

Miranda watched as Matt approached. "So, how'd it go?"

"She's scared," he said, taking the chair opposite her.

"Of what?"

"That Trixie's mixed up in something bad—she's not sure exactly what. She thinks Trixie changed once she started doing business with the Mermaid Fantasea company a few years ago." He paused. "She's also afraid about the future of her camp."

"Did she elaborate?"

"No. All she said was, 'Woman's intuition.' She did tell me the name of the man in the photo on her desk is Mano Sorkin, one of the camp's benefactors. And the yacht is called Mermaid Fantasea . . . with a Roman numeral one."

Miranda leaned back against her chair and folded her arms across her chest. "Now we're finally getting somewhere. Nice work, Matt!"

"I've saved the best for last." He grinned. "She said our mermaid victim looked like a camper who attended her camp a year ago."

Miranda's eyes glowed with excitement.

"And Trixie Monroe was the camper's sponsor."

"You are full of surprises."

The waitress brought over Matt's bill and they both ordered more drinks.

Miranda checked her watch.

"Trixie should be showing up any minute, if Brenda's right." She looked through her binoculars. "Well, a yacht's just pulling into the harbor. That's certainly a promising sign."

"Yeah. I can see it."

"Here," she said, handing Matt the binoculars. "Look at the name on the side."

"Well, I'll be damned. Mermaid Fantasea with a Roman numeral one. The yacht in the picture on Georgia's desk." He paused. "So now we have two Mermaid Fantaseas—number one and number two. Both here at the harbor."

"Yep. So could there be a Mermaid Fantasea number three traveling around out there somewhere?"

"Hmm . . . maybe more."

Matt handed the binoculars back to Miranda as they pondered the possibility that the Mermaid Fantasea Corporation might have a fleet of yachts, and what that might mean.

"Did you happen to ask Georgia if any of her campers were orphans?" asked Miranda.

"No. When she said she didn't know much about their families, I didn't pursue it beyond that." He stared out at the yacht. "Can I have the binoculars again?"

She handed them to him.

"Looks like a man wearing a Panama hat and a tall, attractive woman are on board. Arguing. The woman looks furious. Doesn't look like Trixie Monroe, though. She keeps poking the guy. Ow, that must hurt."

"Let me see," said Miranda, reaching for the binoculars.

"Well, whoever he is, he's had enough. He's just grabbed her wrists but she's pulled away and is zooming down the pier toward the parking lot. I can't see the guy's face very well with that hat, but he's gone belowdecks now."

Miranda set the binoculars down on the table and took a swig of her beer, then picked them up again to focus on Mermaid Fantasea number two. Suddenly she spied a young girl bolting down the ladder on the side of this second yacht, frantically bounding down the pier toward the street, looking over her shoulder, her dark, wavy curls flying wildly.

The girl didn't stop for traffic. Car horns blared as she cut between the vehicles, heading right for the cafe.

The disheveled girl ran through the dining room and out to

the patio, knocking over chairs and bumping into diners and tables, toppling glasses as she barreled toward one of the waitresses.

"Ayúdame, por favor!" she pleaded in Spanish. "Ayúdame! Help, por favor! Help, please!" Her long hair was in tangles. Her short-shorts were smudged with dirt. Her arms and legs were bruised and covered with scratches and dried blood, and tears streamed out of her terrified, black eyes as she clutched the waitress's arm.

Miranda rushed over to the girl and exchanged a few words with the waitress, who was clearly shaken. She put her arm around the girl's bare shoulder and gently ushered her to their table. Miranda was stroking the girl's long hair. She motioned for the waitress to bring a drink over to them.

Matt pulled out chairs for them.

"It's okay", said Miranda. "We're police officers. Can you tell us what happened?" asked Miranda softly. She took a tissue from her purse and handed it to the girl.

The girl wiped her nose while the staff calmed the other diners.

The waitress came over with a glass of iced tea.

"Is there anything else I can do to help?" she asked.

"Yes. Please bring her a cheeseburger."

The girl took a big gulp of iced tea as tears cascaded down her cheeks.

Miranda rubbed her arm until the girl gradually relaxed. "Are you lost?" asked Miranda, leaning in closer.

The girl stared at Miranda, then Matt. She muttered something in Spanish.

Miranda barely knew the language, but enough to ask Habla inglés? The girl shook her head, then pressed her thumb and index finger almost together. "Un poco."

Miranda learned the girl's name was Maria Diaz. She lived in Panama. And she had been kidnapped.

"She said something about being drugged and taken on board a boat," said Miranda, translating for Matt.

"Mermaids," the girl suddenly blurted out.

Matt and Miranda exchanged shocked glances.

"Mermaids, Maria? What about mermaids?" Miranda asked, maintaining a steady voice so as not to alarm the girl further.

The waitress returned with the cheeseburger and set it down in front of Maria, whose dark-brown eyes doubled in size.

"Eat," encouraged Miranda, pointing to the burger and to her own mouth.

Maria took a big bite of the juicy burger and groaned, rolling her doe-like eyes.

"Muchas gracias! Muy bien!" she said through a mouthful of burger, washing it down with a gulp of the iced tea.

"Maria, you mentioned mermaids. What about them?"

Before she could answer, Matt nudged Miranda, gesturing toward the Mermaid Fantasea II and handing her the binoculars.

Trixie Monroe was pacing back and forth, hunched over like an injured animal. A man, with his back to Miranda, was gripping Trixie by her shoulders. They were face-to-face. Miranda wasn't sure whether he was consoling her or berating her.

Something about him seemed familiar.

Then Trixie rolled his hands off her shoulders. An angry exchange ensued before the designer stormed off the yacht and down the pier.

The man quickly disappeared belowdecks.

Miranda followed Trixie through the binoculars, watching her get into her white Mercedes convertible and speed out of the lot.

"She must have boarded the yacht while we were dealing with Maria," said Miranda, setting the binoculars back down on the table and draining her glass of the warm beer.

Matt nodded to the waitress to bring over more drinks.

"Guess nobody's noticed Maria's missing—yet," said Matt.

Miranda picked up the binoculars again and scanned the

yacht. Suddenly a young man with an anxious face stood gazing out at the activity at the harbor.

"Well, someone might have noticed, Matt," she said, handing the binoculars to Maria. She pointed to the boy. "Maria, do you know that boy? Conocerlo?"

Maria looked through the binoculars and nodded. Smiling wide.

"Xander," she said softly, handing the binoculars to Miranda. "Xander. Amigo. Friend."

Miranda watched the young man climb down the ladder and dart across the street through traffic. He rushed into the cafe, scanning the dining room. He was heading for their table when he spotted Maria.

"Maria! Como estas? Como estas?" He stooped down beside her and grasped her hand.

"Xander!"

They hugged. He looked at Miranda. "Puedes ayudarla? Help her?"

"Si. Policia," Miranda said, pointing a finger at herself, then at Matt.

Miranda motioned for him to sit, but he swiftly shook his head. He talked to Maria in Spanish. Miranda couldn't interpret much of what they were saying, but she thought he was explaining that they were police officers and would help her.

Maria also mentioned another name. Mirakakoo.

Xander turned to the two detectives and spoke in spurts of English.

"Quiere madre. Wants mother." He pointed to the yacht. "Kidnapped. Panama. Not safe."

Miranda nodded, glancing at Matt. She patted the seat of the chair again, but he shook his head vigorously.

"Must go. Uncle. Bad man. Come after her."

Miranda pulled a business card from her purse and handed it to him.

"Mirakakoo?" she asked him as he took her card. "Quien es Mirakakoo?"

"Mi mejor amiga." He smiled. "Best friend." He looked at her business card, then looked at her and smiled brightly.

She put her index finger to her ear and little finger to her mouth, signaling "Call me."

Xander nodded.

"Gracias," he said, and kissed Maria on the top of her head. "Cuidate. Be safe," and then he briskly left the cafe and scurried down the promenade in the opposite direction from the yacht.

Maria's eyes filled with tears. She pushed her plate away.

Matt's cell phone rang.

"Detective Selva," he answered.

"It's Georgia Holmes, Detective." Her voice was frantic. "I just got a call from Trixie Monroe. She sounds crazy! She's headed here to the camp. I'm terrified of what might happen. Please come quickly!"

He looked at Miranda, whispered, "Georgia Holmes. Trixie's on her way to the camp."

They both looked at Maria.

"We'll just have to take her with us. Sirens of the Deep maybe the safest place for her right now," said Miranda. "At least now that we suspect our dead mermaid may have attended the camp, perhaps we can use that to our advantage."

"Let's hope Georgia is cooperative," said Matt.

Chapter 28

Xander Montoya walked the promenade, dreading the moment he'd have to return to the yacht, face his uncle, and suffer his punishment. Castro had a vicious temper and would be out of his mind when he realized Maria had escaped from the Mermaid Fantasea. Thankfully, Mirakakoo was recovering nicely on board from her surgery.

He wished he could have stayed with Maria, far away from his uncle and his hideous monster, Python. He'd just have to trust the police to help Maria get back home. He had no doubt that his uncle would never have let Maria ago. And he feared Python would hurt her badly—or worse—if she returned to the yacht.

He knew he would have to return to the yacht eventually, to look after Mirakakoo. Thankfully the doctor in Sarasota had helped her. But she was still recovering from the surgery and would need his help until she got stronger.

Xander blamed Python for giving Mirakakoo drugs and leaving her unsupervised. The cocaine and whatever other substances she was addicted to should have been locked up, far out of her reach. He kicked himself for not having protected her better. The pains in her stomach had been growing worse. He thought that was the reason she had been taking so much medicine over the past few weeks. His uncle had ignored his pleas to get medical help for her—until she almost died. Luckily they had reached Florida when Mirakakoo's condition worsened, so they could take her to the doctor his uncle knew, for surgery.

Xander realized all too well how much trouble they'd all be in if somebody uncovered the despicable deeds his uncle Castro had committed over the years. Castro and Python had worked with cartels that engaged in all manner of unconscionable acts. He had thought about running away many times, but knew he had nowhere to go. He'd gone from foster home to foster home until Castro Montoya had found him roaming the streets in Ecuador and taken him in when he was just six years old.

The beatings he had endured over the years were a trade-off for having a place to live and food to eat. "It's for your own good!" his uncle would scream at him. The beatings, when they weren't too severe, were easier to bear than scrounging for food in garbage cans and aimlessly wandering the dirty, foul-smelling alleyways where rats ran wild. Even if his uncle ordered him to do horrible things every now and then.

But ten years is a long time to suffer such abuse, and the visible scars, as well as the emotional ones, would be with him forever. He longed for the day he could run away.

Soon, he would tell himself, but soon never came. Now that he was almost seventeen, his escape was getting closer. He just needed the right time.

Maybe I should've told the policewoman what was going on. She seemed kind, and she was pretty. And the man with her seemed nice too. He had a nice face. Pale skin—not like mine, all dark and pitted.

"Maybe she would have taken me and Mirakakoo to a safe place," he mumbled as he shuffled amid the tourists meandering along the bayfront.

Xander looked out at the wide swath of water, unsure of how long he'd been walking, or how far. He didn't care. It was comforting to look out at the aquamarine water and watch people laughing and having fun as they went in and out of the small shops along the waterfront.

He stopped to admire the jewelry on display in one of the windows. He checked his pockets, finding he still had the ten dollars he'd found on the ground near the Bolivar Bistro in Panama when his uncle and Python had gone there for dinner one night. He thought Mirakakoo would like the necklace with the bright red beads, so he went inside to ask the price.

It cost more than the ten dollars, so he looked around the shop and found a basket filled with small, colorful stones with words and phrases etched on them, each one different.

He picked up one and rubbed its smooth surface. It said Believe in Miracles.

"How much?" he asked the woman behind the counter.

"Two dollars," she said, and smiled, holding up two fingers.

Xander wondered if the woman was somebody's mother. She looked like what he thought a mother should look like. He wished he could remember his own mother, but she had died soon after he was born. Or at least that's what Castro had told him.

"I buy it," he said, pulling the money from his pocket. He pointed to the words on the stone. He understood enough English to read the words aloud.

"Believe in Miracles," he said, smiling up at the woman.

She looked at him with sparkling, brown eyes. She studied him for a few moments before putting the stone into a small, green mesh bag.

"You take it," she said, handing him the bag, shaking her head when he handed her the money. "My gift to you," pointing first to herself then to Xander.

His eyes danced like he'd just won the lottery.

"Muchas gracias, señora. Muchas gracias," he beamed, waving excitedly at her as he left the shop. Maybe it was time he started believing in miracles, like the stone said.

Suddenly he felt a new lightness spread through him. He hoped Mirakakoo would like the present. She'd been asleep when he'd sneaked off the yacht to go after Maria. But now that Maria was safe and his shopping spree was over, he was ready to return to the yacht to take care of his friend and endure whatever punishment awaited him.

He had overheard his uncle talking on the phone late last night, explaining to someone that a doctor had removed something from Mirakakoo's stomach. Although he didn't understand it, he was happy she was feeling better. He thought his uncle had told Python it was some kind of bird. He wondered how such a thing could have gotten inside her in the first place. "She's recovering on the boat," he'd overheard Castro say on the phone. "We might have to make different arrangements. It poked a hole in her stomach. We couldn't risk taking her to a hospital. Could cause a lot of trouble for us," he had said to the person on the other end.

The closer he got to the yacht, the more Xander's heart pounded. He took a deep breath, staring at the Mermaid Fantasea looming ahead. Nobody was on deck.

He climbed up the ladder and quietly lifted himself over the railing. He looked around and saw Mirakakoo lying on the lounge chair on the far side of the deck. He went over to her, sat down, and handed her the green mesh bag. Then he held her hand and smiled as she opened the bag.

She grinned.

"Cree en los milagros," he told her. Believe in Miracles.

Chapter 29

Matt drove at nearly warp speed, arriving at the mermaid camp in record time. Destina Walker was not at her desk, and the reception room was empty. From behind the closed door to Georgia's office, he and Miranda heard the two woman embroiled in a vicious argument, neither of them able to discern what they were screaming about.

Maria buried her frightened face in Miranda's side and covered her ears. Her body trembling.

"It's okay," said Miranda, smoothing Maria's hair. She jutted her chin toward Matt, signaling him to knock on Georgia's office door.

"You go in first, Matt. I'll stay with Maria until the secretary comes back."

Matt knocked, but the voices were so loud that he had to pound harder. Finally, he opened the door himself, taking the women by surprise. The ferocious fight abruptly ceased.

"Thank God!" exclaimed Georgia. Her face was scarlet. She rushed over to Matt, grabbing his arm and pointing at Trixie. "She's gone crazy! Absolutely bonkers!"

"What's going on?" Matt demanded.

"This maniac has accused me of abusing my campers," said Georgia. "She's claiming that I force them to participate in the talent contest against their will." She let go of Matt's arm and began pacing. "She even said I don't feed the girls properly. That I don't give them enough free time. Nonsense! Complete nonsense!" fumed Georgia. "Nobody loves those girls more than I do. Not even their own families!" She paused, glaring at Trixie before facing Matt. "She said I'm responsible for everything that's going wrong with the camp."

Matt looked at Trixie, her face blistered with rage. Her elegance was gone, replaced by harsh scowls and angry gestures as she stomped around the room in her stilettos.

"It's all such a bloody mess!" shrieked Trixie, "this whole thing! It's way more than I bargained for!" She continued to pace, blowing her anger in and out like a bellows, hysterically scrubbing her head like it was riddled with lice. "None of it's my fault! None of it!"

Georgia looked pleadingly at Matt.

Miranda entered the room and closed the door behind her. She stood beside Matt.

"Georgia's secretary just arrived," she said in a low voice. "I gave her a thumbnail version of Maria's plight and asked if she'd look after her until we're finished in here."

Matt nodded. "They're all yours," he said, relieved that his reinforcement could take over. He took a couple of steps back to not only give Miranda the floor, but to give himself some much-needed space.

"Sounds like you ladies have a lot of pent-up anger," said Miranda. "Care to explain?"

Georgia spread out her arms as if taking flight. "I have no idea what her tirade is all about. She called me an hour ago, out of control. Screaming. Cursing. Saying 'Everything's coming apart.' " She puffed out a breath. "I couldn't understand a thing she was saying. 'Dreadful shenanigans,' she kept muttering."

She paused, glaring at Trixie, giving her a chance to defend herself. But Trixie kept pacing wildly.

"It was like she was possessed," Georgia continued. "'A dead mermaid,' she kept saying. The only thing I could think of was the picture you showed me. Then she blurted out 'Peter's got to fix this!' and 'Fanatics. All of them.' "

She looked at Matt.

"That's why I called you, Detective Selva. How am I supposed to get everything ready for the big event tomorrow night, with her acting like this? She's one of our judges."

Miranda angled her head toward the closed door and mouthed Maria to Matt.

He nodded and left the room to check on her.

"Why don't you both sit down and gather your wits about you. Then each of you can explain what's going on here."

Georgia sat down in the chair behind her desk.

Trixie sat in the chair with the dolphin arms, opposite the director. She folded her arms across her chest, defiant, warning Miranda to tread carefully into the murky waters she was about to wade into.

"Who wants to go first?" asked Miranda calmly.

Trixie sucked in her cheeks and shook her shoulders. Georgia leaned back in her desk chair, her fingers steepled. Each was waiting for the other to speak.

Matt slipped back into the room, nodding at Miranda to let her know that Maria was fine with Destina.

Georgia finally realized that Trixie was refusing to cooperate, so she decided to start.

"I called Detective Selva," said Georgia, glancing at Matt. "I asked if he'd meet with me to discuss my concerns about the camp. After we were finished, we went our separate ways. On my drive back to the camp, I got a frantic call from Trixie," she continued, shooting daggers at the diva, screaming that she was on her way here to confront me—to 'set things straight,' is how she put it. She was rambling like a lunatic! I couldn't follow what she was talking about. I immediately called Detective Selva, figuring he was still fairly close by, since we'd met at a cafe in Tampa." She lowered her head and twiddled her fingers. "I was terrified of what she might do in such an emotional state."

Miranda nodded and shifted her gaze to Trixie, who was rapidly kicking out her long, crossed leg. The sharp point of her shoe was directed toward Miranda, daring her to come closer. Her knuckles were white as she stared at her polished, red nails.

Trixie lifted her cold eyes and stopped jiggling her leg. "You're getting in way over your head, Georgia Holmes. You have no idea what's going on right in front of your eyes," she said through clenched teeth.

There was a knock at the door. Destina peeked in through the crack.

"I was wondering how long you wanted me to stay with Maria?" she asked softly.

Georgia looked puzzled. "Maria?"

"Uh, yes. I thought you knew the detectives had brought a young girl with them," Destina said. "I can watch over her as long as you need."

Puzzled eyes on Miranda, Georgia mumbled, "Okay, Destina. I guess you could show her around the camp until we're through here." Then, to Matt, "Who is Maria?"

Matt cleared his throat and shot Miranda a look.

"I'll fill you in on that later, Ms. Holmes," Miranda said. "It's more important that we get to the source of this argument you two are embroiled in."

Georgia resumed her story.

"Trixie entered into a partnership with the Mermaid Fantasea company several years ago. I only recently found out about some of the . . . details," she said, shooting a scathing look at Trixie. "One of the Mermaid Fantasea partners was the man you saw in the photo on my desk, Mano Sorkin," she said, her eyes automatically shifting to the photo. "In the beginning, everything seemed fine. I was excited when Trixie explained that Mr. Sorkin would help me financially with the camp, since we were struggling after my husband died. And that he would also pay Trixie for supplying the mermaid tails to the campers who couldn't afford them, as part of the cost of the camp. But after a few months of this new arrangement, when a flurry of orders for mermaid tails started coming in, I noticed subtle changes in Trixie."

"Like what?" ask Miranda.

Georgia lifted her shoulders in a half-shrug. "That's just it, Detective. It seemed so insignificant at the time, I didn't pay attention at first. I thought she'd be delighted for the uptick in her business. I was certainly happy for the support for the camp. But when the orders increased so dramatically, I attributed the change in her demeanor to the stress of having to produce so many tails. She was overwhelmed, and it was taking a toll on her."

Miranda looked at Trixie for confirmation, or denial. But the designer was just staring at her nails, crossing and re-crossing her legs.

"Go on, Ms. Holmes," encouraged Miranda.

"When Trixie mentioned the new partnership to me, it sounded like an exciting opportunity for us to expand the camp. Build on the growing fascination for mermaids that seemed to have been dwindling over the past few years."

"So what changed?" asked Matt.

Trixie wiggled again in her chair, growing more agitated.

"It all sounded so wonderful. She told me how the new partners were committed to helping children have a better life. Too many of them were wandering the streets. Nobody to care for them. Orphans, really. The camp would be an ideal place for them to fulfill their dreams. Learn to swim. Meet other children." She paused. "They even suggested they were committed to helping those who were orphans to find homes." She took a deep breath, averting her eyes before looking directly at Matt and Miranda. "But soon, I became more and more suspicious and uncomfortable as little things began to happen."

"Georgia's got it all wrong!" declared Trixie, shooting up from her chair. She slapped both palms hard on Georgia's desk. "I've had enough! You have no right!" she blasted, pounding Georgia's desk with her fist. "You and your fucking camp wouldn't even exist if it wasn't for the Mermaid Fantasea Corporation!

You think this is all fun and games? Well, it's not. It's business! And you can all go to hell!"

Georgia sat aghast, struck silent by Trixie's outrage.

The designer pulled herself up straight, smoothed the front of her pale pink sheath, and strutted like a beauty queen out of the room.

Georgia blew out a breath. Miranda and Matt shared a look.

"We'll get to the bottom of this, Ms. Holmes. Will you be okay for the moment?" asked Matt, going over to the pathetic-looking camp director.

Georgia stared blankly for a few silent moments before shaking her head and looking at Matt. "Who wants to tell me about this girl Maria?"

"We need a favor, Ms. Holmes," said Matt. "Maria was kidnapped in Panama and kept aboard a yacht. A yacht named Mermaid Fantasea."

Georgia gasped. "What?"

"We don't know much more than this at the moment," said Miranda. "But she needs a place to stay until we can make arrangements to get her back home." A pause. "Turns out she was watching for mermaids when she was taken."

"Well, then, what better place for her to seek refuge than at a camp for mermaids?"

Chapter 30

Graham checked his watch, then took his phone from his pocket and dialed Peter Millstine's number. When the call went to voicemail, Graham left a message.

"Peter. It's Graham Waterman. I'd love to take you up on your offer to view your mermaid collection. And your talisman. Especially now that I know the owner," he said playfully. "Please call me with a time that might suit you. I'll be returning to Panama in a couple of days and hope to see your collection before I leave. I'll be around all day."

He was thrilled to have met Peter Millstine and was excited by the prospect of seeing his mermaid belt attributed to the ancient water deity, Masimi Aqua. Peter had asked him to authenticate the talisman, and he was honored to have been asked. The enthusiastic audience who attended his lecture had infused him with new energy and deepened his commitment to continuing his academic research—although seeing Miranda after so many years had dampened his desire to return to Panama. He wondered if he'd be missing out on the joys of the present by devoting so much time to his study of ancient civilizations.

In the frenetic pursuit of technology, where complex gadgets were already easily available to entertain and distract and self-driving cars would soon be the norm, Graham believed deeply that society was draining people of their humanity. He embraced the study of ancient civilizations and their practices as a way to learn from their seemingly less burdensome life. He appreciated their belief in honoring and respecting the mysterious forces in the universe—their guardians and providers. The universe that held magical powers in the sun, moon, stars, and gods.

Yes, battles for position and power took place in ancient times, but those battles were fought for survival amid scarce resources and harsh environments. Drought. Famine. Disease. The basic need for food, shelter, and community superseded the senseless drive to kill innocent people over religious differences, or skin color. The mistreatment of human beings simply because one group declared they were inferior to their own, which had happened for centuries, and was still happening today.

The shorebirds squawked overhead, darting about Bayfront Park as he walked, his mind wandering. He was taking in the aura of Miranda's city, with its high-rise condominiums, smaller ones squeezed between their cement guards.

The grandeur of Sarasota Bay, dotted with large boats, kayaks, and paddleboats, invited carefree motion, while the thatch-roofed, open-air tiki bar was poised to offer food and drink to the hungry and dehydrated. Children were gliding down the slide in the playground as parents watching protectively from wooden benches and dogs chased balls tossed by their devoted owners, all of it drawing Graham's thoughts away from the harsh realities of the past and the despair of the present, to concentrate on the beauty surrounding him in the now.

Still, he couldn't pull his thoughts away from seeing Miranda after so many years had passed. It had stirred emotions that had lain dormant since their breakup, wondering if he could gradually slip back into her life, or if he should even try.

Maybe helping to solve her mermaid mystery was a way in. He was intrigued by the case, and eager to learn more. Not only about her investigation, but about the years she'd spent between college and becoming a homicide detective.

Graham sometimes thought of himself as a different sort of detective, piecing together fragments of the past that would unravel the complexities of human interactions in ancient times, while she pieced together puzzles of the present.

Even though Miranda had shared only bits and pieces of her murder investigation with him, he had learned enough to begin his own research into some of her questions. He loved solving puzzles, and perhaps working on one with his former love might help him heal the hurt he'd carried around with him for so long. Perhaps it would also fill in some holes in both of their lives.

For now he would simply marvel at the scene unfolding around him. He'd dig deeper into his storehouse of reptile symbolism and rituals involving mermaids later.

He sat down on the shallow beach just beyond a cluster of native sea grape with its leathery, green leaves and grape-like fruit, content to just listen to the sounds around him. Laughter. The tide gently swooshing against the curves of the shoreline. The soft beat of music filtering from a distant tour boat.

On the walk back to his hotel, he decided to stop at the tiki bar, Casey's Cabana, for a light bite. The casual, welcoming vibe reminded him of one of his favorite spots in Panama, the Bolivar Bistro and Yacht Club, with its open-air seating and scuffed, wooden bar. Casey's was much smaller, but it was still a good spot to shed some of the melancholy that clung to a corner of his mind.

Peter Millstine sat in his cordovan leather armchair, listening to Graham's voicemail while being entertained by the dazzling array of colorful tropical fish flitting about in his gigantic, custom-made aquarium. He had spent thousands of dollars on the massive aquarium and the exotic fish, imported from Tahiti and other exotic places. The glass rectangle spanned an entire ten-foot-wide wall and stood nine feet high. The tiled mosaic wall behind the aquarium was created to resemble the Great Barrier Reef off the coast of Australia. He loved his fish as much as his collection of mermaid memorabilia.

Whenever he felt overwhelmed, he sought refuge with his aquatic family in his McMansion on Longboat Key. Only briefly would he shift his eyes away from the splendor of his aquarium to admire his collection of objects displayed on shelves and cases around the massive room. His pride swelled more viscerally when he thought about his prized mermaid talisman, locked in a vault upstairs.

He was eager to show it off to the famous professor, as Waterman's authentication of the mermaid belt would add immensely to its value. But he needed to exercise extreme caution when the professor came. Not everything in his collection was available for viewing.

The collector's gaze returned to the aquarium and lingered on the mosaic depiction of the Great Barrier Reef. He recalled a scuba-diving experience he had had many years ago when he was positioning himself to be the premier expert on mermaid folk art and memorabilia. The dramatic encounter he'd had in Australia had embedded itself within him. He promised himself that if he ever became rich enough, he'd re-create the stunning underwater paradise in his own home.

And now that he was a billionaire, he'd kept his promise. He had found an artist who masterfully created the design for the mosaic and then hired a contractor who not only installed the mosaic mural, but also assembled the enormous tank so it would nestle perfectly into the customized alcove specifically designed for it.

During the five years since his massive aquarium was installed, he had gradually added more exotic creatures to his marine family—seahorses, rare tropical fish species, small mounds of coral he'd imported. His love for the ocean and devotion to preserving these creatures' natural habitat was entwined with own existence. His goal to create an environment that would preserve marine life was constantly threatened by the ruthless acts of companies and ignorant people who persisted in dumping toxins and plastic waste into once-pristine waters.

As his passion for protecting sea creatures deepened, he obsessively checked the water in his aquarium to ensure that it was precisely balanced, with all the nutrients necessary to maintain a healthy habitat.

Suddenly Millstine was having second thoughts about having invited the professor to see his collection. He tried to dismiss his worries, as he did not want to anger his close friend, Fernando Morales, who was responsible for inviting the professor to speak to members of the Antiquarian Collectors Group. At the same time, however, he needed to protect the part of his collection that was off limits to anyone's eyes but his own.

He tapped in a number on his iPhone.

"Dr. Waterman. It's Peter Millstine. I'd like to collect you at your hotel to see my Masimi Aqua mermaid belt. I'll call with a time once I know when my meeting will be over."

❧

After getting the collector's call inviting him to his home, Graham busied himself by logging on to his computer for a quick check of his e-mail before Peter picked him up. As usual, junk mail clogged his in-box, despite the filters he'd set up. But the one from his student in Panama, Kai Rendell, caught his attention. Subject: Girl kidnapped near Bolivar Bistro.

He remembered Kai telling him he'd taken a part-time job at the bistro, since it was close to the university. "I could use the extra cash," he had said. Graham and his colleagues enjoyed going to the bistro on weekends, happy to disconnect from the hallways of academia and escape the noise of the city. He knew Jonah MacTavish, the owner, fairly well. "Jonah's a good man," he had told Kai. "Even though he's not an easy one to get to know."

The e-mail attachment contained a copy of a newspaper article published in Panama:

Armando and Estancia Perez, parents of the friend of the alleged kidnapped girl, told the police their daughter and her friend had planned to hide near a small bistro just outside of Panama City. They had planned to watch for mermaids, believing they surfaced at twilight. A tour guide, known to take tourists out on his boat to watch for mermaids, remembered talking to a couple of young girls one day when questioned by police after the girl's parents reported her missing. The tour guide could not provide a good description of the two girls, explaining, "A lot of young girls ask me to take them out to watch for mermaids."

According to the friend of the missing girl, they often went to the harbor after school, hoping they would eventually spot a mermaid. They had contrived a plan to go to the harbor one night, but the two friends apparently had a falling-out, and the missing girl presumably decided to go to the harbor alone.

"Hmm," murmured Graham, ideas circulating in his head. He would call Kai in Panama to learn more while awaiting Peter's call.

Chapter 31

The doorman at the Ritz opened the front door just as Peter drove up in his black Porsche. Graham, who'd been watching just inside the door, stepped out to the covered entrance to greet Peter as he got out of his car.

The collector walked around to shake Graham's hand, warmly patting him on the shoulder. "Good to see you again, Professor," said Peter with a forced grin. Despite the gregarious persona he exhibited to his clients, he was a deeply private and solitary person. Few people in his vast circle of friends and fellow collectors had ever seen his extensive collection. Obsessive, some might say, but he could care less what anybody thought of his peculiar passions. It was for his own pleasure, without exception.

Until now.

"Nice ride," said Graham with a wide smile. "Wish I could afford one of these." Graham quickly realized the collector might consider his remark crass, but it was said in good fun. If Peter didn't have a sense of humor, it didn't matter. He'd be returning to Panama in a couple of days and most likely they'd never meet again.

Graham recalled the collectors he'd met over the years. He'd come to learn that many of them valued the bragging rights of owning the objects more than they appreciated their history. For him it was just the opposite. The history of the objects—not their ownership—is what fascinated him, and was the primary reason he had pursued the study of pre-Columbian artifacts.

With his salary as a professor, he wouldn't even come close to being able to afford any of the objects he'd discovered that eventually made their way into private collections, or museums. "No idol worship for me," he remembered saying when someone asked him why he wasn't a collector. "I prefer studying the people and their customs. I'm happy just to admire them in museums like everybody else."

He looked over at Peter, who seemed distracted, mumbling under his breath.

"Everything okay, Mr. Millstine?"

Peter didn't respond, aside from a rumble in his throat. Graham cleared his own throat loudly enough to get Peter's attention.

"Sorry, Professor. Did you say something? I didn't mean to be rude," Peter said, glancing at his passenger.

"I'm sure you have a lot on your mind. I'm just excited to finally see the mermaid talisman."

"Ah, the talisman," Peter said, happy to be talking about something he loved so dearly. "It's quite exquisite, Professor. I'm interested to hear what you think."

The Porsche passed through an ornate iron gate that opened automatically.

As they approached the palatial house that faced the Gulf of Mexico, Graham took in the landscaped yard that consumed the full width of the front of the house, featuring clusters of coral bougainvillea and a metal sculpture of a great blue heron, standing four feet high at the bottom of the bifurcated stone stairway that led to a wide portico. A pierced turquoise metal globe with dozens of tiny lights poking through hung from the ceiling.

"That's a stunning light," said Graham, admiring the fixture.

"Hmm," said Peter. "Glad you like it. It cost a fortune."

Inside, the dramatic foyer connected to a hallway leading to the modern kitchen and into the dining room. An exquisite

Oriental rug covered the floor under the table. The spacious living room offered several comfortable seating arrangements for conversation.

"Come in, come in," invited Peter, motioning for Graham to sit on one of the leather stools along the center island in the kitchen. He popped the cork on a bottle of 2002 Dom Pérignon Brut that he took from the stainless-steel refrigerator, pouring each of them a glass.

"To mermaids," said Graham, raising his glass.

"To mermaids," echoed Peter, a twitch at the corner of his mouth.

Graham looked around casually, impressed by the sharp, clean lines and sleek contours. Contemporary art adorned almost every wall. The floor-to-ceiling windows in the dining room were free of curtains, enabling the lucky diner facing that direction to have a clear view of the Olympic-size swimming pool surrounded by an impeccable garden filled with tropical plants. These were much grander than the front gardens, rivaling those he'd seen throughout Panama.

"So, where do you want to start?" asked Peter. "The collection, or the gardens?"

Graham had noticed the glass case filled with miniature figurines at the entrance to the dining room.

"The collection," said Graham eagerly. "Perhaps the gardens afterwards, if there's still time? They look magnificent."

Peter laughed and nodded.

"Tell me about those," said Graham, tilting his almost empty champagne flute toward the miniatures.

"Ah," smiled Peter. "Let me top off your drink, and we can start there." He reached for the Dom and filled their glasses before standing in front of the display case.

Graham leaned in for a closer look at the tiny objects perfectly placed on the various shelves. Some were glass; others, stone. And still others were made of gold and silver.

"These exquisite pieces represent the last six years of my life," said Peter, proudly. "This one," he said, picking up a small, brown, tan, and black marbled object from the shelf and handing it to Graham, "is a granite bear dating back to the eighth century. An archaeologist found it inside a small pottery jug that was unearthed in an abandoned mineral mine in Mexico. It's my favorite thing in my entire collection."

Graham's eyebrows flicked high, surprised that a bear, not the mermaid belt, would be Peter's favorite object in his vast collection. But he said nothing as he ran his fingers over the bear's smooth, cool surface. The graceful rise of its back. The shapely slope of its neck. Its impressive luster. He studied the object with the intense eyes of a scholar and researcher, mentally cataloging its superb condition.

"Magnificent!" exclaimed Graham, handing the object back to Peter. "Why is this your favorite?"

An uneasiness spilled into Graham's gut as Peter's gaze bore through him like a drill penetrating a four-by-four. The collector's demeanor had suddenly changed from cordial to haunted. A faraway look filled his eyes when he finally spoke.

"Bear energy," he said softly. "Native Americans believe there are many unanswered questions in life. But each one has an answer." He paused, his eyes now fixed on the small granite bear, as if communing with it. "To this day, the Indians believe that finding answers to these daunting questions lies in the power of bear energy. It is the only kind that can calm the storms raging inside us, that keep the answers locked away. Out of our reach. Keeping us ignorant. And impotent."

Peter stared into Graham's inquisitive gaze, like Buddha searching the soul of his student for signs of true devotion.

"Only by calming the turmoil inside of us will the doors of the Dream Lodge open to reveal our inner self—where all the answers to life's questions are stored," he recited, as a poet might.

Graham nodded. He was beginning to admire the collector.

Peter seemed to dissolve into another dimension for a few seconds before returning the bear to its proper place on the shelf.

Then he picked up another object and handed it to Graham. The miniature terra-cotta jug measured less than an inch high, similar to what you might find in a child's dollhouse, and was inked with images of a bird, a turtle, and what looked like a ram. It appeared to have been hand-painted with black dye. The tiny bird had three black points painted on its crown, like a rooster's comb. A narrow band of green paint circled its neck like a collar. Three tail feathers were painted chalk-white. The bodies of the turtle and the frog were red from the terra cotta bleeding through their surface. Thin black lines outlined their shapes.

"Native American?" questioned Graham.

Peter nodded, his smile playful. "You are correct, Professor. It was excavated just last year in New Mexico. Discovered in an unknown Pueblo grave. A developer had been testing the soil for mineral composition for a planned housing complex when he discovered the gravesite." Peter paused. "You probably know that the peace-loving Pueblo are an ancient race related to the Aztecs?"

Graham nodded.

"Fascinating history," he said, carefully handling the tiny, clay piece. He'd read about such objects but had never seen any firsthand. "The Kuna Indians of Panama and Colombia called their miniature pottery animals fetishes," he said, recalling his faux pas at the cocktail party. He quickly sidestepped it by circling back to their discussion of Indian cultures.

"The Kuna tribe, indigenous to Panama, was known to craft similar animal miniatures for their worship." He smiled at Peter. "And sometimes just for fun. Gifts for children. These ancient tribes seem to have embraced wonderful beliefs and rituals to honor their loved ones, and to keep them safe."

Over the next hour, Peter showed Graham the rest of the miniatures, explaining their significance and, to a certain extent, how he had acquired them. But there were two objects in the collection Peter didn't discuss—a gold filigree frog and a silver tortoise, similar to ones Graham had shown in his slide presentation. Peter's frog was missing an eye, and the tortoise, its shell.

Graham shrugged off the idea that they could in any way be the ones stolen from the museum in Panama. But he decided to explore the possibility, however unreasonable.

"I was wondering about the frog and tortoise miniatures in your collection. I showed photos of similar objects during my presentation. Do you recall those slides?"

Peter cleared his throat. "I'm embarrassed to say, Professor, that I was unable to attend your talk. But Fernando told me you did an extraordinary job of captivating the audience with your presentation."

"I know you are very busy," said Graham, "which is why I so appreciate your willingness to share your collection with me today."

Peter smiled, then said, "Are you ready for the grand finale?"

"Of course!" Graham said, beaming from ear to ear.

Peter led him across the wide hall into a spacious library. The shelves were lined with rare, leather-bound volumes covering everything from classic architecture, pre-Columbian dynasties, and modern art, to mermaid folklore, marine biology, and chemical oceanography. Graham was astounded at the range of titles.

Two club chairs upholstered in red damask graced one side of a walnut coffee table. On the other side sat a sofa with a blue linen slipcover.

"Please, sit down," said Peter, as he opened a cabinet under one of the bookcases. Apparently this is where he stored his safe. Blocking Graham's view, Peter turned the combination lock. With the final click, the safe beeped and Peter opened it, putting on a pair of white cotton gloves that were tucked in the satin pocket on the interior of the door.

Then, he carefully lifted the beaded belt off the cloth-covered shelf and, as if cradling a newborn, he set it gently down on a black velvet pad he'd spread out on the coffee table before Graham's arrival.

Graham's jaw dropped.

"It's absolutely exquisite!" he said, soaking in the extraordinary intricacies of the mermaid talisman. Assorted gemstones adorning the four-inch-wide midsection of the belt sparkled as the recessed LED lights shined down on them. A single row of black pearls formed a garland at the top edge of the belt, while three small oval, gold disks below the pearls separated seven irregularly shaped gems the size of jelly beans. Two rubies, two emeralds, and two garnets flanked a stunning blue sapphire in the center—slightly larger and rounder than the other gemstones. All had been delicately stitched to the front of the belt. Almost invisible threads held pin-sized coral beads in place on a narrow band of sea-green fabric along the lower edges.

"It's . . . it's just . . ." He looked at Peter. "I'm speechless."

Graham's eyes were wide as they roamed every inch of the belt. "It's simply exquisite. So much more breathtaking than how I described it in my article." He studied the gemstones closely. "They're so unique in their clarity, and brilliance. It's just extraordinary! I never imagined it would look this magnificent!"

During his research on the mermaid talisman, Graham had found very little recorded documentation about the precise details of Masimi Aqua and her mermaid's belt. The references he did find had dubious scholarly evidence supporting some of the proposed theories. The few so-called facts he did uncover had concluded that the belt had originally belonged to an ancient tribe living near a now-extinct volcano in Chimborazo, Ecuador. The attribution to the tribe had been based on the unusual gemstones and coral beads known to have been mined in that region.

But the sea-green fabric puzzled Graham. Textiles are fragile and degrade over time, especially when buried in the earth, or when they have contact with water. This belt was in exceptionally fine condition. He made a mental note to pursue that puzzling anomaly going forward.

Graham looked at Peter and pursed his lips as thoughts bounced around in his head.

"I'm sure you're aware, Mr. Millstine, that, during my research, I found a great deal of debate among researchers over the attribution of the belt to Masimi Aqua. Some hypothesize it may have belonged to a water spirit of a different name, under different circumstances—Masimi Wata."

Peter's eyes turned furious. "There's no question that the spirit was Masimi Aqua!"

"I understand. I'm just saying, that, according to that legend, the Achuar tribe was migrating from the Andes northwards, toward Central America," said Graham. "They planned to travel along the coastline where they could fish for food on their journey. Then, one night, the tribe's chief, Tourmalou, was awakened by a shrill cry echoing off a large rock in the darkness of the Pacific Ocean. He walked to the edge of the camp and sat on the beach listening for the sound, curious what kind of strange marine creature could utter such a sorrowful cry."

"That's right," interrupted Peter, excitedly. "The next morning when Tourmalou's people awakened, he told them that a beautiful creature—half-woman, half-fish—had called to him during the night. When he followed her sound, he found her lying on the sand a short distance from their camp. Her silver fins were torn and ragged. She told Tourmalou that she longed to return to the sea, but she couldn't swim back home unless her tail was repaired."

"Please go on," Graham encouraged, eager to add the collector's voice to the academic debate.

"Chief Tourmalou—being a skilled fisherman—got some fishing line from his sack and sewed the torn fins so perfectly she couldn't believe her eyes. The mermaid was so grateful for the chief's kindness that she removed her belt and presented it to him as a gift, instructing him to wear it day and night during his travels. To protect him and his people on their northward journey. She cautioned him that the belt would turn to seaweed if it were stolen, or sold. Only if given as a gift would it remain intact."

Graham nodded. He was familiar with the folktales concerning the talisman that had been passed down through centuries, each generation embellishing the story as time went on. Nobody had ever actually seen the belt, so its description varied from story to story. But the garland of pearls, the center sapphire, and the coral beads remained consistent in each version of the legend. Its magical powers were strong, and only one mermaid—endowed with special gifts—was allowed to wear it.

"I grew more enamored with the Achuar people as I did my research for the talisman," said Graham. He paused, trying to gauge the collector's interest in what he was about to share. "I believe the indigenous people of the Amazon region are still alive and well. Still trying to preserve the rainforest that currently borders Ecuador and Peru, if I'm not mistaken. Are you also interested in the tribe?"

"Yes. Immensely so," said Peter. "I admire their culture, their spirituality. Their belief in dreams and visions. How they incorporate their visions into their daily life." He looked at Graham. "Did you know shamans play a huge role in their culture? The Achuar, like the shamans, believe that turning away from a powerful vision, based on fear, represents a lost opportunity. The opportunity to transform fear into wisdom, drawn from their ancestors' ability to identify a person's true purpose in the world."

Graham's respect for Peter grew as he listened to the collector's depth of understanding about the legend, and his belief in ancient rituals.

"So, Professor," Peter continued, "as you can see, while I'm not a world-famous scholar such as yourself, I do value learning about the legends behind the objects I choose for my collection. And while I embrace the legend of the Achuar tribe, I beg to differ with you: I adhere to the belief that the water princess was indeed Masimi Aqua, not Masimi Wata."

"Well, having the mermaid talisman in your own collection, regardless of whose story you embrace, is quite an accomplishment." Although he knew better, Graham asked his next question anyway. "May I ask how you came by the talisman?"

Peter laughed wildly. "Oh, no, no, no, my dear Professor. That I must never reveal."

"Of course," said Graham. "I assume you know that there are varying accounts of what kind of gemstones were on the belt. Only the pearls, coral beads, and sapphire remain consistent." He wondered just how much Peter knew about that part of the legend. "Nobody really knows what original gems were on the belt when the mermaid presented it to Tourmalou."

Peter remained stone-faced.

"My talisman is authentic, Professor Waterman. I assure you the rubies, emeralds, and garnets with diamonds, peridot, and tourmaline, along with the center sapphire cabochon, pearls, and coral, have been with the talisman for centuries. And I deeply believe they are what originally adorned the belt when presented to the chief by the water spirit—whether her name was Masimi Aqua or Masimi Wata."

"Of course the belt's authentic, Mr. Millstine. I apologize if you thought I was suggesting otherwise." Graham's face was flushed. He felt embarrassed that Peter had called him out on exactly what he was thinking. Graham cleared his throat, continuing with another aspect of the belt's legend that he decided would be less threatening.

"The story claimed the mermaid and the chief had an intimate relationship, and that she traveled the seas, following him on his journeys."

Peter's demeanor turned even more hostile, and Graham instantly realized he had dug a deeper hole for himself, further inflaming the collector's paranoia.

"Seems to me, Professor, that you have issues around sex. Perhaps you are suffering from your own form of fetishism."

Graham decided he had overstayed his welcome.

Apparently Peter had come to the same conclusion. "I'm afraid I have another appointment, so that's all the time I have for now. But let's fill our glasses one more time before we part—on friendly terms."

Graham watched the collector wrap the talisman back in the velvet cloth and return it to the safe. The two men headed back to the kitchen where Peter filled their glasses, then turned to Graham.

"Mermaids are like all legendary figures, Professor. Everybody swears they've seen them, even say they have pictures of them, but nobody's ever been able to prove it beyond a shadow of doubt." Peter's eyes turned glassy as he studied Graham. "But rest assured, my mermaid belt did belong to Chief Tourmalou, and it was a gift from a water deity. I would stake my life on her name being Masimi Aqua."

Graham nodded and smiled, although he still had unanswered questions. He wished he knew how Peter had acquired the talisman, and if it was indeed authentic. While everything about the belt appeared genuine—aside from the near-perfect condition of the green fabric—as an academic and expert in ancient artifacts, it was his duty to do more research after seeing it with his own eyes. The name of the water spirit was less intriguing to him than the belt's provenance. He knew quite well that names changed as legends passed through the generations.

"I'd love to invite you to lunch," Peter said, "but as I said, I have other commitments in town. I'll drop you back at your hotel, or downtown if you prefer. Perhaps we could have dinner before you leave for Panama?" He had no intention of honoring that invitation.

Graham set his still-full champagne glass on the counter. "The hotel would be fine, Mr. Millstine. I'd like to walk around town a bit."

Peter drove to Sarasota and dropped Graham at the entrance to the hotel. Before stepping out of the car, he turned back to Peter. "You didn't show me your mermaids," he said, genuinely disappointed."

Shock washed over Peter's face. "Mermaids?"

"Your mermaid memorabilia—your folk art," clarified Graham. "You said you'd show me your collection when we talked at the cocktail party."

"Ah, of course," nodded Peter, acid churning in his stomach. He pressed his lips tightly together to control his irritation. "Next time," he said lightly, revving the Porsche's engine. "And I'll show you my gardens at the same time."

Graham smiled, nodded, then closed the door of the Porsche, listening to the engine as Peter shifted into gear and zoomed away.

ଓଃ

Peter gripped the steering wheel as he drove. He was angry, his nerves in shreds.

Then he conjured the image of his granite bear and recited in a low, soothing voice as he drove:

Oh, Mighty Bear, invite me into your Cave where I can feel your Energy,

Let the Silence remove the turmoil within me,

Quiet my mind so I can seek the answers to Life's perplexing questions, and

Discover my Inner Knowing, to finally be at Peace,

Ridding me of my ignorance and impotence.

The bear was a gift that had passed through his family for generations. The Mighty Bear chant had been a comfort to him as a young boy whenever the fury inside him swelled. Painful memories of his psychotic mother ridiculing him, citing his list of failures. Never knowing what she expected of him except perfection. Her callous approach to her sensitive son from the day he was born. Chastising him for playing with dolls, while his older brother—a musical prodigy by age nine—got all the attention. A passive, selfish father who ignored him. The Mighty Bear chant had always helped him through those tempestuous times, giving him renewed calm.

Even today, as a wealthy and accomplished adult, deep inside he still felt like a failure. Each time his insecurities broke through, he reached for the granite bear and took it to his private sanctuary, where he'd sit in his favorite armchair, surrounded by his beloved creatures, stroking the object obsessively.

Chapter 32

Mano Sorkin and Castro Montoya were already at the Classico Murano Restaurant in downtown Sarasota, waiting for Peter to arrive. The three men had formed their partnership in the Mermaid Fantasea Corporation several years ago when their paths had crossed at a conference in Costa Rica, sponsored by the International Gem Society. But that chance meeting and their subsequent partnership had less to do with gemology and more to do with propositions and profits.

While Peter's passion for rare gemstones and ancient antiquities had remained steady, Mano and Castro had more ambitious goals in mind for their growing enterprise. Investing in the mermaid industry trumped all their other escapades thus far. When they learned that Peter was a devoted collector of mermaid memorabilia and folk art, they decided to invite him to join their venture.

"It's a very lucrative business, Peter," said Mano, using his skills of persuasion to arouse the collector's appetite for acquiring exquisite merchandise. He eventually introduced Peter to his right-hand woman, Gabriella Navarre, his most valuable resource in creating their network of suppliers and associates around the world.

In the end, it was Trixie Monroe who had convinced Peter that the partnership with Mano and Castro would be an amazing opportunity. Peter had already supported Trixie in establishing Mermaid's Delight in Tampa, so it was no surprise that her fiery spirit, designer pedigree, and ability to open doors had sealed the deal.

None of them could have predicted the paths they would eventually travel as they navigated through the various stages of their evolving partnership. This was on Peter's mind as he drove to the Classico Murano. He was disappointed Trixie would not be joining them this time. Neither would Gabriella, whom he wanted to get to know better. That could be rectified easily enough with a couple of phone calls. And the Festival of Dagon was rapidly approaching—the inauguration of the next phase in their business empire.

Peter checked himself in the mirror as he entered the dining room. He'd been in a foul mood, kicking himself for having invited the professor to come to his home. He knew it had to be done. He wanted his talisman authenticated, and the world-renowned archaeologist was the perfect one to do it.

Get ahold of yourself, chirped the small voice inside his head.

He closed his eyes and recited a few lines of the Mighty Bear chant. Then, he opened his eyes and smiled as he approached their table.

He did not like the look on his partners' faces as he took his seat.

"What the fuck have you done, Peter?" spat Mano. "Your little antics have put us all in danger!"

The meeting on board the Mermaid Fantasea I had upset Gabriella deeply. She was enraged after Captain Moore had informed her that one of the two vessels that had passed through the Panama Canal had been seized by the US Coast Guard. They considered it "suspicious," for some reason, he had told her. The cargo ship was searched soon after it had left the port in Miami. The captain had heard nothing more since that original bulletin.

As tempers flared, the altercation between her and Mano had deteriorated to a poking and shoving match, each one blaming the other for the sudden and potentially catastrophic complication that would jeopardize the Festival of Dagon and imperil the entire Mermaid Fantasea Corporation.

"A lot is hinging on this festival," screamed Trixie when she'd arrived on the yacht after getting Gabriella's message.

"Nobody knows that better than I do," snarled Gabriella.

The two women paced the deck of Mermaid Fantasea I, grumbling to themselves. Then Trixie had abruptly stormed off, her stiletto heel catching the wooden slat of the pier, almost toppling her.

"Fuck," she growled as she headed for the parking lot. "It's time to alert Peter."

The other snafu was Castro's little tart, Mirakakoo. Gabriella had gotten a call from Fernando Morales concerning the emergency surgery he'd had to perform on the young woman, and how shocked he was to have discovered an enameled hummingbird inside her.

"Just stick to the plan and everything will work out," Mano had reassured Gabriella when she became enraged by the news. "You've handled blunders far more serious than this one. You can handle this!"

As CEO of the Mermaid Fantasea Corporation, Mano Sorkin's faith and confidence in Gabriella, his female MacGyver, had never wavered. But these days the world was a much more complicated place to do business internationally. He thought it was time to rein in some of their foreign alliances and focus on the US markets. Despite her loyalty and astute business acumen, Mano was sensing that Gabriella was growing tired, her enthusiasm for power and influence fading since she'd earned her fortune. "It's not any fun anymore, Mano," she had said recently. "I need to get out while I'm still young enough to enjoy the rewards I've earned."

Mano knew that Peter Millstine was key to the transition from the overseas trade to the seemingly unlimited US market. But with opportunity came danger. Especially with Peter's growing obsession with mermaids.

While at first Mano had considered it an amusing hobby, Peter's passion for mermaids had gradually morphed into a mania. He knew that the very rich—he counted himself among them—engaged in many unsavory delights. Their private islands, where sex, drugs, and tyranny reigned. The demonic rituals and hedonistic obsessions of those they called "the men with big boats." But with Peter, it was more than that. He was becoming unhinged, and that was a huge liability.

Castro had warned Mano that Peter was spiraling out of control. But it wasn't until he was confronted with Mirakakoo's near death that he decided it was the last straw, telling Mano one day how Peter had arranged for some thug he knew in Panama to steal a few things from a museum on one of their trips to Central America. He said he had never seen Peter so enamored with an object as he was with that hummingbird. He never knew what happened to it until the night of Mirakakoo's surgery. He had no idea how the object was implanted in her.

Castro declared that night that he would never forgive himself, or Peter, for causing Mirakakoo such pain and suffering. He vowed never to do business with Peter again.

Now, Mano was faced with his own growing doubt over whether his business partners had the ability to execute their plans to expand their mermaid empire. Emergency action would have to be taken.

He picked up the phone and arranged a meeting on board the Mermaid Fantasea I to ensure that the Festival of Dagon would go off without a hitch. Time was running out.

Chapter 33

Huge outdoor video screens were set up in strategic locations around the campgrounds, affording guests attending the end-of-camp celebration the ability to watch the mermaids' graceful underwater ballet from the comfort of the beach chairs they'd brought with them. The cool evening breeze enhanced the mood spreading through the evening air. The almost full moon hanging by invisible threads from the gray-blue sky cast a surreal glow over the lavender tent that covered the stage near the swimming pool. Young girls wearing mermaid tails stunningly adorned with faux gemstones and glitter in a dazzling array of colors posed in a perfect line in front of the expansive swimming pool.

Georgia Holmes's sleek, emerald-colored satin gown shimmered as she strutted across the stage to the podium. The massive crowd roared and applauded enthusiastically as she looked out at everyone who had gathered for the event.

"Good evening ladies, gentlemen, merfolk." She paused and smiled warmly at the audience, then turned to look at the people sitting behind her. "And the judges, who have graciously volunteered their precious time tonight to choose our Queen Mermaid Ambassador." When the applause quieted, Georgia continued.

"The Queen Mermaid Ambassador is the title we bestow on the mermaid who best represents the values and commitment to preserve our waters and the marine life living there." She paused. "Of course, all of our mermaids go out as ambassadors, teaching others about our priceless natural resource—

water—and what we can do, individually, to protect one of our greatest assets."

Whistles floated on the wings of the soft, evening breeze.

"I am proud of what our Mermaid Ambassadors have been able to accomplish after leaving our camp, educating people around the world about the importance of cleaning up our beaches. We all share the responsibility to help maintain the quality of our water and create a pristine underwater environment for the benefit of all marine life."

The crowd stood up, some holding their hands high over their heads as they clapped and cheered before sitting back down.

Georgia raised her arms to quiet the enthusiasm.

"This year, Sirens of the Deep celebrates its twentieth year. A remarkable achievement. And we couldn't have done it without the consistent support of all of you who believe in our camp's mission and entrust your children to us for a few weeks each summer. So, without further ado, fully fledged mermaids will begin the celebration by performing their underwater ballet."

There was a drumroll as the mermaids poised in dive positions around the pool. Their ballet would be broadcast on the outdoor media screens, the underwater lights reflecting through the blue-green water. As the drums softened, cymbals clashed, and in perfect unison, the mermaids arced gracefully into the water, their undulating tails gliding effortlessly through the water, their long hair flowing behind them with each gentle sway.

Matt sat awestruck, mesmerized by the precision and artistry of the aquatic dancers, marveling at how nimbly they manipulated their colorful tails, twirling and bending in perfect synchrony with the music soaring through the night air.

Miranda was equally entranced by the sparkle and vibrant colors. Tears seeped out of her eyes as she thought about her sister, Farrah. How she would have loved seeing the mermaids' graceful moves! She might have been one of them, if life had been kinder to her.

Miranda glanced at Maria Diaz sitting beside her. Maria's wide eyes and broad smile spread through Miranda like honey on warm toast. Thankful for Xander's bravery and Maria's strong will, Miranda took Maria's hand and squeezed it. Maria gave her a beautiful smile.

When the underwater ballet ended and the cheers died down, Georgia announced a fifteen-minute intermission to allow the mermaids to prepare for the next part of the program—the beauty pageant.

Miranda discreetly brushed away her tears and stood up. Matt stood beside her.

"That sure was spectacular, wasn't it?" said a voice from behind them.

Miranda looked over her shoulder and smiled at the clerk from Mermaid's Delight. "Good to see you again, Brenda. Yes, it was amazing." She turned to Maria and said, "Maria, this is Brenda Sinclair. She works in a store that sells mermaid costumes and trinkets."

Maria smiled and reached out her hand to Brenda.

"Hola, Señorita Sinclair," she said with a wide grin.

"Maria loves to watch for mermaids," said Miranda, leaving out the details surrounding her kidnapping and how she had come to be at Georgia's camp.

"Ah," smiled Brenda. "You should come to the shop one day."

A voice on the loudspeaker announced the beauty pageant was about to begin, so guests settled back into their chairs. The judges had already returned to the stage. Dusk had turned to darkness, and spotlights around the stage spilled bright light onto Georgia as she took her spot at the podium. One by one, Georgia introduced each judge—two women, three men.

Miranda nudged Matt and nodded toward the stage. She leaned down for the binoculars in her tote bag and zoomed in on the judges. One looked familiar, but he was partly in shadow. The woman seated at the far left of the row she recognized immediately.

"Trixie's one of the judges," she muttered. "The other woman resembles the one we saw arguing with the man on the yacht yesterday."

Matt looked dumbfounded. "What?"

"Take a good look. Trixie's on the left."

He scanned the judges with the binoculars, pausing to imprint their features on his brain.

"I recognize Trixie, but I'm not sure who the others are."

"We'll soon find out. Georgia's about to make the introductions."

"We are honored to have a panel of distinguished judges with us for this remarkable event," Georgia said proudly. "We are especially pleased to have Mr. Mano Sorkin with us tonight," she said, turning to Mano with a slight nod. He stood up and waved cordially at the crowd before sitting back down. "He's a valued friend of Sirens of the Deep, and he came here all the way from his exotic homeland of Brazil to be one our judges."

"Brazil?" said Matt.

Miranda side-eyed him and shrugged.

"Mr. Sorkin has sponsored many of our campers through the years, helping make their mermaid dreams come true. His generous support, both financial and gifts in kind, have made it possible for the camp to continue with its mission to not only teach campers how to swim, but more importantly, to educate them to be dedicated stewards of our oceans."

The crowd erupted in loud applause.

"Once they have been transformed from mortals into mermaids," she continued, "they become dedicated activists who educate people around the world about threats to our beloved sea creatures."

The crowd applauded again.

"Mr. Sorkin is president of Sorkin Import-Export International Ltd., and has hosted many of our Mermaid Ambassadors aboard his yacht, traveling to distant places to raise awareness of the need to preserve aquatic life."

"Do you think he could be the same man who was hiding in the shrubs, watching the three campers the other day?"

Miranda shrugged. "I'm not sure."

"Could he be the one who argued with Trixie on board the yacht?" Matt asked.

"Not sure. Hats and sunglasses are remarkable disguises. Take another good look at him."

Matt focused the binoculars on Mano, noting his dark, perfectly groomed hair with threads of gray. The firm jaw. Perfectly proportioned features and olive skin.

"I am also deeply honored to introduce Gabriella Navarre, our new judge tonight," Georgia said, resuming the introductions. "On extremely short notice, she was able to replace our regular judge who suddenly became ill this afternoon. Ms. Navarre has been involved with mermaids for many years and embraces the same values we do here at Sirens of the Deep. So, welcome, and thank you, Ms. Navarre, for being here."

Gabriella Navarre remained seated but waved and smiled at the audience.

Miranda nudged Matt for the binoculars. "I'm certain she was the one arguing with the unknown figure on board the yacht, before Trixie showed up," she said.

Miranda noticed a subtle shift in Georgia's demeanor when it was Trixie's turn to be introduced.

"I'm also delighted to introduce another good friend of Sirens of the Deep, the world-renowned designer of exquisite mermaid tails, which a few of our stunning mermaids will be modeling tonight—Trixie Monroe."

Trixie stood up, smiling her practiced smile, then sat back down.

"Finally, we have two more distinguished judges with us on the stage. Peter Millstine, a collector of mermaid memorabilia, and Castro Montoya, a philanthropist and mermaid devotee," she said, smiling and clapping as she turned to face the judges. They stood and bowed before returning to their seats.

Miranda fell back in her seat.

"I can't believe it! Peter Millstine's one of the judges?" She turned to Matt. "Do you remember Georgia mentioning that she knew Peter?"

Matt shook his head. "Why would she?"

"Hmm," said Miranda.

"So, without further ado, let the show begin!" exclaimed Georgia, raising both arms high in the air. Soft music was playing in the background as she glided offstage.

Miranda watched the interaction of the judges carefully during the brief pause, trying to read them. But aside from seeming to engage in light banter, she saw nothing unusual in their behavior.

She leaned in, whispering in Matt's ear, "Keep a close watch on the judges. I have a strange feeling."

"Your incomparable intuition at work again," teased Matt. Miranda elbowed him.

Georgia Holmes returned to the stage and introduced the first camper, who was modeling a magnificent mermaid costume. "Our first mermaid is wearing an emerald-green tail, a matching bikini top with a contrasting band dotted with crystals, and a long necklace of orange coral," said Georgia as the girl turned and strutted in front of the judges. A red silk anemone was pinned behind the mermaid's left ear, and her long, blonde curls dripped over her right shoulder, bouncing gently as she moved. "She is one of our return campers—Chelsea Anderson from Kansas. Her mermaid tail is from our judge Trixie Monroe's very own shop, Mermaid's Delight in Tampa."

"How do they manage to walk wearing a mermaid tail?" asked Matt in Miranda's ear.

"Slits camouflaged in the folds of the tail fins."

Matt nodded and watched the first model as she glided offstage.

The next contestant wore a pale yellow and salmon tail with a pale yellow top covered in sequins.

"Looks like Tammy," Miranda whispered to Matt. "With the turtle—or rather, tortoise—tattoo."

"Our next contestant is Tammy Goodman from North Carolina, modeling a mermaid tail she made herself here at camp."

"Seems like Trixie Monroe might have a protégée," said Matt.

"Interesting idea."

Tammy twisted and twirled before waving and walking offstage as the crowd cheered.

The final contestant floated across the stage.

"Last, but far from least, is our first mermaid to come from faraway Denmark—Lila Bjorg," said Georgia, beaming.

Matt's jaw dropped, amazed at the stunning transformation. Lila's long, platinum hair flowed over her bare shoulder in a single stream, held in place by a delicate purple orchid behind her ear. She was radiant in her purple mermaid tail. A thin swirl of yellow glitter encircled her thin waist and continued in a twist around her hips, ending at the fins. The soft light accentuated the dazzling sequins covering the tail, as if tiny fairies came to life with each step she took.

Matt whispered, "Do you think she doesn't talk much because she doesn't speak English?"

"Highly unlikely," said Miranda. "Most people in foreign countries learn English as their second language. I doubt that's the reason for her silence. Perhaps the more important question is, how did a girl from Denmark come to be here at Georgia's camp?"

"She looks gorgeous, that's for sure," mumbled Matt, his gaze fixed on Lila.

Miranda's heart dropped. She tried to unravel the rare emotion swirling inside her as Matt's words replayed in her head.

Jealousy? she wondered. What am supposed to do with that?

Georgia resumed her place at the podium. "Ladies, gentlemen, and merfolk, this ends the beauty pageant portion of our program. The next, and final, event will be the talent competition. Please remain seated, as it will only take a few minutes for the mermaids to prepare."

When the program resumed, each mermaid performed her special talent, showcasing an impressing range of skills. A heart-wrenching solo about a mermaid and her prince. A flute concerto by C. P. E. Bach. And a recitation from Shakespeare's Venus and Adonis:

What, canst thou talk? . . . Hast thou a tongue?
Thy mermaid's voice hath done me double wrong . . .

"Well, that went way over my head," Matt whispered to Miranda. "Did you get what she meant, about a mermaid doing something wrong?"

Miranda nudged him without comment as Georgia reappeared onstage to announce Lila Bjorg, the final contestant.

Lila looked gorgeous in a costume embellished with silver sequins and Swarovski crystals, hints of coral and apricot hues threaded through the fabric. A violin and bow brushed her thigh as she took her position center stage. She lifted her head and took a calming breath before anchoring the violin under her chin and curling her long fingers around its neck. A soft hum wafted through the outdoor speakers.

Mozart's Violin Sonata in A flowed through the cool night air as if carried on wings of angels to delight the gods. As the last note sailed away, Lila lowered the violin and bow and gazed out at the audience, who sat mesmerized, until one thunderous clap brought everyone to their feet in applause.

"Bravo! Bravo!" rang through the campgrounds.

Lila took several more bows before sailing offstage like a gentle breeze.

Georgia clapped wildly as she made her way back to the podium.

"My, my, my," gushed Georgia. "As you can see, our mermaids have many gifts." The applause gradually ended, and Georgia continued. "Thank you all for coming to this magical event. Now, the judges have the unenviable task of choosing our next Sirens of the Deep Queen Mermaid Ambassador. So relax—take a quick break while the votes are tallied, and then we will announce the winner."

After a short break, Georgia's voice crackled over the loudspeaker. "Attention, please. The judges have chosen the winner. Please return to your seats."

Mano Sorkin took his place beside Georgia at the podium, both smiling out at the expectant crowd.

"Mr. Sorkin, would you please do the honors?" purred Georgia, turning to Mano, her sea-green eyes twinkling like tiny stars.

He glanced at the note card in his tanned, steady hand, the spotlight highlighting the gray strands in his hair.

"Ladies, gentlemen, and . . . merfolk, as Ms. Holmes likes to say," he began, turning to Georgia with a roguish smile, "after much deliberation and animated discussion, we have unanimously agreed on our next Queen Mermaid Ambassador." He paused for dramatic effect. "The mermaid chosen tonight best represents the message Sirens of the Deep has embraced for many years—that we must protect our oceans and marine life for future generations."

He paused to scan the attentive faces in the crowd.

"It's only through education and commitment to changing our destructive ways that we can hope to preserve these precious natural habitats from the double threat of global warming and pollution—the callous disregard for our oceans exhibited by those who toss plastic bottles and other debris into oceans, who dump toxic substances into streams—the danger of the fertilizers that seep into the aquifer and eventually into our waters.

"I urge you all to join the worldwide initiative to clean up the marine environment, embrace research, and actively participate in public campaigns that target political leaders and corporations, urging them to make the right decisions that will protect marine life everywhere," he said in a resounding voice.

"C'mon, c'mon," chanted Brenda, impatient to hear who would be named the next Mermaid Ambassador.

"Ms. Holmes, please invite all the contestants back onstage so we can announce tonight's winner," Sorkin said, glancing at the envelope in his hand.

Georgia motioned for the campers to return to the stage and form a single line.

Mano pulled the card naming the winner out of the envelope. A pleased expression spread over his face.

"I am thrilled to announce that the mermaid who will be crowned Queen Mermaid Ambassador tonight is . . . Lila Bjorg!" Piercing squeals and thunderous cheers burst from the crowd.

Georgia removed the red satin pillow holding the Swarovski-studded crown from the shelf below the podium. The ballet choreographer walked across the stage carrying a bouquet of tropical flowers. Mano Sorkin, carrying a silver trophy, joined them as they approached a shocked Lila Bjorg, frozen among the other contestants.

The choreographer handed the bouquet to Lila.

Georgia lifted the glimmering crown off the pillow. As she reached up to set the crown on Lila's head, Lila collapsed in a dizzying swirl, the flowers dropping like rain on the stage.

Gasps came from the audience. Georgia instantly dropped to her knees beside Lila, fanning her with her hand. Sorkin kneeled beside them, passing the trophy to Trixie, who had rushed to his aid.

"Lila. Lila," Georgia said frantically.

Destina Walker rushed to the stage to assist the director, the choreographer collecting the sparkling crown that had rolled across the floor.

"Give her air! Give her air!" Sorkin yelled desperately. "Stand back, all of you!" he shouted, pushing the startled mermaids out of the way.

"Someone call 911!" screamed Georgia.

The other judges, shocked, watched helplessly.

Miranda and Matt shot out of their seats and raced to the stage. Miranda yelled back to Brenda, "Stay with Maria—and call 911!"

Miranda reached Destina and instructed her to escort the mermaids offstage and watch over them until things settled down.

Matt took Georgia's arm and helped her stand up. "Help is on the way, Ms. Holmes," he said, consoling the distraught director.

Miranda kneeled next to Lila, shoving Sorkin out of the way. "Her pulse is weak," she said, patting the girl's face. "Lila. Lila. Can you hear me?"

Lila groaned.

"Lila, it's Detective Morales. Can you hear me?"

Lila could barely open her eyes. "What . . . ," she said, before the burden of keeping her eyes open was too much for her and she again drifted out of reach.

Ambulance sirens blared through the night air as Miranda took a quick glance at the judges, then leaned in to whisper to Matt. "Aside from Peter, all the other judges have been on board the Mermaid Fantasea yachts. Just not all at the same time."

The ambulance sped across the campground toward the stage. Two EMTs jumped out carrying a stretcher and ran up the steps to the stage, setting it down beside Lila. Miranda and Matt moved out of the way as one EMT put an oxygen mask over Lila's mouth as the other checked her vitals.

"How's she doing?" Miranda asked one of the techs.

"Not good. Her blood pressure's dropping. We need to get her into the ambulance and start an IV. We'll connect with the ER doctor so he can give us some orders."

"Where are you taking her?" snapped Trixie, grabbing the tech's elbow.

"Tampa General."

Trixie stood there, momentarily paralyzed as they lifted Lila onto the stretcher and carried her to the ambulance.

"I'm going with her," Miranda told Matt. "Stay here—see what you can find out, and make sure Georgia's okay. Then meet me at the emergency room as soon as you can."

She raced to the ambulance just as the tech was poised to close the door and jumped on, right before it zoomed away with lights and siren blaring.

Trixie stomped over to Sorkin and grabbed his arm, her face distorted with rage. Gabriella and Castro joined them. They all looked angry and terrified.

"You need to sort this out!" Trixie ordered. "I'm going to Tampa General to be with Lila."

Chapter 34

The emergency department was as hectic as you'd expect for a bustling city. Thugs, addicts who'd overdosed, and young mothers with sick babies sat on benches or lay on gurneys haphazardly spread around the room.

Miranda had to show Dr. Rudy Montgomery her ID before he'd agree to let her stay with Lila while he examined her. A young nurse in the room assisted with the assessment, checking the IV in Lila's arm to make sure it was in place, and recording her vital signs on a chart chained to the bottom of the examining table.

Miranda summarized what had happened at the camp while the doctor and nurse searched for a way to remove the mermaid tail.

"Is there a zipper or something on this thing?" the doctor asked.

"I feel one on the back," said the nurse. "Turn her slightly so I can get a good grip on it."

Dr. Montgomery gently pulled Lila toward him while Miranda watched with heightened concern. The nurse pulled the zipper down all the way and then the doctor gently lowered Lila onto her back where he and the nurse began the tug-of-war with the tail.

Lila groaned. Suddenly her dull, blue eyes flashed open, wild with fear. She bolted upright on the gurney, fighting unknown assailants.

Miranda grabbed her and gently lowered her back down. "It's okay, Lila. It's Detective Morales. I met you at the camp a few days ago. Do you remember?"

Lila squirmed, too little strength to get up again. She looked into Miranda's warm chocolate eyes, nodding.

Miranda brushed Lila's cheek and stroked her hair.

"Dr. Montgomery and"—she looked at the nurse's name tag—"Nurse Williams are here to help you. It's okay. They're removing the tail so you can breathe easier and the doctor can examine you."

"Can you hold the sheet over Lila for privacy as we remove the tail, Detective?" asked Nurse Williams.

Miranda unfolded the sheet and followed the nurse's directions.

They removed the mermaid tail, and Lila slowly relaxed, her legs now set free.

"How did she even get into that thing?" asked Dr. Montgomery, shaking his head. "I'll need you to step out of the room, Detective, while I finish my exam. Nurse Williams will stay with her."

"I'd prefer to stay," said Miranda protectively.

"It's hospital procedure, Detective," explained the nurse. "HIPAA regulations," she added, citing the guidelines established to protect patient confidentiality.

Miranda leaned over and whispered in Lila's ear. "I'll be just outside the curtain, Lila. They're here to help you, so please try to relax. You're safe and in good hands." Miranda gently squeezed Lila's cold hand and stepped beyond the privacy curtain.

She was relieved to see Matt sitting in the waiting room. He jumped up as soon as he saw her.

"How is she?"

"The doctor's finishing his examination now. Hopefully it's nothing serious. Maybe just the heat and excitement at the camp—a combination of the shock of winning and dehydration. They took some blood to run some tests."

Matt nodded.

"The mermaid tail took them by surprise," she noted.

Matt laughed out loud. The momentary lightness sliced

through the tension that had been twisting knots in Miranda's stomach. Matt's presence brightened the dark thoughts stirring inside her. Suddenly she felt ashamed of her jealousy over Matt's remark about Lila's looks.

"Trixie's on her way," said Matt. "She got some resistance from Mano, Gabriella, and Castro. Georgia wanted to come, but I told her it was best for her to stay behind to calm the hysteria at the camp."

"What about Peter Millstine?"

"He didn't stick around. He was particularly agitated after Lila was rushed away. Not sure where he went." Matt took Miranda's elbow and led her to a row of cushioned chairs. "Ah, I think you should know—there's a lot more to your fashion designer than she lets on. Georgia Holmes, too."

Miranda nodded. "Lila, too. I can sense it." She paused. "Something big's going on, Matt. Did you notice anything strange going on among the judges after I left?"

"Like what?"

"I dunno," she replied with a half-shrug. "Just anything . . . suspicious."

Matt thought back to the chaos on and off the stage.

"The audience was obviously shocked. Once things had settled down a bit, Georgia came over to me and confessed she was unnerved by something she'd overheard before Lila was rushed away."

"What'd she hear?"

"She thought she heard Gabriella and Mano talking about 'the dead mermaid.' At least, that's what she thought she heard."

Miranda leaned forward and blew out a full breath.

"She overheard them discussing the newspaper article about our mermaid on Lido Beach," Matt went on. "Georgia is convinced Gabriella knew who the dead girl was."

"What makes her think that?"

"She's certain Gabriella and Trixie Monroe go back a long way. Georgia said she'd never met Gabriella before tonight, but when Mano recommended her to stand in for the regular judge, she said something unlocked in her brain—especially when she overheard Gabriella asking Trixie if the dead girl could be the same one who had stayed at her house a year or so ago, before she mysteriously vanished."

"Vanished?" asked Miranda. "What's that supposed to mean?"

Matt shrugged.

"All Georgia said was that Trixie denied knowing the girl, telling Gabriella she had it all wrong. It's all very suspicious, if you ask me."

"No missing person report filed?"

"Not sure. I'll follow up on that."

Miranda nodded, letting the information sink in. "I'm sure Gabriella is the same woman we saw on the yacht, the one with the Roman numeral one," she said. "That must be the one that belongs to Mano Sorkin."

"Seems like a tight-knit little group, wouldn't you say—all of them connected to the Mermaid Fantasea Corporation in some way?"

"So because Mano vouched for Gabriella, Georgia said she had no reason to question her background, despite never having met her. Did Georgia mention anything about them being partners?" asked Miranda.

Matt shrugged.

"All she knew was that the woman had been involved in what Georgia referred to as 'the mermaid circuit,' as a consultant and program organizer. But she had no idea what kind of relationship she and Mano had, within the Mermaid Fantasea company."

"Mermaid circuit." She shook her head. "Everything's such a jumble, Matt. All very strange indeed."

Mano Sorkin using his yacht for the Queen Ambassador's educational tours and the mysterious connections among the judges—it all reeked of suspicious, if not unsavory, activities in Miranda's mind.

"Brenda said that the custom-made tails Trixie sent to the Mermaid Fantasea company in Miami had increased in number over the past year or so. And Georgia also mentioned that Trixie had become more preoccupied and short-tempered since becoming involved with the company," said Miranda. "She said she has no idea who's ordering all the custom tails." She paused, tapping her index finger against her mouth. "It all smells fishy to me. No pun intended."

"What about Peter Millstine?" mused Matt. "It seems odd that he was a judge. I wonder if Georgia knows him—or was he another stand-in recommended by Mano Sorkin?"

"Hmm . . . I wonder if Peter could be the mysterious figure in the shrubs watching Lila?"

"Oh, there is one more thing I just thought of. As soon as the ambulance left, Trixie raced over to Mano and grabbed his arm, pulling him off to the side. She looked furious, flailing her arms in the air."

"Well, we've seen her tirades before. Remember the catfight in Georgia's office?"

"True. But Georgia was terrified watching the encounter, and she made no effort to intercede. Castro ended up separating them. Trixie stomped over to Georgia and seemed to be reading her the riot act."

"What did Georgia do?"

"Nothing. She just glared at her. Then Trixie stormed offstage." Matt laughed.

"Something funny?"

"Yeah. Trixie. She lost her balance on those high heels and almost fell flat on her face as she bounded across the stage. Georgia made no effort to help her."

Miranda smiled at the image. "That's mean, Matt," she said, unable to disguise her amusement.

"I know," he said. "Once Georgia had things under control, I left to meet you at the hospital. Then Georgia called to warn me Trixie was on her way to Tampa, 'to get Lila,' is how she put it. Apparently she's planning to take her home with her."

"Shit," said Miranda, scanning the waiting room. Trixie was nowhere in sight.

Dr. Montgomery came out in the hallway and motioned for Miranda to return.

"Wait here a minute, Matt. Watch for Trixie."

Miranda walked back to the exam room.

"Lila's a bit shaken, but otherwise she seems fine," said the doctor. He studied Miranda for a few seconds. "She didn't talk at all. I asked her some questions, but I couldn't tell if she didn't understand me, or was too afraid to speak. Can she talk?"

"She's very quiet. Aside from a couple of her friends at the mermaid camp, she hasn't really talked to anybody. She just listens. And watches."

"Well, her lab report came back normal, so she's cleared for discharge. But she'll need rest and quiet for the next few days." He paused. "Does she have family here?"

"I'm not sure about family, Doctor, but I expect between the camp director and her secretary, she'll be looked after until . . ." Until what, exactly, she couldn't say just then.

Dr. Montgomery nodded.

"I'd advise that she not return to the camp until she feels up to it."

Suddenly Trixie Monroe zoomed past Matt and headed straight toward the doctor and Miranda. Matt raced after her, but not before she reached Lila.

Matt mouthed Sorry to Miranda.

"I'm taking Lila home with me," Trixie declared. "And you can't stop me, Detective Morales!"

Lila swung her long legs over the side of the bed, prepared to jump, shaking her head wildly and shrieking, "Nooooooo!"

Chapter 35

Lila Bjorg slept soundly in the queen-size bed in Trixie Monroe's lavishly furnished guest bedroom. Despite Lila's plea to not be discharged into the designer's care, Dr. Montgomery agreed it was probably the best solution, since Lila's family could not be located. The only other option was to discharge her in Georgia's care, since she was already enrolled at the camp. But after giving it some thought, the doctor nixed that option. Lila needed rest, and he felt she would recover more quickly away from the excitement at the camp.

Although Miranda wasn't keen on Lila staying with Trixie, she realized that Georgia Holmes was overwhelmed, dealing with the chaos at the camp, and her assistant, Destina Walker, was tending to Maria Diaz and making plans to send her home. So, Trixie Monroe seemed the logical and most expedient solution, despite Lila's protest.

Dr. Montgomery cautioned both Miranda and Trixie that if Lila suddenly took a turn for the worse, he should be contacted immediately. "She's quite fragile right now."

Miranda reluctantly delivered Lila into Trixie Monroe's hands, knowing that she was not going to be complacent. She would learn more about Lila, as well as Trixie. She was also going to dig deeper into the workings of the Mermaid Fantasea Corporation, and Gabriella Navarre.

Trixie Monroe's housekeeper answered the door when Miranda and Matt showed up unexpectedly. She never invited people inside the house without Trixie's approval, but when they showed their identification, she stepped aside for them to enter.

"My name's Consuela. Miss Trixie is out."

"We're here mainly to see Lila," Miranda said. "She had a . . . bad day yesterday. I was with her in the ambulance and at the hospital. How is she doing this morning?"

The housekeeper relaxed a little and smiled warmly, leading them to the spacious living room to the right of the foyer. She motioned for them to sit down. Modern-style furnishings filled the room. A stunning garden was in view through the wide windows.

Miranda and Matt sat on the sofa as Consuela gave them a report on Lila's condition.

"She had a restless night, and has been sleeping all morning. It's time for her to eat and take her medicine. She hasn't had much of an appetite, but I will check to see if she's awake and willing to talk. Can I get you anything while you wait?"

Matt and Miranda shook their heads and smiled, thanking her before she left.

They looked around the well-appointed room. Oriental rugs. A mix of antiques and modern accessories. Abstract art hanging on the walls.

"What do you think?" asked Matt once the housekeeper was out of range.

"I expected no less of Trixie Monroe," she said.

A tall, purple orchid on the walnut sideboard prompted a memory of a lecture Miranda had attended at the Marie Selby Botanical Gardens in Sarasota. She'd been enchanted with orchids as a child, and visited the Selby Gardens often as an escape from the tense atmosphere at home.

"What do you think?" she asked.

"Well, it's a bit beyond my decorating budget," said Matt. "My condo's decor is a mix of local consignment shop excursions and artwork I bought at the arts-and-craft shows that come to town." He smiled. "But Muscle and I are content in our humble surroundings."

"Ah," she smiled. "You'll have to introduce me to Muscle one day. Maybe if we ever go on that bike ride together."

Consuela entered holding a tray of glasses and a pitcher of lemonade. "Lila's awake, but she prefers not be disturbed," she said softly, pouring each of them a drink.

"I understand," said Miranda. "How does she seem? I know she's not much of a talker, but I was wondering if she mentioned anything about what happened last night at the celebration?"

The housekeeper smiled, sitting down opposite them. "She's one of the few girls her age who doesn't like talking on the phone . . . or at all, actually."

Miranda smiled, wondering if Consuela had children of her own. She wondered how long she'd been Trixie's housekeeper, and how she felt about her employer.

"Have you lived in Tampa long?" asked Miranda.

"I came here on a boat from Cuba with others fleeing to America many years ago. My parents wanted a better life for me and my brother, so they sent us away." She paused, her thoughts drifting to that memory. "Our boat capsized before we made it to shore. My brother and I were the only ones who survived. Except for the captain." She lowered her eyes, tears slipping from their corners. She quickly wiped them away. "The three of us knew how to swim. None of the others did." She dabbed her eyes and wiped her nose with a tissue she took out of her apron pocket. "We tried to help them, but . . ."

She was unable to finish her story.

"That must have been very scary. What happened to the captain?"

"I think the police arrested him for illegally transporting refugees. We never saw him again. We were taken to an orphanage until they could contact our family in Cuba. Officials later told us they couldn't locate them. Then one day, Miss Trixie came to the orphanage and took me with her." She sniffed, then stared directly into Matt's eyes. "But not my brother." She turned her gaze back on Miranda. "I cried every night. Miss Trixie said everything would be okay—that she would go back to the orphanage and get him later. But she never did."

She sighed, twisting the tissue to shreds.

"So you've been living here ever since?" asked Miranda.

"Yes. She said that when she located my parents, they pleaded with her to keep us here, where we'd be safe. To not send us back to Cuba." More tears trailed down her pudgy, brown cheeks. "I learned much later that Miss Trixie never mentioned to my parents that my brother and I weren't together. She said she didn't want to add to their misery." Consuela inhaled a deep breath. "I have no idea where he is now."

The two detectives glanced at each other, then looked up to see Lila standing in the doorway, watching them. They instantly stood up.

Consuela wiped her eyes with the tip of her apron and went to Lila, putting an arm around the girl's slumped, bony shoulders. Lila's pale complexion and slender frame emphasized her vulnerable and fragile state.

"Sit down, Lila, dear," urged Consuela softly, guiding her to a seat near the sofa where Miranda and Matt were sitting.

Miranda studied Lila for a few silent moments. Neither she nor Matt knowing where to start with their questions.

Consuela rubbed Lila's arm, covered by a sheer, long-sleeved pink dressing gown, and whispered in her ear. Lila didn't move and kept her head low, avoiding the detectives' penetrating gaze.

They waited, hoping Lila would speak first.

When she didn't, Miranda took the lead. "How are you feeling?" she asked gently.

Lila slowly lifted her eyes to Miranda, veiled in sadness, fear, and confusion.

"Has she spoken to you, Consuela?" asked Miranda.

Consuela nodded.

Miranda decided she'd tread lightly with Lila, uncertain if she was willing—or even able—to answer her questions. She needed to ask them just the same, even if the girl chose not to answer them. Just seeing Lila's reaction could prove useful.

"I'd like to show you a picture," Miranda began, carefully. "I'm hoping you can tell me if you recognize the girl."

Miranda looked directly at Consuela, whose eyes were wide with alarm.

She continued with utmost sensitivity. "It's really important, Lila."

Lila kept her head low.

"I wouldn't ask if it wasn't important, Lila. We think this girl might have attended Sirens of the Deep, and that you might know her." She paused to give Lila time to process what was being asked of her. "Perhaps you saw her in photos with previous campers? Or maybe she was a friend from home who told you about the mermaid camp?"

Miranda was desperate to ignite any spark in Lila.

Lila searched Miranda's eyes, remembering the detective's kindness, how she had consoled her in the ambulance. "Thank you for staying with me," she said, finally. "You helped me."

Miranda smiled, her heart warmed by Lila's response.

Consuela rubbed Lila's arm and stroked her corn-silk hair.

"May I show you the picture?" asked Miranda.

Lila nodded.

Miranda opened her phone to the cleaned-up image of the Lido Beach mermaid. Although less brutal than earlier images, the pain and suffering was still evident in the close-up of the victim's pallid face. Her features dull and emotionless, her eyes now closed as if she was merely asleep.

"It's not a pretty picture," Miranda cautioned softly, "but if anything about her looks familiar, I hope you'll tell us."

Lila glanced at Matt, who was looking at her supportively.

Miranda moved to sit next to Lila, handing her the phone.

Reluctantly, Lila took it with trembling fingers. She stared at the picture for some time, as if under a ghostly spell, then looked at Miranda with tear-filled eyes.

"Nina," she sobbed. "It's Nina Jorgensen."

Consuela hugged her, rubbing her back to calm the girl's trembling.

Lila pulled away and looked at the detectives. "I didn't know what happened to her. She was my closest friend," she sobbed.

"I think I should take her back upstairs to rest," said Consuela. "This has been very difficult for her." Consuela took Lila's elbow and steadied her as she stood. "I'll be back as soon as I give her some medicine."

"Thank you for your help, Lila," said Miranda, "and thank you, Consuela. We won't take any more of your time. If you need anything, please call me or Detective Selva anytime, day or night."

The housekeeper nodded.

As Consuela guided Lila up the stairs, Lila paused.

"Please take me with you," she pleaded. "The man in the bushes, at the camp. He was one of the judges."

Instantly Matt rushed over to stand beside Miranda.

"Which one, Lila? Mano Sorkin, Castro Montoya, or Peter Millstine?"

"The short one. With very little hair."

Millstine.

Miranda took a business card from her back pocket and slipped into Lila's hand.

"You're going to be okay, Lila. Call me anytime." She looked at Consuela. "I'll leave our business cards on the table in the hallway for you, Consuela."

Matt stood up and joined Miranda. "Will Ms. Monroe be home soon, by any chance?" Matt asked.

The housekeeper shook her head.

"No. She left early this morning. Said she had urgent business in Tampa."

Miranda's instincts kicked in. The dots were suddenly beginning to connect. She decided it was time to have a talk with Peter Millstine.

As she and Matt left Trixie's house, Miranda looked at him with determined eyes.

"I need to go to the collector's house to follow up on a conversation I had with him at the cocktail party."

"I should go with you," he declared.

"No. I'm just taking him up on his invitation," she smiled. "I'll be fine. He wouldn't dare hurt the daughter of one of his closest friends."

Chapter 36

Miranda Googled Peter Millstine and found his company, PM Importers, and a phone number. She wished she had his private number, but refused to contact her father to get it. Keeping her distance from her parents had worked well for many years; seeing them at the cocktail party had only reinforced her disdain for everything they stood for—materialism, greed, selfishness, and arrogance. She would set up a meeting with Peter herself.

The woman's voice on the answering machine confirmed that Miranda had dialed the right number. The message informed her that PM Importers was closed, saying, "If you are calling to schedule a private appointment with Mr. Millstine, please leave a message after the tone."

Miranda definitely wanted a private appointment.

"Mr. Millstine, it's Miranda Morales. I was hoping we could meet so you could show me your extraordinary mermaid collection. Please call me to arrange a time." She left her phone number, then added, "This would be such an honor," hoping that massaging his ego would get her a quicker invitation.

She switched mental gears to her old love, Graham. She wanted to build on what she'd learned from him at his lecture, and thought this would be a good time to see if he could help put together some of the missing pieces of the mermaid puzzle. She knew the risk of seeing him again would make it harder for her to dismiss the feelings that still lingered, but she had to take that chance.

I'll just stay on point—put on my detective's armor. See him as a scholar and ally rather than a former lover and foe.

She blew out a breath and got into her car, wondering whether or not to call him, her thoughts interrupted by an incoming call.

"Detective Morales," she answered curtly.

"Detective, this is Admiral Jordan Brickman of the US Coast Guard office in Tampa. I just got an anonymous call warning us about a freighter that left Miami several hours ago. Apparently there's contraband hidden on board. The caller gave your name and phone number." A brief pause, then, "Our men have already boarded the freighter and found four malnourished, terrified young girls in a metal container labeled PM Importers." Miranda gasped, shivers spinning down her spine.

"Are the girls okay?"

"They appear to be, but they should be examined by a doctor. The Coast Guard is escorting the freighter to port."

"I'm on my way. I imagine Immigration will have to be notified."

"Roger that, Detective. I'll get on it right away."

She called Matt. "Meet me at the US Coast Guard station in Tampa."

"I can be there in about an hour."

The minute she hung up, she had another call.

"Morales."

"Miranda, it's Peter Millstine." His voice was soft but edgy. "I got your message. Let's meet somewhere for a drink."

"I'm on the road right now, Mr. Millstine, but I should be back in Sarasota around four o'clock. Let's meet at Casey's Cabana at Bayfront Park."

"Done! I'll see you at four then."

The US Coast Guard pavilion in Tampa was a small, innocuous cement building at the far end of the Tampa marina. Admiral Brickman greeted her when she identified herself.

"They're pretty scared," he said, leading her to a small room at the end of a narrow hallway where four pathetic-looking girls sat huddled together on a wooden bench. Their sundresses were torn and soiled, their hair in oily, tangled clumps. They looked and smelled like they hadn't bathed in a while. Their frightened eyes froze when Miranda entered the room. Instinctively they clenched each other's hands, squeezing shoulder to shoulder on the bench.

"They've not said a word since we found them," whispered the admiral. "I don't think they speak English. We had a small motorboat transport them from the freighter. Our men will search the cargo hold to see if there are any others hidden away."

Miranda pulled over a chair and sat down in front of the girls. She smiled, leaning forward. "Hola," she said softly. "Mi nombre es Miranda," pointing to herself. "Policía." She smiled and scanned their faces, imagining what they must be feeling. "Hablamos inglés?"

The girls just stared at her blankly, their small hands trembling.

"Have they had anything to eat, Admiral?"

"I've ordered pizza. It should be here any minute."

No sooner had the admiral mentioned pizza than the delivery arrived.

Miranda was relieved to see Matt following close behind the deliveryman. He stood quietly in the doorway until the admiral invited him in with a wave.

"Hey, Matt," greeted Miranda in low tones. "Federal authorities are questioning the captain of the freighter and inspecting the cargo. It's an international shipment, so a lot of higher-ups want to get involved."

He nodded.

"Do you know anything about the girls?"

"Not yet. They haven't said a word. I doubt they speak much English. I tried what little Spanish I knew, but nothing."

Admiral Brickman placed some chairs around the small table and opened the pizza boxes. He looked at Miranda. "Can you take them to the restroom to freshen up?" Neither an order or a question.

She nodded, and took the hand of the youngest-looking girl. The others followed them to the bathroom, and when they returned, Miranda motioned for the girls to sit down at the table.

"Eat. Comer," she said, lifting a slice of pizza to her mouth.

The girls sat still as rocks, stealing glances at each other before one reached into the box and removed a slice. The others quickly dived in like starved animals. After a couple of bites, one girl finally spoke.

"Mi nombre es Della. Hablo un poco d'inglés." She pointed to the other three girls. "Sienna, Katerina, and Mona." She took another big bite of pizza, swallowing it with barely a chew. "Men take us from orphanage." She put her arms behind her back suggesting the men had tied their hands. "Put in bags. Then boat ride. Dump us on ground."

"Did you know the men who took you?"

Della shook her head.

"No. Other boat come. Take us again."

"Take you where?"

She shrugged and looked around the room, pinching her nose to indicate a foul smell. "Ponnos en latas." Seeing Miranda's puzzlement, she struggled to find words in English. "Put us in can." The girl blinked away tears.

Miranda gently rubbed the girl's shoulder.

"Sus nombres? Do you know their names?"

"Uno," said Della. "Snake."

"His name was Snake?"

The girl shook her head, frustrated. "Like snake."

"Hmm," mumbled Miranda.

"Qué orphanage?" asked Matt. Like Miranda, he knew very little Spanish.

"Colombia. Madre de la Esperanza," she said, staring into his eyes. Then she abruptly declared, "Tus ojos bonitos. Your eyes pretty. Azul." Her grin was captivating.

He smiled, a pale blush tinting his face.

"Indigo, actually," chimed in Miranda, sending a small smile his way.

"Indigo," Della repeated excitedly. "I know that word. Si. Indigo!"

They all laughed as tensions relaxed.

Miranda leaned toward Matt and whispered, "I have to make a call to the chief. Immigration's been notified." Her lips pressed together as she scanned the girls' condition. "Not sure how to handle that complication. They really need to see a doctor."

"Okay. I'll stay with them. I think they're feeling a little more comfortable."

When she returned, the pizza boxes were empty and the girls giggling.

"Yum," said Della, tapping her stomach. "Gracias."

Miranda smiled and touched Della lightly on her thin shoulder. Then she turned to Matt and cocked her head toward the outer office. Matt followed.

"I just called Chief Petri. He said the girls should be examined in Tampa. He spoke with someone in Immigration. They'll meet you at Tampa General ER. What we do next will be determined by what Immigration says."

"Do you think Georgia Holmes could take them?" asked Matt.

"Maybe. I'll take them to Tampa General. You stay here, see if you can get in on the questioning of the freighter captain. Find out all you can."

Matt nodded.

"I also called an old friend at the FBI, Damien McMillon. I asked him if he had any information on human trafficking. He couldn't say much, but he did say they have been investigating the rise in international child abductions for a few years. They had some leads, but nothing solid yet. The news of the four girls found on the cargo ship piqued his interest. He'll get back to me once he's had a chance to follow up with his agents."

"The freighter just arrived in port, so we'll be boarding it soon," said Admiral Brickman, interrupting them.

"Okay with you if Detective Selva stays for the interrogation?" Miranda asked.

The admiral nodded. "Sure—if you're okay with taking the girls to the hospital."

"Absolutely," she said.

Chapter 37

The girls got settled in Miranda's car for the drive to Tampa General ER. On one hand Miranda wished Matt was with her, but she knew it was important for him to be present at the interrogation of the freighter captain. She was grateful that Georgia Holmes had agreed to house the four girls, in addition to Maria Diaz. Georgia would come to the emergency room to pick them up and transport them to camp after they'd been cleared for discharge.

Three of the four girls sat quietly in the backseat, while Della sat up front. She spoke some English, so it was easier for Miranda to talk to her about things she might remember about their kidnapping. Della also seemed more mature than the others, despite all of them ranging in age from roughly seven to ten years old.

The radio played softly in the background as the girls chattered in the back, gradually growing more relaxed. Miranda glanced at them in her rearview mirror, wondering what their lives had been like at the Mother of Hope orphanage in Colombia, where Della said they had lived since they were quite young.

"I am the oldest," Della announced proudly.

"How old were you when you went to the orphanage?"

Della put a finger on her mouth, thinking. "Matron say I three. Found me in the garden. I ten now. Gardener see me next morning." She turned to look at her friends in the backseat. "Sienna come when baby. Katerina and Mona sisters. Came together. Katerina two. Mona older. Like me."

Miranda was disturbed by the abrasions she noticed on Della's bare knees. She could only imagine the horror the girls must have experienced at the hands of monsters preying on children. Each girl was pretty in her own way. All of them had intense brown eyes, varying from hazel and amber to dark chocolate and black tea. Their skin tone also varied from pale olive to deep russet, depending on the way the light hit their faces.

Della's complexion was more fair than the others, smooth and creamy, almost Caucasian. Her eyes were an unusual shade of pewter with blue specks, her brown hair streaked with straw-colored strands. Miranda wondered how she had ended up in Colombia. Despite having been kidnapped, locked in a dark container for who knows how long, and now in a strange country—with no idea what was going to happen next—Della seemed more self-assured than the others. Miranda sensed the other girls looked to her for answers. And protection.

"Señora Gretchen asked me to help her. Do chores at orphanage," said Della, picking up their conversation. "Said I do good job." She turned to Miranda and smiled. "She help me learn English."

"Ah. That has come in very handy at the moment, no?" She smiled.

Della laughed and nodded. "Si."

"Does Señora Gretchen have a last name?"

"Kismet."

"That's a very pretty name. You all have pretty names." She paused. "I have to call my partner. It'll just take a minute."

Della checked on the girls in the backseat. Their eyes were closed. She closed hers as she leaned back her head.

"Hey, Miranda," said Matt, answering her call. "How are the girls doing?"

"They're fine. How are things there?"

"The captain of the freighter isn't saying much. Like squeezing blood from a stone."

"One of the girls, Della, told me the name of the matron at the Mother of Hope orphanage is Gretchen Kismet. See what you can find out about her. I assume she's the administrator, but maybe not."

"Okay. What do you want to know?"

"Della said the girls arrived at different times. Katrina and Mona are sisters. I'd like to know more about the way the orphanage is run and who's in charge—whether it's a government or private enterprise."

Matt agreed, and ended the call.

Gretchen Kismet was relieved to hear the girls were safe and being looked after when Matt finally reached her. But she was adamant that she had no idea who could have kidnapped the girls, or why.

"We have close to thirty children in our care. It's a mystery as to how four children could have been taken from here without somebody seeing or hearing something. And why those children?" asked a perplexed Gretchen. "There are at least two people watching over the children at night, more during the day." She explained that the boys and girls sleep in separate quarters, "for obvious reasons." They agreed to keep each other informed of any new developments.

Matt called Miranda back to tell her he was en route to the ER, and that he'd fill her in when he got there.

Her phone rang again. It was Graham.

"Everything okay?" she asked.

"I'm fine, Miranda—just a little unsettled."

"I'm listening."

"I met with Peter Millstine to see his mermaid belt." A long pause. "He seemed . . . withdrawn. Paranoid even? Weird. Like you said. Creepy. Quite different from the man at the cocktail party. Have you spoken to him since then?"

"No," she lied, not wanting to divulge her plan to meet Peter at Casey's Cabana at four o'clock. "But you know how alcohol can change someone's personality. Maybe something was on his mind. Or you're just being overly sensitive."

"Maybe," conceded Graham, "but when he spoke of the mermaid talisman at the party, he was genuinely excited. So willing to talk about it." He paused. "Then, at his house, he showed me this miniature granite bear he took from a glass display case, saying it was his favorite thing in his collection. Which surprised me." Another long pause. "With such a rare and valuable collection, why would a relatively common object like a granite bear be his favorite?"

"Anything else?"

"He also had a filigree frog and tortoise in the glass case with other rare objects. The frog and tortoise resembled the two I showed in my slide presentation. I wondered if they could be the ones stolen from the museum in Panama." Another long pause. "Except one of the frog's pearl eyes and the tortoise's turquoise shell were missing."

"Hmm. That's rather odd. Are you certain the two objects were similar to the ones in your slides?"

"Yes. But even more strange was the dramatic shift in his demeanor when he took the mermaid belt out of the safe and we began discussing it. Suddenly, out of the blue, something dark washed over him."

"Dark?"

He took a deep breath. "Like he was . . . possessed. As if he'd gone into a trance, or was under some demonic spell that had overtaken him."

Possessed. Demonic.

"Did he say anything that caused you concern?"

"No. It was just something about his tone, the menacing glaze in his eyes." He paused. "He became extremely defensive when I told him I had discovered a legend of the talisman that differed slightly from his. He accused me of claiming his talisman was a fake."

"Is it?"

"I highly doubt it. I was merely sharing some academic information about the legend passed down through the generations. The accounts never questioned whether the mermaid belt was real, or that it belonged to a mermaid princess. They only varied when it came to the kind of gemstones that were originally on the belt."

"Listen, I'm tied up right now. Are you free for dinner tonight?" she blurted out, then cringed. She held her breath, not sure whether she wanted him to say yes or no.

Even if the invitation was just business, Graham's optimism bloomed. Could this be a second chance?

"Yes," he finally said.

She blew out a breath.

"Come to my house around seven. I'll make us a reservation for eight o'clock."

Her priority now was to get the girls examined. She'd have to reschedule her appointment with Peter.

She looked in her rearview mirror and smiled when she saw the girls had dozed off. Della, too, had slipped into a nap.

She called Peter and left a message on his answering machine.

"Mr. Millstine, it's Detective Morales. I apologize, but something's come up and I have to reschedule our four o'clock meeting set for today." She clicked off as she pulled into a parking spot near the entrance to the Tampa emergency department.

"We're here," she said, lightly tapping Della's knee. The girls in the backseat were rubbing their eyes. "A nice doctor at the hospital wants to make sure you're all are okay."

Chapter 38

"What are you talking about?" said an outraged Georgia, her hands on her hips, facing Miranda in the Tampa General ER. "I don't know anything about an orphanage, in Colombia or anywhere else, for that matter!" She took a deep breath. "Have you talked to Trixie about this? She's sponsored many girls who attend the camp. I've never asked her where they come from, since she's always assumed full responsibility for them. She's paid their fees and I've just trusted her that the girls were well vetted."

"No, I haven't talked to Trixie. Yet. Do you know if any of the girls Trixie sponsored had tattoos?"

"What?" laughed Georgia. "Tattoos? How would I know that?"

Miranda cleared her throat. "We have reason to believe tattoos might somehow be linked to a case we're investigating," Miranda offered, hoping this might jog Georgia's memory.

"I don't recall any tattoos," she snarled. "And I highly doubt any of my campers came from an orphanage." She pulled back her shoulders. "Sirens of the Deep is expensive, Detective Morales," she said. "Trixie has the money to cover the costs of the camp, and I sincerely doubt she'd stoop to foraging for potential campers to sponsor at an orphanage of all places."

"What about other sponsors?"

"Individuals as well as community organizations will sometimes sponsor a camper if we feel the need to reach out to them. I have no idea if anybody cares whether the camper they sponsor has a tattoo," she huffed.

"I ask because three of your current campers have tattoos, and our Lido Beach victim had one. And they all happen to love mermaids.

"Now that you mention it, I did notice a few of the girls had some kind of marks on their shoulders. What kind of tattoos do they have?"

"Lila has a lizard. Tammy, a tortoise. Gina, a serpent. And our victim, a frog."

"Why would they have chosen such scaly creatures? Why not butterflies, or birds—or mermaids," she said coyly.

Miranda had no idea. Were the tattoos merely a coincidence, or some kind of secret code? And if so, a code for what?

"I've got to run, Ms. Holmes," Miranda said abruptly. "Thank you for taking the girls back to your camp. They've been quite traumatized, but I'm sure they're in good hands now. I'll say good-bye to Della. Detective Selva is on his way and will stay with you."

"Okay," said Georgia. "Make sure you tell the front desk you've authorized me to take them with me."

Matt rushed in just as Miranda was leaving the ER.

"Hey, where are you going?"

"Sorry, Matt. Something's come up. I have to run. Can you help Georgia? The girls are ready to be discharged. You can fill me in on the orphanage administrator later."

Matt shook his head, bewildered. He found a confused camp director seated on one of the hard, wooden chairs in the emergency room. When she saw Matt, her mood lifted. She immediately stood up and greeted him with a demure smile, delighted to see her handsome Hugh Grant.

Dr. Montgomery and Nurse Williams entered the waiting room of the ER. He recognized Matt from Lila Bjorg's visit to the ER.

"I take it you work with Detective Morales?" said the doctor. Matt nodded.

"The girls are in fair condition, considering their ordeal," he said. "They need food, a shower, and some clean clothes. I'm hoping the emotional trauma will diminish once they're able to return to some kind of routine."

Matt nodded. "This is Georgia Holmes, director of Sirens of the Deep mermaid camp. She has graciously agreed to let the girls stay there until other arrangements can be made."

"It's wonderful of you to take care of these girls," Dr. Montgomery said.

Georgia looked at the four girls. "They look so frail," she said. "Are you sure they're okay to go?"

Dr. Montgomery smiled. "I think they'll recover faster once they're away from here."

An attractive woman in her mid-thirties with skin the color of honey entered the room with a warm smile and approached the girls, her eyes bright and engaging.

"This is Martina Torres," said Dr. Montgomery to Georgia and Matt. "She works in our HR department and is fluent in Spanish. I asked her if she had a few minutes to explain to the girls what is going to happen next."

They shook hands and smiled as Matt and Georgia introduced themselves. Then Martina stooped down, smiling at eye level with each girl, reassuring them in Spanish.

"Vas a conocer algunas sirenas," explained Martina.

The girls squealed at the mention of mermaids.

"They are excited to meet some mermaids," she said with a smile. "I explained that you have a camp for mermaids and they are coming to stay with you for a while." She laughed. "They want to know if they can be mermaids?"

She took Georgia aside. "I've contacted the Homeland Security Investigations department within Immigration and Customs Enforcement. They'll send some people to help get the girls returned to their homeland. They've given permission for the girls to stay with you at the camp for the time being, but be prepared for the agents' arrival, to interview the girls."

"I'll do my best to help," said Georgia. She managed a smile despite her concern. "I just hope they don't think we have real mermaids at the camp. I don't want them to be disappointed."

"They understand," nodded Martina. "Perhaps mermaids, even if they're not real, will help them after their ordeal."

Georgia raised an eyebrow and smiled.

"Sounds like they're eager to get on the road," smiled Martina. She handed Georgia and Matt a business card. "Please call me anytime."

"Thank you, Ms. Torres," said Georgia, motioning for the girls to follow her.

Chapter 39

The door to Mermaid's Delight opened with its usual tinkle, the overhead bell alerting Brenda Sinclair that a customer had just arrived. When she looked up, she was puzzled as to why a man the size of a bulldozer would be shopping at a mermaid shop.

"Good afternoon, sir. May I help you?" she asked, keeping her distance while gripping the edge of sales counter.

"Where's Trixie?" he asked gruffly.

Brenda braced herself, debating how best to respond.

"Ms. Monroe has gone out, but she should be back momentarily," she lied, alerting him that she wouldn't be alone for long. Scenes from horror movies she'd seen were flashing through her head. She took a deep, quiet breath to compose herself. "You're welcome to look around until she gets back, if you like," silently praying he'd leave.

His thick neck moved in tandem with his broad shoulders. His long black ponytail was tied with a thin, leather band, stretching down his broad back like a trail of oily petroleum. He grunted like an animal as he roamed the room, stopping briefly to inspect the jewelry in one of the glass cases. A silver charm bracelet caught his eye. Brenda remembered it was the same bracelet Detective Morales had admired on her first visit to the shop.

He pointed to it.

"How much is that one?" he said, his thick finger poking the glass and leaving a greasy smudge.

"Ah," smiled Brenda. "It's one of our signature items. Would you like to see it?" She immediately kicked herself. She would have to unlock the case if he said yes, making it easy for him to steal whatever he was seeking. But she decided she was overreacting. He's just a new customer. Nothing more.

She went over and stood behind the glass counter. "It's on sale. Ninety-nine dollars. Just reduced from one hundred and twenty-five. Sterling silver." Her hands trembled as she unlocked the case and lifted the bracelet off the display, dangling it from her nervous fingers as she told him about the charms.

"The comb and the mirror represent the myth concerning a mermaid's vanity. The seahorse represents—"

"I'll think about it," he said brusquely, thundering down another aisle. His wide-set, dark eyes instantly shot a chill down her spine when he stared at her.

Her fake smile remained frozen on her mouth, the silver bracelet's charms imprinted on her palm from her tight grip on it. Please let another customer come through the door. Please.

The bell on the front door suddenly jingled, startling both of them.

Brenda turned, desperately hoping to see a friendly face. She was disappointed when another stranger entered. Granted, it was a more appealing stranger, who carefully closed the door behind him.

She managed to steady the unease caught in her throat. "Welcome to Mermaid's Delight. May I help you?"

The massive bronze hulk had turned toward the door, a scowl rumbling in his throat.

"What the fuck are you doing here? I thought you were having lunch with Peter and Castro?" said Python.

Mano's eyes blistered with fury. "More to the point, Python, what the fuck are you doing here? You're supposed to be looking after Mirakakoo. Castro's prize. I heard what happened to her." He paused like a diabolical wizard about to banish his worthless assistant to the moors of Scotland. "Or did you conveniently forget about her—again!" He walked toward Python as if stalking a newborn calf. "Or worse yet, did you leave her alone with Castro's good-for-nothing nephew Xander?"

Mano stopped abruptly when he noticed Brenda, fidgeting at one of the display cases. Then, dismissing her, he turned back to Python.

"I asked you, you moron. Explain yourself! What are you doing here?" He poked Python's thick biceps, barely shoving the hulk off balance.

Brenda pretended to busy herself behind the counter as the two men exchanged harsh words and hateful grimaces. Then suddenly, all was silent.

She looked up to see the two men locked in a standoff. Brute strength against executive power. Each prepared to strike.

"Castro is pissed! And, Peter's a damn fool," said Mano, pacing. He stopped, face-to-face with the immovable Python. "You and Castro had better fix this mess! It's not on me or Gabriella!" He swiped his mouth with a crisp, white handkerchief before folding it and returning it to the inside pocket of his unwrinkled linen sport coat. "Trixie and Peter are at the heart of the unraveling. And you and Castro better sort it all out before the Festival of Dagon commences!"

"Excuse me, gentlemen," Brenda said with great trepidation. "Perhaps I can help you . . . are you looking for a gift for that special someone?"

Mano and Python twisted toward Brenda.

"We don't need a gift for anyone," bellowed Python.

"We're here to see Trixie Monroe," snarled Mano, his voice commanding and uncompromising.

"Umm, well, as I told this gentleman, Python," she smiled weakly at the hulk, "Ms. Monroe's out right now, but she's due back any second. If you—"

The phone ringing at the counter startled them. Brenda was unsure whether to answer it or let it go to voicemail. The incessant ring magnified the tension in the air.

Mano cocked his head toward the annoying ring. "Answer it," barked Mano. "If it's Trixie, tell her a couple of friends have stopped by to see her."

Brenda's jittery hand picked up the receiver. The acid in her stomach shooting up to her mouth, stinging as she swallowed.

"Mer . . . Mermaid's Delight," she stuttered through the burn.

"Brenda? What the hell's the matter with you?" growled Trixie.

Mano and Python moved closer to her. She was desperate to signal Trixie that she might be in danger.

"Ah, it's you, Ms. Miranda. The mermaid tail you ordered just arrived."

"What the hell are you talking about, Brenda. This is Trixie!"

"Yes, I know," pretending to laugh. "Why don't you bring Matt with you this time?"

"What the fuck's going on there, Brenda?"

Python shot Brenda a suspicious look. Brenda rolled her eyes at him, pointing at the phone.

"Ms. Monroe should be here at the shop all day. I'm expecting her any minute. She'll call you to arrange your fitting."

"Have you gone mad, Brenda?"

Brenda laughed.

"Of course not, Ms. Miranda. You stay safe. And make sure when you come, Matt comes with you," she laughed.

Trixie hung up, exasperated

"A talkative customer," smiled Brenda. "Trixie designed a mermaid tail for her, but it needs some adjustments. Wants to make sure it fits perfectly."

Mano nudged Python and angled his head toward the door.

"Aren't you going to wait for Ms. Monroe?"

Mano stopped abruptly at the door and turned to face her.

"We'll come back another time."

The overhead bell jingled as the two men left the shop.

Brenda's legs wobbled and she collapsed on the chair behind the counter. She immediately called Trixie, but it went to her voicemail. She left a message.

"I've closed the shop, Ms. Monroe. Two very strange men were here looking for you. One was the size of a gorilla. They both just left. And they weren't happy."

Chapter 40

It was almost eight p.m. when Trixie and Gabriella finally arrived at Mermaid's Delight. The usual lights were on in the shop window, but the CLOSED sign was facing out.

The day had been a trying one. The altercation aboard the Mermaid Fantasea had drained both of them.

"How the fuck did things get so screwed up?" blasted Trixie, throwing her purse on the counter. "I thought you had everything under control. Aren't you supposed to be Mano's fucking MacGyver? The miracle worker?"

"If you're going to point fingers, point them at yourself!" said Gabriella. "The Festival of Dagon will go on. The future of the Mermaid Fantasea Corporation depends on that. It represents everything we—I—have slaved over, and taken huge risks to arrange. It will succeed, come hell or high water!"

Trixie stormed to the back office and turned on the light. She took a bottle of whiskey and two glasses out of the desk drawer.

"Come back here, Gabriella. We could both use a drink."

Gabriella sat down in the chair while Trixie sat on the corner of her desk. Trixie poured each of them a hefty shot of whiskey. Gabriella gulped hers down before Trixie had even poured hers.

"How was I supposed to know the freighter with our cargo had been seized by the Coast Guard after leaving Miami? We don't know the girls' whereabouts, or the fate of the captain. Fuck!" said Gabriella.

"You said getting them out of Panama would be a breeze," snapped Trixie.

"The ship passed through the Panama Canal without a hitch. Somewhere along the way something went wrong."

Gabriella picked up the bottle and poured herself another drink. "What could have happened?" She sniffed the whiskey, then took just a sip this time, looking at Trixie over the rim of the glass.

"Well, Peter better not screw up! The mermaids are integral to the whole celebration of Dagon and the next phase of our expansion."

"I'll make sure things go smoothly on my end."

The two women sat in silence, mulling over the plan as the whiskey settled them.

"We all knew something like this could happen," said Gabriella. "Increased international security on high alert, targeting ships at random, searching for contraband. It was just unfortunate that one of ours got caught."

"Unfortunate?" shrieked Trixie, draining her glass and slamming it down on the desk. "I'd say it's a fucking fiasco!"

Gabriella didn't flinch, her foot bobbing as she carefully calculated potential adjustments to the plan.

"So far authorities have nothing on us. Finding the four girls on the freighter was . . ." She wasn't quite sure what it was, but something had to be done. She looked Trixie in the eyes. "The kidnapped girls have no idea who took them. They were stolen from the orphanage on a moonless night, taken to the cave, and immediately stuffed into burlap sacks that the kidnappers had left in the cave earlier that day."

"I'm not worried about the girls," huffed Trixie. "I'm worried about the captain of the freighter doing us in."

Gabriella laughed and got up to stretch, her smooth, shapely arms tanned and bare. Then she sat back down, crossed her golden legs, and conjured up a plan for handling the disruptive snafu.

"The captain knows nothing about the cargo. My contact in Panama made sure that there would be no way to link that . . . shipment to the Mermaid Fantasea. So, was there a snitch? Or was it just bad luck?"

Trixie got off the desk and checked the clock on the far wall. "I certainly hope you're right. I'm exhausted, and we still have work ahead of us."

"I know I'm right. The mermaid tails need to be loaded on board the yacht tomorrow morning. Mano said he'd take care of transporting Peter and the mermaids to Jewfish Key for the celebration tomorrow night. A whole new era awaits!"

The Bijou Cafe was the epitome of quiet elegance with its starched white tablecloths, subdued candlelight on every table, and French doors separating the smaller, more private dining room from the larger main dining room that looked out onto a small garden, where a pergola was decorated with strands of tiny, globe-shaped white bulbs.

Miranda was having second thoughts about inviting her former flame to dinner, but his lecture had intrigued her. She believed that he might be able to put together some of the puzzle pieces she and Matt had been collecting surrounding their Lido Beach mermaid's death. More importantly, she wanted to ask him about his visit to Peter Millstine's home and his fetish for mermaids.

"This is a lovely restaurant, Miranda," said Graham when he arrived.

"It's one of my favorite restaurants in Sarasota. Consistent quality and a nice ambience." She had a tentative smile on her glossy, full lips. She was remembering the last dinner she had shared with him, when she had expected a marriage proposal and instead was cruelly dumped.

She took a deep breath to quiet the hurt that threatened her resolve.

The waiter greeted them and asked if he could bring them a drink.

"Two Proseccos, please," said Graham, glancing at Miranda, who nodded.

When the waiter returned with the drinks, Graham lifted his glass to Miranda. "To good health and new opportunities."

Miranda fixed her gaze on Graham's sparkling slate-blue eyes and raised her glass. "To good health and new opportunities."

They sipped the Prosecco while staring into each other's questioning eyes. Time froze. Sounds disappeared. Two people locked in memories neither wished to remember.

"So, what do you think of Sarasota?" she asked.

"I can see why you wanted to return. It truly is a paradise."

Miranda smiled. "I love it here. It's so . . . complete."

Graham leaned back in his chair, his eyes fixed on the glow of her flawless face, the chocolate eyes that had captivated him years ago still alluring. She was truly beautiful. Even more so than he remembered.

"Complete? How so?"

She pressed her lips together. "Well, to begin with—" But the waiter had appeared, interrupting the conversation.

Graham ordered a bottle of Cabernet before picking up where she'd left off.

"You were saying how 'complete' Sarasota feels to you."

"Yes," she said, leaning forward, "in that everything I need is here. Great beaches, art, music, theater."

Listening to herself describe her hometown, she realized she didn't really appreciate it as much as she should. Out of the blue, Matt's face sailed into her thoughts.

The waiter returned with the wine. Graham sampled it, and approved. The waiter poured each of them a glass, took their order, and left.

Graham lifted his glass.

"Another toast. Here's to solving your Lido Beach mermaid case. And soon."

She raised her glass. "To Nina," said Miranda.

"Nina?"

"The dead mermaid's name."

"Ah," he sighed.

They clinked glasses, sipped, and leaned back, each studying the other.

"The climate here is quite similar to Panama," he said. "Except perhaps for the amount of rain we get there during the rainy season."

"So I take it you're content living there?" she said.

Graham drained the last of his wine and refilled their glasses.

"Not sure if content is the word. But I love my work."

"Ah," she said.

Good segue.

"I must confess, asking for your help is the main reason for this dinner."

"Right," said Graham, disappointed.

"We're making some progress, but there are still a few pieces I can't quite fit together. One of those is Peter Millstine. Can you fill me in on your visit with him? You mentioned he seemed 'possessed.' "

Graham cleared his throat. "If you'd have been there, you'd know what I mean. Or maybe it was just me." He shrugged.

"What did he do, exactly?" urged Miranda.

He proceeded to describe Peter's dramatic change in demeanor when he talked about his granite bear. "It was like he expected someone to grab it from him, and he was daring them to try. His eyes darkened, in a demonic way. Then he recited—more like chanted—this poem about bear energy, as if cleansing himself of some forbidden act or sinister thought."

Graham paused, studying Miranda's reaction. She just nodded.

"That's what I meant by possessed." Another pause. "And then when I asked him how he had acquired Masimi Aqua's mermaid belt, Peter's eyes narrowed to slits. He stiffened as if preparing for battle. He accused me of questioning the authenticity of the talisman."

Miranda shifted in her chair. "Well, it's not unusual for collectors to protect their sources," she said. "Like journalists. My parents never wanted to divulge how they had acquired certain objects in their collection. It can be a rather secretive, and ruthless, club."

"True. But then there was this otherworldly strangeness when he removed the talisman from the safe and set it on a velvet pad."

"That's exactly how I felt about him at the cocktail party, when my father described Peter's fascination with mermaids as a 'fetish,' " Miranda said.

Graham nodded.

Between bites of food and sips of wine, Miranda and Graham continued to exchange ideas about reptile symbolism, tribal rituals, and the rare objects stolen from the Panama museum that had never been found.

Suddenly, Graham remembered the newspaper article from his graduate student.

He took out his iPhone and opened the e-mail Kai Rendell had sent him. "I got this yesterday and meant to show it to you," he said, handing her the phone.

She set down her fork and gasped when she saw the photo. "Oh my God!"

"What is it?" he asked.

"It's Maria Diaz!" she said, looking across the table at a puzzled Graham. "My partner and I were having lunch in Tampa a couple of days ago when this girl rushed into the cafe. She'd run away from a yacht anchored in the harbor, fearing for her life. She said she'd been kidnapped."

Graham sat speechless as Miranda told him Maria's story. How a young boy named Xander had saved her.

"Where is she now?" asked Graham.

"She's staying at the Sirens of the Deep mermaid camp near Tampa. She desperately wants to return home to Panama, so I'm trying to sort that out with Immigration, since she has no passport. A friend at Homeland Security said it shouldn't be a problem, since our boss has gone up the food chain to get things expedited."

Graham leaned back. "I have an idea how I might help. I'll be returning to Panama in a couple of days. Maybe I can escort her back? You can vouch for me to her family." He paused. "One less thing for you to worry about."

Miranda blew out a breath. "That would be amazing, Graham! Thank you. I have to call the camp director with the good news!"

The waiter appeared, scanning their empty plates.

"Do you have room for dessert, by chance?" he said, smiling.

"Sure. Why not?" she said, although truth be told, she could think of several reasons.

Miranda filled Graham in on everything that had happened in recent days: Maria Diaz's lucky escape from the yacht. Trixie Monroe's mermaid shop. Georgia's camp and the campers with tattoos. The kidnapped girls discovered on the freighter, and Lila Bjorg.

"What we still don't know is how all these things are connected," said Miranda, exasperated.

As the evening wore on and the wine flowed, Miranda's mind turned from mermaids and kidnappings to Graham and their own history. Things began to get fuzzy as she went from merely buzzed to something more.

"I'm really tired. I think it's time to go home," she said.

Graham, who wanted the night to last longer, saw how exhausted she was, as well as how much wine she'd consumed. He was concerned this could take them down a dangerous path.

He nodded to the waiter to bring the check and reached for his wallet.

"No, no . . . this is my treat," she said, her words slurred. "I invited you, remember?" She was leaning against his shoulder, unsteady. "This is bish-ness," she emphasized, reaching into her purse, fumbling, and dropping her wallet on the floor.

The waiter picked it up and gave it to Miranda. Graham handed him his credit card and, taking the opportunity, took Miranda's car keys from her purse.

They left the restaurant soon after.

Graham led her to the passenger door of her red Audi.

She looked at him, confused. "What are you doing?"

"Saving you from a DUI."

"Oh," she mumbled, and plopped down in the passenger seat.

Graham buckled her seat belt and kissed her on the cheek, then got into the driver's seat and started the car.

Chapter 41

Destina Walker held Maria Diaz's hand as she walked up to the entrance to the administration office. She opened the door and guided the girl into the reception area and motioned for her to sit down, smiling as she held up her index finger, gesturing to Maria she'd be right back.

Maria watched as Destina knocked on the camp director's office door and cracked it open.

"Ms. Georgia, Maria's back from our tour."

"How is she?" Georgia whispered, peeking over Destina's shoulder.

"She's fine. But she misses her mother."

"Ah, of course. Understandable."

Georgia opened her door wide and followed Destina to the reception area, sitting down next to Maria.

"Como esta, Maria?" asked Georgia.

Maria smiled. "Muy bien, gracias." But the tone in her soft voice suggested she was anything but fine.

"I have some good news for you," said Georgia, taking Maria's hand. "I called your mother and told her that you were here, safe and sound." She paused, watching the girl's expression brighten.

"Mama?" she squealed. "Mama?"

"Yes," said Georgia, nodding and patting her hand. "Now that you're here, I'll call her back so you can talk to her. She's eager to hear your voice. I'm told we'll be sending you home soon."

Georgia wasn't sure Maria understood what she was saying, but Maria's tight hug was enough.

"Muchas gracias. Muchas gracias." Tears welled up in her dark eyes. "Illyana?"

Georgia and Destina shared a puzzled look.

"Illyana?" asked Georgia.

"Amigo. Friend." Then she grimaced. "Ella esta enojada conmigo," she said, leaving both the camp director and her secretary clueless as to what she'd just said.

"Let's call your mother."

"Mama, Mama, Mama," said an emotional Maria as soon as they'd connected. "I'm so sorry, Mama. I didn't mean . . ."

"Don't worry, my sweet girl. I'm just happy you are safe."

The line went quiet until Maria heard a familiar voice come on the line.

"Illyana?" she shrieked.

"Maria! I'm so happy to hear you're safe. We have so much to talk about when you come home. I'm sorry I didn't go with you. I will never let us be apart again," cried Illyana.

"Si. Si, Illyana. Muchas mermaids," said Maria.

Her mother returned. "Maria, we will see you soon. I love you. Please put Ms. Holmes back on the phone."

Georgia took the phone and said, "I'm here, Ms. Diaz."

"Silvia, please, Ms. Holmes. I am so grateful to you. I don't know how to thank you."

"She's a wonderful young lady, Silvia. I am happy I was able to help."

The two women said their good-byes and ended the call.

"Looks like you might have a welcome home celebration, Maria," said Georgia, looking into Maria's enchanting eyes. "And perhaps one day you and Illyana can come to Sirens of the Deep together and swim with the mermaids."

Maria giggled. "Si, Señora Holmes. Gracias."

Miranda bolted upright in bed. Confused. She scanned her bedroom.

What's making all that racket?

Then she realized the pounding was coming from her front door. She looked at her fully dressed body. Her dress crumpled. Her head throbbing.

"Graham?" she muttered as the fog of last night's dinner broke through. "Graham?" she said, nervously patting the empty space next to her.

She twisted herself out of bed and wobbled to the stairs, gripping the railing. The pounding continued as she peeked into the kitchen, searching for Graham. But he was nowhere to be found.

She opened the front door just as Matt's fist was about to pound again.

"Matt. What's wrong?" Her brows were scrunched, her throat parched.

"What's wrong? What's wrong?" he huffed. Unbelievable. "What's wrong is that I've been trying to call you." He shook his head, surveying her from her bare feet to her crinkled dress, and ending at her bloodshot eyes. He took a calming breath, then angled his head toward the wooden swing on the porch and her shoes beneath it.

"Oh," she said. "I took them off last night."

"I've been trying to reach you since last night. I left messages on your cell phone, even on your house phone. I've been a wreck all night worrying about you." He paused, waiting for an explanation. An apology.

"What time is it?"

Matt checked his watch.

"Eight o'clock. In the morning!" he emphasized. "I drove by your house late last night and saw your car parked out front. A dim light showed through the transom over the door and a light was on upstairs. I figured you must be asleep, or . . ." He didn't finish his thought. "So, I went home." He took another breath. "I was trying to reach you to tell you what I found out late last night."

It was too much, too early, for Miranda to manage right then. She wasn't sure if Graham was anywhere in the house, or if she'd been dreaming. It didn't matter at this point. If he was there, Matt would just have to deal with it.

"Come in, Matt." She held the door open for him. "Would you mind making some coffee while I take a shower? Yesterday was a strange day." And the night even stranger.

As she walked up the stairs, Matt watched her closely.

"Did you sleep in your clothes?"

Miranda turned around and shrugged, then climbed the stairs, leaving a suspicious Matt to make the coffee.

"You know we still have a lot of unanswered questions," he reminded her when she returned to the kitchen. Refreshed, but still not quite herself.

Thoughts of Graham merged with her sense of guilt as she studied Matt. The last thing she remembered before the pounding of Matt's fist on her door a few minutes ago was sitting on the porch swing with Graham the night before.

What happened in the hours between midnight and this morning?

She groaned, "I know. I know." She pressed her fingers against her forehead. "Let's start over. Morning, Matt." She smiled, pouring herself a cup of coffee and taking a sip. "Now that's great coffee!" she said, pointing to her cup.

Matt stared at her, clueless.

"Harrison Ford. Sitting at the table in the Amish family's kitchen in the predawn hours. The movie *Witness*?"

Matt shook his head, battling the anger and frustration swimming inside him.

She took her coffee to the table and sat beside him.

"So, what did you find out last night that was so urgent?"

He stared at his hands before looking up at her again.

"Brenda Sinclair called me late yesterday," he began. "Distraught. Worried about her boss. She said two men came to the shop yesterday looking for her. She described one of them as 'a bulldozer.' " He paused. "The bulldozer's name is Python." Again he paused. "The other is named Mano."

Miranda's eyebrows arched.

"Brenda said they got angry that Trixie wasn't in the shop. And she overheard Python mention the name Castro."

"One of the other judges," murmured Miranda. "The mean uncle that Xander said had kidnapped Maria?"

"Not sure," Matt said, getting up to refill his cup.

"Brenda said Trixie called while the men were there, but she pretended she was talking to you, as if you were a customer. Hoping Trixie would get the hint that something was wrong at the shop."

"What do you think's going on?"

"Whatever it is, we're starting to connect more of the dots," said Matt.

"You're right, Matt. It's all about connections!"

"What do you mean?"

She got up and pulled a legal pad from a kitchen drawer and took it back to the table. She began drawing overlapping circles, writing names in each.

"These circles contain the information we've collected so far, Matt."

Matt nodded without fully comprehending what she was doing. He watched as she added names in the intersecting circles. Pointing. Muttering each name as she added it. Double-checking that she hadn't forgotten anyone, or any detail, critical to the outcome.

"Looks like a Venn diagram."

"It is. We see whose names intersect and then we can figure out what roles they play in this puzzle of ours."

She tapped the pencil against her cheek. What do they have in common besides mermaids?

After a few minutes of scribbling, she shoved the paper in front of Matt.

He grinned at her. "Now we're finally getting somewhere!"

Chapter 42

"Okay, girls," said Georgia, as the four girls followed her from the parking lot to the campgrounds. "Time to get showered and into fresh clothes. We'll stop in my office first. I want you to meet someone."

The girls, soiled and in need of just about everything, and understanding little of what the director was explaining, clumped together behind her and held each other's hands, still frightened by their confinement in the container on the freighter. Fortunately, they'd had the pizza while they were waiting to be transported to the camp.

Destina Walker instantly stood up when Georgia stepped through the door, the girls trailing her. She grimaced at their soiled clothes and bruises.

"Oh, my," mumbled Destina. "What have you here, Miss Georgia?"

"Do you happen to speak Spanish, Destina?" asked Georgia.

"Un poco," smiled Destina.

"Wonderful! Please explain to them that you'll take them to their cottage to get cleaned up and then you'll show them around the camp."

"Well, I'm not sure I know that much Spanish, but I'll do my best," sighed Destina.

Della nodded as Destina summarized the plan. Looking around the room, the girl was awestruck by the colorful mural of sea creatures on the walls. Her eyes glowed like Christmas lights as she giggled at the playful dolphins, bright coral seashells, and tropical fish in rainbow colors. Her gaze locked on a wall clock with a voluptuous mermaid on the dial. She blushed and abruptly turned away.

Destina led them down the pebbled pathway, under the archway, and into the magic. The girls oohed and ahhed as they passed the large swimming pool where some of the campers wore mermaid tails, ready for swim practice.

After they had showered and dressed in clean clothes that Georgia had set on the dresser in the cottage, Destina ushered them to the cafeteria where a buffet service was spread out on a long table, their eyes following the swarm of mermaids who had just finished eating and were leaving the cafeteria.

A soft groan broke through the stillness in the lower cabin of the Mermaid Fantasea II. Xander put his book down on the coffee table in the club room and rushed to the back bedroom where Mirakakoo had been recovering from her surgery.

He knelt down on the floor at her bedside. "Mirakakoo, are you okay?" Xander said in his softest voice, stroking her silky, black hair.

She opened her dark almond eyes and stared at him, then smiled.

"Xander," she sighed. "What has happened to me?" She felt her stomach and the bandage and winced. The pain was better, but not gone. "Help me up," she said.

But Xander shook his head.

"You must rest. You had something inside you. The doctor removed it. You need to take medicine to clear up the infection." He paused. "Rest. I will get you something to eat."

"No," demanded Mirakakoo. "It's better for me to get up and move around. I need to get stronger."

Xander stood up and took her hand, easing her to the edge of bed before helping her stand. He wasn't sure what lay ahead for them as the yacht continued toward Longboat Key.

"How do you feel?" he asked, rubbing her arm. "I have a plan and need you to be strong."

"Better. Still a little sore." She took a couple of pain pills from the bottle on the bedside table and swallowed them with some water. "Take me upstairs. I want to see the blue sky and soaring birds."

He held her by the arm and wrapped his other arm around her narrow waist and helped her stand.

"You are so thin, Mirakakoo. You must eat. You haven't eaten in days."

She smiled. "Okay. We can eat up on the deck and you can tell me all that's happened."

Once Mirakakoo was settled, Xander went downstairs to fix them a sandwich and a pitcher of lemonade. He carried everything up the stairs and set the tray down on the table beside Mirakakoo, who was gazing up at the blue sky. He poured each of them a lemonade and handed one to Mirakakoo, who took a sip.

"Muy bien, Xander. You're so good to me."

He sat down and handed her the mesh bag.

"I saw this in a shop at the harbor in Tampa. I hope you like it."

Mirakakoo opened the bag and took out the smooth, oval stone, tracing the inscription painted on its surface with her slender fingers.

"Cree en los milagros," he said. "Believe in miracles."

"Believe in miracles," she repeated in English. "Hermosa, Xander. Gracias."

Their eyes locked. He squeezed her hand and whispered, "You must believe in miracles, as I do now, Mirakakoo."

He stretched his neck toward her and kissed her on her creamy, pale cheek. Then they leaned back to watch the seagulls flying overhead.

Chapter 43

The Sarasota Yacht Club was humming with preparations for Fashionista Night, a fashion-show fund-raiser in support of the Children's Art Center which brought together the wealthiest and most influential people in the community. Erika Morales had been asked to chair the posh event, the fourth year Erika had agreed to do it, and, she had decided, her last.

Despite her lavish designer gowns, expensive jewelry, and Tuscan-style mansion, Erika Morales longed for a simpler, quieter life, outside the glitz and glamour of Sarasota's elite. Her husband's status as a world-renowned plastic surgeon and his need to keep up appearances had forced her to play the role she'd grown into, but she knew her daughter never wanted anything to do with their lavish lifestyle. "Shallow and materialistic," she muttered to herself, remembering Miranda's disdain.

Erika drummed her perfectly red-painted nails on the crisp white tablecloth in the club's dining room, which looked out at the yachts scattered about the marina. The tightness in her stomach made her second-guess her decision to ask Miranda to join her for lunch. The long pause on Miranda's end of the phone had signaled this wasn't going to be a pleasant meeting. But Miranda had begrudgingly agreed to meet her mother at the club, where her parents had been longtime members, and where her father had kept his boat since she was a child.

The waiter came to Erika's table just as Miranda entered the dining room.

The hostess led Miranda to the small private room where her mother was checking her iPhone.

Erika remained seated. "I wasn't sure you'd come."

The heaviness in her mother's voice loosened the tightness that had been choking Miranda on her drive over the Ringling Bridge to the club. She picked up the starched white napkin and lay it in her lap, brushing it like it was a wrinkle in her skirt, then looked at her mother. The sparkle and intensity she expected to see in her mother's eyes was missing, disappointment and remorse in their place. She looked years older than she remembered, despite having had every type of cosmetic procedure available to delay getting old for as long as possible. Never under her husband's scalpel, however.

"You said you had something on your mind, Mother?" Miranda said, harnessing the contempt that had built up inside her over the years. Although she had buried it by cutting off contact with her parents, seeing her mother's troubled face shook her.

Erika sighed, fidgeting with the napkin.

"What is it, Mother?" Miranda said, hands clasped as she stretched her arms across the table. The muscles tightened around her neck. No matter how much she blamed her parents for her sister's suicide twenty years ago, Erika was still her mother. Unexpectedly, the fear in Erika's eyes pushed Miranda's anger underground, temporarily, at least. She knew it would surface as soon as they parted, but for now, her mother's obvious distress trumped her own hatred.

Erika's eyes suddenly brimmed with tears. She dabbed at them with her napkin, then pressed it against her mouth, muffling an awkward whimper as she looked across at her daughter.

"I'm sorry," mumbled Erika, her voice thick with grief. "I'm so sorry about . . . everything. I should have stood up for you and Farrah when you were young. I should have—"

"Stop it, Mother," Miranda said, instinctively taking her mother's hand, then quickly letting it go. "Those days are past." She momentarily looked down at her lap, knowing this meeting wasn't easy for either of them. Then she looked into her mother's painful gaze. "What's wrong? Why did you want to meet after all this time?"

Erika dabbed her tears and leaned back in her chair, sighing deeply. She stared at Miranda for a few long, silent moments.

"I believe your father's gotten himself into a major mess," she finally confessed, her voice raspy.

Miranda sat up straight. Her mother had her full attention. "What kind of mess?"

Erika took a deep breath and lowered her eyes before looking directly into Miranda's.

"A dangerous one. The work he's been doing in deprived, third-world countries is"—she paused, taking a deeper breath—"is just a cover."

"What?" gasped Miranda. "A cover? For what?"

Erika wondered how to tell her daughter what she'd only recently discovered herself.

"I'm so sorry for everything, Miranda. I've never been strong enough to stand up to him."

Miranda was growing impatient. "Forget about that now, Mother. What do you mean by saying that Daddy's work has been a cover?"

"It's so complicated," said Erika, tears starting up again. "Your father and Peter Millstine have gotten involved with a group of nefarious characters who will stop at nothing to get what they want."

Miranda was stunned by her mother's disclosure. "I . . . I don't understand."

Erika sighed again, shaking her head.

"It's a twisted, ugly story." She paused. "I sensed something had changed when your father began getting phone calls from Central America. At first I thought it was related to his volunteer work there." She began fidgeting with her napkin, averting her eyes, too ashamed to look at her daughter.

"Just start somewhere, Mother," she said, trying to remove the urgency from her tone.

Erika took another deep breath. "It all seemed to start as a small favor."

Miranda's eyes stayed glued on her mother, waiting for something that would make sense. "What kind of favor, Mother?" she asked, her impatience gaining ground.

"A man he met in Central America contacted him about forming a partnership. It all seemed so simple at the beginning. But as time passed, your father became more and more agitated, isolating himself from me." She paused, struggling to look at Miranda. "Turns out the man is the head of powerful cartel in Brazil connected to others all over the world. I think they're involved with smuggling. Somehow your father's involved, but I don't know exactly how, and to what extent."

"Jesus, Mother. What are you saying?" exclaimed Miranda.

Erika finally looked directly into her daughter's eyes. "I don't know the whole story, Miranda. I've overheard bits and pieces from time to time when he's on the phone, or when Peter Millstine stops by. I don't know who all is involved."

"What have you heard that makes you think he's directly involved with smugglers?"

Erika shrugged helplessly. She looked more vulnerable than Miranda had ever seen, and suddenly she felt real pity for her mother, seeing how frail and unguarded she was.

"I don't quite know what to say, Mother," Miranda muttered.

Erika began to sob, and Miranda moved her chair closer to put her arm around her.

"It's okay, Mother. I'm sure there's a logical explanation," Miranda said, although she didn't believe this. "But you have to tell me everything you know."

When Erika regained her composure, she took another deep breath and dabbed her smudged eyes with the napkin. "I'm so, so sorry, Miranda."

"Just tell me what made you worried enough to seek me out."

"When your father left the cocktail reception abruptly the other night, I found out that the emergency he told me he had to attend to involved a young girl. A close friend of his feared it was a ruptured appendix, and he only trusted your father to do the surgery."

Miranda nodded. "Well, he is a surgeon, Mother. Even if his specialty is cosmetic surgery."

"I know. However, when he got home, I heard him yelling downstairs at someone on the phone. At first I thought he was talking to Peter, explaining why he'd had to leave the party. I couldn't follow it all, but I heard him say that he'd just removed a hummingbird that had pierced the patient's insides." She searched her daughter's eyes. "Then he blasted, 'This has got to stop, Castro. You and Peter better sort this out. And soon!' "

Miranda sat up straight in her chair. She needed to stay calm so she could keep her mother calm and focused.

"But why do you think it has something to do with a smuggling cartel?" Miranda asked.

Again Erika paused, trying to get her thoughts in order. She took a drink of water from the glass the waiter had just refilled.

"I heard him say, 'What the hell is going on down there? I thought we agreed that using the girls is too risky. I agreed to do it one time only! As a favor! It's not enough that Peter has an obsession with mermaids. You both have to take everything to extremes.' Then he slammed down the phone and I closed the bedroom door. He didn't come to bed for some time, and I pretended I was asleep when he did."

She stared at Miranda.

Miranda shook her head. Everything her mother was telling her was preposterous. Unthinkable. Outrageous.

"This can't be true, Mother. Maybe you misunderstood. You were upstairs and he was on the phone, downstairs."

Regret distorted Erika's features, seeing how much Miranda had changed—matured. She was stunning. Suddenly, unexpectedly, for the first time she felt proud to be her mother.

"I'm scared, Miranda. About your father. You. The future. There's so much you don't know."

Miranda could do nothing but stare up at the crystal chandelier hanging above them.

Miranda was still reeling from the shock of what her mother had confessed to her, but she needed to file it away in another of her mental compartments for now.

She wanted Matt and Graham to have a chance to talk a bit more before Graham flew home. More than that, she believed Graham had a lot to offer with his expertise in ancient cult practices and mermaid lore. The two men had met unexpectedly, and only briefly. Though Matt had strongly objected, she finally convinced him that Graham might be able to add some clarity to their case.

Graham was already seated at the table in the stunning dining room of Marina Jack, gazing out the window at a flock of seagulls that had just flown across Sarasota Bay when they arrived. He instantly stood up, smiled, and reached out his hand to Matt, giving Miranda a peck on the cheek before they all took their seats.

"Glad you could come, Graham. I wanted Matt to get to know you a little better before you go back to Panama."

She watched the two alpha males sizing each other up. This was a bad idea, she thought.

Matt cleared his throat, then managed a fake smile.

Graham smiled politely.

"Also," she said, clearing her throat, "since you've offered to escort Maria back to Panama, you should at least have some background information." She paused, shifting her eyes to Matt and then back to Graham. "I'm sure you understand that whatever I say is highly confidential, Graham. Nobody knows the details of our case except Matt, me, and our captain."

She glanced at a stone-faced Matt and took a deep breath.

"We're breaking protocol. Big-time. But I think your expertise might be of some help."

"I understand, Miranda."

"We think a powerful cartel is operating here in Sarasota. A cartel involving human trafficking and the smuggling of priceless antiquities. We believe it's tied to cartels in Central and South America, and perhaps other countries as well. We just don't know."

"What does that have to do with your dead mermaid?" Graham asked.

"I have reason to believe Peter Millstine, and my father, might be involved somehow with the cartel."

Graham gasped. "That's absurd. Your father, the humanitarian? You must be mistaken!"

"You never told me that, Miranda!" said Matt, miffed.

"I just learned about it from my mother. She confessed she was worried my father had gotten himself mixed up in something dangerous. She overheard him on the phone after the cocktail party, talking about removing an object from a girl's stomach. She said she had never heard him in such a rage."

"What the hell, Miranda?" said Graham, sitting up straight. "I can't believe your father would be involved with cartels. It's ludicrous. What role, if any, do you think mermaids might play in all of this?"

"The mermaid connection is really difficult to piece together."

"Could it just be a coincidence that your victim was wearing a mermaid costume? Perhaps your case is completely separate from what your mother overheard?"

"We're convinced the mermaid theme is somehow linked directly to the cartel's activities," said Matt. "We just don't know how, or why. The most compelling evidence is Maria, the girl you're escorting back to Panama."

"Ah. What about her?"

"Long story short," said Matt, "she told us she had been kidnapped in Panama while watching for mermaids near a restaurant called Bolivar Bistro."

"Was she wearing a mermaid costume?"

"No," said Miranda. "But the fact that she was kidnapped and taken on board a yacht named the Mermaid Fantasea seems like more than mere coincidence."

"And then we learned there's more than one yacht with that name, and that Maria loved mermaids," said Matt.

Graham shook his head as if to rearrange the information so it would make more sense to him. Then his eyes suddenly turned dark.

"This is weird, but I listened to a discussion a couple of my colleagues were engaged in while we were having lunch in the university cafeteria, before I left for my trip here. One of the professors explained that the body of a young girl had been found in a dumpster on one of the small islands in the archipelago, around Bocas del Toro. During the autopsy, a tiny muslin bag was discovered inside her vagina. The bag contained a small black pearl, later identified as one stolen from a private vault in Japan." He thought about it. "I don't recall the name of the pearl, but apparently it was extremely valuable, and quite rare."

"The Hanadama pearl!" exclaimed Miranda.

"What?" said Graham.

"The black pearl found inside the Lido mermaid. It was thought to have been stolen from the Pearl Science Laboratory of Japan. Turned out it wasn't."

"That's right!" said Matt, astonished. "The Truly black pearl is supposedly a rare pearl harvested from the Akoya oyster."

"Whoa!" said Graham. "How did you know the one in the victim wasn't the—"

"Hanadama pearl," finished Miranda. "Because an expert from Japan flew here specifically to examine it and concluded it wasn't the one stolen from their vault."

"Extraordinary," said Graham, overwhelmed by the complexity of their investigation. "So, what do you know so far? Let's start there."

"Your Venn diagram, Miranda," said Matt.

Miranda nodded, removing the folded drawing from her tote bag. Shoving the place-setting pieces aside, she spread it open on the table.

"Consider this," she said, pointing to various intersecting circles. "Lila Bjorg, one of the campers at Sirens of the Deep, admitted she knew the dead mermaid, Nina Jorgensen, when we showed her a picture. Apparently she and Nina were foster children from the time they were toddlers.

"Then one day a woman came to the foster home in Denmark where the two girls were living. The foster mother and the woman talked in whispers before the woman gave the foster mother a bulging, white envelope. I imagine it contained money in exchange for the foster mother allowing her to take Lila and Nina away with her. They were just nine years old when they were taken."

"Did she say who the woman was?" asked Graham, looking between Miranda and Matt.

"No, but Lila told us that when she saw the female judge onstage during the closing ceremony at Sirens of the Deep, she recognized the judge as the woman who had taken her and Nina that day—Gabriella Navarre," said Miranda, pointing to one of the names in the intersecting circles. "That's why she collapsed."

"So the shock of seeing Gabriella is what traumatized her?"

"Yes. And if my gut is accurate, Trixie Monroe was also involved somehow." Miranda paused again. "That was the reason Lila bristled when Trixie showed up at the hospital to take her home with her."

"Hello," said the waiter, smiling at the threesome.

"Give us a minute, if you don't mind," Miranda smiled.

"Of course."

Graham sat dumbstruck as Miranda went through each of the circles, jabbing her index finger at the critical areas of the Venn diagram—the points where the circles intersected.

At the end of her presentation, Miranda sighed and leaned back in her chair, her mind reeling.

The waiter returned a few moments later to their table. "Hello, again. What can I get you?"

Matt looked at Graham and Miranda. “Three beers?”

Miranda checked her watch and abruptly stood up. “Sorry. I’ve got an appointment to keep.”

Matt’s eyes narrowed. “Where are you going?”

“I just have some things to clear up,” she said vaguely. “You two can share the third beer. I’ll pay the check on my way out.”

“Make that two beers,” said Matt.

She looked over her shoulder as she walked away. *No need to tell them I have a date with Peter Millstine.*

Chapter 44

The eighteen-by-twenty-foot tank rivaled those found at Sarasota's Mote Marine Laboratory & Aquarium. That it was located in someone's private domain was astounding.

It was huge enough to satisfy Peter Millstine's obsession. His passion for sea life and mermaids had only grown over the years, his commitment to them beyond anyone's comprehension.

Peter's chief pleasure was his family of sea creatures. He was captivated by their graceful movement, their varied shapes and colors. He watched them for hours from his cordovan leather armchair in his private enclave. Not only had he spent hundreds of thousands of dollars to have his aquarium custom-designed and expertly installed, he also insisted that the water be free of harmful chemicals, competing with Mother Nature to maintain a pristine aquatic environment. He gloated that he was doing a better job than she was. Especially considering the increased incidence of the harmful algae blooms that cause severe damage to Florida's sea life, when red tide toxins kill not only fish but also marine mammals and birds.

He was grateful that his good friend, Fernando Morales, knew precisely where to find such water to fill the enormous tank—the freshwaters of Puerto Williams in the Chilean Patagonia, near the tip of South America. From day one of the aquarium's completion, Peter had embarked on the complicated arrangements to have that freshwater delivered to his home on a regular basis. The huge expense was worth it. He had learned a long time ago, when he was an orphan rescued from the rough neighborhood he'd wandered as a child by an older, wealthy couple, that one had to take responsibility. The couple had provided him with everything he could have wanted, or imagined. Except love.

Now that he was a billionaire, having followed his father's example of duping people out of their hard-earned money and investing it for his own benefit, he was willing to spend his fortune on whatever he craved.

And he craved mermaids.

Nobody, not even his close friend, Fernando, knew about the private sanctuary in the basement of his palatial mansion overlooking the turquoise Gulf of Mexico. Not even after Fernando had questioned Peter as to why he needed such large amounts of the precious water. Only the builder who'd designed and installed the aquarium knew it existed, and Peter made sure the plans the builder was supposed to submit for approval for the renovations were destroyed. Nothing was more precious to Peter than privacy, and only money—lots of it—could achieve that privilege. He often thought he would go berserk if he didn't have this retreat, a place to go when his partners enraged him—a place to soothe his tattered nerves.

He reminded himself that he had to take his granite bear out of the glass case upstairs and bring it down to his sanctuary with his other treasures. Stroke it as he whispered the Mighty Bear chant and admired his collection. The mermaid belt, however, must stay locked in the safe upstairs until the right time came to move it.

The past week had been especially stressful for him. The tragic death of one of his beloved creatures had unleashed a trail of sorrow. He'd been heartbroken and infuriated as he watched the whole catastrophe erupt that fateful day.

If only he had not stolen the harpoon off Mano's yacht. He was jealous that Trixie had given Mano the antique weapon when she knew how much he loved such artifacts.

If only Python hadn't taken it from the mount on the wall of the Mermaid Fantasea II that fateful day, panicked that Nina would escape, and used the harpoon to strike his beloved mermaid when she jumped overboard during their special excursion. Her final escape from his mermaid menagerie, and her prison.

"Rest in peace, my little darling," he had said softly, tears rolling down his cheeks as the tide swept her away. "What better place for you than to return to the underwater spirit world where you belong."

He had kicked himself for his poor judgment for granting the inquisitive professor's request to see Masimi Aqua's mermaid belt. While he was ecstatic that Dr. Waterman might authenticate the talisman, the visit had upset him more than he realized. He felt violated. He felt he had opened a dangerous window to some unknown danger.

Even more troubling was learning that Fernando had a homicide detective for a daughter, who'd so arrogantly interrogated the professor about fetishes, even suggesting that his interest in mermaids was somehow sexually deviant.

Peter got up and poured himself another cognac, then returned to his favorite chair to marvel at his most recent acquisition, replacing the one he had tragically lost to the sea.

He pressed his hands to the sides of his head to stop the throbbing migraine. The painful headaches were becoming more frequent. He knew they were caused by stress, and his idiot partners, Castro Montoya and Mano Sorkin.

He pushed the button on the CD player next to his chair and turned up the volume, resting his balding head on the back of his padded chair as the Queen of the Night's coloratura aria filled the room, helping him forget his suffering. Shivers ran down his spine as she reached that exquisite moment that only the most daring coloratura sopranos can deliver well.

But even this could not erase his anguish over losing his most beloved Nina.

ଓଃ

Miranda hadn't scheduled an appointment with Peter Millstine on purpose. Surprise can be a detective's best weapon. Her gut told her he would not be an easy mark. He was reclusive, to put it mildly. Weird, for sure. Dangerous? She'd find out soon enough.

As she approached Peter's Tuscan-style mansion, a sense of doom swept over her. But she shrugged it off. She'd been face-to-face in battle with miscreants far more threatening than Peter during her career. She had awards to prove her bravery and accomplishments.

Miranda slowly drove her Audi up the wide driveway, admiring the stately blue heron metal sculpture positioned at the base of the curved stairway leading to the wide portico at the top. A black Porsche and a white Mercedes were parked in front of the mansion.

Looks like he has company.

She got out and climbed the staircase and rang the doorbell.

Trixie Monroe's eyes almost popped out of their sockets when she swung open the door to find Miranda's equally shocked eyes looking back at her.

"Detective Morales," she gasped, pulling back her narrow shoulders. "What are you doing here?"

Before she could answer, Peter stepped in front of Trixie and reached his hand out to Miranda.

"So good of you to stop by, Miranda," he said, the chill in his voice belying his words.

Miranda sensed she had interrupted some clandestine meeting.

"Come in, come in," said Peter, guiding Miranda into the foyer as Trixie stepped back to let them pass.

Trixie decided she'd stay to see what the detective was after, following Peter and Miranda into the kitchen.

Miranda recognized a painting by Joan Miró along one distant wall. Another by Jackson Pollock, and still another by Mark Rothko. The marble floors and Oriental carpets looked elegant and expensive. Her eyes fixed on a glass curio cabinet just inside the dining room. Then she noticed a huge, floor-to-ceiling tapestry covering most of the long hallway below the staircase, presumably leading to the bedrooms. She counted at least three closed doors upstairs as she glanced up.

"May I offer you something to drink, Miranda?" Peter said, motioning for her to sit on one of the stools along the kitchen island.

Miranda shook her head.

Trixie sat down on another vacant stool while Peter refilled her wineglass. He held the bottle up to Miranda. "Sure I can't tempt you?"

"No, thanks," she said. "I'm on duty." She glanced through the large doors leading to the landscaped yard. "Nice swimming pool. Do you swim?"

Peter cleared his throat.

"I used to love scuba-diving when I was young. But now I swim to keep my arthritis at bay. Seems to come with old age." He laughed unconvincingly.

Miranda smiled.

He poured himself a whiskey and motioned for the two women to follow him to the living room. Miranda sat on the sofa, while Peter and Trixie sat in the two armchairs facing her. Miranda leaned forward with her elbows on her knees. "You have a magnificent home, Mr. Millstine."

"Thank you—but please call me Peter. May I call you Miranda?"

"Yes. Of course."

She cleared her throat as she surveyed her adversaries. "I must say, I was surprised to see that both of you served as judges at the Sirens of the Deep celebration. Have you known Georgia Holmes very long?"

"No," said Peter a bit too quickly. "I've known Ms. Holmes for just a short time."

"What about you, Ms. Monroe?" Miranda said.

Trixie sipped her wine and said nothing, her unflinching, green eyes fixed on Miranda.

"Trixie and I first met at an international arts and antique show in France," said Peter, "more than twenty years ago. We realized instantly we had similar interests, and we bonded. Quickly." Our relationship has continued to this day as our mutual interests grew."

Peter's lips trembled as he smiled through his lies.

"Mutual interests?" asked Miranda, her eyes darting between Trixie and Peter, sensing that important details were being left unsaid. "Can you elaborate?" she asked pointedly, leaning back as if she had all the time in the world to hear their stories.

Trixie's gaze turned threatening. She glared at Miranda, then at Peter, then back at Miranda. "Mermaids, of course," said Trixie flatly.

"Excuse me?" said Miranda.

"You heard me, Detective."

Peter pulled a crisp, white handkerchief from his trouser pocket and dabbed a spot of whiskey he'd dripped on his shirt. Blushing.

"Seems like rather a unique interest."

Trixie didn't flinch.

"We discovered we both enjoyed the legends surrounding them." She paused. "I had just begun my foray into fashion design and hoped to open my own studio one day." She forced a smile. "When I mentioned it to Peter, he said he'd be happy to help me achieve my goal."

"How . . . fortunate," said Miranda, skeptical. "I've often heard that artists have to rely on wealthy benefactors if they hope to make a living in the competitive arts market."

Miranda heard a low sound from Trixie. Or maybe she was just imagining it. The more she engaged with the designer, the deeper her suspicions grew. From their first meeting at the mermaid shop, to Trixie's insistence that Lila go home with her from the hospital after her collapse onstage—something just didn't feel right.

Trixie's defensive posture started to ease as the wine took effect.

"I was working in Paris at the time, but Peter and I kept in touch. We realized we loved Florida. He had already established himself as a successful businessman, and he said he was looking to expand." She glanced at Peter and smiled. "And thanks to his guidance and support, I was able to open my first design shop in Bradenton. As my business grew, I decided to move Mermaid's Delight to Tampa, where I could not only custom-design mermaid costumes, but also sell countless accessories along with them."

"Florida's a far cry from Paris," said Miranda. "It must have been quite an adjustment for you."

Trixie's gaze shifted past Miranda, out to the gardens beyond the wide, living room window. She took a deep breath, sighed, and returned her cold eyes to Miranda.

"Life can take unexpected twists and turns, Detective. Lead you to magical places, if you're open to possibilities," she said wistfully. "I believe destiny led me to Peter."

Peter was growing impatient with the detective's questions.

"So, Miranda, what is it exactly that brings you to my home this afternoon?"

"I was in the neighborhood and took the chance you'd be home," Miranda said. "I thought since you offered to show Professor Waterman your talisman, you might be gracious enough to grant me the same honor."

"Ah, the Professor. He did seem to be quite enamored with it."

"I apologize for having to cancel our earlier meeting at Casey's Cabana. I guess I hoped you wouldn't mind an impromptu visit." She smiled. "This is probably a once-in-a-lifetime opportunity to see such a rare object." She hoped her subservience would appeal to the collector's vanity.

But the atmosphere in the room had chilled significantly. The polite cordiality Peter had displayed when he first welcomed Miranda had turned hostile.

The ringing of her phone intensified the tension.

"Excuse me," said Miranda, checking caller ID. "I apologize, but I must take this call."

She stepped out into the hallway as she listened to FBI Special Agent Damien McMillon report on what he'd learned about the freighter seized and searched at the Tampa marina.

"The cargo was being shipped to a company called PM Importers—a business belonging to a Peter Millstine. When we opened one of the crates, we found a corpse inside." He paused. "All the organs were missing."

Miranda clapped a hand over her mouth to muffle her gasp. *Jesus!*

"Miniature figurines and priceless gemstones filled the body cavity. Apparently the crate had been picked up from a wholesale company in Miami called Mermaid Fantasea Corporation. The label identified the sender as Gabriella Navarre. That's all we know so far."

Miranda needed time to recover from this shocking news before rejoining Trixie and Peter.

She lingered in the hallway, pretending to still be on the phone after Agent McMillon had clicked off. She looked at a large tapestry hanging there to distract herself from the gruesome news she'd just received.

A solitary unicorn stood alert in the forest, smaller animals scattered about. Miranda's fingers grazed the smooth, velvety texture of the tapestry's fabric, continuing toward the bound edge on the right side. She felt a small bulge. Curious, she carefully peeked behind the tapestry. A brass medallion, embossed with tiny figures too small for her to identify in the dim light, was fastened to the wall—like a button someone would push, to summon a maid.

Peter's voice called out to her from the living room.

She instinctively let go of the tapestry, allowing it to fall back into position.

"Everything okay?" he called out.

Miranda took a deep breath and stepped back into the room, smiling. She sat down, scanning Trixie and Peter's faces. Her heart was beating faster the more she tried to control its rhythm.

Without preamble, she dived into interrogation mode, making no mention of the shipment and the disemboweled corpse. "Tell me about PM Importers, Gabriella Navarre, and the company in Miami called Mermaid Fantasea Corporation," she said.

Peter's face drained of color, replaced with dread.

Trixie's expression froze as she willed herself not to react. "There's nothing to explain," said Trixie, arrogantly. "Peter's business takes care of importing some of my fashions made abroad into the United States, while Gabriella Navarre markets the merchandise and draws up the agreements between Mermaid's Delight and the buyers. The merchandise is stored in a Miami warehouse until it's time to ship the orders." She challenged Miranda with unblinking, green eyes. "It's as simple as that."

Miranda glared at them, knowing the situation was far from simple.

"I see," she said curtly, realizing she and Peter had set up a roadblock. "Well, it sounds like quite a convenient partnership. Not so easy to come by these days, where everything seems to be done through the Internet and complex online networks."

Peter and Trixie shot each other a look, then Peter rose from the sofa.

"I'm afraid you'll have to excuse us, Detective. Trixie and I have a lot of business to tend to," he said gruffly, gripping Miranda's elbow as he led her to the front door, swinging it wide. "I'm afraid your visit has come at a most inopportune time."

"But I haven't seen your talisman," said Miranda, annoyed at having missed the chance to see, firsthand, the mermaid belt Graham had been able to view.

"Perhaps another day," Peter said blandly, knowing it would be over his dead body.

She stared into Peter's unflinching, cold stare. "Thank you for your time, Peter. You have a stunning home," she said in a conciliatory manner. Wishing she had played her cards differently.

Trixie sauntered over and stood beside Peter, venom turning her green eyes dark.

"Oh, by the way," Miranda added, "that tapestry in your hallway is magnificent. Unicorns are so mysterious, don't you think?"

"Good day, Detective," he said scornfully as he shoved her forward, swiftly closing the door behind her.

He twisted around and glared at Trixie. "Now look what you've done! You're going to ruin everything I've worked for!"

"We've worked for. And I told her nothing. Most of what I did say was all lies."

Trixie took a cleansing breath. "Pull yourself together, Peter. You're heading off the deep end, and we have too much to do for the Festival of Dagon on Sunday night."

Peter stormed back to the kitchen to pour himself another drink.

"What about the girls?" he said, his voice tight and edgy.

"Nothing's changed. The girls will be assembled in due course." A fiendish grin glazed her red lips. "It's going to be spectacular! The detective knows nothing. She's just a small bump in the road. Once you settle down, you'll see that everything is going smoothly."

Peter wasn't convinced, and she knew it.

She collected her purse and stopped at the front door. "Just don't do anything stupid!" she declared before leaving.

The scent of her expensive perfume wafted through the foyer and down the hallway to where Peter stood next to the granite island.

"It better be more than fucking spectacular," he mumbled. He drained his glass like it was water and quickly refilled it.

"I'll be happy to be done with the whole lot of them when all this is over!"

Chapter 45

Brenda Sinclair carefully folded the four custom mermaid tails Trixie had told her to label and set them carefully into the proper boxes. Her boss would be picking up the costumes within the hour for the event on Jewfish Key that evening, ushering in a new era for the mermaid corporation. An exciting new enterprise, although Brenda had no details about the plans. Of course, she hadn't been invited; all Trixie had told her was to label the four boxes she'd set on the counter—Dagon, Oannes, Derceto, and Triton—based on the initials Trixie noted on each lid.

From the outset, Brenda had sensed something was deeply troubling her boss. Her usual calm composure and dazzling green of her eyes were missing, replaced by an overall eerie quality when Brenda told her of the unexpected visit by the two strangers who had shown up at the shop yesterday."

"Ah. So that's why you called me 'Miranda.' To warn me something was wrong," said Trixie, tapping her lips with her index finger. She and Gabriella had been tied up most of the day yesterday, ensuring the final arrangements for the festival were coming together as planned. It had been a rough day, so she had shoved Brenda's confusing phone call to the back of her mind.

Trixie Monroe realized what a loyal employee Brenda was, and smiled.

"Thank you, Brenda. I'm sorry you had to experience that episode at the shop. It's all okay." But deep inside, she had her doubts.

Trixie walked briskly to her office and made a phone call. All Brenda could hear was, "I'll bring the boxes to the yacht within the hour. We'll all go together."

The alarm in Trixie's tone worried Brenda enough that she decided to call Detective Morales to let her know something strange was going on. She feared Trixie was in imminent danger.

❧

Matt checked his watch as he and Graham left the Mote Marine Laboratory on Longboat Key, a few miles across the Ringling Bridge from downtown Sarasota. Miranda had wanted the two of them to "bond." Matt was actually surprised at how quickly they had established a friendship. He decided he'd acted childishly, feeling jealous when he'd seen the professor at Miranda's house.

"What do you imagine Miranda's been up to the past couple of hours?" asked Graham.

Matt shrugged. "I know she wanted to talk to Peter Millstine, but she better not have done that without me." He glanced at Graham. "Knowing her commitment to this case, she's probably been slaving in front of her computer, reading up on his mermaid talisman." He smiled wryly. "No doubt she Googled you and found your article on the mermaid belt."

"I hope there's no pop quiz," he said, laughing. "In any case, your investigation seems pretty complicated."

"That's an understatement. But I sense the wagons are beginning to circle and we're getting close to a major breakthrough."

❧

When the two men arrived at Miranda's house, she had just parked her car and was heading up the steps.

"Hey! Where were you? Everything okay?" asked Matt.

She wasn't happy, judging by her pinched mouth and angry eyes. Something had definitely happened since she'd left them at Marina Jack to go her own way.

"Trouble. Big trouble, I'm afraid," she said, stomping up to the front door and unlocking it. "I'll tell you about it once we get inside and get something to drink."

Matt and Graham followed close behind, exchanging a look.

Miranda dropped her purse and keys on the hall table and walked to the kitchen, pulling out a bottle of wine from the fridge.

"I went to Peter's house," she said, while uncorking the wine.

Matt's eyebrows flared up. "Are you kidding me? Don't you think that was a bit—"

"Stupid?" she said, completing his sentence.

"Dangerous, is what I was going to say."

"It had to be done," she declared, leading them to the patio carrying a tray with wineglasses and a bottle of Sauvignon Blanc. "I don't know what's going on, but I'm certain it's malevolent and involves the mermaid enterprise."

She motioned for them to sit in the two matching deck chairs as she set the tray down on the table. She poured each of them a glass of wine, then sat facing them.

"Trixie Monroe was at Peter's when I got there," she began. "Every muscle in her body tightened when she saw me. Something was up, despite Peter's clumsy charade, pretending my visit was a pleasant surprise."

Miranda was interrupted by her phone.

"Morales," she growled, holding it to her ear.

"It's Damien McMillon, Detective. Are you okay?"

"Sorry. It's been—never mind. What's up?"

"Some disturbing stuff is going on around here," McMillon said. "I spoke at length with the captain of the freighter after Detective Selva left. He said he has no idea who arranged for the transport of the cargo. The paperwork showed only that it originated in Colombia and had passed through the Panama Canal a couple of days ago."

"Go on," said Miranda.

"The captain insisted he had no idea what was in the shipments other than what was stamped on the trunks and crates—'PM Importers. Extremely Fragile.' He was as shocked as everyone else at the sight of the eviscerated corpse when the lid of the crate was removed." He paused. "So upset that he raced to the aft deck and vomited."

"Jesus! Anything else?" she asked, trying to quell the rotten taste hurling up from her stomach. She walked outside to her garden for fresh air, keeping her back turned away from the kitchen to keep the conversation private.

"I got a call a few minutes ago from one of our Interpol agents in Central America. He said two high-ranking officials in the Corbinestro cartel in Colombia had been arrested—Miguel Sorkin and his second in command, Orviedo Montoya, his cousin."

"Jesus," muttered Miranda, shaking her head.

Matt watched from the kitchen, waiting for her to signal him to come out. When she didn't, he turned around.

Graham noticed the change in Matt's demeanor, more personal than professional now. He realized how deeply Matt cared for Miranda—more than just as a partner. He suddenly knew that Miranda felt the same way. Disappointed, he finally had to admit to himself that Miranda had moved on with her life, and it didn't include him.

Miranda sat on the bench in the garden as Damien McMillon continued his report.

"The Colombian authorities have confiscated computers and documents that contain information about Operation Mermaid, an international human trafficking ring—a diabolical cartel with a reputation of being sadistic monsters. They have been high on Interpol's Most Wanted list for the past three years."

Miranda's silence was deafening as she processed his words.

"Are you still there, Detective Morales?"

"Yes, yes. It's hard to take in . . . the magnitude of it all."

"I know. The cartel kidnaps children from streets and back alleys all over the world. They feed and clothe them, get them healthy enough to be sold to the highest bidder. We've yet to uncover the full extent of their network, but so far we've learned they're amping up their game, focusing on Florida and Mexico in the past several months. The two captured cartel leaders have agreed to cooperate with authorities in exchange for complete immunity. Agents have been dispatched to arrest dozens of people the cousins have already fingered."

"Thanks, Damien. You've been a great help. Please keep me updated."

"Roger that. I'll be sure to keep you in the loop," he said, and clicked off.

Miranda took a deep breath and went back inside. She sat down, gulped her wine, and poured another.

"Well?" said an anxious Matt, awaiting details.

"That was my contact at the FBI. He called to let me know that two high-ranking members of a Colombian human-trafficking ring have been taken into custody," she began.

"Christ!" said Graham, blowing out a breath, swiping his hand over his mouth.

"Miguel Sorkin and his cousin, Orviedo Montoya, have agreed to reveal everything about the cartel and their past, current, and future activities in exchange for complete immunity."

"It will take more than immunity to protect them from the cartel's claws. They'll hunt them down like vicious tigers, rip out their tongues for their betrayal," said Matt.

"Or worse," said Graham. "I live in Panama, remember?"

"I'm sure the two cartel leaders are related to Mano Sorkin and Castro Montoya," said Miranda. "We'll need to get to Mano and Castro before word gets to them about this."

Matt saw the fury in her eyes.

"We need to get a warrant immediately to search Peter's house," Miranda said. "Graham, you can stay here." She took the extra house key from her purse and slid to him. "I'm not sure how long this will take, but make yourself at home. Or, you can return to your hotel if you'd prefer."

"Why search Peter's house?" asked Matt. "What do you expect to find?"

"I'll tell you on the way. Call Chief Petri to get us a search warrant, pronto!"

"Be careful, both of you," said Graham.

Chapter 46

Chief Petri called Miranda to say he'd sent someone to meet them at Peter's with the search warrant as she and Matt raced across Ringling Bridge to Longboat Key.

The ornate iron gate at the collector's home was still open. Miranda drove through, and was glad when the officer arrived soon after with the warrant.

When Peter didn't answer the doorbell, Miranda tried the door, and was surprised to find that it was unlocked. She slowly stepped into the wide foyer, Matt following close behind.

"Peter? Peter Millstine? It's Detective Morales." She paused as the two of them poked their heads into the empty, silent rooms. "We have a warrant to search your house," she called out, tilting her head toward the stairs, mouthing *bedrooms* to Matt.

While Matt crept up the stairs, checking his belt to make sure he had his gun handy, Miranda drifted like a panther from the kitchen to the dining room and living room, looking out the windows at the pool and gardens.

Miranda circled around to the foyer, then tiptoed down the long hallway, stopping abruptly in front of the unicorn tapestry that she had admired earlier. The tapestry was no longer hanging flat against the wall, but was now raised a few inches off the floor. She peeked behind the hanging. A hidden door was cracked open. As Matt came back down the stairs, she cocked her head toward the door leading to the basement.

They quietly descended the carpeted stairs, their weapons drawn.

A soft bubbling sound filtered through the otherwise quiet space as they reached the bottom step. Miranda peeked around the edge of the wall at the base of the steps. A muted glow from wall sconces created a serene, yet eerie atmosphere.

The back of Peter's bald head was barely visible as he sat in a leather armchair, facing a gigantic aquarium. The strains of Mozart's Magic Flute filled the room.

Miranda turned to Matt, holding a finger to her lips as they crept along the back wall toward the chair. A soft glow emanated from within the enormous aquarium. They were shocked to see a half-dozen or so mermaids swimming from oyster shell to oyster shell, as if searching for pearls, periodically sucking air from tubes attached at various places along the glass walls before descending, gliding in a monotonous cycle of swimming, rising, sucking, breathing. Their long hair flowed behind them. Their sparkling fins swayed as they moved among the tropical fish, gorgeous in their vibrant blues, bright yellows, deep reds, and stunning oranges, dancing an exquisite un-choreographed underwater ballet.

Miranda cocked her head toward Peter.

Matt nodded, quietly following her lead as they approached the chair from behind.

Peter was sitting in the chair, his eyes open in an unblinking, trance-like stare. A young girl in a rainbow-colored mermaid tail lay flaccid across Peter's lap, her head cradled in his arms, her shapely breasts exposed. A belt adorned with a garland of pearls, glittering gemstones, and tiny coral beads circled her narrow waist.

Miranda gently touched the girl's cheek with the back of her hand, then checked her carotid for a pulse.

"She's warm, but her pulse is weak." She lifted the girl's eyelids but the light was too dim to examine the reaction of her pupils.

"Peter's alive, but his pulse is faint," said Matt, holding the collector's wrist. "His breathing is shallow."

Then, as if awakening from a dream, the mermaid sluggishly opened her eyes and lifted her head slightly. Fear registered when she saw the two strangers standing over her. She tried to get up but was too weak, and fell back against Peter's chest, moaning.

"It's okay," said Miranda, patting her arm, noticing a metal handcuff around her wrist that was connected to the one around Peter's. "We're police officers. We're here to help you," she said softly. "You're going to be okay."

"I'll call 911," said Matt.

"Tell them we'll need multiple ambulances for the mermaids," said Miranda.

Matt made the emergency call, then turned on the bright lights. He glanced at Miranda, squatting beside the dazed mermaid. Peter was moaning.

"Help is on the way," said Matt. "How's the mermaid?"

"Hard to say. Not sure if she's been drugged . . . Peter, too, for that matter."

"I'll check on the mermaids in the aquarium."

He pressed his palm against the glass, alerting the mermaids to his presence. Terrified eyes stared back at him. Some of the mermaids were swimming frantically around the tank, stopping to pound wildly against the glass walls. The tropical fish scattered helter-skelter out of their way. One mermaid shot to the top of the glass cage in a futile effort to climb out, but the walls were too high and the water level too low for her to grab hold of the metal rim.

"We need to get them out, Miranda," yelled Matt.

He rushed over to a narrow slot between the aquarium and the wall where he'd spotted a tall ladder attached to a ceiling rail.

Miranda realized there was nothing more she could do for Peter and his mermaid except pray that help arrived before it was too late. She rushed over to help Matt with the other mermaids.

"Climb up and reach into the water for them," she said. "Your arms are longer than mine. I'll guide them down as you pull each one out."

Suddenly Peter howled when he saw the first mermaid emerge from the tank.

"Get the fuck out of my house!" he growled. The weight of the girl on his lap confined him, and he collapsed in his leather chair.

Miranda moved cautiously up the ladder, reaching for the mermaid. Matt carefully lowered her so Miranda could grab her around the waist and guide her to the floor, where she led the girl to the sofa and sat her down. She wrapped a nearby blanket around the girl's shivering shoulders before returning to the ladder to do it again.

As Matt fished the second mermaid out of the tank, they heard sirens blaring in the distance.

"Thank God!" said Miranda, as she tucked the second mermaid next to the first.

The doors upstairs banged open and somebody yelled, "Police!"

"Down here!" yelled Miranda, racing to the base of the stairs. "Hurry!" she pleaded.

The sound of heavy boots clomping down the steps was music to their ears. She stepped aside to let the EMTs do their jobs. One of them motioned for Matt to come down from the ladder so they could take over.

"Never in a million years would I have imagined something like this," said Miranda, unlocking the breath that had lodged in her lungs. She looked at Matt. The ordeal had taken its toll on him, too. She wanted to hug him, but knew it wasn't the time, or the place.

Chapter 47

"This way," called Destina Walker, looking over her shoulder as the new influx of campers arrived at Sirens of the Deep. Chatter and laughter filled the hallways as it always did on registration day. "Your camp counselors are waiting inside the dining hall to greet you. Please stay in the group you were assigned. They will instruct you about what happens next."

Once the children were with their respective camp counselors, Destina headed back toward the administration building, smiling as she passed by the director sitting on one of the benches facing the flower garden. She went over to her and sat down.

"So, another exciting session ahead," said Destina.

Georgia smiled, but her heart was burdened, and her secretary sensed it.

"Are you okay, Miss Georgia?"

Without looking at Destina, Georgia's eyes scanned the campgrounds, soaking in the serenity and beauty surrounding them and listening to the sounds of the children eager to morph into mermaids.

"You know, Destina," began Georgia softly, "I never tire of hearing the children's laughter. Their excitement about embarking on their transformation from mortal to mythical mermaid." She smiled as she watched one of the girls walk up to an instructor dressed in full mermaid regalia, looking up at her with awe in her eyes. "The lure of the mermaid never dies," she sighed.

"What's troubling you, Miss Georgia?" asked Destina. "I know being responsible for the extra girls rescued from the freighter has been stressful. Plus Maria Diaz—and now Lila Bjorg being back with us. It's put a tremendous burden on you. But they will soon be gone. And everything will be back to normal."

Georgia forced a weary smile.

"I'm happy Maria will be going home to her mother. And grateful that Detective Morales's friend is going to escort her. And, yes, the four girls from the freighter will be returning to Colombia once Immigration has sorted things out with the orphanage. The administrator there said she's hopeful she will find good homes for them after their horrific ordeal."

Destina took Georgia's hand, but said nothing, content to sit quietly with her for however long she needed.

Georgia put her hand on top of her secretary's and smiled.

"Thanks, Destina. You've been wonderful through all of this. I'm really worried about Lila. Not only did she find out that her best friend was murdered, but she also learned the identity of the people responsible for separating them, seeing them face-to-face at the celebration. Imagining the horror surrounding Nina's death." She took a deep, regretful breath. "I had no idea what was going on. How could I not see through it all?" Tears flooded her eyes. "I'm not sure Lila will ever fully recover. She's been through so much."

Destina lowered her head, wondering what their lives had been like before arriving at Sirens of the Deep. No words could lighten Georgia's heavy heart.

She squeezed Georgia's hand and stood up. "I think I should get back to the office and get some of the paperwork done."

"I'll be there shortly."

"Take your time, Miss Georgia."

"Back to work, you old fool," Georgia Holmes muttered to herself. "You have a camp to run."

The Mermaid Fantasea I stood majestically in the Tampa Bay harbor waiting for the custom-made mermaid tails to be brought on board. Trixie Monroe had designed them specifically for the Festival of Dagon celebration to be held at midnight. Dusk was just beginning to settle over the bay, adding a slate-colored sheen to the aquamarine water as the sun slipped toward the horizon, pulling its golden hue with it.

Trixie and Brenda had just arrived with the four boxes of costumes.

Python lumbered down the dock toward them, eyeing Brenda warily. He remembered her from Trixie's shop yesterday.

"I'll take those," he said gruffly, reaching for the two boxes Brenda held. He looked at Trixie holding the other two boxes. "You, follow me," he ordered. "She can go," cocking his head toward Brenda.

Trixie hesitated.

Python twisted around. "C'mon! There's no time to waste," he snarled.

Brenda's heart pounded. She was gripped with fear for her boss's safety.

Trixie let Python get several steps ahead of her, then stopped abruptly.

"Hold on, Python. I forgot to get something from Brenda," she said, walking quickly back to Brenda and discreetly slipping a folded note into her pocket.

"Do you need me to come with you?" Brenda whispered nervously.

"No. Get back to the shop right away," she said quietly as Python twisted around, looking at them with contempt.

Brenda watched Trixie catch up to the bronze hulk on the dock. She stumbled once or twice before finally climbing aboard the yacht.

A beautiful girl with coal-black hair, ivory complexion, and almond eyes looked out from a window on the lower deck. She waved at Brenda. Brenda was too afraid to wave back. A young man stood at the brass railing the next level up, watching everything that was going on.

After Trixie had boarded and disappeared belowdecks, Brenda watched for a time, staring at the two youths as the engine hummed to life. The young man waved to her as the yacht backed out of the slip. Brenda felt brave enough to wave back, now that the yacht was moving. The girl pressed her palm against the window and blew Brenda a kiss.

Brenda waved before heading to the parking lot to drive back to the shop.

As she took the car key out of her pocket, she felt Trixie's note. She took it out to read: Urgent—Danger! Call Detective Morales. Jewfish Key. Midnight tonight.

She gasped. She found Miranda's number in her cell phone and immediately called her, leaving a voicemail when she didn't answer.

"Detective Morales, it's Brenda Sinclair. Trixie's in danger! Call me as soon as you get this. Something's happening at Jewfish Key tonight. Please. She needs your help!"

While Castro Montoya, Mano Sorkin, Gabriella Navarre, and Trixie Monroe talked business over cocktails in the club room of the Fantasea I, they had no idea Xander was devising a plan of his own.

"We'll wait for just the right time," he told Mirakakoo as they sat quietly on the upper deck lounge chairs, en route to Jewfish Key. He turned his soulful eyes to her. She was like a sister to him. He took her hand. "Do you feel strong enough to swim?"

"I think so," she said, rubbing her hand over the incision where the hummingbird had been removed from her stomach. "I have to do it. It's our only chance."

He nodded. "I won't let anything happen to you, Mira. You believe me, don't you?"

"Of course I do, Xander. You always take good care of me."

He nodded and smiled. "Believe in miracles, right?"

Her thin, colorless lips lifted into a wide smile. "Si. Miracles."

ᏨᏒ

As the Mermaid Fantasea I motored from Tampa toward Jewfish Key, Xander spotted lights on the patio of a house at the shoreline of Longboat Key. He was surprised they had made such good time.

"Look, Mira. There's a house over there," he said, pointing. "See the lights on the patio there? Do you see them, Mira?" he said excitedly.

Mirakakoo nodded.

"This is our chance. We must do it before they stop to get the collector at his house. We must do it before we arrive at Jewfish Key. Are you sure you can make it to that house?"

She nodded again. "Don't worry."

"Good," he whispered, kissing the top of her head. "We'll swim toward the dock."

Xander got up and casually walked to the top of the stairs leading to the club room, listening to the voices rising and falling as they argued. He returned to Mirakakoo standing at the rail, looking across the Gulf of Mexico and the house with the lights.

"It's time. We must do it now, before they come back up here," he whispered. "We might not have another chance." He put his finger to his lips, listening for the sounds below. The voices were getting louder. "They'll be distracted for a little while."

He lifted his eyes to the bridge where the captain was focused on navigating through the choppy water. Xander held up his index finger. Un minuto.

Mirakakoo nodded.

They strolled hand in hand to the aft deck like two lovers enjoying the view. It seemed like the moonlight streaming across the Gulf was there for the sole purpose of guiding them toward the shoreline, the white lights, and freedom.

"We'll step over the railing and onto the edge, then dive quickly into the water," Xander whispered.

"I'm scared."

He kissed Mirakakoo's cheek. "It will be okay. We are excellent swimmers. Just head for the lights," he encouraged. "Believe in miracles."

She smiled big.

He looked around one last time and nodded.

"Now."

They held hands tightly as they carefully maneuvered over the railing, hurling themselves into the water. Mirakakoo didn't mean to scream, but the jump was higher and the water colder than she had expected. Xander instantly pulled her underwater, holding onto her hand as they swam, unseen, surfacing only when they thought it would be safe to come up for a breath.

"I don't see anybody," said Xander when he'd popped his head just above the surface. He hoped the muffled noise of the engine and the screech of the shorebirds had covered the sound of her scream. Mira breathed heavily beside him.

"Are you okay to swim a bit farther?" he asked.

"We must," she said, her breathing heavy, her arms growing tired. She ignored the bite from the incision that had not quite healed after her surgery.

"To the lights, then."

Chapter 48

Sound travels across the water, and Robert and Kiera Kingsley, sitting on their patio having cocktails, thought they'd just heard a scream.

"Could just be some noise coming from that enormous yacht out there, Robert," said his wife.

He shrugged. "Probably. You know how the rich like their wild parties."

He got up from his Adirondack chair and gazed out at the sparkling water for a few seconds, listening, then said, "I don't see or hear anything. I'm going in to get the cocktail pitcher and refill the snack tray. Need anything else while I'm at the house?"

"No, thanks," she said, standing up. She walked to the dock where their small boat was tied up. A narrow swath of moonbeam stretched across the water as she looked out at the dancing lights shimmering on the surface of the Gulf. She stood silent on the edge of the dock, listening for sounds. She was certain she heard voices in the distance. She moved closer, turning her ear toward the sound.

"Help! Help! Please help us," a voice called out, an arm waving overhead.

"Hello?" she called. "Who's there?"

Just then Robert came back with the refreshments, set them down on the table, and joined her down at the dock, holding a cocktail for each of them.

"What's wrong? Who are you talking to?"

"Somebody's out there calling for help," she said, taking the glass he handed her and then pointing to the spot where she thought she saw heads bobbing out of the water.

"Get the binoculars off the table on the patio," said Robert. "I'll get a couple of life preservers from the boat."

He jumped into the boat for the two life preservers stored in a small compartment under one of the seats, slipping his arm through the centers. He swiftly jumped into the waist-high water.

Kiera gulped down the cocktail and raced up to the house, empty glass in hand. The glass fell over as she set it down on the table. Her hands were trembling as she grabbed the binoculars, rushing back to the dock where Robert was scouring the surface of the water in the direction where he thought they'd heard the scream.

"There!" pointed Kiera, looking through the binoculars. "The path of moonlight streaming across the water. Two swimmers. About a hundred yards or so away."

"Hello out there! We see you!" Robert called. "I'm throwing you life preservers. We're coming to help you ashore."

"Maybe we should take the boat?" suggested Kiera.

"They'll reach the life preservers by the time we unhitch the boat and start the engine."

Kiera and Robert watched the swimmers' heads bobbing, their arms frantically reaching for the fluorescent orange donuts.

Xander helped Mira put hers over her head before putting on his own. He squeezed Mira's hand. "Okay?" he asked, huffing and puffing as he tried to regain a steady rhythm to his breathing.

"Okay," nodded Mirakakoo.

Kiera and Robert waded out toward them, grabbing the ropes tied to the preservers just as a wave tilted Kiera momentarily off balance.

As the two swimmers reached the dock, Kiera and Robert helped them remove the donuts and led them up to the patio.

Xander looked back across the water. The lights of the Mermaid Fantasea were no longer visible in the distance, the darkness lit only by the pinprick of stars. A large cloud now cloaked the moon.

I do believe in miracles, Xander chanted to himself, his arm around Mira's shivering shoulders.

Kiera had gone to retrieve towels from house. Robert poured them some water when his wife returned with a pitcher and an armful of towels.

"Gracias," said Xander. He pointed to Mira. "Mirakakoo." Then he pointed to himself. "Xander."

Kiera and Robert smiled at them.

"Come. Sit down. Drink—eat," they said, offering them the bowl of snacks.

Xander looked at Mira, who looked much thinner in the moonlight glow that had escaped from the cloud.

"Si, por favor," he said, exhausted.

"I'll make some sandwiches for them," said Kiera, briskly walking up the path toward the house.

"Miracle," murmured Mirakakoo, her eyes bright. Her smile was infectious, clutching the towel around her while she munched on pretzels.

When Kiera returned with a tray of sandwiches and fruit, she whispered to Robert, "We should call 911. I don't think they understand or speak English very well."

"Let's give them a couple of minutes to catch their breath. They don't seem to be in any immediate danger. Maybe they can explain what's going on before we get too mixed up in what might amount to just being a family affair gone wrong."

They sat quietly, studying their unexpected guests, so young and vulnerable.

"I'm going up to the bridge to talk to the captain. See how close we are to Peter's house," said Mano, setting his drink down on the bar and heading for the stairs to the upper deck.

Python, thumbing something on his iPhone, looked up briefly and grunted, while Castro, sitting at the bar drinking a whiskey, glanced at yachting magazines, jiggling his leg.

"Make sure Captain Moore is confident that he can navigate these tricky waters. Submerged objects can cause problems. Especially as we approach Jewfish," said Castro, his anxiety deepening. "As it is your boat, I'm sure you've taken the utmost care in selecting your captain."

Mano had hired this particular captain on Gabriella's recommendation, assuring him he was at the top of his class at the US Naval Academy and had a distinguished career during his years as captain of several fleets. Plus, he was a longtime friend and ally of hers. While Mano was a skilled captain himself, even if not at the level of Gabriella's captain, he didn't trust his own ability to guide the Mermaid Fantasea through uncharted waters. Sandbars and hidden rocks had claimed many a vessel destined for Jewfish Key. This was a once-in-a-lifetime night. Mishaps and blunders were unacceptable. Tomorrow would begin a whole new trajectory for the Mermaid Fantasea Corporation.

Trixie and Gabriella were sitting together on the sofa belowdecks, looking through the pictures of the mermaid tails Trixie had designed for the Festival of Dagon, reviewing how the plan for the celebration would unfold once they arrived at Jewfish Key and unloaded the costumes.

Gabriella called out to Mano as he started up the steps.

"He knows what he's doing, Mano. Don't be so jittery. You're beginning to make me nervous."

Mano scowled without looking back at her.

"Good evening, Mr. Sorkin," smiled the captain. "You are just in time to make a decision."

"Decision?"

"Yes, sir. Whether to go to Jewfish Key first and drop off your friends before stopping for Mr. Millstine, or to pick up your friend and all travel together to the Key." He paused. "Ms. Navarre did happen to mention that she thought it best to go to Jewfish first to unload the costumes and cargo, check on how everything was progressing."

"Ah," said Mano, gazing out at the glittering water. "Good idea. Yes, we'll head to Jewfish first then." He checked his watch. "That way they can get a head start while we go back to collect Peter."

Stars twinkled across the broad, black canopy. A silver path of moonlight seemed to have split the Gulf of Mexico in two: one half for coming, the other for going.

"These aquamarine waters are as gorgeous as any I've crossed," mused Mano.

The captain laughed politely. "Quite breathtaking, I agree."

Mano grew pensive for a moment. Never fully satisfied until he was certain all the dominoes were placed to fall precisely as he had planned.

"I'm sure you'll get us there without incident. The water can be a tricky mistress."

The captain nodded, and Mano returned to the club room to update everyone.

"We're going to Jewfish Key first, to drop off supplies, then the captain and I will pick up Peter. That way the mermaid costumes will be there for the actors to prepare for the performance. Castro and Python can unload the boxes of wine, and you and Trixie can put the finishing touches on the decorations," he said, looking at Gabriella.

Everybody agreed this was the most efficient plan and settled in with their drinks, relaxing before the hullabaloo of the Festival of Dagon and its pageantry.

"I want everything ready when the guests start arriving," declared Mano. "Some may already have arrived." Mano turned to Trixie and Gabriella. "By the way, have either of you heard from Peter today? I've left messages for him about the details for tonight, but so far I've not heard a word from him."

"He'd better be ready!" scowled Gabriella.

"Peter's a perfectionist, Gabriella. You know that," Mano said. "But it's the girls I'm most interested in."

Trixie recalled the heated argument she and Peter had had yesterday—the day Miranda had unexpectedly showed up at his home. No need to upset Mano with that nonsense at a time like this. She was annoyed that the meddlesome detective had questioned them about Peter's import business, and Gabriella Navarre. But what most concerned Trixie was the detective's pointed question concerning the Mermaid Fantasea Corporation. While she felt certain she hadn't divulged anything that would jeopardize the mermaid enterprise's expansion, the detective's pointed questions suggesting she could be a threat to their seamless plans, though the designer could not imagine how.

"I'm sure if there was something wrong, Peter would have called at least one of us," said Trixie, checking the condition of her polished fingernails, a knot growing in her stomach. "He has been wound up tight of late." She paused, growing more agitated. "He's probably fussing obsessively with his mermaid talisman, swooning over his priceless objects," she laughed, snidely.

"No worries, Mano. Trixie and I will take care of things on Jewfish Key until you get back with Peter," said Gabriella. "Everything will go exactly as planned. The Festival of Dagon will be spectacular." She touched Mano's arm and smiled reassuringly. "The beginning of a bolder, better, and more lucrative venture than anything we've embarked on thus far."

Chapter 49

Jewfish Key was hustling like an ant colony by the time the Mermaid Fantasea I anchored at the long dock jutting out from the shoreline. The buzz of guests arriving had electrified the air as everyone pitched in to help wherever they were needed. White wooden lawn chairs had already been positioned under a large, white canvas tent where guests would watch the performance of the mythic Fish God Dagon usher in a new era.

Trixie and Gabriella carried the boxes of mermaid costumes to the master suite in the home reserved for the celebration. They set them on the king-size bed while Python carried boxes of wine to the kitchen. Then they checked that the tiki torches set along the shoreline had been filled with fresh lamp oil. Colorful fresh flowers—bird of paradise, pastel-tinted orchids, blood-red hibiscus—marked the perimeter of the midnight celebration's festivities. Japanese paper lanterns suspended from multicolored ribbons created a rainbow effect inside the tent stretching along the expansive shoreline. Plastic wrap–covered platters laden with fresh fruit, an assortment of seafood on ice bases, and a silver bucket filled with bottles of champagne graced the long buffet table for the feast. The air was crisp as a gentle breeze blew off the majestic Gulf of Mexico.

A ring of small potted palms wrapped with tiny white lights outlined the sandy stage fifteen feet from the tent where the actors would perform the ceremony honoring Dagon—the half-man, half-fish mythical figure that had metamorphosed from that of a god who represented false worship, to a more powerful, positive image of a god devoted to saving marine creatures struggling to survive through the centuries. The new Dagon—god of the aquatic universe—would be born and heralded tonight under a Mermaid Moon. The growing multitude of mermaid ambassadors being groomed to spread the message of hope for a sustainable future for marine life around the world would be indoctrinated this night.

The myth of the mermaid was an ideal platform by which to garner philanthropic support while at the same time engaging in their nefarious charade. A charade that had served the enterprise's despicable crimes of human exploitation and greed, preying on the most innocent and defenseless, robbing children of the precious gifts of love, safety, and a promising future.

"This will be an extraordinary celebration!" declared Trixie, lifting the mermaid tails out of their boxes and holding each one up for Gabriella's inspection before laying them side by side on top of the bedcover, admiring her exquisite handiwork.

"You've outdone yourself, Trixie," gushed Gabriella. "The colors—and adornments! I'd wager these spectacular costumes have exceeded even your own expectations."

"You're wrong, my dear. Each sketch, stitch, thread, and fabric was chosen with an unparalleled sense of composition, color, and vivid imagination. I'm lucky to have such artistic talents in spades."

Gabriella picked up a teal-colored tail off the bed, admiring its feel and weight.

"That's for Dagon," said Trixie, proudly. "I took particular care to ensure that his was an exact copy of the one pictured in my book, *Legends of the Fish Gods and Their Ceremonial Dress.*"

"The namesake of our festival," murmured Gabriella.

She stroked the second one, a cobalt-colored tail. The sequins shimmered as the moonlight drifted into the room through the nearby window. "This one?" she asked.

"Oannes, the solar fish god." Trixie smiled. "A man-head hidden beneath a fish-head, the feet of a man under the fish-tail. When he would come ashore as he traveled, he'd teach mankind how to write, create art, and understand the science of the sea and sky."

Gabriella glanced at Trixie as she picked up the last two mermaid tails, holding one in each hand.

"Derceto and Triton, I assume?"

"I'm impressed you remembered," laughed Trixie. "The coral one is for Derceto. The emerald one, for Triton."

"Everyone's familiar with Triton. Not so much Derceto, though. Me included."

"Ah," sighed Trixie, taking the tail of Derceto from her, hugging it as if it were a child. "How could you forget about Derceto, Gab? The only goddess in our ceremony tonight."

"I've had a lot on my mind lately, or have you forgotten?"

"You don't have to be so snippy about it!" Trixie said. She took a deep breath, then set the tail back down on the bed, admiring it as she recounted the myth. "Derceto evolved from the legendary first mermaid, Atargatis, when the cult of Atargatis traveled from Israel to Greece, where she became Derceto. The constellation Pisces is linked to Atargatis and Derceto."

"Yes. The two fish. Now I remember. She was the goddess of fertility, as I recall. A somewhat tangled story about an egg falling from the sky, and when it washed ashore, Derceto hatched from it."

"Well done," said Trixie. "Now, I have one more surprise."

She took a deep breath as she opened a long, white, rectangular box and gently unfolded the edges of the overlapping tissue paper covering the contents.

"A few accessories to make the magic complete," she said coyly as she slowly removed the gold, three-pronged object and a long, steel pole. She connected the fork-like object to the tip of the pole. "Voila."

"A trident! Perfect!" said Gabriella, as Trixie passed the weapon to her. "It's as light as a feather, even though it looks much . . . heavier."

Trixie laughed.

"I designed it especially for the festival. It's a prototype of the antique trident I gifted Mano for his fiftieth birthday. I found it in an antique shop on one of my trips." Trixie's eyes sparkled, remembering how delighted he'd been to receive such a precious gift. "He said he would find the perfect place for it on his yacht." She tapped her mouth with her finger. "Come to think of it, I don't remember seeing it on the yacht," she muttered. "I'll have to ask him about it later."

"Well, we should get these tails to the actors for a final fitting before the performance," said Gabriella, taking two of the tails while Trixie carried the other two. "The mermaids will look amazing, swimming out to the rocks in the silver moonlight, their songs floating out over the water, signaling the arrival of Dagon and his tribe."

After leaving the costumes with their respective actors, they each poured a glass of wine and took it outside, sitting in two of the chairs set up for the viewing the performance. They were eagerly awaiting the return of Mano, with Peter Millstine on board, so the Festival of Dagon could commence. The expansive sandy beach had been transformed into a surreal landscape where incantations and solemn rituals would soon awaken the aquatic spirits, paying homage to the precious sea creatures, the gods and goddesses who would once again rule the world.

"To the Festival of Dagon," toasted Gabriella. "The Mermaid Fantasea Corporation is finally poised to take over the world. She looked over at Trixie, who was pensive. "Are you okay?"

"I'm worried about Peter," Trixie said. "He's been acting so . . . bizarre lately."

"What do you mean?"

"His obsession with his priceless mermaid collection. His recent withdrawal." She studied Gabriella for a reaction. But, as usual, her face was expressionless. "Seems like ever since he met that professor and showed him his mermaid talisman, he's become quite agitated. Ill-tempered." She paused. "And that damn detective showing up at his home while I was meeting with him, demanding answers to questions surrounding PM Importers and"—she glanced again at Gabriella—"and you."

"What about me?" asked Gabriella, finally showing some facial reaction.

"Who you are. Your background. She had gotten a call while she was at Peter's. When the call ended and she returned to the room, she immediately began barking out all these questions."

"What did you tell her?"

"Nothing. Peter almost had to shove her out the door. But after she left, Peter grew more and more distraught. Pacing. He told me to leave. He wanted to be alone." She glanced at Gabriella, as if asking for an explanation. "I'm afraid his obsession is driving him mad."

Gabriella took a deep breath, drained her wineglass, and refilled it, topping Trixie's off at the same time.

"Look. We have every right to celebrate tonight. It's business. What could they possibly know that would suggest anything other than a company event marking a milestone?"

Chapter 50

Flashing red-and-blue lights from the caravan of police cars and ambulances blared through the serenity of Longboat Key, lighting up the night sky like the rockets' red glare on the Fourth of July. The madness and mayhem had pulled neighbors out of their otherwise peaceful, private mansions. Now they were standing in groups, watching in stunned silence. Shocked that such chaos could be happening in their neighborhood. Unaware that one of their neighbors could be anything but upstanding. Clueless about the sinister activities taking place around them. Protected from the riffraff beyond their walls. Unaware of the bizarre scene unfolding inside their neighbor's house.

Each mermaid rescued from the aquarium was examined by EMTs before transporting them to the ambulances. Chief Petri barking orders at his officers to control the scene outdoors.

"They can't be much older than twelve or thirteen," muttered one of the policemen as he passed Miranda.

"I've seen a lot of weird stuff in my day, but this is off the charts," said another as they assisted the EMTs transferring girls to stretchers who needed them, or walking them to the waiting ambulances.

Chief Petri took Miranda aside. "What the hell happened here, Detective? I mean, I knew you requested a search warrant, but I had no idea something like this was going on."

"Neither did we, Chief. We intended to show Peter the warrant to search his home for artifacts that may have been part of a museum heist in Panama."

"Panama?"

"The Republic of Panama, Chief, not Panama, Florida."

Chief Petri swiped his mouth and shook his head.

They walked over to where a medic was tending to Peter and the girl on his lap. The mermaid still tethered to him with handcuffs.

"Somebody get over her and get these handcuffs off this girl," demanded Chief Petri.

"How are they doing?" Miranda asked the EMT tending to them.

"The mermaid is groggy. Maybe from some kind of sedative? I drew some blood for the lab to test," she said. "Her vitals have stabilized enough for her to be transported to the hospital."

"What about him?" the chief asked, looking at Peter with disgust.

"Again, he's either drugged, or he's having some kind of mental collapse. They're both stabilized enough to be transferred to the hospital for a more thorough evaluation."

"Great," said Miranda, standing back so the techs could load them onto the stretchers.

"Well, what's your take?" Chief Petri asked.

"Short version," said Miranda, glancing at Matt. "We believe Peter Millstine and his partners in the Mermaid Fantasea Corporation have been engaging in human trafficking, theft, kidnapping, and the international transport of stolen museum treasures, to name a few of their hideous crimes. Matt and I suspect something deeper is going on with Peter's business. PM Importers."

"Jesus," mumbled the chief. He grabbed the arm of the female tech who'd examined Peter and the mermaid. "Do whatever it takes to keep them alive!"

She nodded.

The two medics lifted the mermaid onto a stretcher, placing an oxygen mask over her nose and mouth. The handcuff tethering her to Peter prevented their separation.

The policeman nearby took a tool from his belt and snipped the links, separating them.

"Hold on," said Miranda, pulling back the sheet that covered the mermaid to her chin. "I need to remove her belt." She quickly untied the string on one side of the belt and whispered in the mermaid's ear, "You're going to be okay. They're taking you to the hospital." She stepped back and nodded to the EMT. "Go."

The mermaid's eyes fluttered, her breathing erratic as they carried the stretcher upstairs.

Another medic shined a light in Peter's eyes and checked his vital signs, then put an oxygen mask over his mouth and nose. The dazed collector groaned as they lifted him onto the stretcher.

"Take one of the police officers with you," Chief Petri told the medic, nudging the policeman closest to him. "Stay with them until you hear from me."

Miranda snapped a photo of the mermaid's belt and sent it to Graham with a text: Is this the talisman you saw at Peter's?

Almost instantly, Graham texted, Yes.

Only after Miranda sent Graham the text did she notice she had a voicemail. "Detective Morales. It's Brenda Sinclair. Trixie's in danger. Jewfish Key. Midnight. Tonight."

Miranda checked the time. 11:15 p.m.

"Shit," she muttered, then looked at the chief. "Matt and I have to get to Jewfish Key. Something big's going to happen at midnight. And according to my source, at least one person will be in danger."

"I'll arrange for backup," said Chief Petri, eyeing Matt and Miranda. "What else do you need?"

"Jewfish is only accessible when the tide is right," said Miranda, hesitating. "I'll call my contact at FBI. Have him arrange for agents to meet us there. He's been involved since the incidents in Tampa and knows what's going on, perhaps better than we do at this point." She paused. "Call the Coast Guard and see if they can meet us here at Peter's dock. They'll know better than anybody how to get us to Jewfish. Tell them we have no idea what we'll be facing there."

Chief Petri immediately pulled out his phone and made the call.

Miranda tugged Matt's sleeve as they watched the last mermaid rescued from the tank being placed on a stretcher.

"What's happened?" said an exhausted and bewildered Matt.

"Brenda Sinclair left me an urgent message on my phone a few hours ago. With everything that's been going on, I just listened to the voicemail now. She said Trixie's in danger, but didn't say more than that. Only that at midnight something was going to happen on Jewfish."

The chief walked over to Matt and Miranda as the medics carried the last mermaid up the stairs. "The US Coast Guard is on their way. Meet them down at Peter's dock in fifteen minutes."

"Thanks, Chief," said Miranda, checking the time. "We should get to Jewfish in about thirty minutes, depending."

"Why would Trixie be in danger?" asked Matt.

Miranda shrugged. "Whatever it is, let's just hope we're there in time."

Chapter 51

The Coast Guard arrived soon after Matt and Miranda reached Peter's dock and jumped on board.

"FBI Agent McMillon is sending some men familiar with Jewfish Key to meet us there," said Miranda, leaning close to Matt so he could hear her over the engine noise of the Coast Guard's boat. "Whatever's planned could be way bigger than we think."

"What about local law enforcement near Jewfish?" asked Matt.

"I think we'll have enough manpower between the Coast Guard and the FBI agents," said Miranda, shaking her head at the mayhem they'd just left behind as the boat motored away from the dock, an image of Daniel Craig as James Bond, maneuvering a cigarette boat as he chased whatever diabolical monster had just eluded him.

As the Mermaid Fantasea I circled back from Jewfish Key to pick up Peter, Mano stood at the brass railing, scanning the shoreline with his binoculars, not believing his eyes. The red-and-blue flashing lights careening through the landscaped gardens surrounding Peter's house confounded him.

"What the fuck?" he muttered, choked with fear. "Jesus Christ." He called up to the captain and motioned for him to stop the engine.

The captain leaned around the bridge and called, "What's wrong?"

"Just cut the engine," shouted Mano.

Suddenly Mano realized he'd completely forgotten that Xander and Mirakakoo had been on board. He bolted down the steps and scuttled to the lower deck, calling out to them as he searched every nook and cranny. Seeing no sign of them, he sprinted back up to the bridge.

"Did you see if Xander and Mirakakoo got off the yacht with the others at Jewfish Key?"

"No. But I could've missed them while the boxes were being unloaded." said Captain Moore.

"Fuck, fuck, fuck!" Mano said, running his hands through his black hair, trying to remember if he'd seen them leaving the yacht. "Fuck them!" he bellowed, continuing his search of the yacht, yelling their names. But to no avail. "Fuck!" he screamed, rushing back up to the bridge. "Did you see them jump overboard?"

The captain's eyes darkened.

"Of course not, Mr. Sorkin. I certainly would have raised the alarm immediately if I had!"

Mano started pacing wildly. His distress heightened as the blaze of flashing lights continued to strobe through the shrubs and tall grasses at Peter's estate. Every room in the vast Tuscan mansion was illuminated, and spotlights zoomed around the exterior of the house as if a Hollywood movie premiere was occurring, disrupting what had begun as a peaceful Sunday evening.

Where the fuck are they? His panic was spinning out of control, his fears exaggerated by the inexplicable unraveling of his plan.

"What the fuck is happening?" Mano screamed.

"Are you okay, sir?" said the captain, rushing down from the bridge to try to calm Mano.

Mano pulled away, growling.

"Please, Mr. Sorkin. What do you want me to do?"

But Mano mind's was in disarray. He had no idea what arrangements Peter had made concerning the mermaids who were part of the plan.

I knew I shouldn't have left that up to him! fumed Mano silently. "Fuck him and his precious mermaids! The moonlight swim must go on with the ones we have already."

Mano called Gabriella and it went to voicemail. He tried Trixie, this time leaving a message.

"Something's terribly wrong at Peter's. Police and sirens everywhere. Call me back immediately!"

Mano scuttled down to the club room and poured himself a double whiskey, swallowing it and quickly pouring another. "What to do? What to do?" he mumbled, pacing, wiping his sweaty forehead with his handkerchief. "Stay or go? Stay or go?" he chanted like a parrot.

"Change of plans," said Mano when he went back up to the bridge. "Turn back to Jewfish Key, but keep the motor low until we get farther out."

The captain nodded, then said, "What about Mr. Millstine?"

"He's on his own," scowled Mano.

Gabriella raced to the dock at Jewfish Key as Captain Moore secured the Mermaid Fantasea I. She darted from one spot to another, waiting for Mano to emerge, her heart thumping, her mind in turmoil.

"Where the hell have you been? What the fuck's happened?" she said, grabbing Mano's arm the minute he stepped onto the dock. "I tried calling you numerous times but it didn't go through. Where's Peter?"

Mano yanked his arm away, hissing. "We're in deep shit! Police are swarming all over Peter's house," he said, his voice quivering. "I have no idea what the fuck's going on there, but it looks like potentially huge trouble, for all of us!"

Gabriella grabbed his arm again, forcing him to stop, and jerked him around to face her, eye to eye.

"What do you mean? What have you done?" she asked through gritted teeth.

"Me? Me? Do you think I'm the only one involved in this enterprise? So much has happened over the past couple of days, I don't even know where to begin!" He swept his hand through his once perfectly groomed hair. A stray lock fell over his maniacal stare. His hands trembled when he tried to anchor the stray hairs behind his ear.

"What's going on?" said Trixie, scurrying over to them.

"Police cars, ambulances, surrounding Peter's house!" barked Mano. "It's a fucking nightmare!" He scrubbed his head like it was swarming with lice, turned his furious gaze on Trixie. "And on top of it all, Xander and Mirakakoo are missing! Can you imagine what could happen if they get away?"

He began pacing wildly, mumbling under his breath, then stopped abruptly in front of Gabriella.

"You've got to do something, Gabriella. Our entire enterprise is about to implode." He stomped back and forth, wiping his mouth with his hand.

Gabriella huffed, then looked Trixie and Mano square in the eyes.

"Get ahold of yourselves," she said calmly. "What could they know?"

Trixie grabbed Gabriella's shoulders, shaking her as if she were a child's cloth doll. "That damn detective!" she shrieked. "Peter's lost his mind. Ever since the boating accident Castro told me about. Someone Peter loved deeply accidentally fell off the yacht and drowned when they took the Mermaid Fantasea III out one afternoon. I have too much invested to get sucked into Peter's nightmares! We need to abandon this whole mission before it's too late. Get away, out of the country, before they're on to us. Take the yacht and just keep going."

Gabriella was tromping through the sandy beach near the shore, rubbing her chin. She finally twisted toward Mano and Trixie, traipsing behind her.

"No! We will not abandon our plan," she declared. "We'll go on as if nothing's happened," she said calmly, looking at both of them. "We have no idea what's going on at Peter's, but there's no way they can connect what we're doing here tonight with him." Gabriella studied them. "Think about it sensibly. What does anybody really know? All we're doing is having a party. A celebration. No law against that. If someone shows up here, we'll be friendly. Invite them to join us, if they wish." She paused, pondering various scenarios. "It's probably just as well Peter isn't here. They have nothing to tie us to him." She stared at Trixie. "Except you."

"Are you crazy!" screamed Trixie. "Detective Morales asked us about you, Gabriella. And PM Importers, and the Mermaid Fantasea Corporation. I'm sure it won't take her long to tie all of it neatly together."

"We'll just deny any direct involvement with Peter aside from our mutual business interest in mermaids, and Mermaid Fantasea's philanthropic mission to save sea life," Gabriella said, convinced it would work. "The Festival of Dagon must go on!"

She looked at Mano and Trixie.

"Trixie, go tell the actors to get into position for the March of Dagon. Mano, go to the podium and call everyone to their seats. We'll go straight into the opening ceremony. The tribal chiefs can perform the spiritual dance to awaken the aquatic spirits, followed by the arrival of Dagon, Oannes, Derceto, and Triton, who will lead the two mermaids to the shore. They will swim to the rock, where they will await the sacrifice to the Mermaid Moon."

"But, where are the two mermaids?" asked Mano. "We need them. Our clients are expecting them!"

"Don't worry, they're here. I'll get them. They can go around to the back of the house and make their way into the water," said Gabriella. "I arranged for them to be picked up at Georgia's camp." She smiled, pleased with her brilliance. "Lila's fainting spell actually made it easier than I thought it would be, because of all the frenzy."

"Impossible!" spat Mano. "It won't work. So much can go wrong. Shit! Shit! Shit!" he muttered, frazzled. "I think Trixie's right. We should forget the whole thing and get the hell out of here while we still can."

"Just because they're on to Peter," said Gabriella, grabbing Mano's arm, "that doesn't mean they're on to us."

"They will be once Peter starts spilling his guts!" said Mano. "Peter will sacrifice all of us to save himself."

"No!" ordered Gabriella again, this time more forcefully. "I've been through a lot worse than this. Trust me. We can pull this off and then disappear into the foggy mist. Go our separate ways until things cool off." She looked them both in the eye, as calm as a summer breeze. "Now, go, Trixie. Get the actors prepared. Mano, go to the podium." She checked her watch. "It's almost midnight."

Mano blew out a thunderous breath. He felt like his heart was about to burst through his chest. He shifted his dark eyes between the two women, battling the voices screaming inside his head.

"Okay, okay, okay," he said nervously. "Castro and Python can help usher everyone to their seats. I'll instruct the musicians to get ready for the arrival of the tribe and their entourage."

Mano inhaled deeply, as if it might be his last breath, then squeezed his eyes closed, praying for a miracle. Then he opened them and walked toward the podium at the front of the tent.

Chapter 52

It was close to midnight by the time the US Coast Guard dropped the two detectives at Jewfish Key, where torch lights in the distance marked the activity just beyond the shoreline.

Miranda was tense, worried that they might not have the upper hand. She didn't know much apart from Brenda's warning that Trixie might be in danger. What they had discovered at Peter's was alarming, to say the least, but there was no evidence of a direct link between what they'd found at Peter's home and what might await them on Jewfish Key.

"Wait for us on the boat," Miranda told the Coast Guard officer. "Keep a keen eye on that massive yacht in the distance, and alert us if you see any questionable activity."

The officer nodded. "I'll flash the spotlight and sound the horn, if we need backup."

"Just keep still and stay out of sight in the meantime."

The officer gave a thumbs-up as Miranda and Matt stepped onto the dock leading to the sandy beach, crouching like tigers on the hunt as they headed in the direction of the New Age music flowing through the night air. The sound of people taking their seats and the tap of the microphone signaled that whatever was planned was about go live.

As they inched closer to the white canvas tent, Miranda stopped and took Matt's arm.

"We'll watch from here until we get a sense of what's going on," she whispered.

Matt nodded. "Looks like it's just a normal celebration. Maybe a birthday?" He paused. "Do you think Brenda could have been overreacting?"

"I dunno, but going by the decor and the bounty of the spread, it must be for someone very special."

A voice came over the microphone. It was Mano, and he sounded solemn.

"Good evening, Friends of the Sea. We're so delighted you could join us for this unique opportunity to celebrate our mission to protect marine life around the world."

The audience clapped and Mano help up a hand to quiet them.

"While your financial support and volunteer efforts have made our mission a success, it is far from complete. Tonight we welcome a new phase of our Mermaid Fantasea Corporation: educating the world about the necessity of saving our sea creatures and protecting the aquatic environment where they live. In honor of the ancient spirits that have been guardians of this diverse and essential underwater world, we embrace the doctrine passed through generations—the doctrine that enshrined the god we know as Dagon, the Fish God. Dagon, who once symbolized the worship of false objects."

He paused, scanning the awestruck faces in the audience.

"At tonight's Festival of Dagon, we usher in a new era, where Dagon symbolizes the worship of aquatic creatures throughout the world, guided by the goddess of the Mermaid Moon, Moira, guardian of all sea creatures."

He closed his eyes and took a deep breath—more to calm himself than to suggest he was in deep prayer to honor Dagon and Moira. Then he opened them. "So, without further delay, let's welcome Dagon, Oannes, Derceto, and Triton."

The New Age music faded and a trumpet blared. A soft drumbeat followed, giving way to the dreamy sound of panpipes signaling the arrival of the costumed Dagon Fish God, wearing a teal-colored mermaid tail and a high-domed teal hat embellished with glittery stones.

The four costumed fish gods stopped and kneeled, gazing up at the silver Mermaid Moon. A dark cloud passed over its surface, dulling the brightness for a moment. When the full moon reappeared, two mermaids surfaced at the shoreline, their tails shimmering as they posed seductively.

"We have been graced by the presence of these two alluring mermaids," said Mano. "They will swim out to the rock jutting up in the distant water, and sing our praise to the Mermaid Moon."

Matt and Miranda were watching from the sea grape shrubs just beyond. Miranda's eyes widened when she recognized the two mermaids—Gina and Tammy.

She nudged Matt.

"Jesus," he muttered. "What the hell are they doing here?"

"They're obviously more than just campers," whispered Miranda.

"Trixie's girls?"

"Where do you think Tammy learned how to make her own mermaid tail for the pageant?"

"Ah. Trixie's protégé? Gina, too?"

Miranda shrugged.

Trixie Monroe sensed movement and sounds in the distance and walked toward them.

She gasped when Miranda and Matt stepped from behind the shrubs.

"What are you doing here?" she huffed. "This is a private affair. How dare you come here uninvited!"

"I thought you should know. Peter Millstine is unconscious and in the hospital," replied Miranda sharply.

Trixie flinched. "That's impossible!" she said, but her green eyes registered the truth. She stared defiantly at Miranda, expecting an explanation.

Mano had taken notice of Trixie's movement. The crowd was gradually becoming aware of the voices emanating from the nearby shrubs, while the actors and musicians continued as planned, unaware of the disturbance nearby.

Gabriella, watching Trixie from her seat under the tent, got up and walked toward her, not wanting to create a scene, while the puzzled guests gradually shifted their attention from the performance to Gabriella.

Dagon and the gods continued, raising their arms to the moon and chanting, swaying like wheat fields against a gentle wind as the mermaids swam toward the rock.

"You have no right to be here," challenged Gabriella through clenched teeth when she saw the two detectives. She grabbed Trixie's arm. "What's going on?"

Trixie fixed her eyes on Miranda and took a deep breath.

"Detective Morales here claims Peter is unconscious and in the hospital."

Gabriella, adjusting her stance, studied the detectives with unflinching eyes.

"I'm sorry to hear that," she said flatly. "We had hoped he'd be joining us for our celebration. What a shame," she said, clicking her tongue.

Miranda looked past Gabriella to the crowd gathered under the tent, assessing whether anyone appeared to be in imminent danger.

Mano Sorkin was approaching them, his gait unhurried, as if this unexpected visit was nothing out of the ordinary.

"What's going on?" asked Mano, consumed with contempt. His years of dedication and hard work were on the brink of disaster, his corrupt mermaid enterprise about to be exposed, and he had no idea how to stop it. He knew Peter was at the heart of his destruction.

"We know everything," said Miranda. "About the stolen artifacts, and Peter's deranged obsession with mermaids. And about his bizarre aquatic prison where he keeps them for his own twisted pleasure."

"I have no idea what you're talking about," scoffed Mano, flicking his eyes back and forth between Gabriella and Trixie, both women stone-faced.

Miranda took a deep breath. "Young girls, held captive in a monstrous aquarium in Peter's basement. One drugged and near death."

The shock frozen on Mano's face told Miranda he'd had no knowledge of Peter's hideous secret. Trixie, likewise, was aghast. But Gabriella's expression remained emboldened.

"Oh, and we also just learned that a couple not too far from Peter's house have rescued two young people from the water near their home, Xander Montoya and his friend Mirakakoo," continued Miranda. "Apparently they jumped off a luxurious yacht called Mermaid Fantasea."

Mano choked. A long pause followed.

Miranda hoped this outflowing of disturbing details would unnerve Mano enough that he'd confess what perverse and malignant endeavors he and Peter Millstine had been involved in, but Mano just stood there, dazed, like he'd been suddenly transported to another realm of impossible.

"I'm afraid I know absolutely nothing about Peter," said Gabriella. "I just met him recently, during the judging at Sirens of the Deep. I know nothing about his . . . affinity for mermaids," she said.

"What's happened to Peter?" asked Trixie.

"He's been taken to the hospital," said Miranda. "We don't know about his current condition. We do know the truth about what he was doing—the mermaids he kept captive for God knows how long. His collection of what we suspect are rare artifacts stolen from a museum in Panama."

She took a deep breath to curb her urge to strike the designer.

"How could you?" she continued, a breath away from Trixie's face. "How could you just stand by and let all this happen to these young girls? What kind of hideous monster are you?"

Trixie's cold, green eyes brimmed with tears.

"Forget it, Ms. Monroe. Don't pretend to be emotional all of the sudden," said Miranda disdainfully. "You were part of this whole sordid ordeal. If it wasn't for Georgia Holmes, and Brenda Sinclair, whom you treated like a slave, we might never have uncovered the links to the Colombian drug cartel, the kidnapping of young orphans, and Peter Millstine's insane obsession with mermaids."

"Once my lawyers get on the case, Detective Morales, you won't have a snowball's chance in hell of proving any of this," spat Gabriella Navarre, wondering if she had finally reached a point in her life where she wouldn't be able to turn things around.

Then, Miranda heard the rush of feet coming toward them from the dock where the Coast Guard boat had dropped them. Three men in black athletic wear and carrying rifles cautiously approached them.

Miranda relieved to see her friend from the FBI on site.

"Agent McMillon—we're just getting started," she said. "Thanks for the assist."

Suddenly, Castro and Python raced over to them, guns drawn.

"Put the guns down! Now!" ordered Miranda. "You have no place to go! This is the end of the line for all of you."

They stopped on a dime when they saw the black-garbed men with their rifles aimed right at them. Castro and Python dropped their handguns in the sand. One of the agents retrieved the weapons, then stepped back, giving Miranda a wide berth.

"You're all under arrest for aiding and abetting the illegal transport and sale of minors, stolen goods, and kidnapping, to name just a few of the charges," said Miranda, reading them their rights as Matt and the other officers handcuffed them.

"We'll escort them back to Sarasota and meet up with you back there," said Agent McMillon.

"Good. I'll call Chief Petri and bring him up to speed. I suspect we'll need more officers to help question the people here at the festival before they leave the island."

"Stay where you are!" Matt shouted, fending off the rush of curious guests that were scattering hither and yon across the small island, unaware of what was happening. He eventually corralled them and brought them back to the tent, to await questioning.

Agent McMillon looked over his shoulder. "Should I leave one of my agents behind to help?"

"If you choose. Help is already on the way."

A cloud passed over the silver moon. The pageantry of the Festival of Dagon was now in complete disarray, the muted glow of the lanterns dancing in the cool breeze providing a stark reminder that beauty and evil often go hand in hand.

Chapter 53

By the time Detectives Morales and Selva finished questioning the guests at Jewfish Key, it was almost two a.m. Miranda and Matt would be working with international agencies going forward, investigating what had become a complex, multilayered web of drugs, theft, human trafficking, violence, and murder.

"Who would have thought that such horrific things were happening so close to home," said Miranda, shaking her head. She had many questions she was not eager to know the answers to—like, how was her father involved in the operation? What was going to happen to Georgia and her mermaid camp? To Mermaid's Delight and Brenda? And most of all, Lila Bjorg and the other two mermaid campers, Gina and Tammy.

"It's pretty late," said Chief Petri after Miranda had summarized what had just gone down over the phone. "For now the FBI and Interpol will take over. They have a lot more expertise and resources than we do for this type of case."

Miranda and Matt watched as the spectrum of local, state, and international authorities descended on the scene, more support arriving in boats and dinghies.

The Coast Guard boat that had transported them from Peter's dock to Jewfish Key motored them back to Sarasota and dropped them at the marina.

They walked back to Miranda's house, where Matt had left his car.

He walked Miranda up to the front door. A dim light in the front window was on, and Miranda suddenly remembered they had left Graham behind at her house.

She opened the door and called out for Graham, but all was quiet.

She shrugged. "He must have decided to go back to his hotel for a good night's sleep," she said.

"It was good of him to offer to chaperone Miranda back to Panama," said Matt. He was unable to wash away thoughts of what might happen going forward between Miranda and her former love. "Get some sleep," he said. "I'll pick you up in a few hours, and we'll pick up Graham before driving to the camp for Maria."

"What about my car?"

"I'll drive you back to Peter's house once we get the rest of this ordeal behind us," said Matt, blowing out a breath. "See you soon."

They both groaned, knowing they needed sleep but that it would not come easily.

Miranda had plenty on her mind besides the case. So many years of keeping the painful past buried. Her conflicting feelings for Graham. And now, thoughts of Matt. His sensitivity and patience. His commitment. And most of all, his loyalty.

ΩR

Controlled chaos is the only way to describe the pandemonium at Sirens of the Deep when Miranda, Matt, and Graham arrived to collect Maria Diaz the next morning.

Georgia looked tired when she greeted them, but still managed a warm greeting when she was introduced to Graham.

"Pleasure to meet you," said Georgia. "I understand you're escorting Maria back to Panama," she said, motioning for Maria to come over to them.

"This is Professor Waterman, Maria," said Miranda. "He's going to take you home."

"Gracias," she said. Dressed in a pink sundress, Maria was shy, but excited.

"She's all packed," said Georgia. "I also spoke with Gretchen Kismet at the orphanage. She told me she's pretty confident she has found homes for all the girls rescued from the freighter."

"That's wonderful!" said Miranda. The first bright spot in the harrowing journey they'd all been traveling.

Georgia walked with them to Matt's car, and Maria turned to hug Georgia.

"Muchas gracias, Señora Georgia," she smiled. "Gracias por dejar ser una sirena . . . aunque solo sea por un día."

Graham smiled, and translated for the group. "She thanked Ms. Holmes for allowing her to be a mermaid, even if just for a day."

They all laughed, and Maria hugged Georgia again.

"Safe travels, Maria. Maybe we'll see you back here someday," said Georgia, unsure whether the camp would be around should Maria find her way back.

After delivering Graham and Maria to the airport, Matt and Miranda drove to Peter Millstine's house. Tire treads from the many emergency vehicles were a stark reminder of how nothing is ever as it seems. The rich are capable of hiding their propensity for hideous obsessions and unparalleled desire for money and power.

Matt pulled up next to Miranda's car, the engine idling as they sat pensively in the driveway. After some musing, he looked over at her. His indigo eyes were heavy from lack of rest, yet a sparkle still lingered there.

"What a week, huh," she said, turning to the stunning landscape spread before them. The stately heron sculpture at the base of the staircase was undisturbed by the chaos; the birds and butterflies had returned to their favorite spots.

She sighed deeply. "What is it that turns people into monsters, Matt?"

He was quiet for a moment.

"I don't know that anyone can answer that question, Miranda." He thought about the tragedies he had confronted since becoming a homicide detective, and sighed again. "Fortunately there are kind, sensitive people like Georgia Holmes in the world."

Miranda smiled. "I think she has a crush on you."

Matt laughed out loud and elbowed her.

Chapter 54

"So, give me the basic rundown on Operation Mermaid," said Chief Petri, looking across his desk and Matt and Miranda, his long fingers pressed together like a church steeple. "I'll read your detailed report later."

"As far as we know so far, the cartels used the tattoos as a code. Each orphaned girl would receive one as soon as she completed the so-called 'protocol' established by the Corbinestro cartel. The reptile tattoo confirmed the girls' fertility and assured the buyers that those girls, previously shared with potential buyers, had been thoroughly examined and given a 'clean bill of health,' meaning they were disease-free and could bear children, should that be a criterion of a particular buyer."

Chief Petri shifted in his chair, rolling his shoulders in silent disgust.

"What about the two stones discovered inside the victim? And the harpoon?"

Matt cleared his throat. "Excuse me, Chief, but it's actually a trident," he said, glancing at Miranda.

"Okay, trident." His brows crinkled. "What else?"

"After Peter recovered from shock, he agreed to tell the whole story to the FBI in exchange for immunity."

The chief blew out a breath, his eyes black with disdain.

"Concerning the victim, Nina Jorgensen—Peter had chosen her for himself. He'd made a deal with Mano Sorkin that she would not be for sale. Although he kept her captive with the other mermaids in his aquarium, he would take her out on his yacht from time to time."

"Why?"

"A kind of . . . date, I imagine," said Miranda, without inflection.

"What?"

"He told Agent McMillon that he . . . loved her."

The chief shook his head. "Unbelievable."

"According to Peter, Nina was allowed to roam inside his house on occasion," Miranda explained. "One morning, he and Python, Castro's lackey, were loading supplies that would last them a couple of days, traveling on Peter's yacht. Castro was in charge of keeping an eye on her, but apparently something distracted him and he lost sight of her. When he caught up with her, she was peeking at Peter's collection of miniatures in the display cabinet."

She glanced at Matt, picturing the scenario.

"At first Castro thought nothing of it—just innocent curiosity. He knew Peter always kept the case locked. But this time he hadn't. We can only assume that Nina must have panicked when she heard Castro coming up behind her. As she fumbled to return a frog miniature to the shelf, one of the black pearls that formed the frog's eyes fell out. The only thing she could think of was to hide it in her mouth."

"We speculate," said Matt, "that the same thing must have happened with the tortoise's shell, since it was also among Peter's miniature collection. It was too large to stick in her mouth, so her only choice was to hide it in her bikini top."

Miranda nodded, urging him to continue.

"This could explain how it got wedged between the prongs of the trident when it struck her," he concluded.

"The why, and how, is still a mystery," added Miranda.

"The collector never suspected anything?" asked the chief, incredulous.

"Apparently not until much later. In his fury, Peter ordered Python and Castro to come to his house. Peter questioned them vigorously, but Python said he was busy helping load the supplies and blamed it on Castro. Castro, for his own protection, did not mention that he'd seen Nina near his glass cabinet. Peter eventually figured the stones had become loose and had fallen out, and were somewhere in the house. He beat himself up for his carelessness when they never turned up."

"What about the harp—the trident?" asked the chief.

Matt cleared his throat and looked directly into the chief's inquisitive stare.

"As part of his plea bargain, Castro confessed he'd seen Nina put something in her mouth and bikini top, but had no idea what it was. So he kept quiet. Then, once on board Peter's yacht, cruising the Gulf, Nina, terrified, jumped overboard to escape the harsh punishment she knew Peter would dispense once he realized the stones were missing, and that she must have stolen them." She took a breath. "In a fit of rage, Castro alerted Python that she had jumped ship and had already swum quite a distance from the yacht. The only thing Python could think to do was to grab the trident he'd stolen off the wall of Mano's yacht and had hidden on Peter's yacht. 'With great stupidity'—Peter's words," clarified Miranda, "Python somehow attached the trident to Peter's dart gun, and, I guess, hoped for the best."

Chief Petri thought he had heard every possible story during his twenty-five years in law enforcement, but this topped them all.

"It sounds so . . . so preposterous, " he said, blowing out a heavy breath.

Chief Petri needed to know how this maniacal plan had gone on for so long—and, more specifically, how the dead mermaid had ended up on Lido Beach.

"We believe that when the trident struck Nina's chest, the force was so strong that it forced her underwater. A direct hit that certainly Python hadn't expected." Miranda took a deep breath. "Perhaps the gravest mistake Python made was that he had not attached a rope to the trident before he shot it. If he had, he might have been able to retrieve her." She paused. "Maybe even saved her."

"Jesus Christ," sputtered the chief, scrubbing his thinning, gray hair. "Absolutely incredible," he muttered, falling back in his chair.

Miranda and Matt stole a glance at each other and sighed.

"I'm afraid at this point, although many unanswered questions remain, there's not much more to reveal," said Miranda. "If we receive any additional information, we'll add it to our report." She flipped Matt a look. "And, if we learn anything more from the FBI or Interpol, we'll bring you up to speed".

Chief Petri stared at his two detectives, proud of their perseverance in bringing this convoluted and unimaginable plot to a conclusion. He couldn't help but wonder how far the network of human trafficking extended.

"Great job, you two," he said, standing up and reaching out his hand. "You both deserve some time off."

"Thank you, Chief," they said almost in unison as they stood up and shook his hand.

"One more thing, Chief," added Miranda turning back around. "We believe the Mermaid Fantasea Corporation used PM Importers to funnel the girls around the world, to be auctioned off in remote places." She glanced at Matt. "Unfortunately, we expect that a fleet of yachts engaging in these despicable practices will continue to sail the mighty seas at will."

Chief Petri nodded. "Anything else?"

Miranda took a deep breath and stared at the chief.

"My father's been arrested for being a co-conspirator in the mermaid enterprise. And my mother is in the hospital. Attempted suicide." She didn't flinch as she spoke, merely shrugged briefly, as if talking about the weather.

"Miranda! Why didn't you tell me about your mother?" said Matt.

Chief Petri searched Miranda's dark eyes, worried that he might have to order his star detective to take another sabbatical. Perhaps Dr. Belfort would evaluate her again before sending her back into the field, knowing full well that Miranda would vehemently object to the suggestion.

"I only just got word of your father's arrest," said the chief. "I don't know the details aside from the fact that the FBI is investigating his ties to an organization called Doctors for Equal Care." He paused, seeking words that could hardly express his deepest feelings. "I'm truly sorry about your mother. I didn't know."

Chapter 55

The metal door of the Sarasota County morgue swished open, drawing the coroner's immediate attention away from the mural he was painting on the wall leading to his office.

"Well, well, well, detectives," Dr. Rubens said, welcoming them with a warm smile. "I hope you bring happy thoughts here. I've had enough death and disfigurement for a while." He paused. "But then, that's my job. And it's an important one." Raising his paintbrush, he said, "I've taken up painting as a hobby. A kind of antidote to death."

Miranda and Matt smiled.

"Not sure how happy our thoughts are, Dr. Rubens, but at least we're not bringing you news of another tragic death," said Miranda. She coughed, covering her mouth with her arm. "I will never get used to this smell."

"Well, it should smell more like paint today," teased the coroner, setting his paintbrush down on the lid of a gallon of bright coral paint. "So, what do you think?"

The three of them stepped back to evaluate Dr. Rubens's artwork in silence. A stunning mermaid with long, raven hair wearing a blue-sequined tail was poised atop a large rock and staring up at the moonlit night, a lighted path across the water connecting mermaid and moon.

"Why, Dr. Rubens," said Miranda. "I had no idea you were such a talented artist."

"Well, some of them are decals. But I did paint the coral reefs and seashells," he said unabashedly.

"It's phenomenal, Dr. Rubens," said Matt.

"Well," laughed the coroner, "I won't be giving up my day job anytime soon."

He spread his arm wide around the room, showing off the bright, cheery colors on the walls.

"I hired professional painters to dress up this dreary place. Just because the dead end up here doesn't mean the living can't experience a little bit of color to offset their sorrow when they come to this deadly place."

He paused, tapping his lip with his chubby index finger.

"How is it that boring, bland walls, and hard surfaces have come to represent respect for the dead? Don't the dead deserve a bit of pizzazz before they leave their earthly dwelling—to celebrate the good times they surely must have had?"

"I agree, Dr. Rubens," said Miranda with sympathetic smile.

The coroner glanced at Matt and Miranda, searching for what was not being said.

"So, what really brings you back to my morgue?"

"I wanted you to know we suspect the reptile tattoos used on the girls was a code indicating they were fertile. Most likely one of the criteria demanded by the buyers," said Miranda, sadly. "With the various agencies involved in this horrible ordeal, we have a lot more to learn about this complex operation that encompasses multiple countries."

The coroner averted his eyes. His thoughts drifting to a private place. Then, he turned to his painting of the mermaid sitting on the rock. "I will never give up believing that goodness still exists in the world, detectives. If I didn't, I could not show up for work every day."

Miranda and Matt shared a look of mutual understanding.

"Yes, Dr. Rubens. In our line of work, we must find the calm amidst the chaos and debauchery facing us in our line of work." She sighed. Then glanced again at the mural. "I think you may have just inspired me to seek an outlet for my emotions as you seem to have done with this amazing mural as homage to our mermaid."

He nodded. His smile a mix of joy and sadness.

"Well," said Matt, "My dog Muscle helps me cope with the horrors I often take home with me. Dogs make wonderful therapists."

"Hmm," muttered Miranda, glancing at Matt and Dr. Rubens. "Guess it's time for me to meet Muscle…and maybe think about taking an art class."

Acknowledgments

Many people deserve enormous thanks for getting me to publication of my debut novel: my agent Linda Langton for her ongoing support throughout the process; David LeGere and the team and Woodhall Press who opened the door to me; my husband Richard who took time away from his own business to read and make invaluable comments on my manuscript; and my family who believed in me, and who add incredible joy to my life.

About the Author

Pamela Mones is a retired, award-winning journalist for more than a decade. An avid fan of murder mysteries, the idea for *A Deadly Mermaid Fetish* spawned after attending a class on writing murder mysteries. Her lifelong intrigue with the sea, combined with a fascination for mermaids, drew her to feature a mermaid as the victim.

Pamela earned her first writing award in high school for an essay sponsored by The American Legion. She has won awards for her monthly newspaper column, 'Between You and Me'; a short story featuring artist Paul Gauguin's fictional sojourn through Sarasota; and awarded 'Best New Niche Publication' by the Suburban Newspapers of America (SNA) as editor at Chesapeake Publishing Corporation.

She earned a Master's Degree in Communication from Towson University in Maryland, and continued to write in diverse markets. She has published her first children's story, Lavender Bear Goes to the Circus about a lavender-filled, purple bear who longs for an adventure. Her second – Lavender Bear Goes to the Beach.